DEATH
IN
BLACK
AND
WHITE

ALSO BY SG BRYANT

Boss
Taken In

 Simon Bryant grew up on a farm, a soldier settler block in the south-east of South Australia. After graduating with an English literature degree from the University of Adelaide, he has pursued a number of paths, including farming, managing a radio station, working in tourism, and, most recently, an extended spell in the public service in Canberra.

Now retired, he is dedicating his time to a lifelong interest in creative writing, and, in particular, to writing Australian historical fiction.

S G BRYANT

DEATH IN BLACK AND WHITE

BORDER BOOKS

First published in 2022 by Border Books

Canberra ACT 2611

© Simon Bryant 2022

Cover and text design by Sandy Cull, www.sandycull.com

Typesetting by Mike Kuszla

Cover images courtesy of the Pictures Collection, State Library of Victoria
Victoria Park, Collingwood, Accession no: H87.206/149
W. Strickland, Collingwood, Accession no: IAN01/06/95/4

Author portrait by Andrea Bryant Photography

Printed and bound in Australia by Ingram Spark and
Lightning Source Australia

ISBN 978-0-6480375-4-5

FOR MY MATE, DAVE ROBERTS
A COLLINGWOOD TRAGIC ALWAYS

SATURDAY 12 JUNE 1897

HALF-TIME AT THE FOOTY, with the Blues two goals down. And in Effie's view, languishing rather badly against the might of the Collingwood juggernaut. The premiers from last season were flexing their sizeable muscles and the second half loomed ominously.

Effie supposed she should be feeling anxious at her team's precarious position. But somehow, on this balmy June afternoon, cosily settled at the back of the Members' Stand at the MCG, Alfie playing happily at her feet and husband Harry by her side, Effie felt nothing but contentment. The sun was shining, life was good and, who knows, Carlton might even stage a miraculous comeback and seize victory. Stranger things had been known to happen.

She glanced at Harry and saw his attention was focused squarely on devouring a very large meat pie, just delivered to him by his constable, Willie Milton. Taking a break from crowd management duties, Willie had thoughtfully provided for his off-duty boss. Or perhaps it was a case of soft-soaping Harry to build up a bit of future credit. Effie knew Willie had his eye on a promotion to sergeant in the not-too-distant future.

Effie gave Harry a gentle nudge in the ribs and pointed to a trickle of gravy running down his chin. Harry grinned, wiped it quickly with his sleeve, and resumed his attack on the pie. He managed only to turn the trickle into a smear, so she pulled out her handkerchief, leaned over and wiped it away.

'Now now, Inspector Holloway, we can't have you looking disreputable in public, can we? A man of your standing.'

Harry grinned again. He suspected that Effie just enjoyed hearing the sound of his new title, and to be truthful, he didn't mind it either. The promotion had been most welcome, not just for the money, but also for the greater freedom it gave him to pursue his own path at work. In particular, to be more independent of a certain Chief Inspector Marks, his difficult and demanding boss.

'You're looking remarkably happy for a man whose team's behind at half-time,' Effie observed.

'Oh well,' Harry chuckled. 'Where there's life, there's hope.' And he took another large bite.

'Not a lot of hope, if you ask me.'

'It's only two goals,' he reminded her, reaching for his glass and taking a good swig of brown ale. 'But I agree, we're not going too well. It's that damn Sharkey, he's killing us. Never thought I'd say it about a Collingwood man, but that bloke can play footy, that's for sure. What do you reckon, little man?' He tickled young Alfie under the chin.

'More pie, Dadda!' Alfie pleaded, arms outstretched in supplication. Harry chuckled and broke off a chunk of pastry, handing it to him.

'Make sure that's not too hot,' Effie stressed, but more out of habit than concern. It was too late anyway, the piece of pie had already disappeared into Alfie's mouth and he was chewing happily.

'Hello, here they come, back again,' Harry said, pointing to the crowded area below them where the umpires, in the company of a couple of burly policemen, could be seen forcing their way through a milling throng of spectators.

Effie thought how small the officials looked in the company of their giant protectors, and nervous too. The crowd surged threateningly around them as they made their way to the picket gate leading onto the arena. Even from their vantage point on high, Effie could hear the abuse and threats being hurled at the umpires from all sides.

'Are you sure they're safe, Harry?' she asked. 'Those policemen won't be much use if they're attacked.'

Harry shrugged. 'It's a bit of a worry. And it's probably just a matter of time before someone gets hurt. Bad enough for the umpires, but it's getting the players through that mob that's the real problem. It's impossible to keep the crowd away, too many players and not enough of our blokes. You'll see when they come out.'

Effie surveyed the crowd swarming around the umpires as they edged nervously toward the relative safety of the playing arena. 'Some of those men down there look like real larrikins, I wouldn't put anything past them.'

'Oh, it's not just the men we're worried about,' Harry replied. 'It's the hatpin brigade.'

'The hatpin brigade?'

'The well-dressed lady members, that's who I mean. And the Collingwood ladies are notorious for it.'

'For what?' Effie was confused.

'For jabbing the opposition players with their hatpins, that's what. It's getting out of hand, we probably need to arrest a couple and make an example of them. It's assault, after all.'

Effie stared at him. 'You're joking, Harry, surely?'

Harry shrugged again. 'Nope, it's true. Fair dinkum. Look, here come our blokes now. You'll see.'

And sure enough, as the Carlton players, flanked by a small number of police guards, made their way through the crowd, Effie could see that the supporters surging around them were mainly women, most of them adorned with black and white Collingwood regalia. Judging by the angry shouts and threatening gestures, none of them were well-disposed toward the Carlton men. They seemed to be mainly of more mature years and, as Effie noted, mostly very well-hatted.

The police escorts, doubtless aware of the threat, were doing their best to shove the irate matrons out of the way and make a safe path for the Carlton players. The players, like the umpires before them, were pressing their way forward urgently, towards the sanctuary of the playing arena. But Effie could see that the efforts of the constabulary to clear the path were far from successful. The more they roughly shoved the women aside, the more determined the ladies seemed to re-join the fray, pitching forward with umbrellas and other makeshift weapons raised, their indignation no doubt further heightened by the actions of the law. Though she couldn't tell at this distance, Effie had no doubt that some had hatpins at the ready, primed to get in a surreptitious jab should the opportunity arise.

'My goodness!' Effie gasped. 'It almost makes me ashamed to be a woman.'

Harry smiled, but she could see that he was concerned at the carryings-on below. 'Yes, if this kind of thing keeps up, we're going to have to get the league to build a covered race all the way to the gate. Someone's going to get hurt otherwise. And it could be one of our constables too. They're right in the firing line down there.'

On this occasion though, Harry's fears proved groundless. Effie felt a distinct surge of relief as the Carlton players emerged from the crowd onto the arena, apparently unscathed. The Collingwood men were not far behind, and again the ruckus in the crowd around them erupted, but this new roster of ladies was adorned with blue regalia and the hubbub was not quite as intense. It seemed that the Carlton women favoured a more demure brand of assault.

With both contingents now safely on the ground, the game was ready to resume. The players wandered off to their allocated positions and the field umpire, ball in hand, took up his spot in the centre of the ground. On either side of him stood the opposing ruckmen, staring menacingly at each other as they awaited the bouncing of the ball. Around them milled the opposing mid-fielders, pushing and shoving each other in shows of strength. The umpire raised the ball ceremoniously above his head with one hand and blew his whistle with the other. The siren blared and he moved forward, leaning over to bounce the ball.

But then he stopped. And stood upright, looking about him as if something was not quite right. The crowd roared expectantly, urging him to get on with proceedings. But the umpire remained motionless, before taking a step or two forward, towards one of the players.

'What's going on? What's he doing?' Effie asked.

But Harry seemed as mystified as she. 'Not sure,' he replied.

As they watched, the object of the umpire's attention, one of the Collingwood players, suddenly doubled over in apparent distress. The umpire approached him with obvious concern and, leaning over him, placed a comforting hand on his back. As if in reaction to this gesture, the player toppled slowly forward, staggering to retain his footing, but unable to do so, collapsed helplessly onto the ground. There he writhed about, his body contorting, as if in some sort of fit.

'Bloody hell!' Harry exclaimed. 'It's Robbie Sharkey. What's wrong with him?'

By now, players from both sides had gathered around the fallen player and Harry and Effie were unable to see clearly what was going on. A strange hush had come over the crowd. Then the umpire emerged from the pack of players, waving frantically towards the Members' Stand and shouting for help. Within seconds, two officials clad in white, and one bearing a rolled-up stretcher, appeared through the gate and sprinted towards the middle of the ground. They pushed their way into the pack of players, gesticulating at them to stand back. They could be seen to kneel beside the stricken man, who was still thrashing about uncontrollably. With some difficulty, they manoeuvred him onto the stretcher and began hastening from the ground, a Collingwood team mate on either side of the stretcher struggling to control the man's contortions. As they reached the gates, the crowd in the members' enclosure drew back respectfully to let them through. The contrast with the scene just minutes before could not have been more marked.

Like all around them, Effie and Harry were now on their feet, watching as the stricken player was carried through the crowd towards the players' rooms below them. Despite the restraining efforts of his attendants, Sharkey continued to shake violently and thrash about, while at the same time his whole body seemed to be arching weirdly. Effie felt Harry's hand on her arm.

'You'll be all right here with Alfie for a bit, won't you? I think I'm needed down there. Something's badly wrong.'

She placed her hand on his. 'Of course, off you go. I hope that poor boy isn't too ill. What could have happened to him?'

'Not sure, but I don't like the look of it. Could be some sort of epilepsy.' But as he squeezed her hand and turned to make his way down the grandstand steps to the change rooms below, his expression told a different story. Something terrible was clearly unfolding in front of their eyes.

✕

Harry was greatly relieved to find Willie Milton standing at the door of the player change rooms, in the company of a very large, burly constable. They were sternly holding back twenty or thirty people, bustling noisily around the door and demanding entry. Some were claiming official status, others were apparently curious onlookers, or perhaps members of the press, trying to get a first-hand glimpse of this sensational development: Collingwood's star player laid low in mysterious circumstances. No doubt their curiosity was further whetted by the muffled cries coming from behind the closed door.

'Thank God you're here, mate,' Harry exclaimed, as he pushed through the throng. 'These idiots are the last thing we need in there.'

'No worries, boss,' Willie replied. 'I was on duty down on the fence and I followed the stretcher through. Thought I might be needed here.'

'Well done. Who's in there with him?'

'Just the trainers and the Collingwood doc. And one of the Collingwood players. He was getting treatment in the room when Sharkey was brought in. No-one else.'

'We need to get the Collingwood boy out of here, he doesn't need to see this. And let no-one else in, okay? Leave your bloke on the door here and come in with me. He can manage them, can't he?'

'Course he can. Have a look at him. Don't think anyone will get past.'

As Harry and Willie moved to open the door, Harry felt an insistent hand on his shoulder, and turned to find himself confronted by a round-faced, well-dressed young fellow, sporting a red rose in his lapel and a worried expression. Harry recognised Ernie Copeland, the Collingwood Secretary.

'I'd better come in with you, Harry. Robbie looked in a bad way.'

Harry nodded briefly. 'Of course, Ernie. Come in. But just you at this stage, I don't want too many in there until we work out what's going on.'

The three men made their way through the door and into the passageway leading to the rooms. As they closed the door, the cacophony of voices behind them became muted and they became acutely aware of agonised cries coming from the change room ahead. They hurried on, flinging open the half-shut door and bursting into the room.

Harry's worst fears were immediately confirmed. Robert Sharkey lay on a table, thrashing about wildly and screaming with pain. Three trainers were desperately trying to restrain him, but to no avail. His face was barely recognisable, set in a rigid grimace, his cries emanating through clenched teeth. Another man was hovering around him, a tall, stooped fellow unknown to Harry, but presumably the Collingwood doctor. One of Sharkey's team mates, a curly-haired fellow, was standing on the sidelines, staring vacantly at his stricken team mate. Harry motioned to Willie to show the fellow to the door, then turned to the tall man.

'You're the Collingwood doctor?' Harry asked.

The fellow glanced uncertainly at Harry. 'Yes, Ramsgate. Henry Ramsgate,' he replied.

'What have you treated him with?' Harry asked.

Ramsgate stared at Harry. He was pale and sweating and seemed at a loss. 'I haven't really had the chance to give him anything yet. I'm … well, I'm not quite sure what the problem is.'

'Has he had this kind of fit before?' Harry had to shout to make himself heard over Sharkey's cries.

'I don't really know,' Ramsgate managed to reply. Harry could see he was panic-stricken and unfocused.

'Ernie, has he got a history of seizures? Epilepsy?' Harry yelled, turning towards the Collingwood secretary.

'Definitely not! Nothing since he came to us,' Copeland replied. 'And we checked his medical record when we recruited him. Nothing before either.'

'Then it's fairly obvious, I would have thought,' Harry said sharply. 'Poisoning of some sort. First up, we've got to stop these convulsions.'

He barked to the room at large, 'Get some blankets on the floor and get him down from there!' And he joined the three trainers in manoeuvring Sharkey to the floor.

'Quick! Got any chloroform in your bag?' Harry yelled at Ramsgate.

The doctor looked blankly back at Harry, momentarily seeming not to understand the question. Then he gave a start and replied, 'Well, no actually, I don't usually carry it. Not the sort of thing I'd require here.'

Harry turned to Willie Milton. 'For God's sake, go and find Ed Brown, quick as you can. He won't be far away.' For the benefit of Ramsgate, he added, 'He's the Carlton doctor.'

Willie hurried from the room, while Harry turned his attention back to Sharkey, still writhing frantically on the floor. The man was now struggling to get air through his clenched teeth, his breath coming in shallow, desperate gasps.

'We don't have much time,' Harry said to Ramsgate. 'We need to control these spasms. We need chloroform.'

At that moment, as if in answer to his prayers, Willie Milton burst back into the room in the company of a long, thin fellow carrying a brown kitbag. Harry was never more pleased to see his friend, Ed Brown. Nor more thankful that he had recently persuaded Ed to take on the role of honorary club doctor at Carlton.

Normally bashful and reticent, Ed was a man transformed when confronted with a medical emergency. He needed no invitation to come forward and examine Sharkey. Kneeling beside the man, he held an arm steady while he felt for a pulse. He muttered something to himself, then waved his hand in front of Sharkey's face. This action seemed to stimulate further contractions from Sharkey, his neck muscles twitching violently. In between his cries of pain, garbled sounds came from him, as if he was attempting to speak. But no words could be discerned, and foam had begun to ooze from between his clenched teeth. Ed Brown was quickly back on his feet, rummaging in his bag and producing a bottle and a piece of cloth.

'Strychnine poisoning, I'd say,' he said turning to Harry. 'And a large dose, by the look of it. I need you fellows to try to hold him still while I apply chloroform. We may already be too late.'

Harry and the trainers renewed their efforts and, with some difficulty, were able to hold Sharkey steady enough for Ed to apply the chloroform soaked-cloth to his face. Within seconds the convulsions began to ease and the flailing limbs to relax. Ed was now able to apply his stethoscope to the man's chest. He listened carefully for a little while, then straightened. He looked at Harry, shaking his head slowly.

'I want to give him gastric lavage, but I don't dare. His heart is barely beating. The convulsions may have brought on a collapse of the heart. Or it may be that the poison itself has paralysed his heart muscle.'

He leaned over Sharkey again, applying the stethoscope and listening intently for twenty seconds or so. Then he stood up, took a step back, and quietly spoke the words Harry knew were coming. 'He's gone. Nothing more I can do.'

Harry stared at Ed, momentarily dumb-struck. How could this have happened? How could such a tragedy have intruded so abruptly on this pleasant Saturday afternoon? Harry had no immediate answer, but his policeman's instinct pointed in one direction only. This was no accident. This was a deliberate act of evil.

'Right,' he said, regaining his composure and turning to Willie Milton. 'I want this room sealed off. No-one is to enter until it's been thoroughly searched. And this body is to be transported to the morgue under strict police guard. Do your best to make sure no-one sees you leave the ground. Out the back door, I'd suggest. I don't want to start any wild rumours straight away. It's going to be hard enough to contain them later on.'

'And get hold of Crawford Mollison too,' Harry added as an afterthought. 'I want an autopsy done as soon as possible. Tomorrow, if he can manage it.'

Willie nodded and hurried off.

What next, Harry thought, as he looked about the room. And spotted Ernie Copeland, standing immobile against the wall, staring at the dead man on the floor. His normally rosy features had paled and he looked close to tears. The three Collingwood trainers and Henry Ramsgate stood beside him, all in various states of distress. Ed Brown was standing silently on the other side of the room.

'What are we going to do?' Copeland said eventually. Harry assumed the question was directed at him, though Copeland didn't look up, continuing to stare at the dead man.

'Don't worry,' Harry replied quietly. 'We'll take care of the body. And everything else that needs to happen.'

'Of course,' Copeland said, lifting his eyes to Harry for the first time. 'Is there anything you need from us?'

'I've got a couple of questions for you. And for these blokes too. They're your official trainers, I assume?'

'Yes, this is our head trainer, Wally Lee.' He gestured to the tallest of the three, an imposing fellow with an aquiline nose, greying curly hair and an impressive moustache. 'And his assistant, Joey Miller.'

Miller, a small, wiry individual in his forties, blinked nervously at Harry, then quickly shifted his gaze to the floor.

'And this is Jimmy Johnston,' Copeland added, indicating the third trainer, similarly small, but considerably older and more rotund.

'G'day,' Harry said to the group at large. 'I've only got a couple of questions for you blokes now, but I'll want to talk to you again in the next couple of days, I'd reckon.'

Wally Lee looked impassively back at Harry and nodded. His two underlings shuffled and continued to stare at the floor.

Harry went on. 'Before I do though, I need to stress to all of you that you don't breathe a word of this to anyone until after the game. That he's dead, I mean. That includes you, Ernie. You can tell his mates when they come in after the game, but instruct them to keep quiet about it too. Though I realise that'll be difficult to manage.'

'We'll do our best,' Copeland responded. 'But Danny Robinson's probably told them already how crook he is. Was, I mean. He was in here when Robbie was brought in,' he added, in response to Harry's questioning look. The colour had returned to Copeland's features and he had almost resumed his usual efficient air.

'Fair enough. But he wouldn't know yet that Sharkey's dead, would he? And by the way, when you tell them he's gone, I don't want any mention of cause of death. No mention of what you've heard in these rooms about strychnine. Okay?'

'Of course,' Copeland replied, glancing at his colleagues. 'You can rely on us.'

'Good. Now, first up, I assume these are the Collingwood change rooms?'

'They are,' Lee replied immediately. His voice was steady and unwavering.

'We'll need to search them,' Harry said. 'But we should be able to do that before the end of the game. So, no need to move their gear out. Doing that would get in the way of our search anyway.'

'Understood,' Copeland replied.

'Okay,' Harry said. 'Now, is there any way that Robert Sharkey could have been given strychnine by mistake? Either before the game or at half-time?'

'Absolutely not,' Lee replied firmly. We wouldn't have strychnine on the premises.'

'You can guarantee there wouldn't be strychnine pills in your kit anywhere? I know some pharmacists dispense them as a pick-me-up.'

'Definitely not. I don't believe in that, in any circumstances. Too dangerous.' Lee's response was immediate and sure.

'There wouldn't be any lying about anywhere down here for other purposes? To poison rats or other vermin?'

'Not possible. I make sure the room is clean when we come in, and again when we leave. Always.'

'Well then, assuming Ed's diagnosis of strychnine poisoning is confirmed, we can only conclude it was given to him somehow, deliberately and without his knowledge.'

Wal Lee shook his head slowly. 'I can't see how that's possible. Joey and me are the only ones who handle the drinks, and then it's only water. Nothing else.'

Where are the water bottles now?'

'Out on the ground. Where we're meant to be too, actually. One of us should get out there now, we might be needed.'

'Only when I'm finished with you all,' Harry replied sternly, then turned briefly to the burly constable on the door. 'Get one of your boys to get those bottles and bring them down here, would you, Jack. Though I don't expect that's how he got poisoned. Otherwise the whole team would be down, wouldn't they?'

'I suppose so,' Lee replied, and lapsed back into silence. He looked completely mystified.

'Well then,' Harry continued. 'If it wasn't you blokes gave him the strychnine, it must have been someone else. Did any of you notice anyone unusual down here at any time today? Anyone who shouldn't have been here.'

Lee scratched his head and thought for a moment. 'Well, I can't remember anyone unusual. Though I'm not sure we'd notice. We're always busy with the players, and there's always a big crowd of blokes in the rooms before the game. And at half-time, for that matter.'

'Really?' Harry said. 'Who exactly?'

'Oh, you know. Members, friends, supporters and so on.'

'Yes,' Copeland added. 'We like to encourage people to come in and support the lads.'

Harry frowned. 'Sounds like anyone could've been in here and you wouldn't have noticed.'

'Well, I certainly didn't,' Lee responded. 'I was busy doing rub-downs before the game and at half-time. What about you, Joey? Notice anyone suspicious?'

'No, boss,' Miller replied immediately. 'I was busy too, like always. Didn't notice no-one.' And he gave a sideways glance at Harry before resuming his downward stare.

Jimmy Johnston just shook his head and said nothing.

'Fair enough,' Harry conceded. 'Not surprising, I suppose. Well, that's all I've got for you blokes at the moment. I'll let you get back to the game. And I'll say it again. Try to act as normal as possible, at least till after the game finishes. If anyone asks, just say that Sharkey's not well and has been taken off to hospital.'

Copeland frowned. 'It'll be tough for these three blokes, Harry. I'm not sure how they're going to manage it. They're pretty upset.'

'I know, I know it's hard for you all. But do the best you can. It'll be harder for the players if they find out during the game that Sharkey's been killed.'

'Of course, you're quite right.' Copeland looked at Harry carefully, then added, 'The only thing is, given what's happened, I'm wondering whether it's right to continue with the game. Perhaps we should call it off?'

Harry shook his head firmly. 'I don't think so, Ernie. That could lead to all sorts of problems with the crowd. I don't want a riot on my hands as well as this.'

'Yes, of course,' Copeland muttered. 'I should have thought of that. Sorry.'

'Doctor Ramsgate,' Harry continued, turning to the Collingwood doctor, still standing there and looking completely dejected. 'We'll need to interview you in detail pretty soon. But right now, I'll ask you the same question I asked Mr Lee. Do you keep any strychnine with you. For treating players, I mean?'

Ramsgate stared blankly back at Harry. He seemed to be struggling to focus on the question. 'No, no,' he mumbled eventually. 'Of course not.'

'All right then,' Harry continued, addressing the officials at large. 'That'll do for the moment, gentlemen. Again, I need to stress to you all the need for confidentiality. About the possibility of strychnine, and the possibility of murder. That goes for the committee too, Ernie, though I realise you do have a responsibility to brief your president. But no-one else on the committee, not at this stage anyway.'

Copeland nodded grimly. 'You can count on me, Harry.' Then, with a stern glance at his colleagues, he turned and made his way to the door, the others following close behind.

Ed Brown remained in the room, and when the Collingwood officials had left, he turned to Harry. 'If it's all right with you, Harry, I'll accompany the body to the morgue. Just to make sure it's handled properly. And I'll make it my business to talk to Crawford Mollison too, to give him my findings from today. It'll assist with the post mortem.'

'Good idea, Ed. That's appreciated.'

At that moment Willie Milton reappeared, together with a couple of police constables. He reported that all was in readiness to transport the body. An escape route through a side entrance to the grandstand had been identified, and a horse and cart drawn up there ready to take Robert Sharkey to the morgue. Soon the body was concealed within a packing case and hoisted onto the shoulders of the two policemen. Willie and Ed followed them from the room and Harry was suddenly left alone.

He looked around, at the players' clothes hanging on hooks, at the mundane ordinariness of it all. He imagined the scene before the game, only a little while ago, of players and supporters bustling about, laughing and chatting, excited by the contest about to begin. And Harry imagined too, a lone person in that room with murder on his mind, planning his attack on the Collingwood star. Who could it have been? And why? And most puzzlingly, how? How could someone in a crowded room force a fit young man to drink a fatal dose of deadly poison?

But then his thoughts wandered in another direction. What if the poison had been administered to Sharkey somewhere else? In a circumstance where the culprit might be better concealed? And Harry thought of the crush around the players as they came and went from the field of play at the half-time break. He thought of all those women with their hat pins milling around the players, and he wondered whether it might just be possible for a murderer to strike in that crowded area? Worth thinking about, and worth following up, he decided.

As to motive, Harry could readily imagine some very plausible reasons why someone would want to stop Collingwood's best player. And those reasons mostly centred on the exchange of large amounts of money, the curse of illegal gambling which had spread though the sport like a cancer. But the how was something else, something for which Harry had no sensible explanation. At least, not at the moment.

Oh well, he thought, suddenly weary to the bone. Best get on with it, one step at a time. And so, after sending one of the constables off to escort Effie home, Harry began to work his way methodically around the room, searching through clothing, bags and the various boxes and containers used by the trainers. He didn't really expect to find anything. Didn't even really know what he was looking for. What he did know was that whoever was behind this was organised and clever. And desperate too. Desperate enough to kill a man, in broad daylight, before twenty-five thousand witnesses.

✕

Harry Holloway settled back into his cosy old armchair, closed his eyes and tried not to think. He felt completely done in, but his mind didn't want to stop racing. The possible hows and whys of Robbie Sharkey's murder kept bubbling into his consciousness, and none of the options he thought of were at all convincing. Poisoning someone at the MCG, with witnesses present at all times, just didn't seem possible. Unless of course, he'd been poisoned before he arrived at the ground and the strychnine hadn't taken effect until half-time. Perhaps brought about by Sharkey's exertions in the first half. Harry made a mental note to ask Molly about that possibility at the autopsy meeting.

Amid the confusion of his thoughts, Harry was reasonably certain of two things. Firstly, that Ed Brown was right in identifying poisoning by strychnine. Harry, too, had heard enough of the horrible effects of strychnine to know it when he saw it; the terrible convulsions, the clenched jaw and rigid stare, the waking agony of the victim.

Secondly, Harry was increasingly certain that the poisoning was premeditated. He just could not envisage how the strychnine might have been administered accidentally. But if it was deliberate, what motive was there to carry out such a desperate and terrible deed? The most likely answer was it had something to do with illegal gambling on the match? Harry knew that some of the shady figures in the gambling world would go to great lengths to get the result they needed. Bribing players to throw matches had been a sporadic but serious blight on the game for many years. And after all, Sharkey was Collingwood's best player, and getting rid of him would surely go a long way to reversing the result? Not that it actually had done. Collingwood had still won the game, even without Sharkey and the injured Danny Robinson, though it was a close call. Without their star player, Collingwood had laboured and a mere two points separated the two sides at the final siren.

The more he thought about it, the more Harry began to doubt that someone would go as far as murder to influence the outcome of a game. Though perhaps murder was not intended. Perhaps the plan had been to poison Sharkey sufficiently to make him ill and take no further part in the game. Another mental note, to check if Molly could answer that one.

Harry's musings were interrupted by the sound of Effie descending the stairs. She had been in Alfie's room, coaxing him to sleep; the afternoon's drama had clearly had an unsettling effect on him too.

'At last,' she sighed, entering the parlour. 'The poor little tyke wouldn't go down. He kept on asking about the sick man, is he better? I just said, I hope so and not to worry about it.'

'I know how he feels,' Harry replied. 'I'm trying to get Sharkey out of my head too, but he won't leave.'

'Poor darling,' Effie murmured, coming up behind the chair and leaning over to massage his shoulders. 'It'll keep till the morning, try not to think about it. Perhaps this calls for a medicinal brandy. I'm sure we could justify raiding the cabinet.'

Harry sighed. 'I'd better not. I popped in at the Cally for a couple of pots on the way home. But it hasn't helped; I can't switch off. Keep thinking about that poor bloke thrashing around on the floor. And wondering how I'm going to get to the bottom of it all.'

'You will, Harry, you always do.' Effie said, leaning over further to wrap her arms around him and hug him tightly. 'Remember we've got Michael and James coming to dinner tomorrow night. If you're too busy or too tired, I can put them off.'

'No, no,' Harry replied, half turning towards her and taking her hand. 'No, I'll be busy most of the day, I'm meeting with the Collingwood Committee, but tomorrow evening should be good. There's a limit to what I can do on a Sunday anyway. And besides, I always enjoy Michael and James's company. Their world is so different from ours. Well, from mine at least. It'll be good to have my mind taken off the case.'

2

SUNDAY 13 JUNE 1897

AS HE APPROACHED THE handsome bluestone facade of the Grace Darling Hotel, Harry reflected on the significance of this building for the Collingwood footy club. Even more so after he'd made his way inside and entered the hotel's function room, the site of the famous first meeting of the club committee, when it made its decision back in 92 to enter the Victorian Football Association. Who could have foretold that the ultimate glory, a premiership, would come the way of the Magpies within four short years?

Not that the faces of the men seated around the huge, ornately carved table in any way reflected the joy of that recent triumph. Instead the prevailing expressions were of distress, and all looked like they had managed very little sleep the previous night. On many of the faces too, expressions of perplexity, at the presence of police for what was still assumed to be a medical incident.

Though he had never met him, Harry instantly recognised the well-known figure of the President, William Beazley, at the head of the table. Beazley rose as Harry entered the room and strode across to greet him, offering his hand and inviting Harry to be seated at the other end of the table. Willie Milton took a seat behind Harry at a row of chairs placed against the wall, but Beazley motioned him forward.

'Join us at the table, Constable. You mightn't hear us from way back there. There's no standing on ceremony here. We're all in this together.'

'Thank you, Mr Beazley,' Harry replied. 'Constable Milton's not usually this shy.'

Beazley smiled, though somewhat wanly, and continued. 'Well, Inspector, as you can imagine, we're all in a state of shock. It's still hard to believe that this has happened. I'm not sure what we can do to assist you, but whatever we can do, we will.'

'That's appreciated,' Harry replied. 'Thank you. Now, we recognise that …'

'Excuse me for interrupting, Inspector, but I should first introduce you to our committee. Remiss of me not to do so immediately. Our Secretary, Mr Copeland, you know him already, I believe.'

'Yes', said Harry, acknowledging Ernie Copeland, sitting at Beazley's right hand. 'Ernie and I know each other well. We've appreciated his support on a number of footy-related issues we've had to deal with.'

'Next to Ernie is Jeremiah Wingard. Mr Wingard owns the Brunswick Brick Company. One of our local captains of industry.'

Wingard was a tall, upright fellow, in his forties, Harry guessed, with craggy, dark features, a flourishing moustache and a neat goatee beneath.

Beazley continued his introductions. 'Next to Jeremiah is Sir Randolph Thames. Sir Randolph owns the Premier Building Society, one of our great lending institutions and a great supporter of our club. He acts as our treasurer.'

'Good afternoon, Inspector, pleased to meet you,' Sir Randolph said quietly. He was a small, very neat man, immaculately dressed. Like Wingard, he had a prominent moustache and goatee. But where Wingard's features seemed to give an impression of brash self-confidence and strength, Sir Randolph radiated an aura of quieter assurance.

'Then we have Tommy Sherrin, who you probably know already, Inspector.'

'I do indeed. Good to see you Tom.' Sherrin was a solidly built fellow with a carefully waxed handlebar moustache. The game owed much to Tom Sherrin; without him it would not have the unique, oval-shaped leather ball which he had so cleverly developed to suit the nature of Australian Rules.

Beazley continued. 'Then on the other side of the table, Walter Stansforth. Walter is a military man: experience in the British Army in India, among many other distinctions. He now runs a very successful importing business.'

Stansforth was portly and red-faced, well into his sixties, Harry guessed. 'How do you do, Inspector,' he murmured. 'A terrible business, this. Most unfortunate.'

'No doubt you also know Bill Strickland,' Beazley went on. 'Perhaps from his Carlton playing days. As you know, he's our captain and the players' representative on the committee.'

'I still haven't forgiven him for walking out on us at Carlton,' Harry declared, trying to ease the tension in the room. Strickland smiled briefly.

'And finally,' Beazley said. 'We have Doctor Ramsgate, who is also our honorary doctor. I believe Doctor Ramsgate was with you yesterday, assisting with poor Robbie Sharkey.'

Precious little assistance you offered, Harry thought, but nevertheless he politely acknowledged the doctor, before turning to Beazley. 'Thank you, Mr Beazley, for those introductions. And thank you, gentlemen, for agreeing to meet with me at such short notice. Now, I appreciate that this has been a terrible shock for you all, and for the club, and that you all probably wonder what light you can possibly throw on Robert Sharkey's death.'

'Yes,' Sir Randolph said immediately. 'We all saw what happened on the field of course, but beyond that, I can't see how we can help you. And I must say, I'm not certain why the police are involved.'

'Then let me tell you why we're involved,' Harry said solemnly. 'We're urgently investigating the circumstances and the cause of Sharkey's death. And at this stage we're reasonably certain that he died neither of a medical incident, nor through some sort of accidental poisoning. We believe he was murdered.'

'Murdered?' Walter Stansforth exclaimed. 'What do you mean? We assumed Robbie had a seizure or some such. Why are you saying he was murdered? Who would do a thing like that?'

'Perhaps I shouldn't have been quite as definite as that,' Harry replied evenly. 'But we're confident he was poisoned, and I can't see how it was an accident. An autopsy is being undertaken today, probably as we speak in fact. I expect that it will confirm our suspicions.'

A shocked silence ensued around the table as the committee digested Harry's news. Harry too was silent for the moment, calmly surveying the committee members and their various reactions.

Eventually, Beazley spoke again. 'This is the first time most of the committee have heard of possible foul play, Inspector. As per your instructions, the only other people who know of that possibility are the men who were in the room yesterday. And myself. We have also not told the players. Ernie … that is, Mr Copeland, has been assiduous in ensuring your request for secrecy.'

'Good,' Harry replied. 'I appreciate your discretion. But once the pathologist reports to me and the coroner, I'm confident it will be declared a murder by poisoning, and a full investigation will get underway. I'll know by tomorrow and I'll let you know in turn. You'll then be in a position to inform the whole club.'

Beazley sighed. 'If it turns out as you say, it'll be a terrible scandal for the club. One that will be very difficult for us to get over.' And he lapsed into silent contemplation of the table in front of him.

'All the more reason why we need to get to the bottom of it all as quickly as possible,' Harry replied. 'The sooner we find the killer, the sooner the club can get back to some sort of normality. And it would assist us in our investigation if the committee could give me as much background information on Sharkey as you possibly can.'

'Yes, I see.' Beazley paused, stroked his chin, then glanced around the room before turning to Harry again. 'Well, what can we tell you? Robbie was obviously an important part of our club. Our best player. Very popular with our supporters.'

'That much we know already,' Harry observed. 'But what we'd also like to know is how he got on with people at the club. Was he popular? Did he have any enemies?'

'Not that I know of,' Beazley said. 'He always seemed well-liked to me. But I'm probably not the best person to answer that question. Mr Copeland has much more to do with the day-to-day running of the club. And better still, Bill Strickland here. The captain, you know. He's really the one who would know if there were any problems between Sharkey and the players. And with anyone else, for that matter.'

Harry turned to Copeland. 'Ernie, what were your impressions of Sharkey? After all, you must have known him pretty well. You were the driving force behind recruiting him last year, as I understand. The lad from Port Melbourne with loads of talent, and ready to take the next step. And you blokes here at Collingwood turned him into a star.'

Copeland sat silently for a short while, deep in thought. Then he replied, carefully. 'Yes, I suppose I would know him as well as anyone around the place. As you say, I was the one who got him to come over to us and I had quite a bit to do with him, in the first couple of months especially. But you know, I really didn't get to know him that well. He always kept to himself. Not shy, but not a great talker either. Just concentrated on his footy, I suppose, and being the best he could be.'

'Fair enough,' Harry said. 'But how did he get on with the rest of the boys? Was he popular?'

Copeland smiled wryly. 'Well, he was our best player, so he certainly had his team mates' respect. And he was always surrounded by fans at our social functions. Always the centre of attention.'

'Any special friends among his team mates, would you say?'

Copeland thought again for a while. 'Not really. Though I suppose he and Danny Robinson seemed to hang around together quite a bit. Yes, I'd say Danny was the one he spent most time with.' Copeland turned to Strickland. 'Would you agree with that, Bill?'

Strickland nodded slowly. 'Yeah, I think so,' he said. 'Though I agree with you – I reckon he didn't have any real close mates here. He didn't spend a lot of his spare time at the club.'

'Any blues with any of the players?' Harry asked. 'Did you notice anything?'

Harry fancied Strickland shot a quick glance at Copeland before replying, 'Not really, Harry. Nothing major. Just the usual squabbles you always get in clubs. After all, he was the best player here and he knew it. I suppose he'd sometimes let other players know if they did the wrong thing on the ground. But no, nothing major.'

'Good. That's good information. We'll certainly speak to Danny Robinson, now we know they were friendly. What about the rest of you blokes? Anything useful you can add about Sharkey? Again, do you know whether he had any enemies? Any disagreements with anyone around the club?'

There were some exchanged glances around the table, but no-one spoke up. Harry waited for a response. The atmosphere in the room began to grow uncomfortable, until eventually Tom Sherrin broke the silence.

'I'm sorry, Inspector, there's not much we can add. As Mr Copeland indicated, Robbie was a quiet sort of fellow. Not a lot to say for himself, he let his football do the talking for him.' Sherrin paused, then turned to Jeremiah Wingard, sitting across the table. 'What about you, Jeremiah? You seemed to have a bit to do with him, especially early on in his time here. Anything you can add?'

'No, nothing,' Wingard replied gruffly. 'I did my bit to make him feel at home, but I do that with all the players. It's very important that we do. Part of our role, you know.'

'I understand,' Harry said. 'Would you say, Mr Wingard, that Sharkey was happy at the club? Enjoying his time here.'

'As far as I could tell, he was. Put it this way, he never complained to me that he was unhappy.'

'I see.' Harry paused a moment, before turning to the table at large. 'A question now for you all, gentlemen. And a bit of a sensitive one, I suppose. As you all know, the issue of payments to players is one that all the clubs are grappling with at the moment. There are rules that allow you to reimburse some costs to players, but you're not allowed to pay players to play. Which we know can be a problem in attracting players to your club. And retaining them, particularly the star players. Which Robbie Sharkey was, of course.'

'Oh, that wasn't an issue for us,' Copeland replied, promptly and with a degree of certainty. 'We were fully compliant with league rules in regard to all that. You see, when Robbie came to us, Sir Randolph here generously offered him a position in his building society. So he was quite independent financially, quite secure, and no need to worry about money at all. The club didn't pay him a penny.'

'Very generous indeed,' Harry agreed. 'Can I ask, Sir Randolph, what position Sharkey held at your business?'

Thames looked slightly uncomfortable. 'A promotional role, Inspector,

I suppose would be the best way to put it. As a progressive businessman, I'm well aware of the value of effective promotion to sell your product. And as you may be aware, our product is a very popular one in this city. And having the best player of the best football team as its public face is more than helpful for boosting sales even further.'

'No doubt, but what was Sharkey's role in the company exactly? What was he required to do?'

'Oh, a variety of activities,' Thames replied vaguely. 'Be on hand for promotional events, public meetings, that sort of thing. But really, in the main it was to enable us to use his name on our material. And as you can appreciate, that was worth quite a bit to us.'

'I'm sure it was,' Harry agreed. 'But I think what you're telling me is that the job Sharkey had did not really require a lot of his day. He would have had plenty of spare time.'

Thames looked slightly taken aback. 'Well, I suppose you could say that. Though of course, his football commitments would have taken up a fair bit of his time as well. That was one of the advantages of the position he held in our company. He had plenty of time to focus on his football. While still providing a major benefit to our society.'

'Yes, I can see that.' Harry paused, shifting in his chair and glancing briefly at Willy at his side. 'Now, gentlemen,' he resumed, 'another difficult question, but I have to ask it. As you know, there's been much talk of late about the problem of illegal betting on football matches. It's certainly a problem for us, and I assume it's a problem for you blokes too. I know you had that issue with McInerney a couple of years ago.'

Beazley responded, firmly and without hesitation. 'You're right, and the way we dealt with that McInerney fellow shows the attitude we have towards cheats and criminals. Any attempt to throw games or distort results for financial purposes will be met with the same response. You'll note, Inspector, that McInerney still has not returned to the football field, and that's due to our continuing efforts to wipe out cheating.'

Harry nodded. 'Yes, your action against McInerney and his mates was noted and greatly appreciated. I think we told you so at the time. But I'm afraid the stench of illegal gambling on football matches has not disappeared, and there still continue to be rumours circulating.'

'What rumours do you mean?' Beazley asked. 'That players are still trying to influence the result by lying low during games?'

'Among other things. We certainly know there continues to be a lot of gambling on football matches. And where that happens, lots of other unsavoury things can happen too.'

'Inspector, I'm not sure whether you are referring to Mr Wren and his business interests,' Ernie Copeland interceded quickly. 'Just because he's a strong supporter of this club doesn't mean that he involves Collingwood in his business activities. In fact, when you think about it, his relationship with us makes us doubly reassured that he doesn't. Doesn't encourage crooked betting on our games, I mean. He would never gamble on Collingwood losing a game.'

'Ernie, I wasn't making any assertions about Mr Wren. But it's obviously an angle that we have to be aware of. And investigate, in relation to this business with Sharkey.'

'Hang on, Inspector,' Stansforth exclaimed. 'You're not suggesting that someone in our club murdered Robbie in order to affect the result of the game. That doesn't make sense. Surely you should be talking to the Carlton mob if you have any suspicions in that regard. They're the ones who'd be more interested in getting their team up.'

'Not necessarily, in my experience,' Harry replied. 'But anyway, I'm not making any suggestions of any sort. Not at this stage, anyway. It's just that when the best player on the ground is murdered halfway through a match, influencing the result of the game is obviously one motive that must be investigated. And investigate it we will. With an open mind, of course.'

'Indeed you must, Harry,' Copeland agreed. 'We accept that. We just want you to know that this club has been instrumental in setting up structures to tackle the insidious issue of illegal gambling. I'm proud to say that I, along with Bill Strickland, have been responsible for one particular initiative, the Players Code of Conduct, which commits players to proper behaviour, and which is directly aimed at preventing the kind of thing you've raised.'

'Yes, I know of the code,' Harry replied. 'And good on you, it's a great initiative. But like many of these things, I suppose it relies on honesty and openness from the players who sign up to it.'

Beazley smiled wryly. 'You're right, Inspector, we can't force players to do the right thing. But we can at least try to create an environment that encourages them in the right direction.'

Harry sat back, briefly in thought. Then he spoke deliberately. 'As I told you, gentlemen, we're making no definitive conclusions about the cause of death, certainly not until we hear from the pathologist. But it might assist him if you can help me with the events immediately before Sharkey's death. One thing that I did notice, and I know it happens all the time, there was a fair crowd of spectators around the players going into the change rooms at half-time. And lots of poking and prodding, with hat pins and the like.'

'Indeed,' Copeland responded, with some irritation in his voice. 'I wish we could put a stop to it. It's downright dangerous for our players, what some of those women get up to. But short of putting up some sort of enclosure to protect the players and umpires, I'm not sure there's much we can do about it. If I may say so, it seems to have your blokes beat too, Harry, trying to stop it.'

'It's a hell of a problem,' Harry agreed, 'and we're not sure what the answer is either. Short of throwing some of those respectable ladies in the clink, that is. Who knows, it might come to that. But I'm wondering, when the players came in at half-time after fighting their way through that crowd, did anyone, Robbie Sharkey in particular, complain of being jabbed and hurt? More so than usual, that is.'

Copeland was quick to respond. 'Well, I think Henry Ramsgate, Bill Strickland and I were probably the only ones in this room who were also in the change rooms at half-time. I can't say that anyone spoke to me about being jabbed, beyond the usual grumbles about keeping those damn women away from them. Certainly, I can't recall anything at all from Robbie. What about you, Henry? Bill?'

Ramsgate shook his head quickly. 'No, no, nothing at all. No-one said anything to me.'

'Me neither,' Strickland added.

Sherrin leaned forward, 'Are you saying, Inspector, that Robbie was poisoned as he came off the ground. That's a bit far-fetched, isn't it? What're you suggesting, a poison-tipped needle or something?

'Or a hypodermic syringe,' Harry suggested. 'It was bedlam out there, it's possible no-one would have noticed.'

'Blimey!' Jeremiah Wingard exclaimed, giving a low whistle. 'That's a fiendish way to do someone in.'

'Surely it's more likely that someone spiked his drink,' Sherrin continued. 'That would've been much easier to do.'

'It would've been easier,' Harry agreed. 'But strychnine has a very bitter taste. Sharkey would surely have noticed.'

'Strychnine!' Walter Stansforth exclaimed. 'You think it was strychnine, Inspector? That's the first we've heard of that.'

'Oh, sorry,' Harry replied hastily. 'I forgot, you haven't been informed of that yet. Yes, we believe the poison administered to Sharkey was strychnine. But we await the pathologist's report to confirm it.'

'Strychnine with a hypodermic syringe,' Randolph Thames mused, almost to himself. 'It sounds like it was well-planned. A carefully thought-out plot.'

'Hang on,' Harry replied hastily. 'I'm not saying that's necessarily what happened. The hypodermic syringe part, I mean. It's just a theory I wanted to run by you blokes. In case we can help the pathologist with his post-mortem.'

'Yes, of course, we understand,' Beazley replied. 'But it seems like we can't help you, not in this room at least. It's a question you might put to our training staff, Wally Lee and Joey Miller, when you speak to them.'

Harry continued his questions, probing the committee and trying in particular to get a better picture of Robbie Sharkey. Had he been 'not himself' recently? Had he been seen with anyone unusual around the club? How did he get on with his family? Did he bring a girlfriend to social functions at the club?

But his prodding elicited only bland and unexceptional responses. 'No, everything seemed absolutely normal', 'No, Robbie was his usual friendly self.' 'Didn't see much of his family, but he always seemed proud of them. His father's a pharmacist, you know.' But at least on the question of his romantic life, Harry had some success. Robbie did appear to have a lady friend, one Margot Philips, an employee of Doctor Ramsgate. She was a 'classy sort of dame', according to Jeremiah Wingard. As far as Wingard knew, Margot and Robbie were pretty close, had been going together for some time. Good, thought Harry, as he jotted down her details in his notebook. Let's hope she's a bit more forthcoming than these blokes.

After fifteen minutes or so of fruitless interrogation, with very little useful information forthcoming, Harry decided to pull up stumps. He glanced up at the large clock on the wall. 'Well, gentlemen, I reckon I've taken up more than enough of your time. I'll leave you to it.'

'Anything we can do to help, Inspector,' Beazley reiterated. 'We're at your disposal at any time.'

There was murmured agreement from around the room.

'I'd just remind you of the need for your continued discretion,' Harry added, as he rose from the table. 'At least until tomorrow when we hear from the pathologist. If my assessment is correct, it will then become a murder investigation and be public knowledge. Then it's up to you how you inform your players and the rest of the club. Excuse us then, we'll see our own way out.' He took his hat from its resting place on the table and strode from the room, with Willie following.

'What'd you make of all that, boss?' Willie asked, as soon as they were out of earshot.

Harry gave a slight shrug. 'Not a lot really, mate,' he muttered. 'Either Sharkey was a closed book at the club and kept himself entirely to himself, or else the committee is closing ranks and clamming up. I rather suspect the latter.'

'Why would they do that?'

'Oh, I can think of some good reasons. They'd want to protect the image of the club champion. And even more so, the reputation of the club.'

'You think Sharkey was involved in something? Something dodgy?'

'Don't know yet. But if he was poisoned, sure as hell something was going on. Whether he was involved in it or was just an innocent victim, killed because he was too good a footballer, well, that's what we have to find out.'

The two men walked in silence to the police trap waiting outside the Victoria Park gates. As they swung up into it, Harry turned again to his colleague.

'Let's see what tomorrow's autopsy report brings, Willie. We'll see what Molly's got for us. Then we'd better interview the family, I suppose. See how close he really was to them. And after that we'll talk to this Margot woman. She's one I'm pinning my hopes on a bit. If she was that tight with him, she'll be up for finding his killer, I would think. Can't see her holding back. But we'll give her a day or two. No doubt she'll be in a pretty bad way when she gets the news.'

✕

Michael Standish eyed Harry quizzically. 'You're very quiet tonight. Pondering some particularly thorny case? Come on, a penny for your thoughts.' And he smiled an encouraging, but inquiring, smile.

Harry looked up from his bread and butter pudding and replied apologetically. 'Sorry, Mike. You're right, I'm not much company tonight. Got a bit on my mind.'

'It only came up yesterday,' Effie quickly interceded. 'A terrible business, but he can't say anything about it yet. Not until tomorrow, anyway.'

'Oh dear,' Michael said. 'It must be so hard dealing with all these terrible crimes that keep happening in Melbourne. I assume it's a murder, or something equally awful.'

'That much I can reveal,' Harry replied. 'It's not just because it's a murder though. We deal with them all the time, but this one's a bit different. For reasons you'll understand when I can say more, it's getting to me a bit.'

James chimed in, echoing his partner's concern. 'Then we really should make our farewells. You look dog-tired. You've been wonderful hosts, but we don't want to overstay our welcome.'

'You're not going anywhere, James,' Harry insisted, pushing back his chair and getting to his feet. 'Effie's going to take you into the parlour to the comfy chairs, and I'm going out to the kitchen to brew up some coffee and find that bottle of port we put away for special guests. I'm expecting to hear all your gossip from the arts world.' And rising to his feet, he headed off in the direction of the kitchen.

Effie shepherded her friends into their small parlour. 'Don't worry about Harry,' she urged. 'He sometimes needs bringing out of himself when these big cases come along. He actually loves to be diverted by your news. It helps him forget about work for a while.'

'Can I compliment you on dinner, my dear?' Michael said, as he settled himself next to James on the sofa. 'The steak and kidney was delicious. I don't know how you can be such a wonderful cook and a brilliant teacher at the same time.'

'Well, it may shock you to know I wasn't responsible for the steak and kidney pie. That was entirely Harry's doing.'

'Is there no end to the man's talents?' James laughed. 'Michael, that was naughty of you. You shouldn't make assumptions about domestic affairs in this independent household. Effie, feel free to take him to task.'

'I will,' Effie laughed in return. 'Shame on you, Michael, I thought I'd harangued you long enough at school about equality for women. That means sharing the work at home too.'

'Guilty as charged,' Michael confessed. 'It's just that Harry seems such an unlikely gourmet chef. Fiddling around with the right amounts of ingredients, and so forth.'

'Well, that's true,' Effie conceded. 'He's more of a 'throw things together and see what happens' kind of chef. But with surprisingly tasty results, in my experience.'

At this moment, the subject of the culinary conjecture returned, bearing a tray with a large coffee pot, cups and a dusty bottle of port. 'I heard that, Effie Holloway,' he said. 'Definitely a slander on my reputation as a cook. You can expect an appropriate punishment in due course.'

'You know I love your cooking, darling,' Effie said. 'But you must admit you do like to experiment. Even your mother says that, and in her eyes you can do no wrong.'

Harry grinned as he laid out the pot and cups on the occasional table. Then did the honours for his guests, before settling into one of the armchairs, coffee in one hand, port in the other, and his long legs stretched out before him.

'Well then, here we are. Now, what exciting news have you blokes got to offer? You're always up to something.'

Michael glanced across at James before replying. 'Well, we have one exciting bit of news. James has been invited to mount an exhibition later this year.'

'Oh, how exciting!' Effie said. 'Bravo to you, James. And very well deserved. You're a wonderful artist. Where will it be?'

'At the gallery,' James replied, looking somewhat embarrassed. 'The Victorian Artists Society are sponsoring it.'

'He's too modest,' Michael interceded. 'But I'm not. He's brilliant. He'll be the next big thing, mark my words. Move over, Streeton and McCubbin, I say.'

'That's the way,' Harry chuckled. 'Nothing like a bit of confidence. Don't forget our invitations, will you?'

'Don't worry, darling,' Effie responded. 'I'll make sure of that.' She glanced at Michael, suddenly with a more serious expression. 'Did you want to bring up that other matter, Michael? You know, the one you mentioned to me at school.'

Michael shuffled a little on the sofa. 'Oh, we don't want to spoil this lovely evening talking about that. And Harry's had a hard day. It can wait for another time.'

'No, no,' Effie replied. 'It's important. And Harry's always willing to listen and offer some advice if he can. Particularly to good friends like you two. Aren't you, dear?'

'Sure,' Harry replied patiently. 'If I can. Sounds like you might have a bit of legal trouble you want some help with?'

Again Michael glanced at James before replying. 'Well, not really, but it's something we're worried about. Not for us, but for a friend of ours.'

'Come on, Michael,' Effie interrupted. 'Get to the point. You know you can be open with Harry.'

'Yes, dear, I know that,' Michael replied quickly. 'I'm just trying to find the right words. Well, Harry, you know that James and I are members of the Savage Club …'

'I didn't, actually,' Harry replied. 'I think I've heard of that place, but I'm not sure what it's about.'

'You've heard me talk about it, darling,' Effie cut in again. 'It's a club for artists, writers and other people interested in cultural pursuits. Very progressive, it's one of the few clubs around town that allows female members. A lot of my suffragette friends are members. I'm thinking of joining myself.'

'Fair enough,' Harry replied. 'Whatever you reckon, Eff, but I think I'll stick with the front bar of the Cally for the moment. Keep going, Mike. You and James are at the Savage Club. What's next? Something happen there?'

'No, no,' Michael added hastily. 'It's just that we met a young man there who seemed a little lost. And, well, James and I have sort of taken him under our wing. Or should that be wings?'

'Good on you two,' Harry said, taking a generous sip of his port. He added carefully, 'I assume this young fellow has the same … inclinations as you blokes.'

Effie shot Harry a stern look, but Michael was unabashed. 'You're exactly right. I've talked to him at length to make sure he knows his own mind. And I'm sure he does. He's worked out who he is and who he wants to be. His true nature, if you like.'

'And I assume he's well and truly over the age of consent?' Harry added.

'Oh yes, in his early twenties, I think.'

'In that case,' Harry said cheerfully, 'I sympathise. But I'm still not sure what it's got to do with me. Or the law.'

'Well,' Michael went on, again searching for the right words. 'As I said to you, our friend Richard is rather lost. I think he's only just come to terms with his true nature and he's struggling to accept it. He comes from a rather strict background. His father is a very important businessman here in Melbourne, and I think he's making it very difficult for Richard. Reputation and all that, you know.'

Harry raised an eyebrow. 'Yep, I'm sure his old man wouldn't be impressed. I can't imagine a prominent Melbourne businessman would have much patience with a son heading in that direction.'

Michael pressed on. 'The Savage Club is a safe place for him, he's surrounded there by like-minded and responsible people. But I think he's going to other places, and meeting with other people … where he may not be as safe. We're worried that he may be exposing himself to dangerous situations, and that he may come to harm. Or be arrested and thrown in jail. Which would be even worse.'

'Again, I sympathise,' Harry replied. 'But I'm not sure what I, or anyone else in the law, can do to help. It's a sad fact that young blokes in his situation sometimes act desperately and come to harm. And sometimes they put themselves in a position where they can't help but be arrested. And then you have all the consequences that follow.'

'It seems to me that the law is often too keen to arrest them,' Effie said sharply. 'It seems to me that the law is often the problem.'

Harry looked at her fondly. 'Effie dear, within these four walls I can admit that you're probably right. But out in the real world, it's a different matter. You know I can't take the tack that you would like me to. The best I can do is turn a blind eye to things when I can.'

Effie looked at him begrudgingly. 'I suppose you're right. But sometimes I think you should be more prepared to go out on a limb.'

Harry sighed. 'Sometimes I think I should too. And I'm sure you'll keep encouraging me to be braver. But, as far as this young Richard fellow goes, I actually have a suggestion to make.'

Effie's frown relaxed. 'Good. A constructive suggestion, mind. Constructive and helpful.'

'Always,' Harry smiled. 'Well, I know you said his family is strict, and probably not sympathetic to the life he wants to lead. But surely they wouldn't want him to come to any harm?'

'I suppose not,' Michael conceded. 'But apparently, whenever Richard tries to broach the subject, his father refuses to talk about it.'

'I'm not suggesting that,' Harry continued. 'But what if someone else spoke to his father, someone respected in the same social circle he moves in.'

'Oh, would you, Harry?' Effie exclaimed. 'Coming from you, I'm sure Sir Randolph would understand the need to support young Richard.'

'Sir Randolph? That wouldn't be Sir Randolph Thames, by any chance?'

'It would indeed,' Michael replied. 'Do you know him?'

'Would you believe, I met him today in fact. He's on the Collingwood footy club committee.'

'Oh, that's perfect,' Effie said. 'He's bound to listen to you, if he knows who you are.'

'Hang on, Eff, you know there's no way I could get involved. For all the reasons we've just been talking about. No, I was thinking more of a respectable teacher from a very well-known and respected Melbourne family.' Harry cast an enquiring eye in Michael's direction.

'Oh, you mean me,' Michael said. 'Well, perhaps I might have some influence.'

'I'm sure you would,' Harry encouraged. 'Get Sir Randolph to at least accept his son's nature, even if he doesn't like it.'

'Maybe.' Though Michael sounded doubtful. 'If you knew Sir Randolph, you would see my task would be difficult. Sir Randolph is very conservative, very religious and a strict temperance man. I believe he's high up in the Rechabites.'

'By the way,' James cut in, 'I remember now, Richard told us his father was trying to involve him in the Collingwood Club. To keep him away from temptation, was the way his father put it, apparently. I'm not sure it's working.'

Michael looked at Harry curiously. 'Was that part of this new case, Harry? Meeting with the Collingwood Committee, I mean.'

'Can't say, Mike,' Harry replied hastily. 'Actually, I shouldn't have mentioned that meeting at all. You didn't hear about it, lads, okay? Not until tomorrow at least. Then all of Melbourne will know.'

'Understood.' Michael raised his forefinger to his lips. 'Our lips are sealed.'

'Anyway,' James interposed. 'Let's hope we don't have to resort to approaching Sir Randolph. We're still hopeful that Richard will meet the right person and lead a more settled lifestyle.'

Effie turned to him in surprise. 'That doesn't seem likely from what you've been saying. Quite the opposite, in fact.'

'Well, he did indicate to us last time we saw him, that he'd met someone rather special. Though he didn't tell us who it was.'

'Or where he met this person either, I suppose,' Effie said. 'No-one from your group of friends?'

'No.' Michael sounded less positive than James about their friend's new liaison. 'And it could just as easily lead to new problems, I suppose.

If his new friend moves in, you know, dangerous circles.'

'Oh dear, it's all so depressing,' Effie said. 'Why can't the poor boy just lead the life he wants to, without being judged by his family and without living in fear of the law?'

Harry smiled, though rather wearily. 'I know, I know, no need to berate me again.'

'It's all right,' Michael reassured him. 'We know you're doing all you can. It's not your fault the law's the way it is. Now, we don't want to be the cause of a family argument, and we know you've got a big day ahead, so I think it's definitely time we said our farewells.'

'Don't worry,' Harry responded. 'Effie and I have these debates all the time. Keeps life interesting.' And then, in a more serious tone. 'And please, if there's anything that gives you cause to think your friend is in real danger, let me know. You know you can contact me at Russell Street any time.' And, getting to his feet, he shook hands warmly with the two men, before Effie escorted them to the door.

3

MONDAY 14 JUNE 1897

'THIS PLACE ALWAYS GIVES me the creeps,' Willie Milton muttered, as they drove the police trap into the muddy yard at the side of the morgue. A chilling wind had sprung up and was scudding the surface of the Yarra River, next to which the brooding hulk of the morgue and coroner's court nestled.

'Yeah, me too,' Harry agreed, as they tethered the horse and strode towards the small entrance foyer at the rear of the building. 'And believe me, it'll be just as bloody cold in there as it is out here. Colder, probably.'

'Don't let Molly ramble on too much, will you, Harry. Or we'll all get frostbite.'

Harry smiled grimly. 'We'll get it done as quick as we can, mate. No shortcuts though.' And pushing through the entry door, he led the way to one side, into the small post-mortem room.

Doctor Crawford Mollison rose from a chair placed against the wall, laying down his copy of *The Argus* as he did so. Dressed immaculately as ever in morning suit and floral waistcoat, his pomaded hair slicked back tightly to his scalp, the pathologist cut an incongruously dashing figure in the chilly, bare room.

'Greetings, young Harry,' he exclaimed cheerily. 'And to you too, Constable,' he added, nodding amiably in Willie's direction. 'I trust you're both well on this fine morning?'

'Well enough, Molly,' Harry responded, with not quite the same level of bonhomie. 'Hope you've got lots to tell me.'

'I have, I have indeed,' replied Mollison, pointing in the direction of the examination table, where a white sheet was draped over what Harry assumed was Sharkey's corpse. 'Our unfortunate young friend over there met with foul play, I would say.'

Harry nodded slowly. 'No surprises there. And strychnine, would you reckon?'

'Unquestionably strychnine.' Mollison's response was swift and certain. 'I was able to get a decent sample of urine from the bladder and found a very significant concentration of strychnine nitrate therein. I would estimate he was given anything up to one hundred milligrams. A fatal dose, obviously.'

Harry's tone became more animated, as he responded to this news. 'That's interesting. Can we assume then that he would have been given the poison some reasonable time before his death? On account of the time it would take for the stuff to go through him into his bladder?'

'Good thinking, but not necessarily correct. The kidneys actually separate out strychnine from the blood very quickly. The amount I found in the urine could easily have been passed from the kidneys within, say half an hour, or even less, after the poison entered his bloodstream.'

'Hmmm,' Harry mused, 'that doesn't tell us a hell of a lot, does it? Next question then. Any idea how the poison was given to him? For instance, orally? Or even injected?'

Mollison looked at Harry keenly. 'Anything in particular leading you to that second conclusion?'

'Well, it's just that, as per usual, the players were mobbed and prodded with all manner of sharp objects as they came off at half-time. And when they went back on again, for that matter. I'm wondering whether it would have been possible for our murderer to stick Sharkey with a syringe at that time?'

Mollison stood thoughtfully, hands clasped behind his back. 'Yes, I suppose it would be possible. I know that a very small dose of strychnine, injected subcutaneously, can prove fatal. And very quickly too, it's been shown. And that theory would fit with my other findings.'

'And what are those?'

'Well, I found no evidence of strychnine in the stomach at all. Not a trace. And I found a number of bruises on the body. Around the buttocks region. Consistent with poking with sharp objects. And now that I think of it, consistent with poking with an hypodermic syringe as well. Here, I'll show you.' And he approached the examination table and drew back the white sheet.

Robert Sharkey's body lay there, still with a grimace contorting his once-handsome features, and still with his limbs splayed in odd directions. It was almost as if his recent agonies had not yet left him and the peace of death remained elusive. A raw jagged scar ran down the length of his stomach, from breastbone to groin, a result of Mollison's recent examination.

'Bloody hell!' Willie said, drawing away. 'Too soon after breakfast for me.'

'Come on, mate, toughen up,' Harry replied with a grim smile. 'Important you have a good look. It's evidence, after all.'

Mollison smiled indulgently at Willie's discomfort. 'Not a pretty sight, I agree, Constable. But all in a day's work, you know. Here, Harry, give me a hand to turn him on his side.' And with Harry's help, the corpse was re-positioned so that the buttocks were more clearly visible.

A patchwork of small round bruises was spread across Sharkey's rump, most of them a fading dirty yellow against the dead skin. But Mollison pointed at one in particular, standing out a livid purple against its duller companions. A small piece of tissue had been cut from the site.

'That one appears to be the most significant,' he observed. 'Judging by that colouration, I would expect that would have been inflicted more recently, and hence could be the point of entry of the poison. The tissue around the entry point looks to have been traumatised. By the action of the strychnine, perhaps.'

'What are all these other bruises?' Willie wondered aloud. 'His bum looks like it's got the measles.'

'The combined result of hat pins and umbrellas, I suppose,' Harry suggested. 'That's the normal focus of the hat pin ladies, a poke on the bottom as the players go past. What do you think, Molly?'

'A reasonable supposition, Harry. Those lesser bruises look consistent with that kind of activity. And over a period of time too, I'd guess.'

'That makes sense,' Harry agreed. 'It's all the fashion with the ladies at most clubs, I'm afraid. Has been for a while. And Sharkey was the star, so he would have copped a fair swag of it. Now, I see you took a sample from that site. Were you able to test it for strychnine, to establish with certainty that it was injected at that point?'

'Afraid not, old boy. That biopsy showed the presence of strychnine, but not a particularly high concentration. That's not surprising, though. The poison would have disseminated from the point of entry throughout his system quite quickly. Within minutes, perhaps. It's hard to be precise. But to answer your question in a different way, given it's clear that the strychnine wasn't given orally, and given the lack of other marks on the body, I think we can assume that site on the buttocks was the point of entry.'

Harry scratched his head and ruminated, still studying Sharkey's corpse, spread out before them. Eventually he observed, to no-one in particular, 'Well, I suppose we've made some progress. We know now for sure it was strychnine that poisoned him, we know it wasn't given to him orally, and we're pretty certain it was injected into him, possibly while he was coming off the ground. Or going back out again after half-time. Or even perhaps at the start of the game. How does that sound, Molly?'

'All possible scenarios. Though I must say, given the concentration of strychnine in the urine and the fatal outcome, the start of the game might be a bit of a stretch. I'd reckon it couldn't have been any more than an hour before he collapsed.'

Harry nodded slowly. 'Thanks, Molly, you've been extremely helpful. Get your report to me as soon as you can, and we'll get a recommendation off to the coroner.'

'Murder? By a person or persons unknown?' Mollison postulated.

'Got it in one, mate. Keep me informed if you find anything else.' And with a firm handshake and a tip of his hat, Harry turned and strode from the room, Willie Milton close at his heels.

'Blimey, boss,' Willie observed, as they swung up into the police trap. 'I know there's some red-hot supporters out there, but surely no-one's crazy enough to bump off the opposition's best player. And with a syringe out in the open, like you're thinking.'

'Maybe not,' Harry replied thoughtfully. 'But you saw what it was like at the game. Bedlam for the players getting through that mob. It'd be a perfect opportunity for someone to stick a needle into a player going past. I reckon no-one would notice. Maybe not even the player himself, he'd probably just think it was a particularly sharp hat pin.'

'But still there's the question, why? Why would someone go to those lengths, just over a game of football. Surely winning's not worth that much?'

'It might be to someone,' Harry suggested. 'Someone with a major financial investment on the result.'

'I suppose so,' Willie conceded. 'A big punter, perhaps?'

'Perhaps. Or perhaps someone holding the big punter's money?'

'Oh yeah, I see what you mean.' Willie whistled softly and glanced at his boss. 'You talking about John Wren?'

'Well, they say he holds ninety per cent of the footy bets. It'd be logical to start with him.'

Willie looked doubtful. 'Surely not. Wren's a big Collingwood man. Puts a heap of money into the club. He's not going to get their number one man knocked off.'

You wouldn't think so,' Harry said pensively. 'But in my experience, money, and the making of it, is always a bookie's number one priority.'

Then he added, after a further pause; 'Anyway, it'd be well worth our while to pay him a visit. See how the land lies there, at any rate. And in due course, we'll get ourselves down to the Cally for a beer or two, bail up the Ferret and get him to run his sniffer round the place. If this murder's got anything to do with the SP bookies, someone down there may well know something.'

A miserable Monday afternoon at Victoria Park, as two overcoated figures trudged through the muddy expanse that linked Abbott Street to the entrance gates, and then beyond to Collingwood's hallowed turf. Harry Holloway and Willie Milton made their way through the brick entrance archway and headed towards the looming grandstand on their right.

'That's them over there, I reckon,' Willie said, pointing toward four men in the distance, standing in a huddle on the concourse in front of the stand. Harry recognised the tall, slightly stooped figure of Henry Ramsgate, the club doctor, and next to him, Wally Lee, the club's head trainer. The two were leaning in towards each other, obviously engaged in conversation. As they got closer, Harry also recognised Miller and Johnston, the two other trainers at the scene of Sharkey's death.

'Leave the talking to me,' Harry muttered to Willie as they approached the group. 'Just keep an eye out for any strange reactions. Particularly when the subjects of strychnine and syringes come up.'

'G'day, Harry,' Lee ventured, stepping forward to shake Harry's hand. He looked pale and tired, his waistcoat crumpled, his normally neat mane of grey hair unkempt.

'Bad business, Wal,' Harry responded, and the poor fellow looked so shattered that he couldn't help but offer a friendly pat on the shoulder. Then, turning to the club doctor, 'Morning, Doctor Ramsgate, I appreciate you making the time too.'

'Of course, Inspector, happy to be of service. Though I'm not sure there's much we can tell you.' Ramsgate glanced sideways as he spoke, his diffident demeanour suggesting a strong desire to be somewhere else.

'You know these two blokes, of course.' Lee continued, indicating his two offsiders. 'Joe Miller and Jimmy Johnston.'

Harry acknowledged the two with a curt nod, then continued. 'I don't need to tell you blokes, this is a bad business, what happened to Robbie Sharkey. A terrible business. We're treating this investigation with the highest urgency, so I'd appreciate if you could spare the time now to answer a few questions.'

'Of course, we'll tell you all we can,' Lee replied, then quickly added. 'It's been an absolute nightmare, Harry. For the club of course, and for us too. You know, given how he died.'

Harry pressed on. 'You'll recall, Wal, that on the day of the incident I indicated my suspicion that Sharkey had been poisoned with strychnine.'

'Yes,' Lee replied. 'And I indicated to you that we didn't keep strychnine tablets in the club. And that there wouldn't have been any rat poison in the change rooms. Or anywhere where Robbie could have been exposed to it. I'm always very careful about that kind of thing.'

'I remember. But here's the thing. We've now confirmed strychnine poisoning, but apparently it wasn't ingested. Eaten or drunk, that is. And the only other feasible way it could have got into him was by injection. Through a hypodermic syringe.'

'What? Surely not.' Lee stared at Harry in bewilderment, his jaw gaping slightly.

'We're pretty clear on that. Then the next question is, how did it happen? And where? I have to ask, do you keep a syringe in your medical kit, Doctor Ramsgate?'

Ramsgate coloured momentarily. 'Well, as a matter of fact I do. Not for use at the club, you understand. Most certainly not. But occasionally, I do have use for it, for treating certain types of pain in my patients. With morphia, you understand. I find it to be beneficial.'

'But not strychnine?' Harry pressed on. 'By injection, I mean. I understand some doctors prescribe such injections for their patients. For the treatment of muscle injuries.'

'No no,' Ramsgate replied quickly. 'I would never do that. Completely unproven, in my opinion. Verging on quackery, if you ask me.'

'And I take it your equipment has not been interfered with? Or stolen? Your syringe, that is.'

'Not as far as I know.'

'You didn't see anyone near where you keep your kitbag on Saturday? Where do you keep your gear, by the way?'

'Definitely not,' Ramsgate replied hurriedly. 'It's kept in the equipment locker in the rooms. No-one would be able to take it without someone seeing them.'

'Not even when the match was in progress? When I assume the rooms would be empty?' Harry eyed the doctor intently.

'Well, I suppose it might be possible then. But I'm not sure how anyone could get into the rooms. You know… a stranger, I mean.'

'You blokes didn't notice anything,' Harry inquired, turning towards Lee and his two offsiders.

'Most certainly not,' Lee replied immediately. 'What about you, Joey, you didn't notice anything?'

Miller shook his head fervently. 'No, no, I saw nothing. I didn't even know Doctor Ramsgate had a syringe. I've never seen what one looks like, I don't reckon.'

'Me either,' Johnston added.

'Okay,' Harry said. 'But if you don't mind, I'll take your syringe away for testing. You have it here now?'

Ramsgate paused, perhaps considering whether to argue the point, then gave in. 'Very well, if you must. I do have my bag here actually. You realise though, it'll be an inconvenience if I need it on my rounds later today.'

Harry smiled. 'I'm sure you'll manage for a day or so. After all, you indicated you only use it occasionally.'

'Follow me,' said Ramsgate, with the hint of a scowl, as he turned towards the grandstand behind them. 'My bag's in the rooms underneath the stand.'

Harry followed Ramsgate into the rooms while Willie waited with the others. Ramsgate's old brown leather medical bag had been left on a chair in the corner. Harry watched as the doctor rummaged around inside and produced a small silver metal tin. He opened it and silently handed the syringe to Harry.

'Thanks, but if you don't mind, I'll take the container as well. There's spare needles in it, I assume.'

'Yes,' Ramsgate replied curtly. 'Here you are.'

'And there's no other syringes in your bag?' Harry inquired.

'For God's sake, man, what do you take me for? A liar? Here, look if you must.' And he thrust the open bag in front of Harry.

Harry peered into the bag and noted a stethoscope, some rubber tubing, a couple of glass bottles, various jars, and a leather pouch that appeared to contain scissors, a scalpel and other sundry equipment.

'Good, that's all clear then. Thanks for the syringe, we'll have it back to you in a day or so.'

'I should hope so. Is that all you need me for now? I do have work to do.'

'Yep, that'll do for the moment. We'll let you know if we need you for anything else.'

The two men made their way outside to the others. Harry shook Lee's hand and again patted him sympathetically on the shoulder.

'See you later, Wal. Okay, Constable, let's go. We'll let these blokes get back to work.'

✕

'What did you make of all that?' Harry asked Willie, as they made their way out through the Victoria Park gates.

'Not a lot,' Willie replied. 'The doc seemed a bit upset about us questioning him.'

'Yeah, well, you never know, in due course we might need to upset him a bit more. After we have this syringe tested.'

'I'll tell you what though, the skinny little fellow was a bit nervous. And a bit nosy. He was asking me all sorts of questions while you were in the rooms with Ramsgate. Trying to find out if we had any suspects.'

'Who? You mean Joey Miller?'

'That's the one.'

Harry smiled. 'Oh well, it's not every day a famous footballer gets murdered. People are bound to be curious. You told him nothing, I hope.'

'Not a dicky bird, boss. Mum's the word.'

'That's the way.' And Harry gave him a friendly pat on the back, as they approached the police trap drawn up outside the gates.

Twenty-seven, Greeves Street, Collingwood, was one of a row of cottages, all built in the boom times for the aspiring middle class, all largely indistinguishable from each other. Double-fronted villa-style, with a bullnose verandah and white picket fence at the front. And even in the gloom of the gathering dusk, it was obvious that the house was not wearing its twenty years of life terribly well. As he and Willie stood waiting for a response to their knocking, Harry noted the door's already rusting handle and flaking paint.

They heard a soft footfall, the door was opened slightly and a pair of eyes peered timidly out at them.

'Mrs Sharkey?' Harry inquired. 'I'm Inspector Holloway from the Victorian police. I'm here about your son.'

The door opened fully to reveal a small, round, grey-haired woman. She looked up at them with an air that conveyed timidity and sadness in equal measure.

'I'm so sorry for your recent loss,' Harry continued, extending his hand in sympathy. 'I'm in charge of the investigation into your son's death. This is Constable Milton and we would very much like to speak to your family about Robbie, if that's not too painful. Is your husband at home?'

'Yes, and Rachel too. They're both home from work. Come in, Inspector.'

The two men followed Margaret Sharkey down the central passage-way and into a modest parlour. She pointed to a small settee. 'Wait here, I'll get the others.'

She made her way from the parlour, while Harry and Willie perched on the settee. Voices could be heard in a nearby room, and the volume and tone of the male voice indicated that Fraser Sharkey was not particularly happy about their presence. Then the voices stopped and imminently Fraser Sharkey entered the room, followed by his wife and an attractive young woman, who Harry assumed to be their daughter, Rachel.

'This is a very inconvenient time, Inspector. I would have appreciated some notice if you wished to interview us.' Fraser Sharkey stared defiantly at Harry from under beetling brows, his gaunt features fixed in a disapproving frown.

'I'm very sorry, Mr Sharkey,' Harry offered apologetically, rising from the settee and stepping forward. 'But we're pressing ahead as quickly as possible with our investigation into your son's death. We thought it important to talk to you as a priority. You may be able to give us vital information.'

'I doubt it,' Fraser Sharkey replied testily. 'But you're here, we might as well get it out of the way.'

'Thank you,' Harry replied, adding, 'Can we first extend our condolences to you and Mrs Sharkey. And Miss Sharkey too, of course. For your loss. It must be very difficult.'

Rachel Sharkey smiled sadly and murmured a subdued thank you, while Fraser said nothing, still frowning and gesturing to Harry to get things underway. His wife just lowered her eyes, which were red-rimmed and swollen.

Harry invited the women to be seated and Willie rose to make room for them. But they remained standing upright behind Fraser Sharkey, who continued to glare at Harry.

'The first thing I need to advise you,' Harry began, 'is that this is now a murder investigation. I don't think you've been informed of that.'

'Oh no!' exclaimed Margaret Sharkey, blanching and beginning to tremble. 'Surely not? Oh dear. Who would want to hurt our Robbie?' And she half staggered forward and collapsed onto the settee. She began to sob quietly, her head bowed.

Harry glanced at Rachel, who had whitened noticeably and was staring at them in disbelief. She began to sway slightly and Willie hurried forward, taking her arm and guiding her onto the settee by her mother's side.

'Is it certain he was murdered?' Fraser Sharkey asked, his voice quieter now and less belligerent.

'I'm afraid so,' Harry replied. 'He was poisoned. I won't go into the detail now, but we may need to talk about that at a later time.' And Harry gave an almost imperceptible nod towards the settee, to indicate to Fraser Sharkey his wish to spare the ladies any more shocks.

Harry continued. 'First up, I would like you to tell me as much as you can about Robbie. In particular, if you were aware that he had any enemies? Or if he was in trouble in any way?'

Fraser Sharkey let out a snort and shook his head dismissively. 'Well, we wouldn't know, would we? We wouldn't know what he was up to. He didn't bother to come and see us too often, I can tell you. We're only his parents, after all.'

Margaret Sharkey, now calm again, spoke up, quietly but insistently. 'That's not fair, dear. You know he's ... was very busy. At the club ... and the other job with Sir Randolph. He came as often as he could.'

'Nonsense!' Fraser Sharkey retorted. 'Thought he was too good for us, that's what it was. Don't know why. From what I hear, all he was doing was getting into trouble.'

'What sort of trouble would that be?' Harry asked.

'Oh, gambling … and that sort of thing. I don't know really. The club spoke to us about it, but they didn't say much. You'd better talk to them.'

'I have. And will again, no doubt. But that's good information, thank you.' Harry turned to Rachel.

'Now, Miss Sharkey, can I ask you a question or two. Were you on good terms with your brother?'

Rachel gave a tremulous smile, still struggling to control her emotions. She glanced nervously at her father, her hands clasped tightly together. She seemed to be having trouble speaking.

Willie leaned forward and patted her hand comfortingly. 'It's okay, Miss Sharkey, take your time. There's no hurry. Or pressure. But anything you can tell us would be welcome.'

Rachel seemed comforted by Willie's words and glanced gratefully at him. She's certainly very pretty, Harry thought, wondering if Willie's attentions were entirely professional.

'We were close,' she said quietly. 'I loved him very much.' She paused and Harry could see she was fighting off tears. 'He would try to visit me at least once a week. At the shop.'

'You mean, where you work?' Willie asked gently.

'Yes, at Mr Stansforth's shop. In the main street. It's near Father's pharmacy.'

'Robbie got Rachel that job, you know,' Margaret interposed. 'It was very good of him. He didn't have to do it.' And she glanced at her husband. Was there a trace of defiance in that look, Harry wondered.

'Was Robbie close to Mr Stansforth?' Harry asked Rachel. 'I mean, I know that Mr Stansforth would be keen to help him, because Robbie was so important to the club. But would you say they were good friends?'

Rachel contemplated Harry's question, her pretty features puckered as she cast her mind back. 'I wouldn't say so, not particularly. He came mainly to see me. But I suppose he would sometimes chat to Mr Stansforth as well. Out in the back room, you know. I assumed it was football business.'

Harry smiled at her and turned back to Fraser Sharkey. 'I'm wondering, Mr Sharkey, if you had some sort of falling out with your son. I'm wondering if there was a reason he didn't see you as much as you might wish?'

Out of the corner of his eye, Harry caught a glimpse of Margaret Sharkey looking quickly in her husband's direction. But just as quickly she turned back again and stared at the floor in front of her. Fraser Sharkey stood there silently, looking defiantly at Harry for a good few seconds. Then he seemed to make a decision.

'I don't mind admitting, we didn't see eye to eye on everything. I think the football ... and the money ... turned his head. He forgot where he came from, and what his responsibilities were.'

'What exactly do you mean by that?' Harry asked. And again he noticed an imploring look from Margaret in her husband's direction.

'You should tell the Inspector,' she suggested timidly. 'You know, about the money.'

'Be quiet, Margaret!' Fraser Sharkey replied, turning on her fiercely. 'It's a family matter. And it's not relevant.'

'It could well be,' Harry interjected. 'What was it about the money?'

Fraser Sharkey glared at him. 'It was nothing. The young fool came to me to borrow money. I told you, he was up to no good with the gambling.'

'And how much did you give him?' Harry asked.

'I didn't give him a penny,' Fraser Sharkey responded angrily. 'Why should I? He was very well paid. And he refused to help me out when things were a bit tight at the pharmacy. He could go to hell, as far as I was concerned.'

At this, both Margaret and Rachel again broke down and began to weep.

Showing some remorse, Fraser Sharkey softened his tone. 'I'm sorry if that sounds harsh, Inspector. But I felt that giving him money would do him no good. Good money after bad, if you know what I mean. Not that I had much to give him, in any event,' he concluded, and again a note of bitterness entered his voice.

Harry eyed Fraser Sharkey steadily and pushed on. 'You said yourself, Mr Sharkey, that Robbie was earning good money. His gambling problem must have been significant if he had the need to call on you to provide further funds. I assume it was probable that he owed significant sums of money around the town. Was that your impression?'

'Of course it was. I knew he was in trouble. Do you take me for a fool?'

Harry continued calmly. 'Did he indicate to you how much he owed? And who he owed it to?'

'He didn't,' Fraser Sharkey replied. 'That was the first thing I asked him. But he wouldn't say. So I told him there was no way I would even think about bailing him out if he wasn't prepared to be honest with me.'

'Fair enough.' Harry could see that this line of questioning was going nowhere. And there was no point upsetting the two women further. 'I think that'll be all for now. Thank you for seeing me and being so helpful.' And turning to the two women on the settee, he added, 'And I'm sorry to put you through all this at such a painful time for you both.'

Margaret Sharkey smiled weakly and went to rise, no doubt to show them out. 'Don't worry about us, we'll let ourselves out,' Harry reassured her. And he and Willie made their exit, back into the gathering darkness in the street.

'Back to Russell Street, boss?' Willie asked, once they had seated themselves in the police trap.

'Yeah, but only to drop the horse off at the stables. Then I'm going home, I'm done in.'

'Sounds good to me,' Willie replied, sooling their horse into a trot.

'What did you make of that, then?' Harry asked, as they made their way down Lygon Street, back towards the city.

'No love lost between Sharkey and his old man, that's for sure.'

'Yeah,' Harry agreed. 'Fraser Sharkey didn't go to the trouble of hiding that. Mind you, sounds like he might have had some good reasons to be disappointed in young Robbie. Maybe our Collingwood hero really had feet of clay.'

'The gambling, you mean?'

'Yeah, and I think there might be a connection between his gambling, his financial troubles and his death. Don't you reckon?'

'I reckon that's a pretty reasonable theory,' Willie agreed. 'Now we have to find out what the connection is.'

'I think I might start by popping around to Victoria Park tomorrow for training. Ernie Copeland will be there. He's an honest bloke. If I can collar him one on one, he'll tell me if the club knew of any issues with Robbie. I'll get you to do some more checking into Fraser Sharkey and his pharmacy business. Try and find out if he's still got financial problems. Looks like he's had them in the past.'

'Will do, boss.'

'And who knows, your enquiries might mean you have to interview Rachel Starkey again. You seem to have already made a bit of an impression on her.'

Willie glanced quickly across in time to see Harry's brief smile in the light of a passing street lamp. 'You know me, always the perfect gentleman.' Then, in a more serious tone, Willie added, 'But I must say, I felt sorry for the poor girl, losing her brother in those circumstances.

And it seems she was quite attached to him.'

'I think she was,' Harry agreed. 'And I wonder how much more forthcoming she might be about her brother without her father present. Reckon he rules that household with a rod of iron. We might chat to her again, on her own next time. But not just yet. Give her a few days to get over things a bit.'

'Happy to volunteer for that job,' Willie offered.

Again Harry smiled to himself, as they turned into the entrance of the Russell Street headquarters.

4

TUESDAY 15 JUNE 1897

EFFIE TUCKED INTO HER lunchtime sandwich with gusto. The morning's teaching seemed to have made her unusually hungry, and she was suddenly grateful for that extra slice of cake Harry had suggested she put in her lunchbox. Across the table in the Merton Hall common room, Michael Standish was tackling his food in an altogether more circumspect fashion, pausing between bites to return to a book he had in one hand.

'Interesting book?' she ventured.

Michael looked up briefly, nodded, and went back to his reading.

Effie tried a different tack. 'How were your girls this morning? On their best behaviour?'

Michael glanced up again. 'Always,' he replied, with just the hint of a smile. And returned again to his book.

Effie watched him, a prickle of annoyance rising as he continued to ignore her. Finally her self-restraint wilted. 'Oh, put that book down, Michael!' she complained. 'Talk to me. I'm bored.'

Michael smiled and placed the book down on the table. 'Sorry, Effie dear. Very rude of me, I'm sure.'

Effie smiled and took a piece of cake from her lunchbox. 'Well, since we've got the room to ourselves, how about some juicy gossip? I can always rely on you for some delicious titbit or other.'

'Well, let me see. What's been …'

'What about your friend, Richard,' Effie interjected. 'Have you heard any more from him?'

'Nothing recently. We haven't seen him for a week or so now. I must say it was decent of Harry to hear us out the other night. I know he's under a lot of pressure. With this big case and all.'

'Which I can tell you about now,' Effie said. 'Now that it's all public knowledge.'

'I've already heard,' Michael replied. 'Murder at the football! What a scandal! It's all around the town.'

'Oh, you know.' Effie was slightly disappointed. 'Anyway, about your friend, Richard. If you're concerned for him, you don't need to worry about putting Harry under pressure by raising it with him. The injustice that you and your friends have to put up with, it's an important issue. We need to keep reminding Harry about that.'

'Poor Harry,' Michael smiled. 'You certainly keep him on his toes.'

'Poor Harry, my foot,' Effie scoffed. 'Don't worry, he gives as good as he gets.'

'Why do I sense you two enjoy baiting each other?' Michael observed.

Effie just smiled and Michael chuckled, before his face settled into a serious expression.

'You know, there was one thing we didn't raise the other night. About Richard and his new romance, I mean. I didn't really want to bother Harry with it, because I'm not sure there's anything in it.'

'Do tell,' Effie said, leaning forward in her chair.

'Well, Richard told us things are a bit complicated on that front. Apparently, there's a third party involved. And I think Richard's rather worried about it.'

'What do you mean? Does he have a rival for his new friend's affections?'

'That's what we thought too. But I'm not sure. He wouldn't really talk about it. Except to say that he hoped it would turn out for the best, and that we shouldn't worry. But he seemed anxious. And that worried us too.'

Effie frowned. 'It's probably just Richard fretting about his new friend's affections, don't you think?'

'I suppose so,' he said slowly. 'It's just that he seemed, well, rather frightened, I think. That's what concerned us.'

'Well, if you find out any more, and your worries prove to be justified, let me know, won't you? I'll pass it on to Harry.'

Michael reached across and gratefully squeezed Effie's hand. She rose slowly to her feet.

'Well, off to the coalface again. Roll on the end of the day. I can't wait to get home and put my feet up.'

Harry wrapped his greatcoat tightly around himself as he made his way again around the empty gravel embankment encircling Victoria Park. A vicious south-westerly was blowing in, and Harry detected a distinct lack of enthusiasm among the thirty or so figures out on the oval, going through their training routines in the gathering twilight. He continued towards the small open enclosure in front of the grandstand and to the huddled figures standing there, their attention focused on the activity out on the ground. As he got closer, he recognised the solid figure of Ernie Copeland, like Harry, clad extensively against the winter cold. Next to him stood Wal Lee and Lee's sidekick, Joey Miller.

'Evening, gentlemen,' Harry ventured as he joined the group. 'Cold enough for you?'

'Bloody miserable, Harry,' Copeland responded, extending his hand. 'None of us want to be here, I can tell you. And that includes those blokes out there. But there's a game on Saturday. There was some talking of cancelling, but we thought we should push on. Best thing, I think.'

'You're probably right,' Harry agreed. 'Try and keep it as normal as possible.'

'Though of course it doesn't feel normal,' Copeland added. 'Far from it, in fact. Anyway, what can we do for you?'

'Sorry to turn up without warning,' Harry replied. 'There are one or two things I'd like to follow up on though. And I wouldn't mind talking to Bill Strickland too, if he's free. I can wait till after training if he's still taking the boys through their paces.'

'Your timing's good, actually. They're just finishing up now. I think Bill's about to send them on a couple of laps, then they'll come in.'

They watched as Bill Strickland barked orders to his players, sending them off in single file around the boundary line. In his day one of the greatest players to grace the field, Strickland, now in his thirties and his self-declared final season, still cut an imposingly athletic figure. He spotted Copeland's wave and made his way towards them. As he came near, he recognised Harry and came forward, hand extended.

'Good to see you again, Harry.'

Harry shook his hand warmly. 'G'day, Bill. You're moving well. Still looking as fit as ever.'

'Not bad for an old bloke. But believe me, running around on a cold winter's night is getting harder and harder. Just as well the finishing post's in sight, eh?'

Harry smiled. 'Every time I see you, I can't help imagining you with a Carlton jumper on. But no hard feelings, you've done a great job here.'

Strickland shrugged. 'Thanks, Harry. I must say, I've still got a soft spot for the old Blues. But you know, you've only got your committee to blame for me leaving. I would've stayed if they'd made me captain.'

'I know, Bill, I know,' Harry sighed. 'Anyway, let's not dwell on past mistakes, I wanted to have another chat with you and Ernie for five minutes, if you've got time now. Following our meeting the other day.'

'Sure,' Strickland said. 'Happy to talk out here, if you like? Not too cold for you?'

Harry glanced about. Lee and Miller had wandered off to the change rooms to attend to various player requirements, so only he, Copeland and Strickland remained.

'Sure, that's fine,' he said. 'I just wanted to ask you both a few more questions about Robbie Sharkey. I know it's probably quite painful for you, Bill.'

Strickland shrugged again. 'It's painful for all of us, mate. It's hard for the boys to be here, I can tell you. They keep remembering what happened. Bloody awful. But we have to keep going, I suppose. Anyway, ask away. If I can help you find Robbie's killer, that'll mean something at least.'

Harry paused, rubbing his chin and searching for the right way to broach his issues. Best to get straight to the point, he thought.

'From our initial enquiries, it's become apparent to us that Robbie Sharkey liked a bit of a punt. Liked it a lot, apparently. I'm wondering if the club was aware of his gambling and whether it was ever a problem.'

In the gathering dusk, Harry noticed Copeland and Strickland exchange a quick glance, before Copeland responded.

'That's probably something I should comment on first. Bill can add to it if he wants. But to answer your question straight-up, yes, the club was aware Robbie had a problem.'

'So it was affecting his footy? That's how you noticed it, I mean?'

Copeland shook his head. 'Not really. Robbie always kept himself to himself. Never used to talk much about his life outside the club. I never noticed anything wrong with him. Certainly his footy wasn't affected. And he wasn't missing training or anything, was he, Bill?'

'No, no,' Strickland said. 'I never noticed anything either. He was the same as ever around the club, and he certainly never spoke to me about any problems. Not that he would, I reckon. Like Ernie said, he was a pretty quiet sort of bloke. Not shy, just kept to himself.'

'So how did you find out about his gambling?' Harry asked. 'And that he had a problem?'

'Well, we had a tip-off,' Copeland confided. 'Someone came to us, to warn us.'

'Someone close to the club?' Harry asked, though he knew the question was probably unnecessary.

'You could say that.'

Harry raised an eyebrow. 'I reckon I know who that would've been,' he said. 'John Wren, by any chance?'

Copeland smiled wryly. 'You're right, Harry. Not too hard to work that one out, I suppose. Yes, a few months back, John came to us and warned us that Robbie was spending more than he could afford at the tote.'

'And I take it that involved a line of credit that Mr Wren was worried wouldn't be repaid?'

'That's right. Look, I know you blokes take a dim view of John Wren and his operation …'

'Well, I think we're required to,' Harry reminded him. 'What he's doing is strictly against the law, as I'm sure you know.'

Harry detected some semblance of a sigh from Copeland. 'Of course, Harry, you're right. And to be honest, I'm not real keen on what he's doing over there on Johnston Street either. But he's a good friend of this club, you know. And he looks out for us.'

'And he looks out for himself too, no doubt. Coming to you to sort out Robbie Sharkey's gambling problem was a smart move, I imagine. After all, he wouldn't want to have to put the frighteners on Collingwood's star player, would he?'

Copeland sighed, in earnest this time. 'Yeh, that's probably true too, I suppose. But according to John, the word was that Robbie was spending just as much, if not more, with other SP bookies as well. Blokes who might have been more inclined to recoup their money through more forceful means.'

Harry whistled. 'I see. He must have owed a fair swag of money around the town?'

'He must have. We got him in, of course, and quizzed him about it all, but he wouldn't say much. Wouldn't say how much he was in for, nor who he owed it to. But he did promise to cut back his gambling.'

'And did he?'

Copeland shrugged. 'Well, all this happened only a few months ago, so it's probably difficult to tell. But we had no more complaints from John Wren. Whether he was running up debt elsewhere, short of putting someone on his tail around the clock, we couldn't know.'

'No, I suppose not.' Harry turned to Bill Strickland. 'I know you said Sharkey kept pretty much to himself, but did you notice whether he had any special mates at the club? Anyone he used to hang around with in particular. Someone mentioned Danny Robinson the other day.'

Strickland stood for a few moments, hands on hips, staring at the ground. 'I wouldn't say Danny was a special mate,' he replied eventually. 'As I said, Robbie was a bit of a loner. But he and Danny seemed to spend a bit of time together. I'd say the topic of conversation was usually horses. Or dogs, or whatever they were betting on at the time. Not that I'm an expert in that area,' he added hastily.

'Thanks Bill, we'll make a point of speaking to Danny. On another matter, have you had any whiff of anything dodgy going on among the players? I know I can rely on you to give me a straight answer.'

Bill Strickland looked steadily back at Harry. 'What sort of dodgy, Harry? You talking about match-fixing?'

'That's one possibility, among a number of others. You get the drift of what I'm on about?'

'I think I do,' Strickland replied firmly, before adding, 'But I can honestly say that I haven't seen anything along that line in my time here. And this club's done more than any other to deal with those sorts of rackets. Plus, we're always on the lookout for whispers of anything dodgy. We'd let you know straight-up if we found anything.'

'Thanks, Bill, I know you would. I'll let you get back to training now. I'm sure you're keen to put in a few laps.'

Strickland grinned. 'Not likely. These old bones don't need any more wear and tear, I can tell you. I'm knocking off for the night.' And he set off towards the sheds. But after a few paces, he stopped.

'I suppose I should mention that Robbie also seemed to spend a bit of time with Joey Miller. Not mates, but Joey used to hang around him a bit. Not surprising, I suppose, seeing how Robbie was our star player, it'd be natural for Joey to spend a bit more time looking after him. But sometimes it seemed a bit more than that, I'd notice them chatting on the quiet, if you know what I mean.'

'Perhaps Joey's a punter too,' Harry suggested.

'Perhaps he is. I suppose it could have been something like that. Well, mate, if there's anything else you need to ask, you know where to find me.' And he made his way towards the sheds at a leisurely trot.

'Do you want me to get Danny Robinson over now?' Copeland asked, as they watched Strickland wander off into the dusk. 'That's him heading into the sheds now.' He pointed to a solidly built young fellow with curly blond hair. Harry recognised him as the player in the

Collingwood rooms when Sharkey was brought in.

'I don't have time now,' Harry replied quickly. 'Anyway, I don't want to embarrass him by dragging him over here where his mates may see.' And besides, thought Harry, Russell Street might be a more conducive environment to extract relevant information from Robinson. Particularly if it's information he doesn't really want to part with.

'But before I go,' Harry continued, 'is there anything you can tell me about Danny Robinson? And Joey Miller, too, for that matter.'

There was a considerable pause, and Harry peered across at Copeland standing in the gloom, absently treading down a patch of loose turf at his feet.

'There's not much I can tell you about Danny,' he offered eventually. 'He came across to us this year from Williamstown. He was one of their best players and he wanted an opportunity, now they've been kicked out of the new competition. He's okay, I suppose. Bit full of himself sometimes. Too used to being the big shot over there at Williamstown, perhaps. He's had a bit of a rude awakening here, I can tell you. But he's starting to settle down now. Bill's made sure of that.'

'And do you reckon he's been heavily into the horses too, like Robbie? As Bill seemed to suggest.'

'Don't know,' Copeland replied immediately. 'Could be, but we've had no complaints. Nothing from John Wren. Or anyone else for that matter.'

'And Joey Miller?' Harry inquired. 'What's his background?'

'Oh, Joey's all right. Been with us a couple of years. Wal Stansforth recommended him. Miller used to work for him, I think. He's an odd little fellow, but harmless enough. Sometimes thinks he knows more than he actually does though.'

'And did you notice anything between him and Sharkey? Like Bill just mentioned.'

'Oh, that'd be nothing,' Copeland replied airily. 'Just Joey trying to make himself a bit more important by hanging around the star player. I wouldn't read anything into that.'

'You're probably right,' Harry said. 'Thanks for your help, Ernie, I'd better go. Another appointment.'

After shaking Copeland's extended hand, Harry headed back around the gravel concourse towards the gates. As he neared them, a figure materialised from the gloom, heading towards him at a rapid pace. Harry recognised the familiar gait of Willie Milton.

'G'day, boss,' Willie greeted him, puffing slightly from his exertions. 'Glad I caught you.' And he paused for a moment, hands on knees and struggling to regain his breath.

'Blimey, mate,' Harry exclaimed, 'What's the hurry? I was going to catch up with you back at Russell Street.'

'I know, I know,' Willie gasped. 'But I knew you were meeting with Ernie Copeland and something's come up that might be important. Is important, actually.'

'Really? What's happened?'

Willie straightened, still breathing heavily. 'Well, you know how we sent Ramsgate's syringe off to Molly to test for strychnine?'

'Of course. Have you got the result back?'

'Positive.'

'Positive? Is Molly sure?'

'Absolutely certain,' Willie replied. 'Not a shred of doubt. Those were the words he told me to tell you.'

Harry whistled softly. 'Blimey! Starting to look like it could be an inside job, isn't it? You're right, I need to speak to Ernie about this pronto.'

Harry pulled his fob watch from his pocket and peered at it in the dim light. 'But I don't think I can go back and talk to him now. I'm already running late to meet with the Philips woman back at Russell

Street. I'll tell you what, can you go in and see Ernie? See if he can get across to Russell Street tonight for another meeting. After I've talked to Margot Philips.'

'I can do that,' Willie replied, 'but is it really necessary? We can easily arrange to meet with him tomorrow.'

'Yeh, I suppose,' Harry conceded. 'But if it's no trouble to him, I'd prefer to meet tonight. We need to chase this down as quick as we can, and Ernie's best placed to point us in the right direction. But you're right, let him know he should only come if it's convenient. Otherwise, tomorrow will have to do. But no later than that, all right?'

And after patting Willie on the shoulder, Harry hurried off.

✕

There was something about Margot Philips that Harry found disconcerting.

He wondered first whether it was her looks, which would certainly have distracted most men. Sitting there in the interview room at Russell Street, immaculately dressed in a beautifully tailored skirt and blazer, her abundant dark locks swept to one side and framing finely chiselled features, Margot seemed the epitome of society beauty and sophistication. But as Harry reminded himself, he had interviewed plenty of beautiful women in the course of his work and he was pretty much immune to their charms. None of them had the beguiling effect on him that Effie seemed to be able to conjure up at will.

No, Harry realised, it was not Margot's appearance that he found slightly unnerving. It was her manner. Because ten minutes into their conversation, after he had apologised for his lateness, expressed his sincere condolences at her loss and asked whether she was up to answering questions, Harry suddenly realised that his concern for her state of mind was completely unnecessary.

Because Margot Philips was fully in control of her emotions. Calm, almost to the point of detachment, Harry thought.

'Certainly, Inspector,' she replied, in response to his request to ask her questions. 'I've heard that you consider there was foul play, and I'll do everything I can to help you bring Robbie's killer to justice.'

'I appreciate your willingness to talk to us,' Harry replied. 'I was worried that perhaps you might be too distressed to talk so soon after Robbie's death.'

Margot's expression did not change. 'Thank you, I appreciate your consideration. But really, I'm perfectly able to answer your questions.'

'Good. Well then, perhaps we could start by establishing your relationship with Robbie Sharkey.'

Margot looked slightly puzzled. 'What do you mean? We were friends, but I assumed you already know that.'

'Sweethearts, would you say?'

The very faintest hint of a smile played at the corners of Margot's exquisite mouth. 'I'm not sure what you mean by that expression. It's not a term that I would use to describe a relationship. But it's fair to say, I think, that we were close friends. We saw quite a bit of each other.'

Harry was struggling to find the right language in the face of Margot's composed demeanour. 'Let me put it another way, was your relationship a serious one?'

Again, the hint of a smile. 'I'm a serious person, and Robbie was a close friend. So, of course our friendship covered serious matters.'

'Well, did he confide in you? About any troubles he might be having, for example? About anyone he might be having difficulties with.'

Margot paused and eyed Harry intently for a few moments. 'He did confide in me from time to time,' she replied. 'But not about everything, I shouldn't think. Everyone has parts of their lives that they keep to themselves, don't you agree?'

Harry was momentarily flummoxed, but quickly regained his composure. 'I suppose that's right, Miss Philips. Though some more than others, in my experience. But let's stick to what he did talk to you about. Did you know whether he was in any kind of trouble with anyone? I'm thinking in particular about his fondness for gambling.'

Margot Philips leaned back in her chair and placed her hands together in her lap. She sighed.

'Robbie was a very sweet man, Inspector, very kind and generous. And a very warm and entertaining companion. But, like all men, he had his weaknesses. And obviously I'm not surprising you when I say that gambling was one of those weaknesses.'

'And clearly he talked to you about it?'

'He did. Quite often, actually. It wasn't something he was proud of. And he sought my help to try to stop. Or at least to manage it, I suppose. But sadly, with limited success.'

Harry pressed on. 'I've heard he may have owed a lot of money around the town. Did he talk to you about that?'

'In general terms, yes. But not in detail. I was trying to encourage him to pay his creditors and put an end to it. His gambling, that is.'

'Did he involve you in his gambling activities? Take you to the race track, for example.'

Margot raised an elegant eyebrow. 'Hardly, Inspector. I can assure you, that isn't part of my world. But it was certainly part of Robbie's.'

Harry leaned forward slightly and eyed Margot quizzically. 'I'm actually wondering, Miss Philips, what is your world? Or at least, what part of your world did you share with Robbie Sharkey?'

Margot returned Harry's gaze, her calm expression unaltered. 'Do you mean, how did we spend our time together?'

'That's what I mean.'

'Well, let's see. I suppose we attended quite a lot of club functions together. And we enjoyed dining together. We shared a taste in good food. And I was beginning to involve him in the arts. Musical theatre, and a little taste of serious theatre. It was new to him, but I think he enjoyed it. We used to joke that I would make a cultured man of him.'

'Did it worry you that there were some parts of his life he didn't share with you?'

'Not at all, Inspector. There were many parts of my life he wasn't involved in as well. We were both quite comfortable with that.'

'Speaking of your life, Miss Philips, I understand you're employed by Doctor Ramsgate?'

'Yes, I manage Doctor Ramsgate's surgery in Collins Street. It's how I met Robbie actually. I attended a Collingwood club function with Henry.'

Harry pressed on. 'So, what does your job involve? Managing inventory, I suppose. Including medicines?'

'It does,' Margot confirmed. 'Among a number of other responsibilities.'

Harry gazed at her intently, thought for a moment or two, then spoke again. 'Well, that's about as much information as I need for the moment, Miss Philips. We'll be in touch again if we need to speak to you further.' And he rose and extended his hand.

Margot Philips' handshake was firm and confident: Harry was surprised by the casual strength of her grip. And he could not help but be impressed by the grace and elegance of her bearing, as she bade him farewell and strode confidently from the room.

✕

Harry pulled out his notebook to record his impressions of the meeting. He scribbled down the key points of Margot Philips' evidence, then sat deep in thought for a few minutes, only stirring when the door opened and Willie appeared to inform him that Ernie Copeland was outside. Harry rose and strode out into the corridor.

'Come in, Ernie. Sorry to drag you back in at this ungodly hour. I told Willie to tell you it could wait until tomorrow.'

Copeland smiled and shrugged. 'Don't worry, your man made it clear I wasn't being forced to come in tonight. But I reckoned it must be important for you to want to see me again so soon, so here I am. Now, what's come up?'

'Well, it is important, actually. Because we've got the results back on that test we did on the syringe. And it's come back positive.'

Copeland looked confused. 'I'm sorry, Harry, you've lost me. What are you talking about?'

'Oh, that's right, you weren't there, were you? When I met with Henry Ramsgate and your trainers, I took away Ramsgate's hypodermic syringe. We've since had it tested, and it's come back showing traces of strychnine.'

Copeland stared at him, open-mouthed. 'What does that mean? Does it implicate Henry Ramsgate?'

'No, not necessarily. But I think it does prove, quite conclusively, that we've found the murder weapon.'

Copeland again looked puzzled. 'But couldn't it just mean that Henry had administered strychnine at some recent time with that syringe? To one of his patients?'

Harry shook his head. 'Apparently not. Ramsgate was quite emphatic that he never treats any of his patients with strychnine. And certainly not by injection.'

'Oh, I see.' Copeland spoke slowly and deliberately as he took in the implications of Harry's news. 'So you think …'

'It looks like an inside job, I'm afraid. It appears that someone has entered your clubrooms before or during the game, stolen the syringe, and somehow found a way to inject Robbie Sharkey with a lethal dose of strychnine.'

'You mean, in the crowd at half time? Like you were suggesting to the committee?'

'That seems to be one plausible explanation,' Harry agreed. 'At this stage, anyway. Someone concealed in that mob that were jabbing the players with hat pins.'

Copeland sat deep in thought, staring at the far wall. 'You know,' he said eventually, 'if that theory's correct – how he was injected, I mean – that would exonerate a number of our people. Like Henry Ramsgate and our trainers, for example. They would have been present with the team through that whole half-time period. They couldn't have been sneaking off to conceal themselves in the mob around the players.'

'That's true,' Harry said. 'On top of that, they would have been noticed by someone, you would think. Though it doesn't necessarily absolve them from taking the syringe and giving it to someone else to carry out the murder.'

'My goodness, Harry! Surely you wouldn't think one of our blokes capable of that?'

'Well, it certainly looks like someone has used that syringe to inject Robbie. And it must have been someone in the club, unless someone from the Carlton staff or someone not involved with either club snuck into the rooms and took the syringe.'

'You're right,' Copeland conceded, sounding decidedly dejected. 'As you know, the Carlton rooms are completely separate from ours. It's hard to imagine how someone from Carlton, or a complete stranger, could get in or out of our rooms without being seen.'

'Particularly since they would need to know where to go to get the syringe from Ramsgate's bag,' Harry added. 'And they would need to sneak back later and replace the syringe in the bag. All completely unseen by any of your people. Highly unlikely, I would say.'

Copeland stared at the floor in front of Harry's desk, head bowed. 'I just can't believe that any of our people would be capable of such a thing. And why? Why would they want to do in poor Robbie Sharkey? A young fellow with his whole life in front of him. I just can't understand it.' He shook his head slowly and looked up, almost beseechingly, as if imploring Harry to reassure him that it was all a bad dream.

Harry offered what little comfort he could. 'It's a terrible thing all right, but if there's a bad apple in your barrel, we must all work together to root it out, as quick as we can. For everyone's sake.'

Copeland sat up and pulled himself together. 'You're right, Harry, of course,' he declared, a new note of determination in his voice. 'Good on you, we appreciate having you on the case. And I can tell you, the resources of the Collingwood Football Club are entirely at your disposal to find the bastard who did this.'

'I'm pleased to hear that,' Harry replied. 'Because this latest finding means that we'll be focussing a lot of our attention in this investigation on the club, and on the personnel involved with the club. So we'll need your full cooperation, Ernie. You and I will need to work together closely.'

'I understand, Harry. I'm available whenever you need me.'

Copeland rose, shook Harry's hand and left the office. Harry watched the departing figure. Copeland's step, if not exactly jaunty, was at least back to its familiar bustling confidence, a confidence well-justified by an already legendary string of achievements in the football world. Good, thought Harry, we'll need Ernie back at his best to help us with this one.

✕

'She's an odd one, that Margot Philips,' Harry observed to Effie, as he pulled off his boots and placed them at a safe distance from the fire to dry off.

Effie looked up from marking papers. 'I think I understand you pretty well, Harry Holloway, but I'm not yet up to reading your mind. Who is Margot Philips?'

'Oh, sorry,' Harry replied with a smile. 'She was Robbie Sharkey's girlfriend. At least, I think she was. I interviewed her today.'

Effie looked puzzled. 'Think she was. Why do you say that? She either was or she wasn't.'

'Well, she was certainly stepping out with him. She told me that much. But I was left wondering how close their relationship really was.'

'What made you think that?' Effie asked.

'Well, it's just that …' Harry paused, choosing his words carefully. 'It's just that she didn't have the reaction I expected to Robbie's death.'

'What do you mean?' Effie put her pen down and pushed the marking to one side.

'Well, I suppose she wasn't as upset as I'd expected. No tears, no breaking down. Nothing.'

Effie's eyes narrowed. 'You mean she didn't behave like a woman is meant to behave in that situation. All weak and helpless. Just because she's showing some strength in the face of this tragedy, that makes her odd in your book? Harry Holloway, you need to broaden your horizons, I think. There is such a thing as a strong, independent woman.'

Harry raised his hands in mock surrender. 'Don't worry, Eff, I've had plenty of practice appreciating the independent woman. But it's not that. It's just that she didn't seem as passionate about Sharkey, and as upset by his death, as I thought she would be.'

'Well, perhaps she wasn't. Perhaps they were just good friends. Just because a woman is stepping out with a fellow, doesn't mean he's the love of her life.'

Harry sunk into his favourite armchair, beer in hand. 'You know, my dear, that's a very good point. And when I think about it, that's exactly how she came across. As a good friend to Robbie. And you're quite right, that doesn't make her odd at all.'

Effie smiled and leaned over to kiss him affectionately. 'I'm glad I've got you back on the right track.' Then, leaning back, she eyed him again and asked, 'By the way, this Margot person, is she good looking?'

Harry looked at her again, in some surprise. 'Well yes, I suppose she is. But how relevant is that to my perspective on the independent woman?'

'Oh, it's not important,' Effie replied vaguely. 'Just trying to build up a picture of her in my mind.'

'Well, if it'll help, she is rather striking. Darkish features, bumps in the right places, all that sort of thing. I would say very feminine, but strong with it. Athletic, I mean. She looks like she might be a sportswoman of some sort.'

'She sounds interesting,' Effie observed. 'Think I'd like to meet her sometime. Perhaps I'll ask Lydia if she knows her. Or knows of her.'

Harry grinned. 'All in the name of building up that better picture, I assume?'

Effie looked at him sharply. 'Harry Holloway, I hope you don't think I'm jealous of this Margot person. That wasn't behind my question at all. I'm not that shallow.'

'Of course not, my dear, I would never suggest such a thing. Besides, you know I've only got eyes for you. And always will.'

'Well, just make sure it stays that way.' Effie's voice was stern, but the twinkle in her eye gave her away. 'Anyway,' she added, 'that's enough of your day. You know, I spoke to Michael again today.'

'Oh, yes.' Harry leaned back and shut his eyes. He had a fair idea of what was coming.

'Now, darling, I know you're tired, but you've got to focus on this.'

Harry's eyes remained shut. 'I'm focused. I assume this is about Michael's friend?'

'Yes, Richard Thames, the young man whose father is connected to Collingwood. The one who's just discovered himself. You know the one I mean.'

'I do. Last I heard he'd just met the love of his life. Do you have more news?'

'I do. Michael and James are really worried about him. It seems there's a third party involved.'

Harry's eyes half-opened and he squinted at Effie. 'What do you mean 'a third party'? Does he have a rival?'

'I think that's what's going on,' Effie responded uncertainly. 'But Michael and James aren't sure.'

Harry looked puzzled. 'I'm not quite sure how that concerns me. Or the law. Competing for someone's affections isn't a crime, the last I heard. Though strictly speaking, in this case it probably is. But you know what I mean.'

'I know, I know, but it's just that Michael said the poor fellow is terribly upset. And even afraid. That's how he described it to me.'

Harry sighed, sat up, and took his wife's hand. 'Effie, I'm not sure what's going on with Michael's young friend, but whatever it is, it's certainly not enough to warrant our involvement. I mean, from what you've told me, there's absolutely no indication the fellow's in any danger. We just can't do anything, I'm afraid.'

Effie smiled bleakly. 'I know, darling. I just have a feeling about this, that's all. I always trust Michael's judgement and he's genuinely worried.'

Harry took a contemplative swig of beer. 'How about this then? The best I can do is talk to his father. I'll need to talk to Sir Randolph soon anyway, given he employed Sharkey in his business. Tell you what, I'll slip into the conversation a couple of questions about his son. See what he thinks about the young fellow's state of mind. From the sound of it, young Richard won't be confiding in him, but at least his father might give me a steer on whether his son's generally happy about life at the moment. Or otherwise. What do you think?'

'Would you, darling? That would be wonderful,' Effie replied, brightening visibly. 'Michael will be very grateful.' And she kissed him lightly.

Harry gazed at Effie affectionately. 'You know, my dear, I thought Margot Philips was good-looking, but she's not a patch on you. No-one is.'

And with that, he put his empty glass on the side table, rose to his feet and took his wife in his arms. Effie kissed him again, more passionately this time.

'Harry Holloway, you devil, you know the old saying, don't you?'

'And what might that be?'

'Flattery will get you everywhere.'

5

'YOU MEAN YOU'VE NEVER been to John Wren's tote before?' Harry asked Willie, as they made their way down Johnston Street, Collingwood's bustling commercial heartland. He glanced across at his constable in some astonishment, almost as he was in the presence of an alien, recently arrived from another planet.

'Can't say I have,' Willie confessed. 'Either in an official or a sporting capacity.'

'Well,' Harry confided, 'you're in for an educational experience, mate. I can confidently say there's nothing like it in Melbourne. The tote won't be operating today, but at least we'll see where it all happens.'

'Yeah, I gotta say I'm a bit excited to see what all the fuss is about. I'm surprised though, that Wren's prepared to meet us there. Thought he wouldn't be too keen on that. After all the raids there's been.'

Harry grinned. 'Don't worry, I got word to him and he's expecting us. And as I said, there's no tote today so there'll be no incriminating evidence lying around. We'll just be meeting with John Wren the tobacconist.'

Willie grinned too. 'Oh, that's right, it's a tobacconist shop, isn't it?'

'At the front, Willie. But a bit different out the back.'

They continued their walk down Johnston Street, enjoying the unusually warm winter's morning, before Willie turned to his boss again.

'Aren't you a bit worried, turning up at Wren's like this?'

Harry glanced at his offsider. 'What do you mean? There won't be any trouble. As I said, Wren's expecting us and he knows who I am. We're on reasonably civil terms.'

'That's not what I mean. Aren't you concerned the word might get around, among the powers that be, I mean, that you're too friendly with John Wren? And too familiar with his operation. And maybe too soft on it too. I mean, after all, everyone knows you like a punt.'

Harry gave a wry smile. 'A man's got to have at least one vice, mate. And that's mine. And, to tell the truth, I don't see too much harm in what Wren's doing. Providing a service to the public, as much as anything. I know it's strictly illegal, and we're meant to enforce the law from time to time. But not today, I think you'll find there's nothing there to give us cause to make an arrest. And anyway, we're here on a murder enquiry. Nothing to do with what's going on at the tote. But I'll take your words of caution on board. I'll play it straight down the line.'

Willie persisted. 'I've heard that some of his strong-arm tactics are a bit over the top though. You wouldn't turn a blind eye to that, would you?'

'That's a different story altogether. Any of that sort of carry-on we need to come down on hard, for sure. But as far as the tote itself goes, if the government's so worried about it, they should set up their own tote. Compete him out of business.'

'Too many wowsers in the big house for that to happen,' Willie observed.

Harry chuckled. 'You're right there, mate.' And left it at that.

'You know I'm not one of them, Boss,' Willie added. 'A wowser, I mean. Actually, I agree with what you say, about the tote and all that.

But there are some up the line who might have a different opinion. At least, that's what the word is around the station.'

Harry chuckled. 'I know who you're talking about, mate. I'm well aware that Chief Inspector Marks has a different view on these matters. But I'm a big boy, I can look after myself.

'Anyway, here we are,' he added, coming to a halt outside an unprepossessing, double-fronted tobacconist shop.

'Through here?' Willie suggested, indicating the front door.

'No, mate. That used to be the entrance, but it's closed off now. Too much traffic. The real shop is out the back these days, actually mostly in the yard behind the shop. Follow me.'

And Harry set off down the lane at the side of the building. They made their way alongside a tall stone wall, then turned and followed the wall down Sackville Street to the back of the residence. Harry knocked loudly on a stout door set into the wall. It opened a few inches, sufficient for them to see a burly, dark-haired, roughly dressed fellow peering out at them. 'Yeah, watcha want?' he demanded.

'Harry Holloway to see Mr Wren,' Harry replied calmly. 'He's expecting me.'

'Oh yeah, right.' And the door opened a little further, enough to allow them to squeeze through. 'This way,' their guide instructed, after securely bolting the door behind them.

He led them across a smallish courtyard, towards yet another wall on the far side.

'Is this where the tote happens?' Willie whispered to Harry.

'No, mate,' Harry whispered back. 'This is the lookout yard. Mr Wren believes in safety first.'

Sure enough, they were led through another door into a larger courtyard where a number of tables and chairs were set out, rather incongruously, around the perimeter. The courtyard was completely empty of any customers, and the tables were bare.

'Believe me,' Harry whispered out of the side of his mouth. 'I've seen it a lot busier than this.'

Willie smiled and said nothing.

They continued through the second courtyard, then through another door on the far side. They found themselves in a long, dim corridor, obviously the rear of the tobacconist's premises. Half-way down this corridor, they came to a door on their left. Their guide knocked and a muffled voice invited them to enter.

'You go in,' the fellow muttered. 'I'll wait here.'

They entered a small, sparsely furnished room, which obviously served as John Wren's office, though very little in the way of records or papers could be seen in the small bookshelf which ran along one wall. Wren rose from his desk and came around to greet them. He was small in stature, clean-shaven and his hair, pushed back from his forehead, had a ginger tint. He was slightly stooping in stature as he came forward. He had an almost gnome-like quality, reinforced by prominent ears and a large, slightly crooked nose.

'Morning, Harry,' Wren said, rather softly and with a slight inclination of his head.

'G'day, John,' Harry replied. 'Fairly quiet around here today. Tobacconist trade a bit slow?'

'Always quiet on a Wednesday,' Wren replied, ignoring Harry's attempt at humour. 'Just settling up a few accounts from the weekend.' He pointed to a couple of chairs in front of his desk, and Harry and Willie took this as an invitation to be seated.

'Who's this, then?' Wren continued, returning to his desk and glancing in Willie's direction.

'Constable Willie Milton,' Harry announced. 'Don't worry, Willie's here as an observer only. He won't be taking notes or anything like that.'

Wren leaned back slightly in his chair and surveyed Harry with the faintest hint of suspicion. 'This meeting's off the record, right?' he said. 'I'll deny I said anything, if you try to use what I say against me. Regarding my business activities, I mean.'

Harry returned his gaze steadily. 'Don't worry, John. I'm not interested in your business activities today, except how they might relate to the death of Robbie Sharkey. If you're honest with me about Sharkey and his dealings with you, I can guarantee I won't be looking to finger you for your dealings with your other customers. You can trust me on that score.'

Wren said nothing, simply nodding his agreement to the arrangement.

'Terrible thing about young Sharkey,' Harry continued. 'A real shock for the club.'

'Yes, it was,' Wren agreed, then lapsed into silence again.

'He was a customer of yours, I understand?'

Wren nodded again, fixing Harry with a wary stare.

'A big customer, by all accounts?'

'Big enough,' Wren replied, a hint of defiance in his voice.

'Big enough to be a bit of a problem, I hear. Ernie Copeland told me you came to him, to warn the club about the problem.'

Wren stared hard at Harry, who sat calmly, waiting for a response.

Finally, Wren leaned forward and spoke softly. 'Well, it was a problem, because Sharkey was owing me more than he could afford to owe. I run some credit accounts, but they're not unlimited.'

'And why was that something you wanted to warn the club about?'

'That's fairly obvious, isn't it? I'm a Collingwood man, and I didn't want our best player in that sort of trouble.'

'And I suppose you didn't want to expose the club's best player to your normal debt collection methods. Am I right?'

Wren's expression became surly. 'I'm allowed to collect money from blokes who owe it to me. Nothing wrong with that, is there?'

'Nothing wrong with that, John. Provided it's within the boundaries of the law. We wouldn't want your good name to be associated with standover tactics, would we?' And Harry smiled pleasantly.

Wren scowled and sat in silence, his chin thrust out defiantly.

'Who's your debt collector, by the way? Our escort?' Harry gestured over his shoulder in the direction of the door.

'That's him,' Wren confided. 'One of them, at least.'

'Does he have a name?'

'Bill Hanrahan.'

'And did you encourage Mr Hanrahan to have a chat with Robbie, in regard to his financial problem?'

'I got Bill to talk to him. Give him fair warning. Pay up. That's all, just a talk. But Sharkey wouldn't listen, said he'd pay me back when he was good and ready. So I refused to give him any more credit.'

'So I take it he died owing you a heap of money?'

'As it turns out, no. That's the funny thing. He turned up here about three months ago and settled his account. In full. I couldn't believe it.'

Willie leaned forward and spoke. 'Can we ask how much he owed?'

'About a hundred quid,' Wren replied, glancing disdainfully at Willie before turning back to address Harry. 'Thought I'd never see that again, I can tell you. Anyway, once bitten, twice shy. I refused to give him any more credit. Cash only after that.'

'And he continued to do business with you?' Harry asked.

'For a while, yeah. But he stopped coming here about a month ago. I assumed it was because he'd run out of cash and gone off elsewhere, where he could get credit. Plenty of people less scrupulous than me, y'know. Anyway, good riddance, I thought. He was a good footballer, but he was a fair bit of trouble. For me and the club. I can't abide blokes who carry on with his sort of caper.'

'And what sort of caper would that be, John?'

Wren fixed Harry with a steely glare. 'Oh, you know, boozing and playing around. That sort of thing. I can't stand blokes who can't control themselves. He was our best footballer, he should have been setting an example to his team mates. And to the whole Collingwood community, for that matter. It's not right.'

Harry just shrugged and said flippantly, 'Oh well, John, we've all got our weaknesses.' But he was taking careful note of what Wren had to say. His account lined up pretty well with Ernie Copeland's story. They both had the ring of truth about them. No point in pursuing that line of questioning any further.

'I suppose you would have been holding quite a bit on Saturday's game?' Harry suggested.

Wren looked at him suspiciously. 'What do you mean?'

'It's okay, this is all off the record,' Harry reiterated. 'I'm investigating a murder, as I said, and I'm not interested in nailing your betting operations. You can be open with me.'

'All right then,' Wren said begrudgingly. 'It's just that I have to be careful. There's a few in the force out to get me, as you know.'

'Well, I'm not one of them. At least, not at this moment. Now, back to my question, were there big bets on the Pies' game last Saturday.'

'Always are. It's one of the biggest games of the season.'

'Plenty backing Collingwood, I suppose,' Harry continued. 'Last year's premiers. Lots of one-eyed punters around here, I know for a fact.'

'More money on the Blues, actually,' Wren replied. 'I was laying them pretty heavy. Thought they had no chance. Plenty of punters happy to take my odds, I can tell you.'

'Really?' Harry was surprised. 'Is that dinkum?'

'I'll show you my books if you like. I had twice the payout if Carlton got up. So that's hardly a reason for me to have our best player knocked off, is it?'

'No, it certainly isn't,' Harry agreed. 'But it would be a good incentive for one of those punters backing Carlton to do something a bit drastic.'

Wren snorted in derision. 'Come on, Harry, I was holding a few biggish bets, but nothing big enough to warrant that sort of caper.'

Thinking about it, Harry had to admit it seemed unlikely. 'Maybe you're right,' he conceded. 'But I might need to come back to you for more information, from your sheets on the game. Depending on how our investigations go.'

Wren looked at him anxiously. 'Hell, Harry, that might be a problem. If they got into the wrong hands, I mean.'

'All in confidence,' Harry reassured him. 'They'd go no further than me.'

'Well, all right. I trust you, I suppose.'

'Good. That's probably a good time for us to be going then. On a note of mutual trust. Thanks for your time, John. I assume our escort's waiting for us?'

Wren simply nodded at them, still wearing a slightly worried expression, before returning his attention to the papers on his desk. The interview was obviously over.

Harry and Willie found the hulking Hanrahan outside in the corridor. Without a word, he headed off down the corridor, motioning them to follow. Passing an open door on their left, Harry paused briefly and glanced inside. This was the settling room, where Wren's man was either paying out or collecting bets made on credit. Harry immediately recognised the client in the room, hunched over a desk in conversation with Wren's clerk. It was the gaunt, stooped figure of Henry Ramsgate. Ramsgate glanced in his direction, but gave no show of recognition, hurriedly turning away from Harry.

'Well, well,' Harry muttered to himself, as he strode to catch up with Hanrahan. 'I wonder which team Doctor Ramsgate was backing on Saturday.'

⨯

Effie reclined on Lydia's elegant couch and sipped her tea. Her monthly afternoon tea at Lydia Smith's Toorak terrace house was a highly anticipated event in Effie's life. Alfie was safely ensconced with Harry's mum, Millie, until dinner time, and this was Effie's opportunity for a good hour or two of uninterrupted gossip with her close friend. Subjects usually ranged across their shared interest in both the arts world and the suffragette movement, and always included, from Lydia's side at least, a fair smattering of the controversies and scandals of the day.

But on this occasion, despite Lydia's reportage containing its usual intriguing array of diverting snippets, Effie found herself somewhat less than usually captivated.

'What's the matter, darling?' Lydia inquired, breaking off her account of a particularly scandalous affair, involving one of Melbourne's leading parliamentarians. 'You don't seem yourself today.'

'I'm sorry, dear, I am a bit preoccupied. It's all this business that Michael's been dealing with. I think one of their friends is in some kind of trouble.'

Lydia leaned over and patted her friend on the knee. 'Well then, spill the beans. No point in keeping it to yourself. Two heads are better than one, and all that.'

So Effie blurted out the whole story that Michael had relayed to her about Richard Thames, his problems with his family, the difficult decisions he was facing in his life, and the possible danger he might be exposing himself to.

'We've raised all this with Harry,' she concluded. 'But there's nothing he can do. There's nothing concrete to go on, he says. And he's right, I know that. It may all be quite innocent. Well, perhaps not innocent, but at least innocuous. And besides, Harry's snowed under at the moment on this terrible Sharkey case. You know, the Collingwood footballer who was murdered.'

'Oh yes, of course,' Lydia said. 'It's the talk of the town at the moment. My Ed's told me all about it. He was the one who tried to treat the poor man, you know.'

'That's right, Harry told me that he had to call on Ed. He said the Collingwood doctor was quite useless.'

'You know Harry's probably quite right,' Lydia continued. 'About Michael's friend, I mean. The details are a bit vague.'

'I know,' Effie sighed. 'I'd best try to put it out of my mind. It's just that I trust Michael's judgement, and he and James seem quite worried about the young man. And it's just so wrong, so unjust, that he should face such bigotry and possible danger, just because of who he is. But you're right, there's nothing to be done, I suppose.'

'What are you talking about?' Lydia exclaimed suddenly. 'There's everything to be done. If the details are too vague, then we'd better un-vague them.'

'What do you mean?' Effie said, looking with some astonishment at her friend.

'I mean we need to meet with Richard Thames and extract the facts from him. Then we can make a proper judgement as to whether we're dealing with a lovestruck puppy, or if there is really something there that should interest your Harry. Either way, I'm sure we can do something to help the young fellow and lift his spirits. And we would set your friend Michael's mind at rest.'

'Really?' This course of action was something that had never occurred to Effie.

'Yes, really. And post-haste, I would suggest. Why don't we try and organise something for Friday afternoon? We could go to the Hopetoun Tea Rooms after work. Or even to the Federal coffee palace. Though perhaps that might be too grand. A bit overwhelming for the young man.'

But Effie was still trying to get her head around the concept of meeting with Richard. 'But, dear, I don't know Richard Thames, and even if I could contact him, I'm not sure he's going to pour his heart out to two strange women.'

Lydia smiled brightly. 'No problem, darling, I'm sure Michael Standish could contact him and organise to meet on Friday. At the tea rooms, definitely the best choice. And if Michael and James are there, that will help to put him at ease. Then leave the rest up to me. I can assure you my sympathetic touch has been known to melt hearts of stone. Or perhaps in this case that should be, strengthen faint hearts. Anyway, I'll have him confiding in me in no time.'

Effie looked doubtfully at her friend. 'I'm sure you mean well, dear, but won't Richard be rather upset that Michael has told us all about his troubles? We're two strangers to him, after all.'

'Don't worry,' Lydia reassured. 'I'll invent a satisfactory reason for us to meet with him. Is he interested in the arts at all?'

'Well, Michael said he's a budding actor.'

'Perfect!' Lydia exclaimed. 'We want to meet with him to help him into the acting profession. Through my extensive network of contacts in the theatre business.'

'Well,' Effie replied slowly, a significant touch of doubt still lingering, 'I suppose it can't do any harm. And at least he'll be gratified that we care about him, I suppose.'

'That's the spirit,' Lydia enthused. 'Lydia Smith to the rescue. Now stop brooding and pay attention while I finish telling you about that old goat, McHenry, and his carry-on with that actress. Without a lie, I tell you she's young enough to be his grand-daughter.'

✕

It turned out that Doris Smith lived at 39 Malmsbury Street, Kew. Harry had got her address from the Carlton members list, and it came as something of a surprise to discover that she inhabited this conspicuously genteel street in this genteel suburb.

The Dorrie Smith he knew could be seen at Carlton games, kitted out in outlandish blue and white regalia, hurling abuse at the opposition and the umpire. It was the same Dorrie he'd had cause, on a number of occasions, to eject from the ground on account of her unruly behaviour. It was the same Dorrie who was a leading light in the Carlton hat pin brigade. And, on the face of it, the Dorrie he knew at the football seemed extremely unlikely to be the inhabitant of the imposing Queen Anne villa that he found at number thirty-nine.

And when he knocked firmly on the equally imposing oak door, and was greeted by a pleasant matron, demurely but smartly dressed in a pale grey twin set and tweed skirt, he was forced to take a second look to make sure he hadn't come to the wrong address.

But yes, it was Dorrie. Dorrie transformed, but Dorrie nevertheless. And she was obviously chuffed to see him.

'Harry, what a pleasant surprise,' she exclaimed jovially. 'What brings you to this neck of the woods? Come in, come in. Would you like a cuppa? Or something a little stronger, a sherry perhaps?'

'Good of you, Dorrie, but no thanks. Still on duty, I'm afraid. Actually, I'm here about our investigation into Robbie Sharkey's murder.'

'Oh yes, of course.' Dorrie's smile disappeared. 'A terrible business. What's the world coming to, eh? You know, I'd love to help you, but I'm not sure how that might be.'

'It's a long shot, but I'm hoping you might have noticed something at the half-time break. I know you and your friends like to gather at the gate when the players come off. To, well, you know, barrack and so forth.'

'Hmm.' Dorrie's tone became more cautious. 'I know you fellows think we get up to mischief, but I'm not part of that business, I promise.'

'I know, Dorrie, I know. But let's go inside and talk about it, shall we?'

'Of course, duckie. Very rude of me. Come on in.' And she ushered him into a spacious foyer, closing the door behind them.

'Who's that?' came a muffled male voice from somewhere within the distant recesses of the house.

'Don't worry, love,' Dorrie shouted back. 'It's for me. Won't be long.'

And turning conspiratorially to Harry, she whispered, 'Let's go into my sewing room. Just here on the left. I don't tell Peter everything that goes on at the footy. You know what lawyers are like, always worried about the look of things and their reputations. He might get a bit nervous if he knew about everything I get up to.'

Harry just grinned and followed her into the room, obviously Dorrie's private domain, judging from the Carlton paraphernalia adorning the walls. 'Now then,' she said, after closing the door and settling them into two cosy armchairs. 'What did you want to talk about?'

'Well, one line of investigation we're looking at is that Sharkey might have been poisoned as he was going onto or coming off the ground. Either before the game or at half-time.'

Dorrie's eyes widened. 'Goodness me, Harry, how awful! Well, I would never have believed it. But how? How could he be poisoned like that?'

'Good question. What we're thinking is that someone might have injected him with an hypodermic syringe. In amongst the crowd. And that he wouldn't necessarily have noticed, given that he and the other players were getting poked with hat pins at the same time.'

Dorrie's expression turned from amazement to alarm. 'I hope you don't think I was one of those women. With the hat pins, I mean. I'm always keen for a bit of verbal advice to the opposition, but I draw the line at poking them, I promise. I might have stepped over the line once or twice in the past, but that was a long time ago.'

'I'm not here to accuse you of assault, Dorrie. I just want to know whether you saw anyone, or anything unusual, last Saturday.'

Dorrie relaxed perceptibly and sank back into the plush armchair. She gazed contemplatively at the large Carlton banner on the wall, her brow puckered in thought. 'Well, I'm not sure I can help much, Harry. You see, I was at the player's gate, but only when they came off at half-time. Before the game and after half-time I was back in my seat. Organising the girls to cheer our boys on as they came out.'

'Very commendable. But did you notice anything or anyone as the players came off? Particularly anything unusual near the Collingwood blokes.'

Again Dorrie sat pondering, before replying. 'Not really. I was actually quite close to the Collingwood lads as they came off. I was intending to give them a bit of friendly advice. But I didn't notice anyone, or anything unusual, I must say. And thinking about it, I don't think anyone could have got to Robbie Sharkey, at that time, anyway.'

'Oh, why's that?'

'Well, I was intending to give Sharkey a bit of what for. On account of him playing so well. So I was on the lookout for him. But he didn't come off with the other players, he came in at the end, when the crowd around them had kind off broken up. He was with a trainer, so I thought he might have been injured. I suggested as much to him, but he didn't hear me. Too busy talking to the trainer.' Dorrie sounded slightly disappointed that her abuse had been in vain.

'Right,' Harry replied, scribbling in his notebook. 'And what did the trainer look like. Was it Wal Lee? Big bloke?'

'No, little fellow. Looked a bit like a weasel.' Dorrie's eyes grew wide again. 'Perhaps Sharkey was already crook. Perhaps he was already poisoned.'

'Perhaps. Always a possibility. Thanks, Dorrie, I'll follow that lead up. Very helpful.'

Dorrie sat back, smiling benignly at Harry. 'Glad to assist. Is there anything else you need to know?'

Harry put his notebook in his pocket and took his hat from the side table. 'No, that's all for today, I think. I'll bid you goodnight. Hope I haven't caused any matrimonial problems, by turning up here unannounced.'

Dorrie winked at him as she quickly shepherded him out the front door. 'He'll never know, love. It's our little secret, eh?'

'Fair enough,' Harry agreed. Then added, as he turned to leave, 'And remember, always keep your hat pin on your head. You wouldn't want to lose that blue and white headdress, would you? It's a work of art.'

Dorrie just grinned and said nothing as she quickly retreated into the house, closing the door firmly behind her.

✕

Harry watched Willie weave his way through the crowded bar, two large pots of the Caledonian's finest in hand.

'Here you go, boss,' Willie said, plonking himself down in the booth opposite Harry and pushing one of the beers across the table. 'I think we both need this.'

'You're right there, mate,' Harry agreed, taking a large swig. He leaned back against the faded red leather upholstery and briefly surveyed the scene around them. The front bar of the Cally was its usual six o'clock self – noisy, smoky and crowded. The perfect environment for a confidential review of the day's events.

'What did you make of our meeting with Mr Wren?' he asked, leaning in towards his colleague, and taking another sup on his beer.

'Well,' Willie replied, 'it's obvious Sharkey had a gambling problem. That was fairly clear. And it looks like he got himself on the wrong side of the profit and loss ledger.'

'You're right on both counts, I'd say.'

Willie took a contemplative sip on his beer, then spoke again. 'Do you believe Wren when he said he got his standover man to just give him a talking to? I reckon that bloke Hanrahan only knows one way to persuade the customers to pay up. And it's not through a friendly chat.'

'Yeah, he wasn't the nicest bloke you'd ever want to meet, was he? But actually, I believe Wren, on that score anyway. I'm pretty sure he wouldn't come at having Collingwood's best player roughed up. Not even on account of a hundred quid.'

'If that's all it was. Could have been more.'

'Could have been,' Harry conceded. 'But even so. One thing I found interesting though, was that Sharkey was suddenly able to pay off the debt in full. He seems to have come across another source of income all of a sudden.'

Willie nodded. 'Yeah. Where did that come from, I wonder? A big win on the neddies?'

Harry ran his finger round the rim of his glass, watching as the drops of moisture ran down its side.

'Maybe, but unlikely, judging by his usual punting form. It's also possible he got paid for doing some promotional event at the building society. It seems as though his arrangement with Sir Randolph worked in that kind of way. Or maybe Sir Randolph, or some other benefactor, gave him the money to help him out of a tight spot. I'll check with Sir Randolph, and with Ernie Copeland too. Though I reckon they wouldn't be too keen to spill the beans on any extra payments. We know it happens all the time with the better players, but clubs run the risk of being accused of breaking league rules, so they keep pretty quiet about it. But wherever the money came from, it seems like Sharkey didn't learn his lesson. He didn't stop spending it. Not according to Wren, at any rate.'

'Seems like our Mr Sharkey was a bit of a desperate character,' Willie observed.

'Well, he's certainly not the character the committee was making him out to be,' Harry agreed. 'I've got a feeling that the more we look into this, the more we'll find that the real Robbie Sharkey was someone entirely different.'

'By the way,' Willie said, 'How did you get on with your Carlton supporter? Y'know, the old girl you hoped might have seen something in the crowd at the gate.'

Harry shrugged. 'Dorrie, you mean? Nah, nothing. She was only there when they came off after half-time, and she saw nothing. Except she did notice Sharkey came off late. And according to Dorrie, he wasn't mobbed at all, and couldn't have been jabbed then.'

'Ah well, it could still have been when they were coming back out. Though maybe your syringe-in-the-crowd theory is looking a bit less likely.'

'Dunno. Maybe. But we'll still keep it in mind as one possibility.' Harry finished his beer and looked across at Willie.

'My shout, I reckon. Come on, mate, you're dragging the chain there.'

Willie raised his glass and downed its contents with one gulp. 'Cheers, boss. One for the road, eh? I'll get 'em.'

'Thanks mate, but I'll pay,' Harry replied, extracting a note from his pocket and placing it in front of his constable. Willie set off, empty glasses in hand, in the direction of the bar.

Harry glanced around the crowded room, taking in the familiar post-work swill, exclusively male and in this pub at least, overwhelmingly working men, winding down after their hard day's labour. Many of them could be identified from their respective workplaces: the Fosters brewery blokes by the brownish patina to their clothes, whereas the workers from the nearby Hoffman's brickworks had a slight reddish tinge, from the dust they were exposed to all day long.

There were some exceptions to the domination of manual labourers though. Harry's attention was drawn in particular to two figures sitting in a far corner of the room. One was large, florid and flamboyantly dressed, none other than the notorious SP bookie, George Winton, who Harry had often witnessed operating from the front bar of the Cally.

Winton was making no attempt to hide his strictly illegal activity. Apart from his very noticeable garb, Winton was ostentatiously engaged in making entries into a large ledger, while his companion, obviously his bag man, dealt with a steady stream of customers, either handing over cash, or receiving it from his large brown kitbag.

Harry couldn't care less about Winton's activities: he viewed SP bookmaking simply as a failure of the government to give the working man a decent opportunity for a bit of entertainment. If Wren, Winton and their like were prepared to fill the gap, he wasn't going to go out of his way to stop them. Unless, of course, he was ordered to, which in fact had happened from time to time over the years. And if his boss, Winston Marks, had his way, would still be happening, on a very regular basis. Fortunately, the head man, the new police commissioner, was more sensible and was generally prepared to turn a blind eye, even under pressure from the more puritanical elements of Parliament.

Harry's interest was more strongly piqued by another figure, hovering in the background in Winton's vicinity. This fellow was Winton's diametric opposite; drab where Winton was flamboyant, slight where Winton was substantial, furtive where Winton was raucous. Harry waved casually in his direction, and miraculously the little fellow's attention instantly diverted from Winton's activities. He snuck a quick peek over at Harry, then surreptitiously made his way across the room, arriving at Harry's side in concert with Willie, returning with their beers.

'G'day, Ferret,' Harry said cheerily, pulling out a vacant chair and patting its seat in invitation.

'G'day, Inspector,' the Ferret muttered, sidling into the chair, and peering out at Harry from underneath a large, battered trilby. He glanced suspiciously across at Willie, who smiled in return.

'This is what they might call a happy coincidence,' Harry observed. 'Bumping into you tonight, that is.'

'How come?' The Ferret's suspicious demeanour remained.

'Because you've now got the opportunity to earn an honest quid. Two actually, if you can find the info I'm after.'

'Now you're talkin', Inspector.' A gleam appeared in the Ferret's eye, and he leaned forward toward Harry in anticipation. 'What d'you need to know? I'm your man.'

'Well, Ferret, I've heard on the grapevine that there were some fairly large bets placed around the traps on Saturday's Carlton–Collingwood game. I'm keen to know if there were any real big goes, particularly on Carlton to win. Might have been placed with our friend, big George over there. Or any of the other SPs around town. But I'll save you a bit of work, don't worry about checking out Johnny Wren. That's all done.'

A sly grin spread across the Ferret's pinched features. 'I reckon I know what this is about. You reckon somebody's done in that Sharkey kid to swing the result. Well, didn't work, did it?'

'No, it didn't,' Harry concurred. 'But it went close in the end. And there's no need for you to worry about the whys and wherefores of this job, Ferret. Just do what I ask you to do and leave the detective work to Willie and me.'

'Righto, Inspector. I'll get back to you in a couple of days or so. And I'll tell you what, I'll scout around and find out whether anyone's talking about Sharkey and what happened to him. Might be able to do your job for you.'

'Good idea,' Harry agreed. 'That sort of info could be very useful.'

'I reckon that sort of offer's worth payment in advance,' the Ferret suggested hopefully.

'Sorry, Ferret, usual terms. Half now, half on delivery of the goods.' And Harry pulled a pound note from his pocket and placed it on the table.

Willie hardly had time to register the appearance of the money before it was gone, secreted into the depths of the Ferret's oversized coat with remarkable alacrity.

'I'll be here on Saturday after the game,' Harry said. 'Should be enough time for you to find out a bit, I would think. I'll see you then.'

The Ferret needed no further invitation. In one movement he was up from his chair and dissolving back into the crowded room. Harry took a long sup on his pint and winked at Willie.

'Let's hope that's two quid well spent.'

'Reckon it is,' Willie said. 'If there's one person in this town that could get that sort of lowdown, it's the Ferret.' And he joined Harry in focusing on the merits of the beer.

'So, what's next, boss?' Willie continued, having temporarily quenched his thirst. 'We gonna keep chasing down this gambling connection?'

Harry nodded slowly. 'It seems the most likely motive at this stage, I suppose,' he said. 'I've organised for Ramsgate to come in first thing. Just want to find out how much of a gambler he is, and whether he was linked with Sharkey's gambling connections at all. Probably just a coincidence we saw him at Wren's joint, but you never know. And I want to find out a bit more about who had access to that syringe on Saturday too. Then I'm going to interview Joey Miller. You know, that little offsider to Wal Lee. Apparently, he seemed to hang around Sharkey a fair bit. And he had as much opportunity as anyone, I suppose. May be nothing in it, but we'll see.'

'Fair enough,' Willie said. 'What say we divide our forces for a bit? I thought I could go out and talk to that Stansforth bloke. You know, the committee man.'

Harry eyed his colleague keenly. 'He's the bloke that Rachel Sharkey works for, isn't he?'

'Now that you mention it, yes, I suppose that's right,' Willie replied airily.

'Any reason in particular for interviewing him first up?' Harry asked quizzically, an eyebrow extending upward. 'Ahead of, say, Jeremiah Wingard or Sir Randolph?'

'No, no reason. We have to start somewhere, I suppose.'

'Very reasonable answer,' Harry replied, a smile beginning to crease the corners of his mouth. 'Just make sure you don't get waylaid talking to his attractive young assistant, eh?'

'I'll try not to,' Willie grinned. Then more seriously: 'Though she may be able to offer some background on Sharkey that we haven't come across. And you can trust me to deal with her carefully. I know it's a bloody tough time for her.'

Harry replied, serious now too. 'Yeh, sure mate. I know you'd be sympathetic. And it seems like she was close to her brother, so you're right. She might be able to give us some useful information.'

'I'll get right onto it,' Willie replied, with obvious enthusiasm.

✕

6

THURSDAY 17 JUNE 1897

'I CAN'T SEE THE relevance of that question, Inspector. What's wrong with having a little flutter now and again?' Henry Ramsgate was doing his best to be defiant, but the slight tremor in his voice betrayed him. And his discomfort at being called to Russell Street to be interviewed was palpable.

'Well, of course it's technically illegal, but I'm not too concerned about that,' Harry reassured him, leaning back comfortably in his chair. 'What I would be concerned about though, is if those little flutters multiplied and turned into big flutters. Financially embarrassing flutters. Financially embarrassing, even for a professional man such as yourself. Particularly if they also involved placing bets on the football.'

Ramsgate flushed and replied indignantly. 'I resent that implication, Inspector. I can assure you that my betting has never put me in a compromised position. I never bet on any game that Collingwood is playing.'

'Not sure that I accused you of betting for or against Collingwood,' Harry replied amiably. 'But it's reassuring to hear you don't, in any case.' He paused to study the good doctor in more detail. He fancied he saw sweat materialising on Ramsgate's brow. And his expression as he stared warily back at Harry conveyed his profound unease. Not the look of a man with nothing to hide.

'You can take my word for it,' Ramsgate continued, clearly taking Harry's pointed silence and interrogating gaze for disbelief. 'Just the occasional flutter.'

'Happy to take your word for it,' Harry replied, his demeanour as calm as ever. 'Though of course I don't need to. I can get all the information I need about your betting history from Mr Wren.'

Ramsgate shot him a nervous glance. 'Surely that information is confidential,' he protested. 'A breach of my privacy.'

Harry chortled. 'Hardly, mate. It's all evidence of illegal behaviour, after all. But John Wren and I have a certain understanding. I'm prepared to overlook his entrepreneurial activities, if he assists me with information on this murder case. Which, as you may guess, I regard as a bit more important.'

'But how is me having a few bets got anything to do with the Sharkey case?' Ramsgate's voice now had a definite edge of panic.

'Probably nothing,' Harry replied. 'But I'll be the judge of that. Now, do I have to call in Mr Wren, or are you going to be truthful with me about the extent of your gambling? Because I'm pretty confident it's been more than the occasional flutter. How much more is what I want to know.' The genial tone had evaporated, and Harry now fixed the Doctor with an expectant stare.

Ramsgate's show of nervous defiance disappeared completely, replaced by timid resignation. 'All right, the amount I wager may be a little more than I indicated. But I've never been financially embarrassed. I've always paid my bets on time, and I've never extended my credit, I assure you. Check with John Wren, if you must.'

Harry eyed him steadily. 'That won't be necessary at this stage. But you might help me with a bit more detail. Did you have a wager on the

Carlton game last weekend?'

'No, definitely not!' Ramsgate declared adamantly. 'I told you, I never bet on games where our boys are playing.'

'But perhaps on other games?'

Ramsgate's shoulders slumped. 'Sometimes,' he muttered, almost under his breath.

Harry shook his head slowly. 'Not good, Doctor, not good. Not good for an official in your position to be involved in betting activity on the football in any way.'

'I know, I know,' Ramsgate acknowledged, head bowed.

'I won't take it any further now,' Harry said, eyeing Ramsgate thoughtfully. 'Let's just call it a friendly warning, eh? But there are a couple of other matters I want to explore with you.'

'Certainly, Inspector. Absolutely. What do you want to know?' Ramsgate's relief at the change of subject was tangible.

'Well, while we're still on the subject of gambling, it's becoming clear to us that Robert Sharkey liked a punt as well. In fact, we know his punting was out of control, to the point where he was spending far more than he could afford. Were you aware that he was a big-time gambler? Did you see him around John Wren's place at all?'

Ramsgate looked at him carefully. 'I think most of us around the club knew that Sharkey was a pretty serious gambler. Those of us who spent a bit of time there, I mean. He and Danny Robinson were the two. Always talking about the horses and what was going to win.'

'And the footy? Did they talk about betting on the footy?'

Again Ramsgate surveyed Harry cautiously. 'I don't think so. Not that I heard, anyway.'

'And my second question? Did you ever see him at the tote?'

'Occasionally on a Saturday. Not in the footy season, of course. But I assume when he was playing, he'd be going in during the week to lay his bets. Less chance of me coming across him then.'

That all makes sense, Harry thought. And it fits with what we already know. Now let's see if he wants to be just as straight about last Saturday.

'Now, I want to get a bit more detail about the events surrounding Sharkey's death. I recall when we spoke last, you indicated that you kept your medical bag in the equipment locker in the clubrooms when you weren't using it?'

'Yes, that's correct.'

And what else was in the locker?'

'Oh, all our other supplies. Tape, bandages, disinfectants, that sort of thing. Mainly for our medical and training staff.' Ramsgate coughed and cleared his throat.

'You okay, Mr Ramsgate? Glass of water?' Harry asked considerately.

'No, no, I'm all right,' Ramsgate, replied, producing a handkerchief and wiping his brow.

Harry smiled at the doctor and resumed. 'So all your training staff would know you kept your medical bag there, in that locker?'

'Yes, certainly. There was no secret about it.'

'And all the players as well, I assume?'

'Yes, I suppose so. Players would occasionally help themselves to tape or other equipment. They would see my bag in there, I suppose.'

'In fact, anyone who regularly spent time in the change rooms before or during a game?'

'Yes, probably.'

Harry leaned forward, with a stare that was not quite accusatory. 'Now, just to be clear again. About your movements I mean. You put your kitbag in the locker before the game?'

'Yes, that's correct.'

'And it stayed there for the duration of the game? You didn't take it out to the boundary? In case it was needed during the match?'

'No, I always leave it in the change rooms for safekeeping. The trainers have all the equipment that's needed to treat players out on the ground. Tape, bandages, smelling salts, and so on. In their own bag. I consider that if an injury is serious enough to warrant my attention, the player should be taken, or stretchered, down to the rooms. Like Sharkey was on Saturday.'

Harry eyed Ramsgate closely. Why not ask the question, he thought. 'Excuse my bluntness, Doctor, but it seemed to me that the situation with Robbie proved a bit too much for you. Is that a fair call?'

Ramsgate coloured and glanced away. But he returned his gaze to Harry as he replied.

'I'm ashamed to say you're right, Inspector. I have to admit I panicked. I've seen strychnine poisoning before, but it was many years ago. And Sharkey's seizure was so unusual, and so severe, it completely confused me at the time. I should have known what it was, I admit that. Thank goodness Ed Brown was there. A first-class doctor, I'm in his debt.'

'You're right, he is a first-class doctor,' Harry agreed. "Thank you for your honesty, there's plenty who would never admit to what you just have. Don't worry, you'll learn from the experience. It made no difference to the outcome anyway, as it turned out.'

Ramsgate said nothing, just sat there looking disconsolate, head bowed. Time to put him out of his misery, Harry thought.

'That'll do for today,' he said briskly. 'I appreciate your cooperation.'

Ramsgate rose quickly to his feet and beat a hasty retreat, his relief at being dismissed very evident. Harry watched him go, then rose and left the room too. Now let's see what Joey Miller has to say, he thought to himself. But first a cuppa. And he wandered off to find the tea lady.

✕

Joey Miller fidgeted in his chair in the Russell Street interview room. Harry was taking his time to begin the interview, sitting back in his chair on the other side of the table and turning over the pages of his notebook, examining the entries in some detail. In reality there was nothing of relevance in those pages, but sometimes Harry liked to give the impression of copious (and incriminating) information at hand, just to keep his customers on their toes. At Harry's side, Willie Milton sat at his ease, smiling pleasantly at Miller, who seemed to be growing more uneasy by the second. Willie was well used to this technique of Harry's.

'Right,' Harry began eventually, placing the open notebook on the table in front of him. 'Thanks for coming in, Joey. First up, I just want to confirm some background about you and your involvement with the Collingwood footy club.' He paused and looked at Miller, who swallowed hard and shuffled again in his seat.

'That okay with you?' Harry asked cheerfully.

'Ask me anything you like. I got nothing to hide.' Miller's tone was an attempt at defiance, but Harry detected a quaver in his voice that spoke to him of the man's anxiety.

'Now, we understand from Mr Copeland that you've been at the club for a couple of years. And that Mr Stansforth was good enough to recommend you for the job?'

'That's right.'

'I'm wondering why Mr Stansforth was able to do that? Did you work for him previously?'

'Yeah, that's right. We would have worked together for a couple of years, I suppose. Maybe more.'

Harry glanced at Miller in mild surprise. 'Worked together? You mean you worked for him for a couple of years.'

'No,' Miller replied immediately, and with a degree of pique. 'I meant what I said. We worked together. We were sort of … partners.'

Harry's surprised expression remained, but he continued. 'And when would this have been?'

Miller gazed out the window and thought for a while. 'Oh, maybe six years ago. Thereabouts.'

'And what line of business did you share?'

Miller stared at Harry and said nothing for a few moments. He seemed to be weighing up his response, and how much he should reveal. Eventually he settled for very little.

'A medical business,' he replied, and left it at that.

Again Harry was surprised. And intrigued. 'A medical business? What exactly does that mean, Joey? As far as I know, neither of you are doctors.'

Miller eyed Harry and replied, again in a slightly annoyed tone. 'You don't have to be a doctor to know how to treat people. Doctors often get it wrong and charge a fortune for their trouble.'

Harry was quickly learning a lot about Joey Miller, and Walter Stansforth too, for that matter. A touch of flattery might kick things along a bit further.

'That sounds very interesting,' he ventured. 'What techniques were you and Walter Stansforth using. I hear there's some exciting developments in the field of … medical treatments.'

Miller sat up straighter and leaned forward a little. 'Medical electro-therapeutics,' he confided proudly. 'It was all the rage in Europe. Still is, they tell me.'

'I'm not sure I've come across that method,' Harry suggested. 'What exactly does it involve?'

'Well,' Miller said, a definite note of enthusiasm now in his voice. 'It's really the treatment of disease though the hypodermic injection of organic liquids, extracted from certain glands. Mr Stansforth learned it, he told me, from the famous Professor Brown-Sequard. In Europe.'

'Organic liquids?' Harry was genuinely intrigued now. He glanced at Willie whose features were suffused with an air of incredulity.

'Yes, organic liquids. Extracted from animals' glands. From sheep and cattle, from their, you know, knackers.'

'Blimey!' Willie muttered under his breath.

'So how did that go?' Harry asked. 'I mean, did you cure people? Did you get plenty of customers?'

'It was going pretty well,' Miller said. Then, in a more sullen tone. "We struck a bit of trouble though.'

'What sort of trouble?'

Miller hesitated. 'Someone got … crook.'

'No bloody wonder,' Willie murmured.

'How crook?' Harry pressed on.

'Quite crook.' Miller was noncommittal. 'Anyway, for one reason or another, we had to get out of the business.'

'Well, that was a bit of bad luck,' Harry suggested.

His sarcasm was lost on Miller.

'Yeh, it was,' he sighed. 'Awful bad luck. We was on a winner there.'

Harry leaned forward in his chair. 'And whose job was it to do the injecting, Joey? Yours?'

'Yeh, that's right,' Miller replied cautiously.

'Funny thing though, when we were talking to you the other day, you said you hardly knew what a hypodermic syringe looked like. I got the very distinct impression you wouldn't know one end from the other. But you must have been quite an expert at it after two years' experience.'

Miller looked confused. 'Did I say that?' Then, after a longish pause, 'What I should have said is, it's been so long since I used one, now I'd hardly know what one looks like.'

Willie could contain himself no longer. 'Oh, so that's what you meant to say,' he exclaimed, eyebrows raised, and voice dripping with sarcasm. 'Very reasonable explanation, but you seem to have a bit of a problem with your memory. I'd see a doctor about that, if I were you.'

Miller said nothing, just sat sullenly, his gaze shifting nervously back and forth between the two policemen.

Harry changed tack. 'Let's turn to last Saturday, were you in the change rooms alone at any time, either before or during the game?'

Miller shook his head. 'I don't think so.' He shuffled nervously on his seat. 'Though, come to think of it, I might've been. Actually, I can't remember whether I was or not. Y'see I'm often called on to go down there and get something or other. Supplies, tape, that sort of thing. So, like I said, I might've been.'

'Willie's right, you do have a problem with your memory, Joey. Just give me a straight answer, were you or weren't you in the rooms alone?' Harry persevered, his exasperation growing. 'Is it a yes or no?'

'I don't think I was,' Miller reiterated. 'Though, like I said, I can't be sure, I might've had to go down there to get something. And I was down there after half-time because Danny Robinson had a sore hammy and I had to give him a rub-down.'

'So you were in the club rooms when they brought Sharkey down on the stretcher?'

'Yeah, Wal and Jimmy brought him down. Hell of a shock to see him like that, I can tell you.'

'No doubt,' Harry agreed. Then, giving up on that line of questioning, 'How well did you know Robbie Sharkey? The word is you seemed to spend a fair bit of time with him.'

'What's wrong with that?' Miller replied. 'I mean, he was our best player. It was my job to look after him.'

'You were noticed chatting to him as he was coming off at half-time,' Harry continued. 'What was that all about?'

Miller's eyes darted between the two. 'Oh, nothing much. He had a sore calf, wanted a rub-down.'

'So you gave him a rub-down in the half-time break?'

Miller thought for a few seconds. 'Actually, I don't think I did. I remember he said it came good and he didn't need one after all. Then I had to work on Danny Robinson.'

'Fair enough,' Harry sighed, and scrawled 'LIAR' in very large letters in his notebook. 'Finally, are you a punter? On the horses? Or the football?'

'No, I'm not.' Miller replied emphatically.

'Not familiar with John Wren's tote?'

'I've heard of it. Never been there.'

'Never?'

Miller looked nervously at Harry. 'Well, maybe once or twice. I can't really remember.'

'There you go again with the poor memory,' Willie cut in. 'You really do need to work on that.'

Miller scowled at Willie and said nothing.

Harry smiled genially and slapped the desk in front of him. 'All right, that's all we need for the moment. Don't leave town, we might want to call on you again.'

Miller rose abruptly from his chair and scurried from the room without so much as a backward glance. Harry watched him go, then turned to Willie.

'Well, what do you make of that? A bit to work on there, I would think.'

'Yeah,' Willie agreed. 'He's a strange one. Wouldn't lie straight in bed, I don't reckon. But not sure he'd have the bottle to do Sharkey in. And I'm struggling to think what sort of motive he'd have for killing him. I can't see him as a hit man.'

'Mmm,' Harry mused. 'I think I agree. But either he's got a very nervous constitution or he's hiding something. Question is, what's he up to? And has it got anything to do with Sharkey? I think we need to make a few more inquiries about Mr Miller.'

'By the way,' Willie interceded, 'You asked me to check up on Fraser Sharkey.'

'Of course. What did you find?'

'Well, the club confirmed what we already know. That there was no love lost between Sharkey and his son. Apparently, he was never seen around the club at all. Turns out he's another temperance man, in the Rechabites apparently.'

'That's interesting,' Harry mused. 'Same as Sir Randolph.'

'That's not too surprising,' Willie replied. There's lots of blokes in the Rechabites. It's pretty popular with the temperance folk. Anyway, I also did a bit of digging about Fraser Sharkey's financial affairs. Remember he said the business was in a bit of trouble and he went to Robbie to bail him out. Turns out it was a big bit of trouble, a few years back when the recession really hit. Almost lost his house apparently, and he's still pretty much mortgaged to the hilt. No wonder he was down on Robbie for not helping him out and for blowing all his money on the neddies. And whatever else he blew it on.'

'I see,' Harry replied. 'Fraser had good reason to be disappointed, I suppose. And angry. And from what we saw the other day, that anger hasn't gone away.'

✕

Clem and Millie Holloway lived in a rented workman's cottage at 254 Barkly Road, a small, single-fronted duplex, and an easy walk from Clem's work at the Hoffman Brickworks in Dawson Street. It was a bit more of a hike from Harry's place at Pleasance Street, half an hour or so, but one which Harry or Effie were regularly required to make to pick up young Alfie after work each day.

Not that they minded: Millie's devotion to her grandson knew no bounds and was returned in equal measure by the little fellow. Altogether, a very satisfactory arrangement, even if Clem expressed his annoyance from time to time, when dinner was running late because Millie was too busy keeping Alfie amused.

Normally it was Effie who picked up Alfie from her in-laws; her hours were far more regular than Harry's. But this morning she had asked if he wouldn't mind meeting her there and walking home together. She'd been feeling a little tired recently and would appreciate the company. Harry was more than happy to accommodate her request – the Sharkey investigation was hectic, but it could wait until the morning. He had asked if she was feeling a bit under the weather, but she had reassured him that all was well; just the pressure of school at the moment.

Harry glanced at his fob watch as he opened the door to number 254. Six o'clock, the old man would be just home from work. And indeed he was, pulling off his boots in the tiny lobby while his grandson tugged enthusiastically on his rather dusty shirt.

'Come and see what I drawed, Granpa,' he commanded.

'Soon, Alfie, soon mate,' Clem promised. 'Just let me get me working gear off first, eh? Oh, g'day, Harry,' he added, noticing his son standing in the doorway.

'Leave Granpa alone, mate,' Harry suggested. 'Mum will have a fit if you get some of that dirt on you.'

Alfie needed no further invitation, propelling himself at Harry, who scooped him up and tossed him lightly in the air. Alfie gave a squeal of delight and demanded a repeat flight.

'One more,' Harry agreed, 'and that'll do. Why don't you go and get that drawing and show me how clever you are?'

'Tough day, Dad?' Harry enquired, after Alfie had dashed off on his mission. His father was as wiry and tough as they came, but thirty-five years at the brickworks were starting to wear him down. He wasn't quite as upright as he'd always been, and now there was always a tired look around his eyes, particularly after a punishing day's work.

'Same as ever, son, same as ever,' Clem replied wearily. 'Doesn't get any easier.'

'That's for sure. Just make sure you're not pushing it too hard, eh? You're a foreman, you should be getting the younger blokes to do the hard graft.'

'I can keep up, don't worry about that. I've got responsibilities. And I'm grateful just to have the job. Plenty of blokes been laid off down there, y'know. The building trade's doing it tough these days, and when they're not building houses, they're not buying bricks either.'

'You're right there, Dad. Anyway, are the ladies about? Effie said she'd meet me here.'

Clem pointed in the direction of the door. 'In the parlour, I think. Millie said she made your missus put her feet up. Thought she was looking a bit done in.'

'I'll go see how she is,' Harry said, making his way to the passage door, just as his son came barrelling through, paper in hand. Harry scooped him up again, much to Alfie's delight, and the two made their way down the passage.

'I'll just wash up,' Clem called after him, and Harry waved acknowledgement with his free hand.

A coal fire was burning in the parlour hearth and Effie was luxuriating in front of it, seated in the best armchair and legs extended on a small cushioned stool. She smiled cheerfully at Harry.

'Blimey, you're doing it in style there!' Harry observed, grinning. 'I heard you were down and out, but you don't look too bad.'

'Your mum's spoiling me, like she always does. And she's pretty good at it. I don't really want to go home now.'

'Your wife works too hard,' Millie Holloway said firmly, looking up from where she was hanging up the washing on a clothes horse near the fire. 'Holding down a job and looking after the little one as well. No wonder she gets tuckered out.'

'She'd be lost without her teaching, mum. Wouldn't know what to do with herself, would you, darling?'

'I would not,' Effie agreed, and smiled again.

'Time for a beer before you go?' Clem suggested to Harry, making an appearance at the parlour door. 'I want to talk to you about something.'

'Okay, but just one,' Harry agreed. 'We'd better get home soon. It's my turn to cook, and I can't keep those sausages waiting.'

Clem disappeared into the kitchen and returned with a glass of beer in each hand. 'Cheers, son, get this into you. Now, how's the investigation going. It's a hell of business, that poor young Collingwood fella.'

'It is,' Harry agreed, taking the beer and perching on the armchair wing by his wife's side. 'We're making progress, but nowhere near an arrest yet. It's gonna be a tough one to crack.'

'The boys at the brickworks are all talking about it. They're all Magpie men down there, of course. Shocking thing for the club.'

'Speaking of Magpie men, I spoke to your boss the other day. Jeremiah Wingard. He's on the committee.'

'Yeh, I know,' Clem replied. 'He seems pretty cut up about it. Called a meeting and spoke to all the blokes about it. They were all a bit down, y'know.'

'That was good of him,' Harry observed.

'Yeh, well, he's a good bloke.'

'Fair enough,' Harry said. 'Good to work for too?'

'Good enough,' Clem said non-committedly. 'I got no complaints.'

'I don't suppose you'd see that much of him,' Harry suggested. 'Him being the big boss and all.'

'No, he's not like that,' Clem replied firmly. 'Down in the yard every morning, regular as clockwork. Doesn't mind getting his hands dirty, neither. He'll pitch in with the blokes when it's needed.'

'Sounds like the kind of boss everyone should have,' Harry observed, thinking about his own very much hands-off superior.

Effie looked up at him and smiled; the ironic reference to Chief Inspector Marks was not lost on her.

'We'd better get going,' said Harry, draining his glass. 'But before we do, you said there was something you wanted to talk to me about?'

'Oh yeh, that's right, almost forgot.' Then, lowering his voice slightly and turning away from the women, 'The Plumpton's on Sunday at Moonee Valley, and I'm taking Bess along. Want to come?'

Before Harry had a chance to reply, Effie cut in. 'I heard that! No way you're going to a coursing event, Harry Holloway. You know my attitude to that so-called sport. It's horrible and cruel.'

'Hang on …' Harry began, but got no further as Effie continued her tirade. 'I mean it! It's barbaric! It should be banned.'

'Don't be like that, dear,' Millie interceded gently. 'Clem loves that dog, and it's really the only chance she gets to have a decent run. She just loves getting out there and running with the other dogs. Think of her.'

Effie was not persuaded. 'I'm thinking of the poor hares, actually. Torn to pieces by those dogs, and no hope of escape.'

'That's not right, love!' Clem said indignantly. 'Most of the hares get away. They get a big start on the dogs and most of them get through the escape hatches before the dogs get anywhere near them.'

'Dad's actually right, Eff,' Harry added, endeavouring to pour oil on troubled waters.

'It's the ones that don't get away that concern me,' Effie replied. 'I don't know how you can go and watch it.'

Harry shrugged. 'To tell the truth, I'm not that keen on it. Much rather be watching the neddies any day. But it's important to Dad, and besides, every punter in Collingwood will be there, and I wouldn't mind having a nose around and asking a few questions about Sharkey. You never know what might turn up.'

Effie eyed him suspiciously. 'I hope you're not just making that up, Harry. It better not be just an excuse. But if it's important to the investigation, I suppose I'll overlook you going. But just this once, mind.'

Harry loved his wife's fiery indignation, and in truth he shared her abhorrence of blood sport. And coursing certainly fitted into that category. But he knew how Clem loved to show off his prized greyhound. And who knows, there might be some titbits of good information to be picked up.

'Thanks, darling,' he murmured, stroking her arm affectionately. 'Now, sorry to say, it's time to leave your cosy spot and head for home. Your reward will be my sausages and eggs, well worth the effort.'

'See you Sunday then, Son,' Clem called out, as Harry hoisted Alfie into his pram, and he and Effie made their exit. 'It'll be a great day!'

'Sure thing, Dad,' Harry called back, taking care not to inject too much enthusiasm into his voice. By his side, he felt Effie stiffen in disapproval.

✕

7

THE OFFICES OF THE Premier Building Society were in Collins Street, just down the road from the Queen Street intersection. Built in the seventies housing boom, the ornate four-story edifice, topped with a faux bell tower, was obviously designed with greatness in mind, but seemed somehow diminished, squeezed as it was between even more imposing buildings on either side. And after only twenty or so years, it was beginning to fade prematurely: pigeon droppings festooned the upper parapets and the once brilliant sandstone facade was now a dirty grey.

As he made his way through the front doors, Harry wondered whether the Premier Building Society had weathered the recent recession and housing collapse just as poorly. Might be worth a question or two of Sir Randolph in passing.

The interior of the building complemented the unprepossessing exterior. It was certainly no hive of activity: in fact, the only sign of life could be heard from the offices on the left of the hallway, where a glass door was emblazoned with the society's name. Elsewhere on the ground floor all appeared to be empty.

Making his way through the glass door, Harry was greeted by a young clerk who escorted him down the length of the large room, occupied by rows of desks at which the staff of the society laboured assiduously. At the end of the room, he was shown into a small foyer, where a rather stern-looking woman peered up at him from behind her desk.

'Do you have an appointment with Sir Randolph?' she asked sharply.

'I'm Harry Holloway, to see Sir Randolph,' Harry replied cheerfully. 'Inspector Holloway, that is, from the Melbourne CIB. I think I'm expected.'

'I know nothing about it. I'll see,' the woman replied, with no hint of a smile disturbing her granite features.

She disappeared through a frosted glass door by her desk and reappeared shortly after. She glanced at Harry's typically rumpled attire disdainfully.

'Sir Randolph will see you now. Through there.' With a slight inclination of her head in the direction of the door, she dismissed Harry from her orbit, sat down and resumed her attention to the ledger she had been working in.

'Much obliged,' Harry murmured as he walked past and entered Sir Randolph's office.

The interior of this room was a step up in style and luxury from the mundane facilities occupied by his staff. Sir Randolph was obviously not going to allow straitened circumstances to impact his accustomed level of comfort.

The gentleman in question rose from behind an imposing desk and came forward to shake Harry's hand. He was just as neat and self-assured as when Harry first met him; not a hair out of place and immaculately dressed.

'Good morning, Inspector,' he ventured. 'Please be seated. Would you like a cup of tea?'

'That sounds like a good idea,' Harry agreed readily, parking himself in a leather armchair in front of the desk.

'Very good. I'll just ask Miss Jackson to oblige.'

'I'm surprised you'd dare,' Harry observed drily. 'Not sure I'd have the nerve.'

Sir Randolph chuckled. 'You'll have to excuse her. Like the rest of us, she's been rather struggling to get used to our, shall we say, reduced circumstances. But she's a loyal and willing employee. Been with me for many years.'

'I couldn't help but notice that things seemed a bit quiet when I came in,' Harry said. 'I suppose you've been hit by the recession, like everyone else.'

'We have,' Sir Randolph replied, and Harry fancied there was an almost imperceptible sigh. 'But we're hanging on, Inspector. I don't intend to let this downturn defeat me.'

'Good for you,' Harry said. 'But I must say I'm surprised that your business has been hit so badly. As one of the more successful building societies around town, I mean.'

Sir Randolph eyed Harry steadily. 'I'm a cautious man by nature. Always have been, it's been a key to my success over the years. But I've been forced to keep up with some of these Johnny-come-lately permanents, with their reckless borrowing and lending practices. It was the only way we could keep our customers. We overstretched ourselves, I'm afraid. Now we're paying the price.'

Harry shrugged. 'No comfort, I know, but there's plenty of others in the same boat. Tough times, I'm afraid.'

'Yes. But I'm sorry, Inspector, I've forgotten our tea. Excuse me a moment.' And he rang a small bell on his desk, whereupon the severe Miss Jackson promptly appeared in the doorway in response. Harry noticed that she was markedly more civil to Sir Anthony than she had been to him, even to the extent of offering a slice of cake to accompany their tea. Sir Randolph accepted the offer graciously.

'Now,' Sir Randolph continued, 'what's the purpose of your visit today?'

'Background information on Robert Sharkey is what we're looking for at the moment, Sir Randolph. In particular, I'm after a bit more detail on the arrangement you had with him to promote your society.'

'What sort of detail, Inspector?'

'Well, for a start, exactly how much he was paid. And what his duties were?'

Sir Randolph stroked his chin and thought for a moment. 'Ten pound a week was the agreed salary.'

Harry pressed on. 'On average, how many hours a week did that take up?'

Sir Randolph looked slightly uncomfortable. 'Oh, I don't know,' he replied vaguely. 'Perhaps ten to twenty hours. It varied quite a bit.'

Harry scribbled down the amount in his notebook, writing next to it, *Probably less.* He looked up again at Sir Randolph.

'And that's all he was paid? No bonuses, no little extras?'

Sir Randolph now looked distinctly uncomfortable, glancing away briefly, then rubbing his chin distractedly. He seemed to be struggling with a decision.

'I'll find out if there were extra payments,' Harry persisted. 'I'm sure some others in the club knew about it. Ernie Copeland, for example.'

Sir Randolph sighed and raised his hands, as if in resignation. 'You're right, Ernie does know about it, and I'm sure he'd be straight with you. And I will be too. Sharkey was being paid a little extra. A bonus payment, if you like.'

'How much exactly?'

'An extra ten pounds.'

'One off, or regularly?'

'Weekly, actually,' Sir Randolph replied off-handedly, as if it was neither here nor there.

Harry raised an eyebrow. 'So he was actually being paid double his nominal salary. I bet that wasn't well known around the place.'

Sir Randolph sighed again. 'No, you're right. Ernie told me to keep quiet about it. Apparently, the league takes a dim view of payments just to play football. They're meant to be amateurs, after all. And we would struggle to justify the payment on what he was doing for my business. Though ultimately, that's how we would need to characterise it, if we had to.'

'And I take it Sharkey was the one who was chasing the extra money? You and the club weren't just feeling particularly generous?'

'He was actually quite aggressive about it. Said we needed to pay him or he was off to the Shinboners.'

'And when did all this happen?'

'A bit over a year ago,' Sir Randolph replied, without hesitation. 'The middle of last season.'

'Are you sure about that?' Harry looked slightly puzzled. 'You're not getting mixed up, are you? With earlier this season?'

Sir Randolph looked at him with some bemusement. 'I know I'm getting on a bit, but I haven't lost all my wits yet. It was definitely during last season, because we thought we needed to keep him to have a chance at the premiership. And as it turned out, we did. Besides, I ought to know. After all, I've been the one who's been forking out that extra ten pound a week for a year or so.'

Harry smiled slightly. 'Yes, I suppose you should. But tell me, did Sharkey come back to you at the beginning of this season for another pay rise?'

Sir Randolph raised his eyebrows in mild surprise. 'How did you know that, Inspector? In fact, he did. For a considerably larger sum this time. But I'd had enough of his shenanigans, and besides, I couldn't afford any more. I called his bluff, and he went away. Pretty angry he was, too, I can tell you.'

Now it was Harry's turn to raise his eyebrows. 'I see. All these demands must have caused a bit of bad feeling between you and Sharkey. All in all, he probably wasn't your favourite person around the club. Would that be a fair statement?'

Sir Randolph leaned forward slightly in his chair and replied firmly, 'I don't mind admitting to you, I didn't like the fellow very much at all. I thought he was greedy and selfish. And I didn't approve of his lifestyle, what I knew of it at least.'

'Oh, and what in particular did you disapprove of?'

'I know he was a gambler. And a drinker too, I've been told. I disapprove strongly of both those activities. As you probably know, I'm in the Order of Rechabites.'

'Yes, I did know that,' Harry said. 'Each to his own, I hear the Rechabites do good charitable work. What interests me though is why you forked out all that extra money for Sharkey if you disliked him so much?'

'I did it for the club,' Sir Randolph replied promptly. 'The club is a very important part of my life. It's a wonderful organisation: great family values and great people. People like Bill Beazley and Ernie Copeland, and Bill Strickland too. They're the salt of the earth, with the amount of work they put in for Collingwood. And all unpaid, of course. Not like Robert Sharkey, I might add. Putting up with his demands was a small price to pay if it would contribute to the club's success, and to the pleasure that would give people like Bill and Ernie.'

Harry looked at the list of questions and issues written in his notebook. He was satisfied he had covered everything. Then he suddenly remembered his promise to Effie.

'Speaking of family values, I believe your son is now involved in the club, in some capacity. You must be pleased with that?'

Sir Randolph frowned slightly. He looked down at his desk, and appeared to ponder some papers there, before looking up at Harry again.

'My son has gone astray in his life, Inspector.' He spoke quietly, but with an anxious intensity. 'Been led astray, I should say. He fell into bad company, and I feared for the salvation of his soul. To tell the truth, there have been times when I feared for his sanity, such were the depths to which he sank, and the … the depravity into which he had been led. I thought introducing him into the club and exposing him to the fine values the club promotes, could be helpful in curing the aberrant impulses that had taken hold of him.'

Harry knew exactly what the 'aberrant impulses' were, but saw no need to cause pain to Sir Randolph by probing further on that front.

'And your son has enjoyed mixing in the club?' he ventured politely, looking to wind up this obviously painful topic for Sir Randolph. But to his surprise, Sir Randolph brightened considerably as he answered.

'I'm pleased to say, I think it's been a success. My colleagues at the club, everyone really, have gone out of their way to make him welcome. And Richard seems to be happier and more settled than he's been for a long time. I'm hopeful that he's on the way back to a normal life. The last time I saw him he seemed much more like his old self, more like the boy he was before this malignant influence came into his life.'

'I'm pleased to hear it.' But Harry was surprised at Sir Randolph's optimism. From what Effie had told him, Richard Thames was very far from returning to a normal life. But at least Harry had some positive news to report back to his wife.

'I've taken up enough of your time, Sir Randolph,' he concluded, closing his notebook and getting to his feet. Sir Randolph rose and came out from behind the desk to shake his hand.

'There is one thing,' he said, as he grasped Harry's hand. 'One favour I would ask of you, Inspector. That you keep the fact of our extra payments to Robert Sharkey confidential. All the clubs make these payments, one way or another. It's a complete farce of a system. But the league is keen to find a scapegoat in the name of amateurism, and they wouldn't hesitate to attempt to sanction Collingwood, if they found out about it. I would hate to be the cause of a major problem for the club.'

Harry rubbed his chin. 'Look, you've been honest with me, and I'll be honest with you. I've got no inclination whatsoever to report the club to the league, that's entirely between you and them. But if it turns out that these extra payments are relevant in some way to our investigations, and to Robbie Sharkey's death, it's going to be inevitable that it gets out. That's all I can offer you.'

'That's a fair response,' Sir Randolph agreed, as he led him to the door. 'And of course you're right, the issue of bonus payments is nothing compared to the death of that young man.'

✕

'Something's come up,' Effie exclaimed breathlessly, as she stepped from the kerb outside the Merton Hall gates and hoisted herself into the hansom cab next to Lydia.

'What do you mean?' her friend said, somewhat alarmed at Effie's flustered state. 'Is our rendezvous with Michael and his friend still on, or shall I send the cabbie back to my place for afternoon tea?'

'No, it's still happening, but Michael visited him last night to arrange things and found him in a terrible state. Completely distraught, shattered in fact. Something awful has happened to him, but he can't, or won't, say what.'

'Oh, that is bad news,' Lydia sympathised. 'Perhaps his love affair hasn't blossomed the way he would wish.'

'No, no!' Effie declared emphatically. 'Michael thinks it's something worse than that. Far worse. He said Richard was almost hysterical.'

'Goodness me, it's a wonder he's agreed to go ahead with our meeting at all, if he's in that kind of state.'

'He has agreed, but reluctantly, according to Michael. And only because Michael stressed to him the opportunity for his acting career. I hope you're not going to fill his head with expectations that can't be met. You do actually have good contacts in the business, I hope.'

Lydia rolled her eyes in mock outrage. 'Effie Holloway, how could you doubt me? Believe me, I'm in touch with quite a few people who could help him. Harry Rickards, for example. He's a great pal and he's always on the lookout for exciting new talent.'

Effie sighed and replied. 'From what Michael said, I doubt whether the poor young man is up to auditioning for Mr Rickards at the moment. He sounds dreadful. I'm not even sure whether there's any point in us meeting with him.'

'What do you mean?' Lydia said. 'It sounds to me as though he has an awful lot he needs to get off his chest.'

'I don't know,' Effie countered. 'He wouldn't reveal anything to Michael, why would he unburden himself to two complete strangers?'

'You may be right. But on the other hand, it's often the case that people under great stress can talk to strangers better than they can to friends. Particularly if those strangers are sympathetic. And we know how to be sympathetic par excellence, don't we, dear?'

'I suppose we do.' But Effie's tone betrayed her lingering doubts about Lydia's theory.

Nevertheless, in due course they had made their way down Collins Street, and their horse was reined in outside the fashionable frontage of the Hopetoun Tea Rooms. And waiting on the footpath was Michael Standish, in the company of a well-dressed young man. An extraordinarily handsome young man, Effie realised, as she studied him more closely. Dark features, with a shock of black, neatly groomed hair, and full lips. Though Richard Thames' good looks were blemished by eyes that were red-rimmed and bloodshot, Effie observed, as Michael introduced them.

'It's lovely to meet you, Richard,' Lydia began warmly, immediately taking charge of the conversation. 'Michael has told us about your acting ambitions, and I have a number of colleagues in the business on the lookout for new talent. I hope you don't mind me initiating this meeting.'

'No … of course not,' Richard replied, and Effie could see he was struggling to maintain his composure. 'I … I appreciate your interest.'

'Good,' Lydia replied, her manner kind but firm. 'Let's get out of the cold then and enjoy some of the Hopetoun's delicious afternoon tea. I have arranged a private room for us, where we can talk freely. You can tell us about yourself, as much as you care to. But don't feel under any pressure at all, we just want to help you. In your career, that is.' And taking his arm, she gave it a comforting pat, and led the way into the Hopetoun, Michael and Effie exchanging glances as they followed behind.

Soon they were ensconced in their private room, tea served and a large multi-tiered cake stand placed in front of them, replete with tiny sandwiches, cakes and other delightful petits fours. All the while, Lydia held court on the Melbourne theatrical scene, describing to Richard the excitement and vibrancy therein, and how it could be an absolutely wonderful career for a young man with flair and creative ambition. Richard appeared to listen politely as Lydia talked. But Effie could see that underneath he was distracted and nervous, and she found herself hoping that Lydia was sensitive to the poor young man's distress.

She need not have worried. After a suitable amount of attention to the ostensible reason for their meeting, Lydia paused, smiled sympathetically, and placed her hand gently on Richard's.

'I know you're interested in what I've been saying, but I can also see that something is troubling you.' Lydia spoke softly, but warmly, and now took his hand in both of hers.

'You know,' she added gently, 'it's often a great relief to get distressing thoughts off your chest. To confide your concerns in others who, we can assure you, are sympathetic to your circumstances and … desires.'

Richard said nothing, just glanced quickly at Michael, who nodded his affirmation. Richard hung his head, apparently thinking on Lydia's words. Lydia continued to stroke his hand gently.

'Thank you,' Richard eventually managed to say. 'I really …' But he couldn't continue. He took his hand from Lydia's and covered his face as fierce sobs began wracking his whole body. Lydia got to her feet and went around the table to him, holding his head against her breast, as his unrestrained sobs continued. Effie added her sympathy, reaching across the table and stroking Richard's shoulder.

'There, there,' Lydia murmured, as if to a child. 'Don't hold back, you'll feel better for a good cry.'

Richard hung his head silently as the tears continued, but then he managed to regain some control, lifting his head and freeing himself from Lydia's embrace. 'Don't worry,' he declared, a renewed strength to his voice, and a degree of bitterness as well. 'I've done plenty of crying in the past few days. It hasn't helped much yet.' Then he added quickly, 'But I apologise. I don't mean to seem ungrateful, it's really very nice of you to be so concerned.'

'What is troubling you, my friend,' Michael now interposed himself into the conversation, just as gently. 'Lydia is right, you know, it will help to open your heart. You can trust us, Effie and Lydia know of your situation and they're entirely sympathetic.'

'Is it … is it about your special friend?' Lydia asked quietly. 'Michael told us that you had … formed a close relationship.'

Richard looked at her blankly, then seemed to comprehend her meaning. He nodded mutely.

'Is there a problem?' Lydia continued. 'A falling out?'

'No,' Richard replied dully. 'He is dead. Murdered.'

His three companions stared at him, shocked and incredulous. But before they could question him further, Richard continued. 'You might as well know. It was Robbie. Robbie Sharkey. I couldn't reveal it before, but now, what does it matter? His reputation doesn't matter anymore. Except, I suppose, to his family.'

'And to the club too, I imagine,' Effie added, almost thinking aloud.

'I don't care about the club,' Richard retorted fiercely. 'The club made it impossible for us to be together.'

Effie was still struggling to come to terms with what Richard had revealed. 'Are you sure about your friendship with Robbie?' she inquired. 'I appreciate your feelings were very strong, but were they returned? Sometimes it's hard to tell these things. Were you … intimate?' She felt a flush of embarrassment and guilt, that she was prying into his private life. But they had to be certain.

'Do you mean, did we make love together? The answer is no, Robbie was too afraid we'd be caught out. And his career would then be over, wouldn't it?'

'Then how could you really know?' Effie persevered. 'Did he give you any other indication that his feelings were … of that kind?'

Richard looked puzzled. 'What do you mean?' Then, with a hint of anger in his voice, 'Oh, I understand, you think I'm a silly boy, infatuated with a famous man, and dreaming up something that wasn't there. Well, that's not how it was. We weren't intimate in that way, but there was no mistaking his feelings for me, I assure you. Would any number of stolen, passionate kisses be enough to convince you?'

Effie glanced at Michael and Lydia, then back at Richard. 'I don't want to distress you further, Richard,' she said tentatively. 'But it's possible your friendship may have a bearing on what happened to Robbie. You know, we should probably inform the authorities about your relationship.'

'No! What could it possibly have to do with his death? How could it? No-one knew about our friendship.' Richard was clearly having second thoughts about the damage to Robbie Sharkey's reputation. And perhaps to his own.

'I'm sorry,' Effie replied, gently but firmly. 'You're probably right, but we really can't conceal it from the police. I'll tell you what, my husband is Inspector Harry Holloway and he's in charge of the investigation. I'll tell him of our conversation and ask him to keep it in confidence, unless it turns out to be relevant to the case. How does that sound?'

Richard sighed resignedly. 'I suppose you're right, you can't hide it from the police. I accept that. And what you've suggested sounds fair. It's just that I couldn't bear for what was between us to become just an item of gossip and scandal. You know, at the club … and elsewhere. It would make it so hard for my parents.'

'We understand your concern completely,' Michael reassured him. 'Don't worry, you can trust Harry to treat it all sensitively. He's a first-class chap. Now, I'm sorry to revive painful memories any further, but there is one thing I was wondering about.'

Richard looked at him inquiringly.

'You mentioned to James and me that there was a third person involved in your friendship with Robbie, and we got the impression that it was causing you distress. Is that something we can help with?'

Richard glanced at Michael, then shook his head. 'No, no,' he replied immediately, 'That was nothing to do with Robbie and me. I'm sorry if I gave you that impression. It was just that another person said some things that … that weren't welcome. But I'm sure it was nothing, I was probably being foolish and misunderstood his meaning. And intentions. He was probably just being kind. And as I said, it had nothing to do with Robbie and me.'

'So you don't want to talk about that?' Effie persisted.

'No, there's no need,' Richard replied, as a nervous smile passed fleetingly over his face.

'And of course, we respect your judgement on that,' Lydia interceded, patting him on the hand again. 'You've been very brave in these awful circumstances. We're so sorry for your loss.'

Her kind words seemed to precipitate Richard to lose control of his emotions again. His bottom lip began to quiver and tears welled.

Michael looked to ease his distress. 'You know we're here to support you whenever you need it,' he reassured him. 'But is there anyone else you can call on for comfort? Your parents?'

Richard shook his head emphatically. 'I can't talk to them. They're aware of the person I am, or at least my father is. And he's not sympathetic, not for a moment. He regards it as a sickness. Even worse, an abomination.'

'I'm sure he doesn't think that badly of you,' Michael murmured, but with little conviction. 'Anyway, James and I will make it our business to help you through this dreadful time. What say we call on you Sunday afternoon, and then we'll take you out to dinner? We'd do it tomorrow night, but unfortunately we have a prior engagement with friends. One that we cannot get out of.'

'That's very kind of you,' Richard replied, a hint of animation in his voice revealing his gratitude. 'I'll look forward to that very much.'

'Shall we say four o'clock?'

'Four o'clock would be perfect. I'll expect you then.'

'Good, that's settled then,' Lydia said, rising to her feet. 'Now, we must go, but remember too that Effie and I are here to help you at any time. And if there's anything else that occurs to you that may be related to Robbie's murder, or indeed if there's anything that's troubling you, Inspector Holloway at Russell Street is someone you can trust completely.'

'Thank you,' Richard murmured, getting to his feet also, and accepting warm hugs from Lydia and Effie in turn, as well as a heartfelt handshake from Michael. 'Thank you again, so much. I have felt utterly wretched since it happened. Now, at least, I feel that I'm not alone. And that there's some people who understand me and know what I'm going through.'

✕

Walter Stansforth's shop at 282 Chapel Street was located in the very fashionable Prahran Arcade, surrounded by a collection of couturiers, milliners and other ladies' fashion providers. More incongruously, Willie Milton noted, there was also a billiards saloon and a Turkish bath house, and at the entrance to the arcade, facing out onto the street, the Arcade Club Hotel.

Stansforth's shop proudly displayed his name stuccoed above the entrance, and below that the intriguing descriptor, *Exotic Interior Design*. That should get the customers in, Willie thought, as he pushed open the opulent glass door.

A golden light suffused the interior of the shop, showing off to fine effect the oriental hangings and rugs draped around the walls, and the many expensive-looking fittings, mouldings, lanterns and other paraphernalia displayed on racks and shelves throughout the room. Although he had never been to one, Willie imagined the effect was meant to be akin to an oriental bazaar.

Behind the counter at the far end of the shop stood Rachel Starkey, almost hidden by this cornucopia of fashionable decoration. She smiled shyly as she recognised Willie.

'Good morning, Constable,' she murmured quietly, then fell silent, eyes downcast.

Willie took charge. 'Good morning to you, Miss Sharkey. I'm sorry to intrude, I know it must be very difficult for you at the moment. Please accept my sympathies again.'

Rachel nodded, raising her eyes briefly to meet his.

'I'm here to talk to your boss, Mr Stansforth. Is he in at the moment?'

Rachel shook her head. 'I'm sorry,' she said. 'He's not in at the moment. Can I give him a message from you?'

'Are you expecting him back soon?' Willie persevered.

Rachel glanced up at the large wall clock, which read half past eleven. 'I'm not sure. He may go straight to lunch when he's finished his appointment.'

'Okay, what would be the best time to get hold of him then?'

Rachel flushed slightly as she replied, 'I don't know really. He's ... often out.'

Willie looked at her closely and noted her confusion. 'Is he in the Arcade pub perhaps?'

Rachel nodded silently. Don't worry, Willie thought, you haven't betrayed the boss. At the same time, he felt an unprofessional surge of elation at the prospect of spending even a few minutes alone with her.

'Never mind,' he said soothingly. 'Might be best if we organise for him to come down to Russell Street. I'll get out of your hair then,

Miss Starkey. Let you get back to work.' Then, glancing around at the empty shop, 'Though since it's quiet at the moment, would you mind if I ask you a couple of questions? Nothing too difficult, just some background information.'

'It normally gets a little busier after lunch,' Rachel said. 'So I think it would be all right with Mr Stansforth. For you to ask me questions, I mean.' And she coloured slightly again, no doubt wondering if she had offended the law.

Willie smiled at her reassuringly. 'Don't worry, I'll take the blame if he objects to me being here. Though I'm sure he'd be keen for you to cooperate.'

Rachel returned his smile nervously. 'I'm sorry. I didn't mean to imply that it's up to him. I'd be happy to talk to you.'

'And I'd be happy to talk to you too,' Willie replied. Then, glancing around, 'It's an interesting shop he has here. Quite unusual stuff. Is there much demand for it?'

'Oh yes,' Rachel confided, 'At least, there used to be. It was all the rage for a while, among the fashionable ladies. But it's been quieter this year. I think Mr Stansforth is a little worried.'

'Well, I'm sure things will pick up,' Willie reassured her. Then glancing around, he added, 'Expensive looking stuff, that's for sure.'

'More than I could afford, by a long way. A lot of it's imported, you know. From India and other places.'

'Don't reckon an underpaid cop could afford it, either,' Willie said, then changed the subject. 'What's he like, Mr Stansforth? A good boss?'

Rachel hesitated before replying. 'I'm very grateful for the position. It's quite a good wage.'

'And he treats you well?'

Again Rachel faltered, before replying, 'Oh yes, I suppose.'

Willie looked at her more closely. 'But he could treat you better? Yes?'

Rachel's eyes rounded as she considered her reply. 'It's just that sometimes … sometimes it's not very pleasant. Particularly when he comes back to the shop and there's no-one else here.'

Willie was careful not to show his welling anger. 'You mean he … takes liberties?'

Rachel simply nodded, eyes down again. 'It's not too bad. It's just talk. I do my best to ignore it.'

'It's still not right. You shouldn't have to put up with it,' he said, more firmly now. 'If it upsets you, or if he does anything worse, come and see me, and I'll make sure he's dealt with.'

Rachel smiled timidly. 'Thank you, that's very kind of you. But I'm grateful for the job, and Mr Stansforth might be displeased if he thought I was complaining to you.'

'Don't worry about that, I'd make sure he got the message in the right way. And I'm sure he doesn't want to cross the law. You won't lose your job, you can be sure of that.'

'Thank you,' Rachel said, obviously relieved. 'It's not really that I like the job a great deal, it's just that my family needs my income, and I know Father would be upset if I lost my position. It's rather tough for everyone these days. As you know, I suppose.'

'So you'd rather be doing something else?' Willie ventured, conversationally. A few more minutes with Rachel would surely be justifiable. After all, he'd already learned quite a bit from her about Walter Stansforth and his business.

'Do you mean for a job?' she asked.

'Yeah,' Willie replied. 'What would be your ideal job? If you had the choice?'

Rachel gave a slightly embarrassed smile. 'That's easy. I'd like to be a teacher. It's something I've always dreamed of. But that'll never happen, of course,' she added, apologetically.

'Why not?' Willie asked. 'I reckon you'd make a terrific teacher.'

Rachel shrugged. 'I don't know. I wouldn't have the first idea how to become one.'

Willie had a flash of inspiration. 'I'll tell you what. The boss's wife is a teacher. I'm sure she'd be happy to meet with you and explain how to get into that game.'

'Oh no,' Rachel said, 'I couldn't impose like that. I'm sure she's too busy to meet with me.'

'Don't worry,' Willie reassured her. 'She's just like the boss; a real corker. And she's what the boss calls an 'independent woman'. I know she'd like nothing more than to recruit another female into the ranks.'

'That would be wonderful,' Rachel exclaimed, real excitement now in her voice. 'I'd love to meet with her. If she's happy to, of course. Thank you.'

'That's settled then,' Willie said firmly. 'Now, Miss Sharkey, I'd better go. I've wasted enough of your time.'

'Not at all,' Rachel insisted. 'It's good to think of future possibilities. It takes my mind off everything that's happened.'

'That's the spirit,' Willie said, and turned to go. Then he had another thought.

'Seeing as how the shop's still empty, can I ask you one more question? Does the boss keep any poisons out the back by any chance? To deal with vermin and the like?'

'I don't know,' Rachel replied, an alarmed look appearing. 'I don't go out the back very often. I know he's complained about rats in the past.'

'Would you mind if I have a quick peek out there? Don't be concerned, I'm not expecting to find anything incriminating, if that's what you're worried about. Just routine, really.'

'This way then,' Rachel said, leading him to the doorway behind the counter. They passed into what was obviously a storeroom, quite large with a number of wooden racks around the walls, all stacked with merchandise of one kind or another. In one corner stood a small open cupboard in which were stored a variety of bottles and jars. Rachel pointed at it.

'That's where the cleaning stuff is. We have a cleaner come in once a week for the shop. If there's any poison here it'll be in that cupboard.'

It was obvious to Willie that the cleaner was not employed out here in the store room: a coating of dust lined those shelves that were empty, and rodent droppings were evident in a number of places. He peered at the various bottles and jars on the cupboard shelves. Some were similarly covered in dust: those in regular use were cleaner.

'Here we go!' he exclaimed, picking one of the clean bottles off the shelf. It was labelled 'Pure strychnine powder' underneath a large red 'POISON' sign. Willie peered at the contents, about half full.

'Think I'll take this with me,' he said to Rachel. 'Could be evidence.'

Rachel was staring at him, wide-eyed. 'Do you think …' she began, then faltered.

Willie saw her anxious expression and quickly reassured her. 'No, no, most probably not, if you're wondering if this was the poison used in the murder. Probably just used to kill rats, as we thought. But I'll take it with me nevertheless. We'll let Mr Stansforth know when we catch up with him, though you can tell him if he asks where it went.'

A bell tinkled in the shop next door and Rachel started.

'Oh dear, that's a customer. Excuse me, Constable.' And she turned to go back into the shop.

'No problem, all done here.' And as he followed her, he added, 'By the way, you can call me Willie, if you want. Most people do.'

Rachel flashed a quick smile back at him as she hurried through the door. A fashionably dressed matron was waiting, tapping on the countertop impatiently.

'Sorry to hold you up, madam,' Willie offered breezily, as he strolled past. 'The young lady here has been very helpful assisting me on police business. All routine, I can assure you. She'll be delighted to attend to you now, I'm sure.'

And as the matron turned to Rachel, Willie gave Rachel a little wave and mouthed a silent 'thank you'.

✕

'What? Surely not! Are you certain?' Harry turned from hanging his coat and looked at his wife in disbelief.

'I'm absolutely certain,' Effie declared. 'I couldn't be more certain. And I have witnesses. Ask Michael and Lydia, if you like.'

'You didn't misinterpret what the lad said? Maybe they were just good friends.' Harry reached for the rum bottle. He needed something to warm his extremities, chilled by the biting winter cold outside.

'No possibility of misinterpretation, my darling, I can assure you. Richard couldn't have been more certain. He was in love with Robbie Sharkey and Robbie Sharkey was in love with him. They were planning a future together. At least, they were talking about it.'

Harry remained incredulous. Settling himself down in the armchair with a decent tot of rum in hand, he eyed Effie doubtfully. 'Look, I haven't met the lad, but from what I hear from Michael and James he seems a bit unworldly, a bit naive. Perhaps he's mistaken a friendly overture from Sharkey for something else? Is that a possibility?'

Effie returned her husband's interrogating gaze with a slightly scornful look. 'I don't think a passionate kiss could be misinterpreted, do you? Actually, a number of passionate kisses. And that's what Richard says happened. And whatever he is, I'm positive Richard Thames isn't a liar.'

Harry whistled softly. 'Well no, that doesn't seem to leave much doubt. And I trust your judgement, dear, I really do. I'm just staggered by it, that's all. A complete turn-up.'

Harry lapsed into silence, sipping on his rum and thinking. Then he resumed speaking, almost musing aloud rather than speaking to Effie. 'But y'know, when I think about it, it does make sense, in a funny kind of way. It would explain Margot Philips's puzzling reaction and the way she talked about Sharkey. Perhaps she was just a good friend.'

'Yes,' Effie agreed. 'I think that's exactly what she was.'

'Well, one thing's for sure, I'm going back to talk to our Miss Philips again, and this time we're going to get the whole story. I expect that'll confirm what you've just told me, Eff.'

'There's nothing to confirm,' Effie replied, a little indignantly. 'I've told you all there is to tell. There's absolutely no doubt about Richard Thames and Robbie Sharkey. Don't you believe me?'

'Of course I do,' Harry replied hastily. 'Just my policeman's training, I'm afraid. Always needing to hear it straight from the horse's mouth. Corroborating evidence, and all that.'

'I suppose so,' Effie conceded. 'As long as you're not doubting my woman's judgement on these things.'

'Heaven forbid!' Harry raised his hands in mock surrender. 'By the way, I've got a bit of news you might find interesting. I might have found you a recruit.'

'A recruit? A recruit for what?' Effie's interest was piqued.

'Well, Willie Milton was talking to Robbie Sharkey's sister, Rachel. I've met her and she seems a lovely young girl. Willie certainly thinks so, that's for sure. Anyway, she currently works as a shop assistant, but it turns out she really wants to be a teacher. Willie's dropped your name to her as a good contact. I told him you'd be happy to have a chat with her and point her in the right direction.'

'Of course I would!' Effie exclaimed. 'I'm sure we could organise something. I think Miss Hensley might be prepared to take on Miss Sharkey in some sort of role while she works her way through teachers' college. After all, Merton Hall is proving very popular, and the number of girls enrolling is going up quite a bit.' Then she eyed Harry again, wondering.

'This isn't another one of Willie's flights of fancy, is it? He's not just trying to impress this young lass? Are you sure she's serious?'

Harry smiled. 'I take your point and I'm sure Willie was strongly encouraging her. But I'm also pretty sure she's serious about it. And from what Willie says, she's very much under the thumb of a strict, religious father. Reminds me of how you described your family history to me, actually. I'd say if anyone needs to get away from a domineering father and strike out on her own, it's Rachel Sharkey.'

'It certainly sounds that way.' Harry's description of Rachel's circumstances had indeed struck a sympathetic chord with Effie. She was now full steam ahead.

'We should organise for me to meet with her as soon as possible.'

'We should, but carefully, I reckon. As I said, her dear papa keeps a pretty tight rein on her, so we need to be all proper and correct. I reckon an invite to have dinner at home with Inspector Holloway and his charming wife would do the trick. And if Constable Milton happens to show up uninvited then who's to know and who's to care. Because Willie won't speak to me again if I don't let him in on it.'

'Wonderful! What about this Sunday? No time like the present.'

Harry laughed quietly. 'Too soon, I reckon. Got to have time to go through the proper channels. And besides, as you know, I've promised the old man I'd go to the Plumpton with him this Sunday. To watch Black Bess in action.'

'Oh, that's right.' There was disappointment in Effie's voice. 'Well, make sure you set it up as soon as possible. No excuses.'

'No excuses indeed, my love. I'll get onto it as a matter of priority.'

'Thank you, darling,' Effie replied. If there was one thing she could count on, it was Harry's word. If he said it was going to happen, it inevitably would. Impulsively, she leaned down to him, still slouched in his favourite armchair, and kissed him. The kiss lingered and turned from grateful to passionate.

'Alfie in bed?' Harry murmured.

'In bed and fast asleep,' she whispered in reply.

'Good,' he said rousing himself from the depths of the chair. 'I think we might have an appointment upstairs, don't you?'

'I think we might,' Effie agreed, and took his hand.

8

SATURDAY 19 JUNE 1897

'PREPARE YOURSELF, MATE,' Harry warned Willie, as they made their way through the labyrinthine passages beneath the MCG. 'You're about to enter the rarified atmosphere of the members' dining room.'

'Don't remind me about food. I'm starving, I could murder a steak and kidney pie.'

'Don't worry, I reckon they'll have finished their tucker by now. You won't be tempted to nick the food off the president's plate.'

The banter between the two lapsed as they approached the large oak door, inscribed with '*Members' Dining Room*' in gold lettering. Harry's tone became serious.

'Now, it'll be interesting to see how they react to my news. They'll all plead complete ignorance, of course, but someone may know more about Sharkey than they're letting on. Just keep a sharp eye on all their reactions, and don't be afraid to interrupt me if you need to press a point with any of them.'

As the two men entered the room, they saw their timing was precise. The committee seemed to have just finished lunch, their empty plates in front of them, and were now focussing on their port and cigars. Harry's quick scan of the room indicated that all were present, except for Bill Strickland who must have been off preparing for the game. Harry noticed that Henry Ramsgate was seated at one side of the table among his fellow committee members. Obviously he played no part in pre-match preparations.

William Beazley rose from his seat at the head of the table and came forward to greet them. 'Welcome, Inspector. Constable. We got word through Ernie that you were coming. Take a seat.' Indicating two empty chairs at the other end of the table.

'Thank you,' Harry replied. 'And sorry to interrupt your lunch.'

'That's perfectly all right,' Beazley replied. 'No doubt you have your reasons for this meeting. Naturally we're keen to hear your news.'

'Well yes, there has been an important development and, as you can appreciate, we're keen to push on as quickly as possible. Plus, we felt this would be a good opportunity to catch you all together. We realise you're all busy men.'

'Of course, Inspector, of course. And it's opportune from our perspective too. Because there's also been a development from our end that may be important.'

'Really?' Harry eyed the president questioningly.

'But your news first, perhaps.'

'All right.' Harry paused for a moment to gather his thoughts. 'It's a rather delicate matter, and one that I'll ask you to keep in confidence. It's information that you may find difficult to believe, and perhaps also find … distasteful. But I'll get straight to the point.'

'Please do.'

Harry sensed that all eyes in the room were now closely, and expectantly, concentrated on him.

'Well, we have it on very reliable advice that Robert Sharkey was … I believe the modern term for it is 'homosexual'. You might be more familiar with the term 'sexual deviant'.'

There was dead silence from the members. The only sound that could be heard was the faint rumble of voices from the gathering crowd in the grandstand above their heads. The committee appeared to be having difficulty processing what Harry had just said.

Eventually Walter Stansforth spoke. 'Inspector, are you saying that Robbie Sharkey was a pervert?'

Harry nodded silently, surveying their faces.

A peal of laughter erupted from one side of the table. 'Absolute rubbish!' exclaimed Tom Sherrin. 'I'm afraid someone's been pulling your leg, Inspector.'

'I don't think so,' Harry replied calmly.

'You're not seriously suggesting that about a Collingwood footballer, are you? One of our best players.' This from Jeremiah Wingard, who was fixing Harry with a disbelieving stare.

'That's exactly what I'm saying,' Harry replied emphatically, but by now he was struggling to be heard. A cacophony of voices reverberated through the room, the tone a mixture of anger and incredulity.

'Gentlemen, please!' A stentorian voice rang out from the head of the table. William Beazley had risen to his feet and had both arms in the air. The hubbub died away. 'Gentlemen, could you please be quiet and hear the inspector out. Can I remind you that the police are investigating Robbie Sharkey's death and that this new information may be important in that investigation. Please give the inspector the courtesy of your attention.' Then, resuming his seat and turning toward Harry, Beazley added, 'Now, this is indeed a staggering proposition. I do hope you have reliable evidence to back up your claim.'

Bloody hell, Harry thought, I hope Effie has got this right. Then aloud, 'Mr President, I believe our information is accurate. We have a witness that we can trust, though we need to verify their evidence, and we'll do that as soon as possible. That's in fact why I'm talking to you gentlemen today, in the hope that you may have information that can confirm what others have told us.' And Harry paused, waiting for a further response.

There was absolute silence. Harry noticed Sir Randolph Thames staring at him with a strange expression on his face. Was it alarm? Panic? Fear? Harry couldn't tell, but Sir Randolph was certainly far from his usual equanimous self. Worth a try, thought Harry.

'Sir Randolph, you employed Robbie Sharkey. You would have had as much to do with him as anyone in this room. Did you have any inkling that this kind of … preference was in his nature.'

Sir Randolph shook his head emphatically. 'Certainly not!' he exclaimed, his voice cracking slightly. He cleared his throat and continued. 'I can assure you, Inspector, that if what you allege is true, I wouldn't have employed him.'

'Nor would this club countenance such behaviour,' Jeremiah Wingard said. 'If we'd known, we'd have shown him the door quick smart. Assuming that what you say is true, of course. Which I, for one, doubt very much.'

Harry looked around the group. 'Well, it seems this has come as something of a surprise to all of you. Can I assume then that you can't enlighten me further on that side of things?'

'It would appear we can't, Inspector,' Beazley replied.

Of all those present, it was he who seemed to be taking this startling news with the greatest degree of calm.

At that moment there was a knock on the door. It opened and the tousled white head of Jim Johnston, the Collingwood trainer, popped into view. He settled his attention on Ernie Copeland and silently hurried in. He whispered something in Copeland's ear, then scurried out again. Copeland looked at the president.

'Something we need to hear, Ernie?' Beazley asked.

'I'm afraid so, Mr President,' Copeland replied.

'Afraid? That doesn't sound too good," Harry said. 'Has something come up? Something I should know about?'

'Possibly,' Copeland replied. 'We're not sure yet.'

'Let's hear it then, Ernie,' Beazley said. 'I assume it's about Joey Miller.'

Copeland shifted slightly in his seat. 'Yes, it is. The thing is, Harry, Joey Miller hasn't turned up for the game today. Jimmy Johnston just confirmed to me that he's still not here, and the game's only half an hour away. It's very unlike him, he's normally extremely punctual.'

'I see. And you've made enquiries of all your staff?'

'Yes. No-one's heard anything from him.'

Harry nodded slowly. 'Well, Ernie, I can guarantee that's a development we're definitely interested in. It's something we'll look into straight away. Of course, it's possible he might just be held up by something, but that sounds like an unlikely coincidence. And from what you say, his absence is out of character.'

'Yes, it's very unlike him.' Copeland's worried expression grew more pronounced.

'I suppose the first place to look for him might be his home,' Harry surmised. 'After all, there may be an innocent explanation for him not showing up today. I suppose you've got his address somewhere?'

'Bound to have it on file,' Beazley asserted confidently. 'Could you get it to the inspector forthwith, Ernie?'

Copeland hesitated, then turned to Harry. 'That might be a bit difficult. The contact address he's given us is a small flat around the corner from the Eastern Market. His wife lives there, she has a stall at the market of an evening, I believe. But Joey's given us the impression in recent times that he's no longer living with her and has moved out into separate digs. Where that might be, I've no idea.'

Harry frowned slightly. 'I see. That's interesting news too. Well, I suppose we need to catch up with his missus first, at any rate. She may be able to tell us his whereabouts. Is he still on friendly terms with her, do you know?'

'Not sure,' Copeland replied. 'Hard to tell with Joey. He doesn't give too much away.'

'You said his wife's at the Eastern Market. Where would we find her there?'

'I believe she's a fortune teller by trade,' Copeland replied. 'Goes by the name Madame Zera, I'm told. I think her real name's Maud, as far as I can recall. But if you look for Madame Zera, you'll find her. It won't be hard.'

'Much obliged, Ernie,' Harry said.

'What do you think, Inspector?' Stansforth asked. 'Is Joey a suspect? It doesn't look good, does it?'

Harry shrugged noncommittally. 'Well, given I've only just found out about him going missing, it's very hard for me to say, Mr Stansforth. I mean, I suppose it could be interpreted as suspicious behaviour, but, as I said before, there may be an innocent explanation for it.'

'That's enough, Walter,' Beazley interceded forcefully. 'Let's not tell Inspector Holloway how to do his job. We're here to help him, not to speculate about Joey Miller, or anyone else for that matter.'

Suitably chastised, Stansforth relapsed into silence. Harry nodded politely in the president's direction. Beazley spoke again.

'Inspector, is there anything else you need? I don't want to cut you short, but there's a football match out there for us to watch very soon. Life must go on.'

'Of course, Mr Beazley,' Harry acknowledged, 'but there is one other matter the committee might be able to help us with.'

'Certainly, Inspector.'

'Well, we have it from a reliable source that Robbie Sharkey came into a very considerable amount of money earlier this year. Above and beyond his salary with Sir Randolph's business. I've already raised this matter with Sir Randolph, and he indicated that he made no additional payment to Sharkey in that timeframe. We're wondering if any of you other gentlemen have any information of additional payments made to Sharkey earlier this season.'

An uncomfortable silence settled over the room. Eventually the president responded. 'I think I can assure you, Inspector, there has been no payment from this club to Mr Sharkey, apart from his salary with Sir Randolph.'

'I think it's fairly obvious where the money came from, Inspector,' Jeremiah Wingard said, glancing at his colleagues as he spoke.

Harry said nothing, eying Wingard inquiringly.

'We all know Robbie was a gambler,' Wingard continued. 'And a pretty sizeable one at that. I know he lost quite a bit, but if you lose big, you can also sometimes win big. Surely that's what's happened?'

'Perhaps that was it,' Harry replied quietly. 'It's a possibility we've already thought of. But we wanted to see if there was any other explanation. Thank you, gentlemen, that'll be all. I'll let you get to your seats for the game.'

Harry rose, took up his hat, shook hands firmly with both Beazley and Copeland and, with Willie Milton in tow, made his way from the room. Behind him the committee sat in silence. But as the two policemen closed the door behind them and began to make their way back down the passage, a hubbub of raised voices emanated from the room behind them. Harry wondered whether the topic of conversation centred on Joey Miller's disappearance or Robbie Sharkey's sexual leanings.

And he wondered too whether there really was complete ignorance within the room of Sharkey's secret. Unlikely, he thought, surely someone would have noticed something. Was the committee's universally professed ignorance an attempt to conceal the terrible scandal of it all? Or was it perhaps that someone on the committee had other reasons for feigning ignorance?

✕

'What do you reckon, Harry? Have we got our man?' Willie asked his boss.

But Harry's attention was distracted as he scanned the noisy environs of the Caledonian front bar. 'Sorry, mate,' he replied, turning his attention back to his constable. 'Didn't catch that. I'm on the lookout for the Ferret. Remember we said we'd find him here tonight.'

'Don't worry, the Ferret will find us if there's a quid in it. I was saying, do you reckon Miller's our man?'

Harry supped on his beer and considered Willie's proposition. 'Dunno,' he ventured, as he wiped some foam from his chin. 'If Sharkey was injected at half-time, I can't see how Miller could have done it, given he seems to have been in the clubrooms all that time. Of course, he may be in cahoots with someone else and is now getting cold feet. And of course, there may be another possibility.'

'Yeah, that he's just got a hangover. Or crook guts or something, and he'll turn up tomorrow, right as rain.'

'That too,' Harry agreed. 'But I was thinking of another possibility, that he knows too much about what happened to Sharkey, and someone's done something about it.'

Willie whistled softly. 'Right. You mean he's been done in?'

'It's a possibility. One of the options. Which makes it doubly important that we track him down quick smart. If it turns out he's just nursing a hangover at home, so much the better. But we need to get onto the job of finding him first thing tomorrow. I had wanted to catch up with the Philips woman then, but she can wait 'til Monday.'

'Right. Though I'm not sure where we start, boss. No-one seems to know where his digs are.'

'I'd say Madame Zera should be our first port of call. She might know where he lives. She'll be at the market tonight if she's got a stall there. I reckon we should hotfoot it round there pronto. No time like the present. Soon as we track down the Ferret and hear what he's found out.'

'You're right. Hopefully she'll be in the know. Then we can look for her old man tomorrow.'

Harry rubbed his chin thoughtfully. 'Yeah, sounds like a reasonable plan. That might take up most of tomorrow though. Which will put me in the bad books with the old man. I promised to go to the Plumpton at Moonee Valley with him tomorrow. His dog's in the field and he reckons it's got a good chance of winning.'

'I'm happy to chase down Miller if you need to go to the coursing.' There was an eager note in Willie's voice and Harry smiled briefly at his enthusiasm.

'Mate, I appreciate the offer and I'm sure I could leave it in your capable hands. But this could be an important lead and I can't really justify heading out to Moonee Valley in these circumstances, just to watch the woofers doing their thing. So, we'll catch up with Madame Zera tonight and if that leads us to chasing down Miller tonight or tomorrow, so be it.'

'Fair enough.' Willie sounded a little disappointed.

At that moment, Harry's attention was captured by a movement in the crowded bar. 'Let's make ourselves a bit less noticeable,' he suggested. 'We've got company.' And pulling his hat a little further down over his eyes, he slid along the bench until he was against the wall at the farthest end of the booth. Willie did likewise and next thing the Ferret materialised alongside them, sliding surreptitiously into the booth and peering out at Harry from beneath his tattered trilby.

'Evening, Ferret,' Harry said cheerily. 'Had a lucrative day at the track?'

The Ferret scowled slightly. 'Backed a winner or two,' he muttered. 'What's it to you?'

'Nothing really, just making polite conversation. So, what have you got for me, Ferret? Any news on Robbie Sharkey's death? What are the punters saying?'

'Nah, nothin' much,' the Ferret replied. 'No-one knows what happened to him. Best guess it was likely a hit man for one of the bookies.'

And perhaps it was, Harry thought. But I need to know a bit more, though I doubt the Ferret is the man to take into my confidence. But I suppose I have to try him out, so here goes.

'Tell me,' he began leaning forward confidentially. 'I don't suppose any of your contacts made any comment about Sharkey's taste in women? Or lack of taste, if you know what I mean?'

The Ferret eyed Harry blankly. 'What you talkin' about? I know he used to hang around with that posh sheila. Not showin' much taste there, if you ask me.'

'Here's the thing, Ferret,' Harry said. 'There was a rumour going round that he liked the boys more than the girls, in that department. You know, as far as his romantic inclinations went. Just a rumour though. Probably untrue, though we have to check it out.'

The Ferret let out a little cackle of glee. 'Bugger me, Harry, are you sayin' he was a nancy? Well, bugger me again.'

'I'm saying that was the rumour. Hear anything along that line in your enquiries?'

'Wish I had,' the Ferret replied, with a lewd grin. 'Would've given me a good laugh. But you gotta be jokin', Harry. Robbie Sharkey a nancy-boy? Someone's been havin' you on, mate.'

'Probably right, Ferret. As I said, just a rumour. Forget I raised it.'

Harry was surprised that word of Sharkey's sexual preferences hadn't got out. He obviously kept his private life very private. And at the same time, a faint quiver of doubt ran through Harry. That perhaps Effie's informant, young Richard Thames, was delusional after all. Or that his story was a complete fabrication. But then, just as quickly, he put the doubt out of his mind. He trusted Effie's judgement on the matter. And Michael's too, for that matter.

He turned his attention back to the Ferret. 'Well, it seems to me that you haven't told me much at all,' he said. 'And that's bad news for you. For your bank balance, I mean. Hardly worth that second quid, what you've told me so far.'

The Ferret's expression transformed instantly, from a lewd smirk to wide-eyed alarm. 'Don't worry,' he said hastily.' I've got some other stuff that's worth every penny of a quid. Probably worth two, actually.'

'I'll believe it when I hear it. Righto mate, spit it out.'

The Ferret glanced quickly around, leaned conspiratorially across the table and spoke from behind his hand. 'They tell me that big George over there was holding some big money on Collingwood to win against the Blues.' With a flick of his thumb he indicated a far corner of the bar where the burly figure of George Winton, resplendent in a floral waistcoat, could be seen, seated at a table, his large ledger in front of him.

'Nothing unusual in that, Ferret,' Harry observed. 'Plenty of strong Magpie supporters in this neck of the woods. 'I'm sure his odds would have been fairly skinny, and he would have laid off a fair bit too.'

'That's the funny thing,' the Ferret continued. 'They reckon his odds weren't skinny at all. They reckon he was takin' the Pies on. Stood to lose a bucket of dough if they got up. You never know what that might tempt a man to do.' And he winked knowingly at Harry.

'Maybe,' Harry conceded. 'Not much to go on there, though. Speculation mainly. But I suppose it's worth a quid. Here you go, don't spend it all at once.' And he placed a pound note on the table.

Instantly it disappeared into the Ferret's possession, and equally quickly he was gone, melting back into the crowded bar without so much as a thank you. Harry shook his head.

'Hmm, not sure what we can take from that, Willie,' he confided. 'Sounds pretty much like business as usual for our friend George over there. But it was interesting he was taking on a Collingwood win. He must have known something the rest of the footy world didn't know. On form, the Maggies were dead-set certainties. Think it's time to have a chat with Mr Winton.'

Downing the dregs of his pot, Harry squeezed out of the booth and made his way across the room.

'G'day, George,' he said casually, as he eased himself into a vacant chair at George's table. 'Still hard at work, I see.'

Winton slammed the ledger shut and slid it out of view under the table, all in the one motion. Then he recognised Harry.

'Bloody hell, Harry, it's you! You had me worried for a moment there. Thought it might have been one of your more legalistic colleagues.'

'No, just me. And this is my offsider, Constable Milton. Don't worry, we're not here to close you down.'

'I know you wouldn't do that, Harry. What can I do for you, then? Perhaps you're interested in a wager. Happy to take your money anytime.'

'Now now, George, you know me. I'm sworn off gambling for life. I've seen the light.'

'Of course. Forgive me, it'd slipped my mind.'

'Now, George, I won't linger here tonight, your regulars might find it a bit off-putting to have a rozzer hanging about. But I want to have a chat with you about your business dealings. In particular, your interest in the Collingwood-Carlton game last Saturday.

Winton's expression instantly changed from genial to guarded. 'This is about Robbie Sharkey's murder, isn't it? I heard you were on the case.'

'Not sure why you think Sharkey's murder's got anything to do with your business activities,' Harry replied. 'Unless one of your customers was trying to manipulate the result. Or unless you were, for that matter.' And he smiled amiably at Winton.

'That's an outrageous allegation,' Winton protested, his tone now one of high dudgeon. 'How dare you accuse me of such a thing,'

'I'm not accusing you of anything, George,' Harry reassured. 'But the possibility of a gambling link to Sharkey's death is one we need to follow up.' He added in a lower tone, 'I'm sure we don't want your customers here to be alarmed by such a possibility, so why don't you pop into the station sometime soon. Then we can chat with a little more freedom.'

'All right then,' Winton agreed quickly. 'But only under sufferance, mind. Doesn't mean I'm accepting the false insinuations you just made.'

Harry smiled and rose to his feet. 'Good, glad to see you're cooperating. Constable Milton here will be in touch to set up a time. He knows where to find you, of course. Here at the office, naturally.'

And the two policemen rose and strolled from the bar.

Winton scowled and returned to his ledger. Around him a gaggle of potential customers lurked, for the moment at a safe distance, pending the complete disappearance of the law, before moving forward to resume their business transactions.

When Harry and Willie arrived at the Bourke Street entrance, the Eastern Market had already transformed itself, with the daytime sale of farm produce replaced by stalls catering for the Saturday night entertainment of out-and-about Melburnians.

There were gaudy clothing displays, side by side with cheap jewellers. Hawkers of household wares and other sundry bric-a-brac touted their offerings. Various culinary delights were also on offer, while in the walkways, magicians, tricksters and other conmen plied their trade. And at every corner, musicians serenaded the masses.

Harry surveyed the crowded scene before them. 'Well, she's here somewhere, mate. Only one way to find out where.' And they set off through the market in search of Madame Zera's stall.

One lap around the market's perimeter bore no success, so they entered the huge central pavilion, where the smaller stallholders were set up in rows of canvas tents offering their wares to the world. Halfway along one of these rows, Willie grabbed Harry's sleeve and pointed. Sure enough, there she was: 'Madame Zera, Phrenologist', displayed in faded red and gold lettering above the entrance to one of the tents. Business looked to be good; half a dozen or more prospective clients hung around the entrance, waiting for their turn to have their future divined.

'Bewdy!' Harry exclaimed, weaving through the gathered customers and ignoring their indignant complaints for him to get to the back of the line. 'Looks like we've struck gold.' And he pushed aside the slim lace curtain across the entrance to the tent.

It was rather dark inside, so they heard the reaction to their entrance before their eyes had time to adjust to the gloom. 'Bloody hell! Can't you wait your turn, you stupid idjits!'

Then, by the light of a flickering candle, they detected the figure of Madame Zera, exotically dressed in full gypsy regalia, with wild, flaming, improbably red hair haloing her weather-beaten face. She still had her hands on the head of her current victim, a blowsy, blonde woman of indeterminate years.

'You must be Madame Zera?' Harry cheerily suggested to the gypsy lady.

Madame Zera, displaying a mysteriously perceptive awareness of the presence of the law, responded tersely. 'What if I am, copper?' Then, slipping back into character for the benefit of her client, and adopting a more conciliatory tone, 'I am indeed ze famed Madame Zera, mein good sir. Vould you like to see ze future?'

'Not right now, madam, we've got other priorities,' Harry replied. Then turning to the blonde woman, 'If you could wait outside, love, Madame Zera will resume her consultation directly. We just need to have a little chat first.'

Willie took the confused woman's arm, led her to the entrance, gently eased her out, pulled the lace curtain back across, and took up sentry duty.

'Okay Maud,' Harry resumed. 'Time to talk. I'm Inspector Holloway, CIB.'

Madame Zera bridled. 'You can't do this. You got nothing on me, my business is all above board. I got a licence!'

'I didn't say you didn't have one,' Harry replied.

'Look,' Maud Miller continued. 'All that … misunderstanding, that was years ago. I've turned over a new leaf, I don't do that sort of stuff anymore.'

Interesting, Harry thought. Might follow that up later. 'Don't worry,' he spoke, 'We're not after you. It's your better half, Joey Miller, we're more interested in. Interested in finding him, actually.'

'Gawd, what's that silly bugger been up to now?' Maud exclaimed sharply. 'Can't keep himself out of trouble!'

Interesting again, Harry thought. 'It's all right, Maud,' he said 'He's not necessarily in trouble. But he is a person of interest in the Sharkey murder, and he seems to have gone missing. Temporarily, we hope.'

At the mention of Sharkey, Maud's weathered features blanched noticeably, and she dropped any further attempt at bravado. 'Oh gawd,' she muttered, almost under her breath. Then to Harry, 'I'm sorry, I can't help you. I would if I could, but Joey and me, we sort of don't live together anymore.'

'Yeah, I know that,' Harry replied. 'But I thought you might know where he does live now.'

'No, 'fraid not,' Maud replied quickly. 'No idea.'

'Not on friendly terms anymore?' Harry suggested.

'Oh, I wouldn't say that,' Maud replied vaguely. 'He calls around to see me now and again. It's just that we had a bit of trouble a while back and we fell out for a while. We've never really bothered to get back together.'

Harry rubbed his chin, eyeing Maud quizzically. She seemed to be telling the truth, but on the other hand, Harry reckoned she might also be an accomplished liar.

'Now, Maud,' he continued, 'I hope you're not giving us the run-around here. Protecting Joey for some reason. Because we'll find out and we might be interested in revisiting that other problem you had.'

'No, no! Honestly, I dunno where he is. God's honour, I'm telling the truth.'

'All right, I'll believe you. For now. But if Joey comes visiting, make sure you tell him we want to talk to him urgently. Far better for him to turn himself in, than we have to waste time and effort tracking him down.'

'Yes, absolutely,' Maud agreed meekly. 'I'll be sure to tell him that. If I see him, that is.'

'Good,' Harry said firmly. 'Now, we'll let you get back to your client. Hope you find more on her head than dandruff.'

Maud grinned feebly at Harry's witticism and adjusted her wig. 'Thank you, Sir, much obliged.'

Harry joined Willie at the tent's entrance and announced to the small crowd waiting there, 'Okay folks, Madame Zera's back on the job. Our apologies for making you wait.'

'What do you reckon?' he quizzed Willie, as they made their way from the markets, through the now rowdy throng of Saturday night revellers. 'Is she telling porkies or not?'

Willie shrugged. 'Hard to tell. But you certainly put the wind up her. She's obviously not a great fan of the law. Bit of a rogue, I'd suggest.'

'Yeah,' Harry mused. 'And the same could be said for Joey, too, I'd reckon. But how much of a rogue? Not sure about that. He might be mixed up in the Sharkey murder, but I can't see him actually doing it. Not sure how he could, actually.'

'Maybe he was mixed up in it along with someone else?' Willie suggested.

'That's a possibility, for sure,' Harry agreed. 'Probably at the top of our theories, for the moment. But right now, we've got no idea where he lives, or even if he's still there. So, let's wait a day, and see if he turns up. It's still possible that him going missing might be completely innocent. If he hasn't surfaced by Monday, we'll ramp up our search then.'

'Fair enough. So you'll get to see your old man's dog chasing the hares tomorrow, after all.'

'Yeah. But right now, I'm going home to see my darling wife. And see if she's saved me a bit of pudding. What about you, mate?'

'Back to the pub for a while, I reckon. Another pint or two wouldn't go astray.'

'Oh, for the life of a free-and-easy bachelor,' Harry joked. But it's not what he felt. The promise of a Saturday night in Effie's company was more attractive than anything else he could imagine.

✕

9

SUNDAY 20 JUNE 1897

'HOW'S SHE GONNA GO, Dad? Confident?'

Clem Holloway looked up from a final brush of Bess's sleek black coat. 'Reckon so, son. As good a chance as any.'

Harry knelt briefly and rubbed the greyhound's ears, while Clem continued his grooming. Bess nuzzled against Harry, her tail wagging furiously at this unexpected pleasure.

They were in the public enclosure of the Mooney Valley Plumpton course: in reality, nothing more than a roped-off area at one end of a windswept paddock in the middle of the Moonee Valley racecourse. To one side of this public area another small enclosure was set up, fifty yards or so square and fenced with wire mesh. This was the hare enclosure, where a number of animals were securely held, ready to be released into the chase paddock, one at a time, for each heat. The chase paddock stretched out in front of them, two hundred yards or so in length, at the end of which was another enclosure. This was the hares' sanctuary which, if they managed to outrun the dogs, they could enter through a number of small openings in the netting fence.

In truth, Harry was not at all comfortable with the concept of coursing, particularly this very artificial Plumpton variety. He had tried to rationalise the practice as just another form of hunting, a very natural thing for the human species to revel in. But, when you really thought about it, it was far removed from that primal instinct. The more he considered it, the more it just seemed like an exercise in cruelty, and he found himself more and more being swayed towards Effie's view on the sport. But the old man loved it and argued with Harry that the hares more often than not escaped their pursuers, and even that they probably enjoyed the chase as much as the dogs themselves. Harry privately thought such arguments an exercise in self-deception, but he resisted the urge to argue with Clem, instead trying to enjoy his father's excitement and pleasure when Bess competed, and when she outpaced her rival to win her heat. Still, Harry couldn't avoid looking away when, as frequently happened, the dogs bested the hare and tore it to pieces.

Harry's misgivings were obviously not shared by the other members of the public in his vicinity, who were mingling excitedly about, in expectation of the upcoming contest. And a curious mix they were too: country gentlemen and ladies, immaculately dressed in the best sporting style, cheek by jowl with every manner of spiv and ne'er-do-well, all with an eye on a quick quid to be made. The bookmaking fraternity were also well represented, having commandeered one corner of the spectator enclosure to set up their boards, bags and other paraphernalia. They were already on the job, shouting their odds for the first heat, due to start in ten minutes or so.

With Clem's first heat still some time away, Harry decided to go for a wander through the crowd, first paying a visit to the bookmakers' area. No sign of John Wren, which was no surprise. He was bound to be at church on a Sunday, but Harry noticed a couple of his offsiders running a book in his stead. And lurking nearby was the slightly menacing figure of Bill Hanrahan, as always on hand to manage any customer disputes.

Further along, Harry spotted George Winton's board, with the proprietor here in person, as florid and bulbous as ever, drumming up business for the first heat in strident tones.

'G'day George!' Harry called out. 'Good to see you again so soon.'

Winton glanced at Harry, nodded surreptitiously and turned back quickly to his spruiking. Clearly, he considered the presence and jovial greeting of a well-known detective not particularly good for business.

'I'll see you this week!' Harry shouted above the din. 'At Russell Street!' And took a degree of perverse pleasure in Winton's further obvious discomfort. Another brief, surly nod from Winton was the only acknowledgement that he had registered Harry's words. Harry smiled to himself and moved on.

As he did so, he noticed that Hanrahan had drifted away from John Wren's people and was now standing in a far corner of the enclosure, in animated conversation with another man. His companion was a young, strongly built fellow who was standing with his back to Harry, but whose solid bearing and curly blond locks were vaguely familiar. Then, as he turned slightly into profile, Harry recognised Danny Robinson, the Collingwood footballer he had seen several nights before at training.

No surprise, I suppose, Harry thought, remembering Ernie Copeland describing him as a gambling mate of Robbie Sharkey. Still, he pondered, it might be useful to bail him up for a chat here. Catch him on the hop, so he has less opportunity to hide anything. That is, if he has anything to hide.

But Harry didn't join the two men immediately. Instead he melted back inconspicuously into the crowd. Something about the exchange between the two had captured his attention and intrigued him. He had a distinct impression that the encounter was hostile, and this was reinforced as he watched them in conversation. Hanrahan was clearly the aggressor, leaning into Robinson threateningly and from time to time emphasising his message with a forceful poke in the chest. Not that Robinson was cowed. Far from it. He was standing squarely up to Hanrahan and eyeing him directly as he put his side of the argument. Then, with a final angry shake of his fist, Hanrahan abruptly ended the meeting, turning on his heel and striding off. Robinson was left standing there, watching his burly inquisitor heading off into the crowd.

'G'day there,' Harry said, quickly approaching before Robinson had a chance to move on. 'You're Danny Robinson, aren't you?'

Robinson turned toward him, anger still etched on his features. 'I am, mate. What's it to you?'

'Harry Holloway, CIB,' Harry replied, producing his badge and waving it in front of Robinson. 'I saw you on the training track the other night, when I was talking to Ernie Copeland.'

'Oh, that's right, Ernie mentioned that you might want to see me.' Robinson's reply showed no sign of nervousness, though there was a guarded tone in his voice.

'Look, Danny,' Harry said, 'to save you the bother of coming into Russell Street, or me coming out to Victoria Park again, why don't we have a chat right here? Have you got ten minutes to spare?'

'Mate, I'm here to relax and enjoy myself, not to have a flamin' interview with the coppers.' But then Robinson paused, weighing up the pros and cons of Harry's proposal. 'But I suppose what you say makes sense. We might as well get it out of the way now. But only ten minutes, mind, I've got a wager on the second heat, and I don't want to miss that.'

'Fair enough,' Harry agreed. 'Why don't we find a quiet spot where we can talk privately? And where you won't be seen consorting with the law.'

'I don't give a stuff who sees me talking to the law. I've got nothing to hide.' But Robinson allowed himself to be led away to a secluded corner of the enclosure, behind the wooden shed on stilts that served as the judge's tower.

'I notice you were having a bit of a blue with Bill Hanrahan back there,' Harry began. 'Nothing too serious, I hope.'

Robinson looked at Harry for a second or two, then shook his head. 'Nah, just the usual. Bill putting the screws on, doing his boss's dirty work. Show me someone who's had a friendly conversation with Bill Hanrahan and I'll show you a liar.' And he laughed sourly.

'Yeah, he doesn't seem an overly pleasant sort of bloke,' Harry observed. 'But, let's get down to business. I wanted to ask you a few questions about Robbie Sharkey. From what Ernie says, you were probably his best mate among the players.'

Robinson shrugged. 'I dunno about that. I wouldn't say we were the best of mates, but we both liked a punt, I suppose. We talked about punting a bit. And we went to the track together, when we weren't playing footy. But I've only known him a little while, only since I moved over to Collingwood.'

'All right then, but from what you saw, what sort of punter would you say Robbie was? I mean, did he gamble a fair bit?'

Robinson laughed, again without humour. 'I'd say he was a bloody stupid punter,' he said emphatically.

'Really?' Harry responded. 'What do you mean by that?'

'I mean that he bet big on horses that couldn't win. And he bet too much, more than he could afford.'

Harry looked at him keenly. 'But I suppose that's just a matter of opinion. About whether a horse could win or not. Clearly he thought the horses he backed could win.'

Robinson gave Harry a scornful glance. 'That's bloody obvious; he wouldn't back a horse if he didn't think it could win. But what I mean is, he always made risky bets. Nothing wrong with having a flutter on a long shot, but he did it too much. And he put too much money on, he never seemed to realise that long shots are long shots for a reason. He didn't win too many, I can tell you.'

'So, from what you saw, he wasn't real successful as a punter?'

'That's one way of putting it. Hopeless is another.'

Harry eyed Robinson keenly. 'We've been told that Robbie came into a fair swag of money a few months ago. Enough to pay off his debts, we understand. Do you know if he had a big win on the neddies? One of those long shots finally come home?'

Robinson shook his head. 'Not as far as I can recall. He did have the occasional winner, but nothing real big. Though he wouldn't necessarily have told me if he did. He was like that, Robbie, didn't like to give much away. Even when it was good news.'

Harry set off on another tack, though he suspected that this new line of inquiry would probably not bear fruit either. 'And did you mix much socially with Robbie? Away from the track, I mean.'

Robinson shook his head. 'Nah. We went down to the pub a few times after the races, but that's about it. Had a few beers together, but he never talked much about anything except racing. And footy.'

'You didn't ever chat about other things? Like the girls you might be chasing? A couple of good-looking blokes like you two, I thought that'd be on the agenda, for sure.'

Robinson paused and thought a few moments, as he remembered his time with Sharkey. 'Nah, don't think so. It was funny, really. I tried to talk to him a few times. You know, about sheilas and such like. But I could tell he wasn't interested in talking about things like that. He was, what do they say, he was a closed book.'

I could enlighten you about why he didn't want to talk about sheilas, Harry thought, and momentarily considered revealing the truth to Robinson. To gauge whether Danny had any inkling of Sharkey's true nature. But he decided to keep that one under his hat for the moment. Robinson seemed to have no knowledge. And anyway, the facts were bound to come out eventually, perhaps sooner if any of the committee members lacked discretion. Then the Sharkey family would have to deal with the shame and social opprobrium that would come with the revelations. And the Thames family too, for that matter. No need to hasten that day of reckoning.

'While I've got you here,' Harry said, 'I'd also like to ask you about last Saturday. You know, the day of Robbie's death. Just some general questions we're asking everyone.'

Robinson nodded and waited expectantly, apparently unperturbed.

'I'm just wondering whether you noticed anything unusual during the day. Particularly when you came off at half-time and went back on again after the break.'

'What do you mean?' Robinson asked, a slightly puzzled expression appearing. 'Do you mean when we were walking off? And walking back on?'

'That's right. And particularly when you had to make your way through the crowd. Running the gauntlet of the hat-pin ladies. Did you see anything, or anyone, unusual among those women?'

Robinson stared absently into the distance as he considered Harry's question, before replying. 'Well, to tell the truth, I wouldn't have noticed anything. We're always too busy getting through those bloody women without getting a pin stuck up our arses, to worry about spotting anyone in the crowd. So the answer to your question is no, I didn't see anything unusual coming off the ground. And I didn't after half-time either, because I didn't go back out. I did a hammy just before the break. I got a rub-down from Joey Miller, but it didn't come good, so I was still in the rooms after half-time. Trying to stretch it. I was still there when they brought Robbie down. Bloody awful, that was.'

'Yes, I remember,' Harry said. 'Actually, I'm trying to understand why you were still in the rooms then. I would have thought you would've gone out to watch the game, hammy or no hammy.'

'Well, I would have,' Robinson replied. 'Gone back out to the bench, that is. Except that Miller was meant give me a rub-down at half-time, but I couldn't find him. Until we were almost due to go out. I was a bit crook at him for that, I can tell you.'

'Any idea where he might have been?' Harry asked.

'No idea. Someone said he might be giving Sharkey a rub-down, but I'm pretty sure that he didn't. But he eventually turned up anyway and got to work on my hammy. Not that it mattered, I was too sore to play on anyway.'

'Fair enough,' Harry said. 'Well, Danny, I've kept you away from your punting long enough. Thanks for your help.' And he watched as Danny made a beeline towards the cluster of bookies.

I wonder whether you're any cleverer in your punting than Sharkey had been, Harry mused. In Harry's mind, there was no such person as a successful punter, himself included. The secret was to limit your losses, something that Sharkey was obviously incapable of doing.

He made his way back to the owners' area, bracing himself for what was always an ambivalent experience, alternating between admiring the speed and grace of the greyhounds as they flew across the paddock, and turning away in disgust when they were too speedy and seized their frantically fleeing quarry.

✕

The little terrace house at thirty-two, Pleasance Street, looked particularly inviting to Harry as he made his way down the street through the chilly gloom. He noted with approval the curl of smoke rising from the chimney, portending a warm, cosy parlour. Add to that

Effie's promise of roast lamb with the trimmings, preceded by a tot or two of rum to enhance the warming process, and all would be well with the world again. Or as well as could be expected, given the level of pressure he was feeling from the Sharkey investigation.

As he neared the front gate, he became aware that a hansom cab drawn up in the street was stationed right outside his house. Harry waved to the cabbie, sitting rugged up against the cold, and had a quick peek inside. Empty; it seemed that the Holloways had a visitor. Hoping against hope that it wasn't someone from the station on official business that would keep him away from his roast lamb, Harry strode up the garden path. He had only just shut the front door and was in the process of removing his coat and scarf, when Effie appeared in the passageway.

Before he had a chance to greet her, she exclaimed breathlessly, 'Darling, something terrible has happened!' and seized his hand in hers.

Such drama was decidedly unEffie-like, and Harry's thoughts immediately flew to his son. Visions of fatal accidents flashed into his mind.

'What is it?' he asked quickly. 'Is Alfie all right?'

Effie placed a reassuring hand on his shoulder. 'No, no, nothing like that, Alfie is perfectly fine. He's upstairs, having a little sleep before dinner.'

'What then?' Harry's next thought was for his parents, but that was at a slightly lower level of anxiety. He could manage that news.

But that was not it. 'It's Richard,' Effie exclaimed. 'He's gone missing!'

Harry scanned his memory for Richards, among family, friends and acquaintances, but drew a blank. 'Richard? What Richard?'

'You know, Michael and James's friend, Richard. The one whose father is at Collingwood. You know, we told you about him.'

'Of course, now I remember. Sorry, I was thinking closer to home.'

'Sorry, darling, I didn't mean to alarm you.' And she gave him an apologetic kiss. 'Michael and James turned up a little while ago with the news. They're terribly worried.'

By now Harry had slipped back into calm, investigative mode. 'Right then, let's hear it from the horse's mouth, before we go any further.'

He shepherded Effie back down the passage and into the parlour. Michael was waiting there, perched upright on their sofa. He looked on edge. James was seated in the armchair, and he too looked uncomfortable and worried.

'Sorry to disturb you on a Sunday night, Harry,' Michael apologised. 'You must get sick of work interrupting your family life. But I thought you should know about this straight away.'

'That's all right, mate,' Harry reassured him. 'So, what's happened? Effie said Richard Thames has gone missing.'

'Yes, and it's most unlike him. When Effie and I saw him two days ago, I told him James and I would call on him today at four o'clock. But he wasn't there. We knocked and called, but no answer. We managed to speak to a neighbour, and she said she hadn't seen him all day. We waited for ages but no sign of him. So we came straight around here.'

Harry walked over to the window and stroked his chin thoughtfully. He turned towards Michael, 'Any chance he might have got the time wrong? Or the date, for that matter?'

'Absolutely not. I was very specific about it. The time and the day. Wasn't I, Effie?'

'Yes, it was quite clear,' Effie agreed. 'And Richard seemed very pleased about it. I suppose to help take his mind off things.'

'That seems fairly clear-cut then,' Harry said, 'Now, is there a chance he might have been called away at short notice? Perhaps his parents took him back to their place. They might have been worried about his state of mind.'

'How could they know about his state of mind?' Effie exclaimed. 'Remember, he felt he couldn't talk to them about … about his true feelings. Why would they be worried about him?'

Harry's thoughts returned to the committee luncheon and Randolph Thames's odd expression when Harry revealed the startling news about Robbie Sharkey. Had he guessed what was going on? Had he confronted his son and discovered his secret? And then taken him away, to support him in his time of grief? Or perhaps to make another attempt at remedying the affliction which Sir Randolph believed was infecting his son?

'It's possible that his father might have guessed Richard's feelings for Robbie Sharkey,' he suggested. 'I informed the committee yesterday of what Richard told you two. I didn't mention Richard by name, but Sir Randolph might have put two and two together. He's no fool.'

'Well, I suppose that's a possibility,' Michael agreed, and Harry thought he looked slightly relieved at this hypothesis. 'I hope you're right. I was thinking of other awful possibilities. That he has done himself harm. Or gone off and done something rash, out of desperation.'

'What do you mean?' Effie asked. 'What do you mean by 'something rash'?'

Michael glanced at Effie, and replied gently, 'Effie dear, in our world, young men are sometimes tempted to seek relief from the stress of their secret lives by indulging in … casual encounters. Often dangerous encounters. There are many others who hate the way we are and find pleasure in exacting violence on us.'

Effie shuddered. 'Oh dear, that's terrible. But surely that's not Richard. Surely he wouldn't do something like that.'

Michael shrugged. 'I hope he wouldn't. Let's hope his disappearance is quite innocent, as Harry suggested might be the case.'

'Let's hope so indeed,' Harry echoed. 'Now, we can't get to the bottom of it tonight, but here's what I propose to do. I'll get my men onto it first thing tomorrow. I'll send someone round to Richard's place to see if he's turned up, and I'll check with Sir Randolph to see if he knows anything. How does that sound?'

'That sounds good,' Michael said. 'We really appreciate your support on this, Harry. I know most policemen wouldn't be as sympathetic.'

Harry waved his hand dismissively. 'Oh, I don't know about that. All part of the job.'

'Don't be so bashful, darling,' Effie chimed in. 'We all know you're wonderful.'

'Hear, hear!' James said, as he and Michael rose to leave. And after a grateful shaking of hands, they made their departure.

Harry and Effie returned to the kitchen and the enticing aroma of roast lamb. Harry realised just how hungry he was.

'I'll go wake the little fellow, shall I?' he suggested.

'Yes please, darling. I'll organise dinner.' Then, as he began to climb the stairs, she added, 'You do think Richard's all right, don't you? You weren't just saying that?'

'I hope so, dear. More often than not, there's a perfectly innocent explanation for someone not showing up when they're meant to.' But his words were spoken without conviction, and he couldn't escape an inner anxiety that all was not well.

10

MONDAY 21 JUNE 1897

'FOR GOD'S SAKE, HOLLOWAY, what the hell are you playing at, with this codswallop about Sharkey?'

An apoplectic Chief Inspector Winston Marks was the last thing Harry needed this Monday morning, but there was no getting away from it. It was just something to be endured.

'I had it on very good authority, sir,' he explained, as deferentially as he could manage.

'And whose authority might that be?' Marks asked suspiciously, eying Harry sternly from under beetling brows.

Harry remembered Effie's promise to Richard Thames, that she would try to ensure his relationship with Sharkey remained a secret. But in this circumstance, that promise could not be kept.

'Actually, Sir, my informant was Richard Thames, Sir Randolph's son.'

'What? Randolph's boy! How the hell would he know anything about Robert Sharkey?'

Harry breathed deeply and continued. 'Richard Thames claims he and Sharkey had a romantic attachment.'

'What? Absolute rubbish! Everyone knows the lad's not right in the head, been a problem for Randolph for ages, I hear. Making out that a

Collingwood footballer is some sort of queen, what a load of nonsense! The boy's a fantasist, that's what he is. And the worst thing is, you believed him.'

So much for keeping the Starkey revelation confidential, Harry thought. And he wondered who had fed Marks the information. Could have been anyone on the committee, he realised.

'We don't necessarily believe him,' Harry ventured, seeking to calm the waters. 'But it's a line of inquiry we're following up. Among others.'

'Correction, Holloway, you are not following up on it. If I hear you're asking any more questions on that subject, there'll be trouble. You'll turn the force into a laughing stock, that's what'll happen.' And he stared threateningly at Harry, as if daring him to challenge this ultimatum.

'Very well, sir, I'll no longer make that assumption about Robert Sharkey. Unless I get corroborating evidence, that is. But I do need to continue looking into Richard Thames, because he's been reported missing. I'm sure Sir Randolph would want us to make enquiries.'

Scarcely mollified, Marks continued to stare angrily at Harry. 'Well, if you need to look for him, I suppose you must. But not you personally, mind. Because the boy is sure to turn up directly. These temperamental types are always off on some jaunt or other. I want you to focus on the real issues in this case, because from what I hear you're making precious little progress.'

'And what do you see as the real issues, sir?' Harry asked, trying to avoid any hint of sarcasm in his voice.

Marks looked at him suspiciously, then suggested sourly, 'You could start with finding that fellow, Miller. He seems to be the one, if you ask me. And what about that jumped-up little mick, Wren? I'd wager he's involved too. I wouldn't put anything past him, the little crook. Openly breaking the law and poncing around like the grand Pooh-Bah.'

'I'm making enquiries in regard to Miller, sir. As for Mr Wren, there's no evidence yet as to any involvement by him in this business. And to be fair, he's hardly likely to bump off the star player of the team he supports so much.'

This was hardly the response that Marks was looking for. He glowered at Harry but said nothing.

'Will that be all, sir?' Harry continued, as calmly and politely as ever.

'For the moment, Holloway, for the moment. But I'm not happy with the progress of this investigation, I can tell you. And if I hear of you getting side-tracked down any other ridiculous rabbit holes, there'll be hell to pay. Do I make myself clear?'

'Perfectly clear, sir,' Harry replied, rising to his feet. But he was premature, Marks had another ace up his sleeve.

'Before you go, Holloway, there's one other thing.'

Harry suppressed a sigh and reluctantly resumed his seat.

'I have it on good authority that you've been consorting with known criminals.'

'What?' Harry stared wide-eyed at Marks, genuinely mystified.

'You don't deny that you were seen meeting with a certain George Winton in the Caledonian Hotel? A George Winton who is a known illegal bookmaker. And that you were meeting with him while he was in the course of his illegal activities?'

Oh, bloody hell, thought Harry, as the penny dropped. Looks like I'm not the only one with spies out there. 'That was a necessary interview in the course of my investigation, sir,' he explained. 'In fact, I've summoned him into the station for a further interview. He's already given me important relevant information.'

'Summon him into the station, by all means, but don't have friendly chats with him in a public house, particularly when he's in the process of conducting illegal activity. It's not a good look for the force. Am I clear?'

'Perfectly clear, sir,' Harry muttered, the taste of humble pie sticking in his craw. 'Will that be all now?'

'For the moment,' Marks replied curtly, turning to some papers on his desk to indicate the meeting was over.

Harry made his way from the office and encountered Willie Milton, hovering outside the door and wearing a worried expression.

'Everything all right?' he inquired in a loud whisper. 'Seemed to be getting a bit heated in there. On one side, at least.'

Harry only raised his eyebrows and pointed down the corridor, to the sanctuary of his office. Once they were ensconced there, he leaned back in his chair, closed his eyes and sighed.

'Well, that was a predictable response, I suppose,' he muttered.

'To what?'

'To what Richard Thames had to say. If you thought the committee struggled with the notion of Sharkey as homosexual, it was nothing to the chief's reaction. But I must say, it was interesting that he heard about it so quick. So much for keeping it in confidence.'

'I'm not surprised,' Willie suggested. 'Melbourne Club gossip, they've got nothing better to do with themselves there.'

'That's what I thought too,' Harry agreed. 'But I'm not sure why anyone on the committee would want to let that gossip out. Not exactly painting the club in a good light. On top of all the scandal with Sharkey's murder.'

'Oh, I don't know,' Willie replied. 'Most of them would probably think it couldn't possibly be true, so they'd be dismissing it as a load of nonsense. Pretty much the same way the chief has.'

'I suppose so,' Harry said thoughtfully. 'Anyway, back to business. We need to follow up on Richard Thames this morning. And I'm not allowed to have anything to do with him, it seems. So, it's over to you, mate.'

'Sure thing,' Willie responded. 'You want me to go and check at his premises?'

'Yeah, he's in Kew somewhere.' Harry rummaged through a pile of papers on his desk. 'Michael Standish gave me the address. It's here somewhere. Ah, here we are, 36 Highfield Grove, Kew. He's in a town house there, apparently. Belongs to the old man, I suppose.'

'I'm onto it,' Willie said, rising from his chair.

'Hang on, wait a sec. I don't want to be too dramatic, but just in case you come across the worst, a description might be useful. Early twenties, and from what Effie told me, dark hair, dark features, hair neat and combed down. Handsome was the term she used.'

Willie eyed him quizzically. 'You think someone's got it in for him?'

'Nah, not really. He's probably safe and sound at home, I'd reckon, but I suppose it's best to be prepared, just in case.'

'Of course.'

'If you don't find him there, go round to the parents' house,' Harry added. 'They might know something. I've got Sir Randolph's address here somewhere, too.' Harry did some more rummaging in his chaotic pile of papers.

'Here you are, mate. Off you go now. I've got Margot Philips coming in soon. Time to sort out a few home truths about her and Sharkey, I think.'

✕

Margot Philips was as cool and composed as ever, sitting at ease in the Russell Street interview room and smiling calmly at Harry as he took his seat opposite. Again Harry found himself slightly unsettled by her presence. There was something in the way she looked at him with that expression of wry, slightly amused detachment that he found oddly disconcerting.

Resolving to put such unsettling thoughts out of his mind, he decided on a formal approach. 'Good morning, Miss Philips, thank you for agreeing to another interview, and at short notice.'

Margot Philips smiled at him. 'Goodness me, Inspector, we're very proper this morning. You know, I feel like we're old friends already. Surely a little less formality will do. I'm comfortable with Margot, and … Harry?'

Harry reddened slightly but was determined not to be out-positioned. 'Margot it is. And Harry is just fine too. Now, I won't take up much of your time, I appreciate you're a busy woman.'

'Thank you, Harry. I appreciate your appreciation.'

'So let's talk about the nature of your relationship with Robbie Sharkey. We sort of skirted around it last time we met, but perhaps I was a bit too … proper to get to the real point of my question.'

Margot smiled archly.

Harry cleared his throat. 'To be blunt, was your relationship with Rob Sharkey a romantic one? A sexual one?'

There was no hint of reticence in Margot's reply. 'No, it wasn't. We were simply friends.'

Harry sighed. 'You could have told me that the first time. It would have helped my investigation a bit.'

Margot smiled again. She seemed to be enjoying the conversation. 'Well, as you yourself just indicated, Harry, you never really put the question to me. I don't think I answered any of your other questions untruthfully.'

'You're right, my fault, I suppose. But since we're now getting right to the point, here's another straight question. Were you aware that Robbie was attracted to men? Sexually, I mean.'

Margot nodded, and replied with more than a hint of sadness. 'Of course I was. Robbie confided in me a lot about that subject. He was terribly confused and conflicted about his sexuality. I hope that I was of some use in helping him to come to terms with it.'

Harry was beginning to appreciate Margot's directness and honesty. 'I'm starting to understand that he must have been a troubled man. But I have certain information that he'd formed a relationship shortly before his death that might have helped him reconcile his feelings. A relationship with a certain young man.'

Margot responded immediately. 'Yes, he did. The love of his life, I think. From what he told me, anyway. But you know, he wouldn't tell me who it was. He said it was too risky for the other man for anyone to know. I tried to persuade him that he needed to confide in his friends. And be more honest with himself too. You know, honest about that part of his nature.'

'I suppose he had to be careful,' Harry suggested. 'A man in his position, I mean. It must've been very difficult for him.'

'Yes, it was,' Margot replied. 'He was very troubled. I think that's what caused him to go astray in other ways. With the gambling and so forth.'

Harry leaned back in his chair. He was now genuinely grateful to Margot. At least, Effie's information had been completely validated and he could confidently proceed on the basis that it was all true. 'I take it you would be prepared to testify as to what you've told me?'

'If it comes to that,' she replied promptly. 'Will it, Harry? Come to that, I mean.'

'Not sure, to be truthful,' Harry replied. 'There're a few threads to Robbie Sharkey's story, and at this stage I'm not sure how they're connected. Or if they're connected.'

'Oh well, 'Margot said. 'I hope I was helpful. I really liked Robbie. We were odd friends in a way, I suppose, but friends nevertheless.'

'I hope you don't mind me dwelling on that for a bit,' Harry ventured.

'But I'm intrigued about the nature of your friendship. You're right, it does seem like an unlikely friendship. Robbie being a footballing legend and mad gambler, and you, if you don't mind me saying, a sophisticated, intelligent woman. I can't quite see why you became close friends.'

Margot sat quietly for a few moments, gazing into the distance, apparently weighing things up in her mind. Then she turned back to Harry. 'I'm happy to tell you this, Harry, because I think I trust you, and it might help to put things in perspective. But what I'm about to tell you has nothing to do with Robbie's death, so I want you to keep it in confidence.'

Harry had a fair inkling as to what was coming and was happy to adhere to her condition. 'Of course, if it's got nothing to do with the case, I won't reveal it to anyone.'

'As I think I told you, I met Robbie at a charity do, put on by Randolph Thames. I was there as a partner for Henry Ramsgate. As you know, he's my boss, and he sometimes invites me along to these functions when he needs a woman on his arm. He's not married, you know, still lives with his mother. Anyway, the room was full of rich businessmen and other high society types. Poor Robbie was like a fish out of water, so I befriended him out of sympathy. And surprisingly, I found I liked him. He had a natural intelligence and a great sense of fun. He made me laugh. And he seemed to like me too, though I quickly sensed that he wasn't interested in me as a woman. If you know what I mean.'

Harry just nodded and Margot continued. 'But that didn't really worry me, because you see, I wasn't interested in him as a man, either. My interests ... lie in other directions. As far as that goes.'

'Yes, I see,' Harry said.

'And Robbie and I both came to the realisation, separately I think, that becoming friends, and being seen out together in public, could be quite useful to the both of us. In keeping rumours at bay. You know what people are like, Harry.'

'Yes, of course, it would have been a good arrangement for you both. I can see that.' The relationship now made perfect sense. Oddly, he found himself thinking about Effie, and how she would probably enjoy Margot's company.

Margot smiled and gathered her purse. 'Will that be all then, Harry?'

'Yes,' Harry replied, rising and shaking her hand. 'Thank you again, you've been very helpful.'

She took his offered hand and grasped it firmly, fixing him with a pleasant smile.

Inexplicably, Harry found himself blurting out, 'You should meet my wife sometime, I think you'd have a lot in common. She's very interested in … women's issues.'

Margot's smile broadened slightly. 'Thank you, Harry, I think I'd like that.'

And with those words, Margot Philips made her way from the Russell Street interview room, leaving Inspector Harry Holloway standing there alone. He felt himself re-energised, and more than ever determined to find Robbie Sharkey's murderer.

✕

George Winton's usually genial nature seemed to have deserted him as he sat in surly silence in the Russell Street interview room. He looked up sourly as Harry entered, before resuming an air of pained indifference. Harry wondered whether Winton's mood indicated some discomfort with being grilled about Robbie Sharkey, or was simply a natural antipathy to revealing any of his business affairs to the law.

'Afternoon George,' Harry began jovially. 'Good of you to spare us the time for a chat. I know you're a busy man.'

'Spare us the soft-soap,' Winton replied. 'You know I'm only here under sufferance. It's a complete waste of my time and yours, as you'll find out. But so be it, I've got nothing to hide. Just get on with it, if you wouldn't mind.'

'Fair enough. As I mentioned Saturday, we're interested in who bet what on the Carlton–Collingwood game, when Rob Sharkey was killed. You see, we think there's a possibility that his death might be connected with some attempt to fix the result of the game. Unsuccessfully, as it turned out. And with due respect to your reputation, every man and his dog knows you're a bookie who, shall we say, sometimes strays outside the strict bounds of the law. At the moment I'm not focussed on investigating your betting operations per se. But I will be if I suspect your activities had anything to do with the murder of Robbie Sharkey.'

'Bit far-fetched, your theory, isn't it?' Winton eyed him coldly. 'I mean, that a bloke could be done in by a punter for a few quid.'

'Possibly,' Harry conceded. 'But on the other hand, a footballer being murdered during a game in front of twenty-five thousand witnesses might seem far-fetched too. Until it happened.'

'I suppose so,' Winton mumbled, and continued to stare at the table in front of him.

'And of course, we might be talking about a bit more than a few quid, George. Quite a bit more.'

Winton sniffed and sat in sulky silence, so Harry continued. 'So, with that in mind, George, I'm wondering if you carried any particularly large bets that day? On either team, Collingwood or Carlton.'

Winton looked up in surprise. 'What do you mean? It wouldn't make sense for a punter to knock off Sharkey if they were betting on Collingwood. What would be the point of that?'

'No point at all,' Harry agreed. 'But it would make sense for a bookie to get rid of the Magpies' star player, if that bookie was holding a particularly large bet on Collingwood to win. Don't you agree?'

Winton's ruddy complexion flushed a deeper hue of mottled purple. He said nothing.

'So, George, back to my question. Were you holding any particularly large wagers on that game?'

'I might have. I'm not sure. I run a pretty big operation, as you know. I'm one of this town's biggest.'

'I'm aware of that,' Harry continued patiently. 'But if your memory's no good, I can of course examine your ledger. And if you're not keeping a ledger, or if I find it's been altered or nobbled, then of course, I might be inclined to run you in for illegal betting. I might get serious about your bookmaking operations. Very serious, perhaps.'

Winton glared at him for some time. Harry gazed back at him pleasantly. Winton eventually shrugged and replied. 'All right then, now you mention it, there was one particularly large bet on that game.'

'Go on. Who was it, and how much?'

'Well, as a matter of fact, it was Robbie Sharkey himself. He placed a hundred quid on the game.'

Harry whistled softly. 'That's a hell of a wager. On Collingwood, I suppose.'

'Naturally. Who else would he bet on?'

'Well, we've seen a few examples of players throwing games because they've bet on the opposition. Jack McInerney comes to mind. But that's clearly not the case here. Anyway, it was a great result for you, wasn't it?'

Winton scowled at Harry. 'What do you mean it was a great result for me? Collingwood won, didn't they?'

'Yeah, but Sharkey's not around to collect his winnings, is he? And I assume you've got no intention of paying out to his estate?'

Winton's scowl remained, but there was also alarm on his face. 'I dunno,' he mumbled eventually. 'I haven't gone into that yet.'

'Reckon we might be interested in going into it, George. Might be an interesting legal conundrum. But not yet, we've got other fish to fry at the moment. Though I wouldn't be spending Sharkey's winnings, if I were you. Put the cash in a safe place under the bed.'

Perhaps realising the full implications of his position, Winton suddenly turned to a more conciliatory approach. 'Hell, Harry, you can't think I had anything to do with Sharkey getting done in. I mean, how would I do it, for a start?'

'That leads me to my next question, actually,' Harry continued evenly. 'You don't happen to know a fellow by the name of Joey Miller, do you?'

'Never heard of him,' Winton declared vehemently. And a trifle too promptly, Harry thought. Then Winton added, 'Who is this Miller bloke anyway?'

'A Collingwood trainer, actually. And someone we're interested in. But unfortunately, he's disappeared. Done a runner, maybe?' Harry raised an eyebrow in Winton's direction.

'How would I know anything about that? Like I told you, I never heard of him.' And Winton reassumed his air of indignant silence.

'Anyone else around the club that you're friendly with? Any particular mates over at Collingwood?'

'Oh, I dunno,' Winton replied vaguely. 'I suppose a few of them might have a punt with me from time to time.'

Harry tried a stab in the dark. 'If you're having trouble with your memory, George, perhaps I can assist. Does the name, Henry Ramsgate, ring a bell? Doctor Henry Ramsgate?'

'Ramsgate. Now that you mention it, yeah. Tall, skinny fella. Bit of a strange fish. He's a regular. Why, you reckon he's got something to do with Sharkey?'

'Not necessarily. Just someone we've interviewed in the course of our investigation.'

That's enough, Harry thought. A bit to go on there. 'Well, George, you're free to go. But we may be needing you again, so don't disappear on us, or anything like that.'

Winton rose to his feet, adjusted his jacket around his portly frame, and put on his best injured demeanour. 'Fair dinkum, Harry, if you think I had anything to do with it, you're barking up the wrong tree. You should be off chasing after the real suspects. Like this Joey Miller bloke.'

'The one you've never heard of,' Harry reminded him. 'Don't worry, we're on that trail too. We'll catch up with Mr Miller, and we'll be asking him the same question we asked you.'

Winton paused. 'What question d'you mean?'

'Whether you two know each other. We'll see what he's got to say to that.'

✕

Harry bounced his son on his knee and glanced across at Effie, who was sitting at the dining table, steadily working her way through a small pile of exercise books.

'It's been a frustrating day, but at least the meeting with Margot Philips went well,' he mused.

Effie glanced up from her books. 'By 'frustrating', I assume you mean that you haven't found Richard Thames yet?'

'We haven't,' Harry replied sombrely. 'And I'm starting to get a bit concerned. I sent Willie over to Richard's house, and then to his parents, but nothing. He wasn't at home and his parents haven't heard from him.'

Effie closed the book she was marking and looked sympathetically at her husband. 'Oh dear, that doesn't sound good at all.'

'It doesn't,' Harry agreed. 'And to make matters worse, Willie found his place unlocked and no sign of Richard when he had a look inside. That's not necessarily suspicious, but it's still worrying.'

'Something has happened to him, I know it,' Effie lamented. 'And it's all to do with Collingwood and Robert Sharkey. I told you I was worried. You know, after what Michael said. You should have taken us more seriously.'

'I did take you seriously, Eff,' Harry responded wearily, cuddling his suddenly sleepy son in his arms. 'It's just that I couldn't justify taking any action at that stage, on the basis of what we knew.'

'Really?' Effie queried. 'Are you sure it wasn't because that idiot boss of yours wouldn't allow it, and you weren't prepared to take him on?'

Harry sighed and replied, as calmly as he could manage, 'Come on, Eff, that's hardly fair. You're right about Marks, he's a fool of the first order, but I can guarantee you I'm not scared of him. If I could've taken action to protect Richard Thames at that time, I would've.'

'I'm sorry, darling,' Effie replied, suddenly remorseful. 'I know you would have. It's just that it's so upsetting. That people like Richard are subject to such stigma. And to such dangers as well. It's just not fair.'

'Couldn't agree more,' Harry sighed.

'What are you going to do now? How are you going to find him?'

Again Harry sighed. 'Not sure, Eff. Trouble is, the places he might have gone are often not known to us. They're kept secret, for obvious reasons. But I've got my blokes on the beat looking in all the places we do know about. Where we know men of that ... inclination are known to congregate. But, to be honest, I'm not expecting they'll find him.'

'You said something about meeting, what's her name, Margot Philips?' Effie said. 'Robert Sharkey's mystery companion. The independent woman you couldn't quite understand.'

'Oh yes,' Harry smiled briefly. 'Yes, it did go well. You'll be happy to know she's not so mysterious to me anymore.'

'How so?' Effie leaned back in her chair and surveyed her husband with a critical eye.

'Well, she made clear to me that she was just good friends with Sharkey. As you suggested, they were just companions.'

'Ha! I told you so! Next time, you should listen to your wife, Harry Holloway.'

Harry grinned. 'Fair enough.' He thought about Margot again, and wondered whether he should reveal more to Effie. I should, he thought, she's an enlightened woman.

'She also told me something else,' he continued. 'In confidence, actually, but I know you'll keep it to yourself.'

'I would hope you can trust me to do that,' Effie replied. 'I love a good gossip, but I can also keep a secret when required.'

'Well, one of the reasons she was just a good companion to Sharkey, rather than romantically involved, was that she … she doesn't see men in a romantic way.'

Effie eyed him quizzically. 'What are you trying to say, Harry? Are you saying she told you she's a lesbian?'

'Well, yes, that's what I was getting at,' Harry replied, a trifle taken aback. 'Does that shock you?'

'Of course not, you silly man,' Effie smilingly chided him. 'What do you take me for, some sort of naive young girl? Lots of the women I've mixed with in the suffragette movement are of that inclination. Like Michael and James, and Richard Thames too, they have to hide their true feelings when they're out in the world. Our movement is one of the few places where those women can be open about themselves.'

Harry shook his head in self-admonishment. 'Sorry, dear, sorry for misjudging you. I'm the naive one, actually, not remembering how independent and worldly-wise you are. But you know, in my more enlightened moments, I do appreciate your ... your acceptance of people. It's why I love you so much.'

Effie smiled lovingly back. 'Apology accepted, darling. And compliment gratefully received.'

'By the way,' Harry remembered, 'I'm not sure why I raised it, but I mentioned to Margot that you might be interested in meeting her. Perhaps I realised that you two might be kindred spirits.'

'I think I would be interested,' Effie replied. 'She sounds a very interesting person. She certainly seems to have intrigued my husband, which is a good indicator of an interesting character. What's her profession?'

'She works for Henry Ramsgate. You know, the Collingwood doctor. That's how she met Sharkey. She runs the office, she tells me. Very efficiently, I shouldn't wonder.'

Effie reopened her exercise book, but paused before taking up her pencil. 'Ramsgate, he's the one you were telling me about, isn't he? The one who was so hopeless when you were trying to help poor Robbie Sharkey in the change rooms?'

'The very one. You're right, he was hopeless. Actually, he's apologised for that performance. Claims he was panic-stricken.'

'And you believe him?' Effie's tone had become mildly suspicious.

'Not sure. There's a couple of things about him that interest me. He's a regular gambler. I spotted him when I went out to Wren's tote. He's also a regular customer of George Winton. And he's a confirmed bachelor, still lives with his mother, I'm informed. Nothing wrong with either of those facts, I suppose, but the other thing about him is that he seemed quite nervous when I interviewed him. Nervous and defensive, as if he had something to hide. Would be handy to find out what that something is.'

Effie's interest was now thoroughly piqued. 'I'd be keeping a very close eye on him, if I were you. He sounds very suspicious. And let's face it, he had the means, and the skill, to inject Robbie Sharkey.'

'Maybe, but I'm still not sure how he could have achieved it.' Harry was a lot less enthusiastic than Effie. But she was now off and running.

'What if he was deliberately hopeless in those change rooms? What if he made out he didn't know what to do, so that Robbie would die before someone treated him properly?'

'Interesting theory,' Harry replied. 'Might be worth following up.' But he didn't sound totally convinced.

'Harry Holloway, I hope you're not underestimating your wife's deductive powers yet again. Haven't you learnt that I'm more often right than wrong?'

Harry grinned as he tugged his forelock in mock obeisance. 'Blimey, Eff, you're getting as good as the boss at ordering me about.' Then, in a more serious vein, 'But, you're right, Henry Ramsgate does need to be further investigated. Along with a number of other possibilities.'

Effie gave what sounded to Harry like a reasonably satisfied grunt and returned to her books. Left alone, Harry glanced down at Alfie, resting in his arms and long since asleep. He rose gently, made his way upstairs to Alfie's bedroom, and put the little fellow in his cot. He lingered for five minutes, enjoying the sight of his blissfully sleeping son.

Returning to the dining room, he pulled out his tatty old notebook and began to scribble. Not just his record of the day's events, but also some musings on those other angles that were running through his head.

✕

11

TUESDAY 22 JUNE 1897

HARRY HOLLOWAY LEANED BACK in his chair, clasped his hands behind his head and closed his eyes.

All in all, yesterday had been quite satisfactory. He was particularly pleased with the meeting with Margot Philips. The mystery of her seemingly odd relationship with Sharkey had been cleared up. Her explanation now made perfect sense to him. They were two prominent people in their respective spheres, but at the same time outsiders in those circles. They were covering for each other, providing safe public personas to protect them from what would be otherwise certain public condemnation.

And what of George Winton? It was a strange coincidence that Sharkey was killed the same day he was playing to win big money. Was Winton up to that sort of desperation? He was a scoundrel, no doubt about that, but murder? Surely not. If his intention was to prevent Collingwood winning, he could have ordered one of his ruffians to beat up Sharkey and put him out of action. Still, it would be interesting to see what Joey Miller had to say about Winton. Assuming they could eventually find the missing trainer.

Harry's reverie was interrupted by a growing awareness of footsteps approaching his office. And rapidly approaching, from the sound of it. Abruptly the door was flung open and Willie Milton appeared, breathing heavily.

'Strike me, Willie,' Harry exclaimed. 'Ever heard of knocking? What's up?'

Willie's usual casual demeanour was gone, his expression one of alarm and concern. 'Boss, we've just had a telephone call from the St Kilda station.'

'And?'

'They said there was some bloke walking his dog this morning and he came across a body. Over at Albert Park, half-hidden in some bushes down by the lake. The St Kilda boys hot-footed it down there as soon as it was reported. Not a pretty sight, apparently. And from what they said, the description fits pretty well with that Thames bloke. From what you told me. Young bloke, dark hair, plastered down, and might have been good looking, as far as they could tell. Though they said it was a bit hard to describe him, he was a bit of a mess, apparently.'

Harry felt a slight shiver run through him. It wasn't so much a feeling of dread at dealing with a gruesome murder scene; he was more than used to dealing with that kind of situation. Rather he was gripped by the apprehension that the dead man was indeed Richard Thames, with the complications that would mean for the Sharkey investigation. And he was thinking too of the impact it would have on the Thames family. And on Effie, Michael and James, for that matter.

But then he checked himself. Nothing was confirmed, there was no point in getting ahead of himself. Just deal with the situation one step at a time.

'Right,' he said briskly, taking his hat from his desk. 'Who's down there now? Have they got someone on guard? I hope they haven't moved anything.'

'First question I asked,' Willie reassured him. 'They told me they've done it by the book. Nothing touched, everything just as they found it. They've got a bloke waiting for us at Queen's Road and another copper looking after the body. Keeping the nosey parkers at bay.'

'We'll need someone to identify the body,' Harry muttered, thinking aloud. 'If it's Thames, that is.'

'You think it might be?'

'Who knows, but I'd say there's a reasonable chance.' Harry paused for a moment, thinking hard. Sir Randolph was the logical witness to take, but Harry hesitated. What if it wasn't Richard Thames? Plenty of dark-haired young men in the city, and why put Sir Randolph through unnecessary pain and anxiety if it wasn't his son? If it turned out for the worst, he would be called on anyway, and at least they could prepare him for the ordeal and soften the blow a little. No, a better idea would be to take Michael Standish. He would still be a reliable witness and besides, the school at Commercial Road was quite near Albert Park.

'Come on,' he instructed Willie, throwing open the door. 'Let's find a trap and get going. We can pick up Michael Standish on the way. He'll be at school at this time of day, and I'm sure he can arrange to get away for a while. Effie can organise cover for him.'

Dark clouds were gathering and rain threatened, as Harry, Willie and Michael Standish followed Constable Jim Redmond towards the lake shoreline. Although it was only three in the afternoon, the darkening sky enshrouded Albert Park in a sombre cloak, and the copse of low shrubby trees that ran around the edge of this part of the lake loomed brooding and sinister. Everything about the depressing scene instilled in Harry a gathering sense of foreboding.

As the trio got closer to the shore, they saw another policeman standing on guard at one end of the belt of trees. A small group of boys were congregated a little way off, pointing and talking excitedly among themselves.

'Jack, this is Inspector Holloway from CIB,' Constable Redmond called out to his colleague on guard as they approached.

Constable Jack Hill straightened to attention and pointed back into the thicket. 'The body's in there, sir, just as we found it.'

'Let's have a look,' Harry said grimly and followed the constable into the tree line.

Some twenty yards or so in, they came across it, the body of a young man, fully clothed, lying in the thick shrubbery. Harry carefully leaned over and examined the body. It was lying front down, but the man's neck was twisted at an odd angle, so that the face was exposed. Harry wondered if the poor fellow's neck had been broken. The face, though clearly visible, might not be easily identifiable, Harry realised, as he examined the swollen and bloodied features. He looked back up at Michael and motioned him forward.

Michael gave a small gasp as he joined Harry and looked closely at the dead man's face. He stood up quickly and moved back. Harry looked at him and Michael simply gave a small nod of the head.

'Yes,' he said quietly. 'It's Richard.'

Harry put his hand on Michael's arm. 'You're sure? He's been badly beaten.'

'Quite sure.'

'I'm very sorry,' Harry said, speaking quietly too. He turned to the police constables. 'It's pretty well concealed in here. I'm not sure how your dog walker came across the body. He wouldn't have seen it walking past.'

Constable Hill replied, 'Just a fluke, apparently. He told me his dog disappeared into the bushes and wouldn't come out. When he went in to drag the mutt out, he came across him sniffing around this. Scared the hell out of him, he said.'

Harry bent over the body again. Richard Thames' skull had been smashed in, and coagulated blood had stuck to the hair around the gaping wound. His stylish clothes were also daubed with blood, as well as with considerable amounts of mud and dirt.

'What do you blokes reckon happened here?' Harry inquired of his colleagues. At the same time, he gave a tug on Willie's sleeve, to indicate the question was not addressed to him.

'I'd say it's fairly obvious,' Constable Redman replied. 'Of a night time, this area's a well-known hang-out for nancy-boys and other deviants. I'd say this young fellow's in the club and he's come here looking for a bit of fun. He's met a likely prospect, they've gone into the bushes for a bit of a tug, and somehow or other things went wrong. Turned nasty on him. I know that some young thugs think it's a good night's entertainment to bash a nancy or two of a Saturday night.'

'Yes,' Harry said slowly. 'That would be a logical conclusion, I suppose. Particularly if you knew that Richard Thames was of that persuasion.'

'There you go,' Redmond declared with a degree of self-satisfaction. 'Right, first time.'

'Maybe. And maybe not.' Harry turned to Michael. 'From what you've told me, Thames wasn't in the habit of indulging in this sort of random activity. Correct?'

Michael shook his head slowly. 'No, certainly not recently. It's the very thing that James and I have been warning him against. And he would never have done this after he met Robert. But I don't know, after the murder, given his state of mind, he might have done something impulsive and stupid.'

'I suppose he could have. From what you say, he was in a state of desperation. Of course, another possibility is that he could have been meeting a particular person here,' Harry mused. 'For a purpose not necessarily sexual.' He glanced around at the windswept landscape, the long line of the lake, and the expanse of open ground leading down to this line of trees. 'Though it does seem an odd sort of place for a meeting, doesn't it? Particularly on a cold winter's day or night.' He pondered again as he surveyed the landscape around them.

In particular, his attention focused through the trees, back up towards Albert Road where their police trap was tethered. 'Tell me, you fellows, how hard would it be to transport a body to this spot? Albert Road looks the closest point of entry. What do you reckon? Too risky?'

'Depends what time of the day or night,' Constable Redmond replied. 'It's normally fairly quiet down here, particularly in the winter time. That's why the nancy-boys like to do their business here, not much chance of mistaken identity, if you get my drift. But they'd all be gone by eight o'clock, too cold for them after that. In the middle of the night there'd be no-one here.'

Could someone bring a cart or buggy into this general area?'

'I can't see why not. There's plenty of gaps in the fence up there by the road. In the middle of the night it'd be pitch black. Safe as houses, I'd reckon.'

'Right,' Harry replied slowly. Then he wandered back through the thicket to where they had entered, looking closely at the ground all the while. He turned to Willie, who had followed him as he walked.

'It's a bit hard to tell, mate, because we've been tramping in, and our clod-hopping friends here have been going back and forth as well. Not to mention the witness and his dog. But it seems to me that something has been dragged through here. See how the ground there has been smoothed and the grass rubbed away. And those little shrubs on either side almost broken right off.'

Willie peered more closely at the scene. 'Yeah, you could be right.' Though Willie's concurrence seemed more on the speculative side of things.

'Here's what we'll do then,' Harry said decisively. 'You organise with our two mates there to get the body transported to the morgue. Then I want you to get hold of Mollison, as quick as possible. Tell him I want him down to the morgue today. Don't think we need a cause of death, that's fairly obvious. But I do want him to give me an estimate of time of death. And any other evidence he can find. I'll meet him there first thing in the morning.'

'Righto, boss. What are you going to do now?'

'I've got a hunch. I'm going back to Thames's apartment to have a closer look. I think that unlocked door might signify something. But first I'm going to wander round here for a bit. See if I can find any cart tracks. Or anything else interesting. Get them to pick me up in an hour and take me back to his apartment. No later.'

'What about the family? Who's going to tell Sir Randolph?'

'Last job on my list for tonight,' Harry replied grimly. 'I'm not looking forward to it. Now, off you go, mate. We'd better get cracking.'

'I'm onto it, Boss,' Willie declared, as he headed off to summon his colleagues.

'And by the way,' Harry called after him, 'Get someone to put the fear of God into those kids over there. I don't want them hanging around and getting in my way.'

✕

The Thames family residence was a huge Italianate mansion in Camberwell, a testament to the boom times enjoyed by the Premier

Building Society in the seventies and eighties. At the front of the house, a circular gravelled driveway wound around a lush lawn, fringed with a miniature box hedge.

With some trepidation, Harry made his way through the evening gloom, mounted the marble front steps and approached the towering front door, set back under a spacious, ornately decorated verandah. He gave the brass bell pull a firm tug. A very small voice within him hoped that Sir Randolph would not be at home. This was the part of the job he disliked most. He hated the knowledge, as he began his spiel, of the impending horror he was about to deliver upon the relative. And then the feeling of powerlessness as he watched them crumble in the wake of his news.

But of course, Sir Randolph was at home. Where else would he be, given his son's disappearance, but at home doing his best to comfort a distraught wife, while both hoped against improbable hope that the worst possible news would not result. So Harry was ushered into a small drawing room by a liveried servant and invited to take a seat while Sir Randolph was fetched. Harry tried to rehearse the best words he should use to lessen the blow. A futile exercise, he quickly decided, and resolved instead to be as brief, direct and honest as he possibly could.

Within a very short space of time, Harry heard a rapid footfall approaching from the depths of the house. The urgency in the steps told Harry it must be Sir Randolph, and indeed it was. The door was flung open and Sir Randolph hurried in, ashen-faced. He scanned Harry's face expectantly, as if he was afraid to ask the question they both knew was the reason for Harry's arrival.

'Good evening, Sir Randolph,' Harry began, in as even a tone as he could muster. 'I have news of your son, Richard. I am wondering though, whether it would be appropriate for your wife to be present to hear it?'

'No, Inspector,' Sir Randolph replied, his tone curiously wooden, as if he had divined the news that was coming and resigned himself to it. 'She is too afraid of the possibilities to meet with you. I will tell her of any news you may have.'

'Very well,' Harry replied. 'In that case I will come straight to the point. I regret to have to tell you, sir, that your son is deceased. His body has been found and identified by a close friend. I did not call on you to identify the body, to avoid distress to you in case the person we found was not Richard. But regrettably it is.'

Sir Randolph staggered slightly, but quickly righted himself. He turned away from Harry and stared out the window into the immaculate front garden. Harry stood quietly by while the seconds, then the minutes, ticked by. Eventually Sir Randolph spoke, in a low voice and still staring out into the garden.

'Am I able to see the body, Inspector? Just in case ... in case a mistake has been made.'

'Most certainly, sir,' Harry replied quickly. 'That can be arranged first thing in the morning. Though we are very certain that it is your son. And I must warn you there was a good deal of violence inflicted on him. It will be upsetting for you.'

Harry thought he detected a shudder run through Sir Randolph, but the reply was immediate. 'I still wish to see him.' Then, after a short pause, 'From what you say, he was killed ... by another, rather than ...?' His voice trailed off and he stared inquiringly at Harry.

Harry momentarily struggled to comprehend the gist of Sir Randolph's words, before replying. 'It was definitely murder. Of that, there's no doubt. He was attacked at his home, we suspect.'

At these words, Sir Randolph quickly turned away again and Harry saw him convulse with muffled sobs. He briefly wondered whether he had been too frank with Sir Randolph, but he needed to be if he was to prepare him for the ordeal of witnessing his son's battered corpse.

'I have already organised a pathologist's examination, and that is being undertaken as we speak,' Harry continued, seeking to turn the conversation to more procedural matters. 'I expect we can arrange for the body to be delivered to you quickly, so you can get on with funeral arrangements.'

Then thinking perhaps that this was too unfeeling, he added, 'Sir Randolph, I am deeply sorry for your family's loss. Rest assured, I'll do my utmost to apprehend the person responsible for Richard's murder.'

Sir Randolph nodded slowly and looked Harry directly in the eye, 'Thank you, Inspector, I appreciate your words. And I will do everything I can to assist.' He was now dry-eyed and calm, and a steely resolve had crept into his voice.

'Good, your full cooperation will be greatly appreciated. But I won't trouble you with any questions here and now. No doubt you'll appreciate a little time to come to terms with what has happened.'

Sir Randolph cut him off quickly. 'No, Inspector, the sooner you begin your investigation, the better. I am fully prepared to answer any initial questions you may have.'

Harry was mildly surprised at the speed with which Sir Randolph had composed himself, but perhaps this was his way of coping with the shocking news. 'Very well, sir, if you feel you are up to it.'

'I am.' Again Sir Randolph's tone was resolved.

'Well then,' Harry continued, 'Let me begin by asking whether you are aware of any enemies Richard may have had?'

'Of course not. He was a very gentle, kind boy. Always. He didn't have an enemy in the world. But really, I don't know why you ask that question. Surely you realise what has happened to Richard.'

'I don't quite understand what you're getting at, sir.' Though Harry had more than an inkling of what Sir Randolph was getting at.

'This is the work of some deranged pervert! A random stranger!' Sir Randolph declared, his anger welling. 'The boy has put himself in harm's way yet again, and this is what has happened. It is unfathomable. How could he be so stupid?'

'That may be,' Harry replied carefully, 'But it's not yet proven. Until then, we'll keep an open mind. We'll look at all possibilities.'

'What other possibilities could there be?' Sir Randolph exclaimed, his voice rising in frustration. 'Inspector, my son had an illness, a terrible illness, that compelled him towards unnatural acts. I thought we had guided him away from that mad path, and that he was coming to his senses. But I was wrong. He clearly relapsed into perversion and paid the price. That is where you should be directing your efforts, Inspector, to the haunts where these foul creatures like to gather.'

'And we will, sir, we will,' Harry reassured him. 'But as I said, we'll look at other possibilities too. For example, that Richard's death may be connected to the murder of Robert Sharkey.'

Sir Randolph stared at Harry in disbelief. 'Surely not!' he exclaimed. 'Inspector, I heard what you said about Sharkey, that he was similarly afflicted as my son. But my impression was you think Sharkey's death was somehow connected with criminal goings-on within the club. Surely you don't think Richard was involved with such activity. Or that someone connected with the club would wish him harm.'

'It's possible,' Harry replied quietly. 'As I said, we're keeping an open mind.'

Sir Randolph shook his head slowly in bewilderment. And distress too, Harry could see. 'Well, Inspector,' Sir Randolph said wearily, 'I suppose you must do your job. By the book, as they say. But believe me, I will be proven right, of that I am certain. Your murderer will be shown to be some debauched creature, a prowler of the night, who has killed my son purely out of some perverted lust.'

Harry simply nodded. He had made his point and could take it no further. No point in probing further tonight. He again offered his sympathies and urged Sir Randolph to make immediate contact if anything occurred to him that might be at all relevant to his son's death. Then he left the stricken man to get on with the dreadful business of relaying the tragic news to his wife, a task that seemed to Harry to be beyond the strength of anyone to endure.

12

WEDNESDAY 23 JUNE 1897

CRAWFORD MOLLISON, as dapper as ever, presented an incongruous image within the gloomy confines of the morgue's autopsy room. When Harry entered, Mollison was standing by the body of Richard Thames, laid out on the examination table with all but his head covered by a white sheet.

Harry hailed the pathologist. 'G'day Molly, punctual as ever, I see. I take it you finished the job last night?'

Mollison nodded. 'Well and truly. But it was getting a bit dull by the time I finished, so I've had another quick once-over this morning. Just to satisfy myself with what I found last night.'

'And you were here when Willie Milton came by with the father, Sir Randolph?'

'Yes. The poor fellow took it badly. As you can see, I've done my best to conceal the worst, but still dreadful for him, no doubt.'

'Can't be helped,' Harry said quietly. 'Anyway, I take it you've confirmed last night's examination.'

'Yes, I don't think I missed anything.'

'Well, give me the details then,' Harry said, turning towards the corpse. 'Pretty awful business, this one. No prizes for guessing cause of death, eh?'

'No indeed. Blunt force trauma to the head. A wooden cudgel of some sort, possibly. Or more likely, just a piece of timber. I found a few timber fragments in the skull. Maybe oak, though I can't be certain. Either way, it was delivered with a great deal of force. Killed him instantly, more or less, I would imagine.'

Harry nodded, as he peered at the congealed mess entangled in Richard Thames's dark locks. 'More importantly, I need to know when he was killed. Can you give me a reasonably accurate timeframe?'

'Well, as you know, Harry, estimating time of death is far from an exact science. Though we continue to make scientific leaps forward in that regard. An important element of assessing time of death is knowing the ambient temperature that the body was exposed to. So, the first thing we have to assess is where he was killed, at Albert Park or somewhere else. I take it you have your suspicions he may have been transported there?'

'That's right. I think he might have been done in at his own residence, and then taken to Albert Park. Have you had a look at that piece of carpet I sent through last night? It might help answer that question.'

'You're right, it does,' Mollison replied. 'There was nothing on the surface, which appeared to have been recently cleaned. Still very slightly damp. But deep within the pile I found significant traces of blood. And I can confirm it matches the blood of this poor fellow. So I think your suggested hypothesis about the location of the murder is probably accurate.'

'Good,' Harry said. 'I think it's likely he was transported to Albert Park in the middle of the night. I reckon Saturday night. Is that a reasonable guess?'

'Reasonable indeed, Harry. I took temperatures from various orifices and, allowing for cold daytime temperatures and near-freezing nights, my opinion is that the body could well have been in situ since Saturday night. He was certainly killed more than two days ago. Rigor mortis has more or less completely dissipated.'

'Thanks, Molly, that's very useful,' Harry said. 'Here's where we're up to then. He was killed at home on Saturday, time unknown, then late Saturday night carted to Albert Park and dragged through the bushes to the site where he was eventually found. Correct?'

Mollison nodded. 'My examination fully supports that hypothesis. The amount and nature of the dirt on the clothing indicate the body was dragged a reasonable distance, over varying kinds of soil. And I found evidence of plant matter from at least three different species on the clothing, indicating the body was dragged through that thicket and collected plant matter along the way.'

'Right then,' Harry said, 'That all seems pretty clear.'

'Not much doubt at all,' Mollison agreed. 'And by the way, speaking of the clothing, there was one other finding you might be interested in.'

'Yes?' Harry asked expectantly.

'I found some fine dust on the clothing of the deceased. Not really visible to the naked eye, but very apparent under the microscope.'

Harry shrugged. 'Perhaps a dirty piece of bag or cloth was thrown over the body when it was transported. It must have been concealed for the trip, I imagine. Doesn't really tell us much, does it?'

'Perhaps not,' Mollison agreed. 'Except that the dust was quite unusual. Appears to be red in colour. Like clay soil. Can't think of anywhere near Albert Park that has soil that colour, can you?'

'Not offhand,' Harry replied. 'Though neither of us are experts in the soil types of Melbourne. Unless that happens to be another string to your bow, Molly. Anyway, I'll bear that finding in mind. Bag up the clothing and register it, just in case.'

'Will do. That's all you need for now?'

Harry remembered another musing that had been wandering around his mind. 'There is one other thing. Just a thought really. Probably of no significance.'

'What's that, Harry?'

'It's about your examination of Robert Sharkey's body,' Harry replied. 'There was one aspect of that I've been thinking about, and I wouldn't mind checking your opinion. It's about those bruises on his buttocks.'

'That's right. The ladies who poke.'

'Yeah, probably, but I was wondering if it could have been something else. After all, there were lots of those older bruises.'

'There are lots of ladies who poke too, they tell me,' Mollison replied. 'But undoubtedly anything sharp, or even not so sharp, could cause a similar result. Even football sprigs, I suppose. Impossible to be more precise than that, I'm afraid, given the obvious age of the bruises. Sorry, Harry, that probably wasn't much help.'

Harry grinned and patted Mollison on the shoulder. 'Don't worry, Molly, you're always helpful. You're a boon to the force. We're lucky to have you.'

And Harry made his way from the room, leaving a suitably complimented pathologist in his wake.

✕

Harry sipped on a cup of tea and ruminated on the events of the past twenty-four hours. The more he thought about it, the more certain he was that Richard Thames's death was somehow linked to Sharkey's murder. But the how and the why still eluded him. Was Thames killed because of his relationship with Sharkey? Or did he know too much about Sharkey's death and the reasons for his murder?

Effie paused from the task of persuading Alfie into his nightshirt. 'You know, I feel so sorry for Richard's parents,' she said, breaking into Harry's reverie. 'They must be completely shattered.'

'Sir Randolph certainly took it hard,' Harry said. 'I feel for the poor fellow. He has a strong character, there's no doubt about that, but this would break any man.'

Effie nestled Alfie into a soft cushion on the couch next to her, where he lay contentedly, eyelids already sagging towards sleep. She glanced at Harry enquiringly. 'From what you say, he clearly thinks that Richard was killed in a random attack. By some stranger, in a casual encounter. But you don't think so?'

'No, not really,' Harry replied thoughtfully. 'I mean, it's possible that he was seeking a casual sexual encounter, though it seems out of character, especially given what's just happened to Sharkey. But the thing is, transporting Richard's body, that's not the work of a stranger. Why would a random killer go to that much trouble to make it look like a random killing? Doesn't make any sense, really. Plus, there was nothing taken from the premises, so that eliminates the possibility of murder and robbery.'

'Do you think it's connected with Robbie Sharkey? And Collingwood?'

'Probably,' Harry agreed, but with a cautious note in his voice. 'I'm not absolutely certain, but it's looking that way. I suppose there are other possibilities, though it seems too much of a coincidence to me.'

'I'm certain of something, though,' Effie declared.

Harry looked up at her, a surprised expression on his face. 'What's that, Eff?'

'What's happened to Richard makes me even more certain you should be looking at that Ramsgate fellow.'

Harry sighed inwardly and adopted a patient tone. 'And why is that, dearest?'

'Don't patronise me, Harry Holloway,' Effie retorted. 'I know that tone of voice.'

'Sorry,' Harry murmured. 'I just can't quite see the connection.'

'Well, I can. I think this now points even more obviously to him. We've agreed he had the means to kill Sharkey, now we have the motive. Sexual jealousy!'

'But we don't even know whether Ramsgate is that way inclined,' Harry objected.

'Well, we know he's unmarried. And still lives with his mother. It's a perfectly reasonable assumption to make.'

Harry shrugged. 'But it's still an assumption, Eff. Look, Ramsgate's a part of the investigation, and of course we haven't discounted him. But I'm trying to keep an open mind on all this. We need evidence.'

Effie shook her head in irritation. 'Really, Harry, sometimes I think you disagree with me just for the sake of it. You're very contrary sometimes, you know.'

Harry briefly thought about mentioning a black pot and a kettle, but quickly decided that was not a good idea. He simply smiled at Effie and went back to his cup of tea.

Still feeling somewhat miffed, Effie rose to her feet, a now soundly sleeping Alfie still in her arms. She turned to make her way upstairs, but Harry had already intercepted her.

'Leave the young bloke to me,' he suggested, taking the sleeping child from her. 'Take the weight of your pins. You must've had a big day, you look a bit worn out.'

✕

13

THURSDAY 24 JUNE 1897

'I THOUGHT I TOLD you to stay away from investigating that young deviant?' Winston Marks stared balefully across the desk at Harry, arms folded in a hostile pose.

Most days, Harry was prepared to patiently tolerate his boss's prejudices and obtuseness, but today was not one of them. He'd had enough. The grim find down by the lake had affected him more than usual.

'I know you did,' he replied steadily, taking care to look Marks directly in the eye. 'But I'm not sure what you expect me to do when the son of one of Melbourne's most eminent businessmen is brutally murdered. Besides, I'm growing more certain that his death is connected to Sharkey's in some way.'

'There you go again,' Marks scoffed. 'Still on that same ridiculous fantasy. For God's sake, man, you can't make wild assumptions, based on hearsay from a fellow who's obviously mentally unbalanced. Was mentally unbalanced, I mean. Evidence, Inspector, that's what you need to go on, not hearsay.'

'I do have a corroborating witness, actually,' Harry declared, doing his level best to stay calm. 'About Sharkey's sexual preference, I mean.'

'And who would that be?' Marks eyed him suspiciously.

Harry remembered his promise to Margot that he would keep the reality of her relationship with Sharkey confidential. He looked at Marks again. Damn it, he thought, I'm happy to wear the heat from this idiot.

'I'm sorry, sir, I promised my informant that I wouldn't reveal their identity, unless required to do so in court. I think I need to honour that promise.'

Marks's glare became even more angry, his complexion incandescent. 'Damn it, Holloway, that's close to insubordination! You'd better be right about your so-called informant. Their information had better be reliable.'

'It is, sir,' Harry confirmed, again speaking quietly and resolutely. 'And while I'm not as certain about the connection of Richard Thames's death to Sharkey's murder, there appear to be some very strong links. We absolutely need to look into it.'

'Look, I know it's a damn shame what happened to the lad.' Marks's tone had become slightly less antagonistic. 'I must say, I feel sorry for old Randolph, after all he's had to put up with that boy. But it's fairly obvious, isn't it? The young fellow's gone down there to Albert Park for devious purposes and put himself in harm's way. He's got no-one else to blame if things went wrong and he's been done in. These are not nice people we're dealing with, you know.'

'Well, actually, sir, I don't think that's what happened.'

'What? What do you mean? What else could it be?'

'On Tuesday night, I conducted a detailed search of Richard Thames' apartment, sir. And I found significant traces of blood, in a carpet in his living room. An attempt had been made to clean it up, but there was plenty left in the pile. I sent it off to Crawford Mollison for analysis, and he confirmed it matched Richard Thames's blood type.'

Marks stared silently at Harry. He was obviously not prepared to acknowledge Harry's acumen and fine work, but Harry could see that Marks now recognised the truth of his account of Richard Thames's death. He had achieved a win on that front, at least.

'Be that as it may, Holloway, you still need to get moving on Sharkey's murder. I'm getting a lot of pressure about it from on high. People can't go around killing star footballers with impunity.'

'I appreciate that, sir, and we're working hard on the case, I can assure you.'

'But you don't seem to be making any progress!' Marks exclaimed, and Harry could see he was working up another head of steam. 'I mean, we know it was strychnine, but we still don't have a clue about how it was given to him. And why, for that matter.'

'We know it was injected,' Harry replied. 'And we have some reasonably accurate boundaries as to when it must have been injected. What we don't know is where and by whom. I agree, sir, that's unsatisfactory, but we will narrow it down, and we will resolve it, I can assure you.'

Marks said nothing, simply emitting a scornful harrumph to indicate his displeasure at Harry's progress.

'As to motive,' Harry continued, undeterred, 'Our two main directions of inquiry are the gambling angle and the homosexual angle. We know that Robert Sharkey was involved in both activities, and we know that both activities can, and often do, have an element of criminality about them. So that's where we're focussing our efforts currently.'

'Not very successfully, it seems. When the hell are you going to catch up with that Miller fellow? Seems to me that once you catch him, you solve the case. If he's not the killer, he certainly knows who is.'

'I agree, he's pivotal to the case and we need to get hold of him. We've already interviewed his wife. She claims not to know where he's holed up, but I have my suspicions she might be protecting him. I intend to go back to her and apply more pressure. There are others, too, who seem to have had a relationship with him. Walter Stansforth, for example.'

'Don't worry about any others,' Marks directed. 'Just find Miller. I don't care if you have to put the heavies on his wife to find out. She's not going to complain to anyone. Or not to anyone who matters, at any rate.'

Harry just nodded and waited for the next volley. Marks said nothing, so Harry quickly took his chance.

'I'd better get moving, sir. I've actually got an interview with Walter Stansforth today. I'd best get organised for it. So, will that be all?'

But apparently the meeting was already over. Marks dismissed him with a wave of his hand, not bothering to look up as he returned to the papers on his desk.

✕

'You really didn't have to come, y'know, Willie. I could have taken care of it by myself.'

Willie glanced across at his boss. 'Well, I thought it was quite an important meeting, and since I've already been on the premises, I thought I might be able to help.'

Harry smiled. 'That's an interesting argument, mate. I'll tell you what, why don't I grill Stansforth in the back room, and I'll leave you to follow up with Miss Sharkey out the front? Just in case you missed anything the first time round.'

Willie glanced across again and smiled too. 'I know you're having a go at me, but I'm happy to be part of the joke,' he replied. 'More than happy.'

'Fair enough,' Harry laughed. 'But there is something you can keep an eye on. I'll be probably a half hour or so with Stansforth out the back. If you could keep an eye on the number of customers in that time, that would be handy. Four o'clock on a Friday arvo should be quite busy, if the business is doing well. It'll be interesting to see how many come through the door.'

'I'm on the job, boss, count on me,' Willie declared, reining in the police pony outside number 282, Chapel Street. 'Are you sure Stansforth is going to be here? From what Rachel said, he's at the pub most of the time.'

'Ernie Copeland assured me I'd find him here at four, so let's hope he's right.'

And right he was. But only just, Harry reckoned, judging from the reek of alcohol evident on the person of Walter Stansforth as he came forward to greet them. He seemed even more florid and bulbous than Harry remembered. Rachel Sharkey was also in attendance, considerably brighter than when Harry had last seen her, some colour back in her cheeks. She's really very pretty, Harry thought. No wonder Willie's a bit keen.

'Good of you to make the time to meet us,' Harry began. 'No doubt you're a very busy man.'

Harry was aware of Willie shooting him an incredulous glance, but Stansforth had no hesitation in agreeing. 'Always, Inspector, always. But always happy to make time for you chaps. This Sharkey business has been dreadful for the club. And, of course, for Miss Sharkey here and her family.'

'Indeed,' Harry replied. 'I'll tell you what, why don't you and I head out the back for a chat, and I'll leave Miss Sharkey and Constable Milton here. Just in case he has any follow-up questions for her. And he's under strict instructions not to get in the way when she's dealing with customers.'

Stansforth nodded vaguely. Rachel Starkey blushed and gave Willie a nervous smile.

Stansforth's storeroom was indeed as grubby as Willie had described it. But at least there was a small round table and a couple of chairs that seemed moderately clean. The two men seated themselves on either side of it. A whisky haze continued to waft into Harry's orbit.

'Now, Inspector, what would you like to know?' Stansforth began, leaning confidentially in towards Harry. 'Though I doubt there's much I can inform you about Sharkey that others haven't already told you.'

'Actually,' Harry replied, 'I'm more interested in getting a bit of detail from you about Joey Miller.'

'Really?' Stansforth replied, somewhat taken aback.

'Yes, the trainer who's gone missing. As you appreciate, we're very keen to know his whereabouts.'

'Can't help you there,' Stansforth replied quickly. 'I wouldn't have a clue where he is. I would have told Ernie if I did.'

'I realise that. But I'm also interested in your past dealings with him. I understand that you were in business with him at one time.'

'What? Who told you that? Joey Miller?'

'Yes, he indicated that you and he had some sort of medical practice. A few years back.'

'No, not really,' Stansforth replied hastily. 'That is, Joey had a business of that kind, a sort of medical business, I suppose you could call it, but I wasn't really involved.'

'But he said you and he were partners,' Harry replied calmly, now watching Stansforth intently. 'That's not how you saw it?'

'Well, I wouldn't describe us as partners,' Stansforth insisted. 'No, not all. I mean, I did invest a small amount of capital in the venture, but that's all. Joey, Mr Miller, was the active participant in the business.'

'I see,' Harry continued, 'And according to Miller, the business ran into difficulties. Something about harm to a patient. Were there legal proceedings, perhaps?'

Stansforth shifted in his seat and glanced about him. Veins stood out in his forehead. 'I can't really remember, Inspector. As I said, I was only an investor in the business. But I can vaguely recall something happening. Not that I would put too much faith in Joey's account, if I were you. He does have a vivid imagination.'

'You mean he wasn't telling the truth?'

'Well, I don't know about that. But he has been known to garnish the facts, if I can put it that way. I discovered, during my brief business interaction with him, that Joey Miller is not a very reliable character.'

'That's interesting,' Harry observed. 'That you question his reliability. But not sufficiently, it would seem, to prevent you from recommending him for a job with Collingwood?'

Stansforth squirmed in his seat again. 'Oh well, it's not a very important position at the club. He's well supervised, he can't get into much trouble.'

'But why put him up for the job at all, given your past experience with him? There'd be plenty of others looking to make a few quid doing the training job.'

Stansforth stared at Harry, his mouth slightly open and eyes bulging. Harry gazed pleasantly back.

'I suppose … I suppose I just took pity on him,' Stansforth offered eventually. 'He told me he'd fallen on hard times, so I thought perhaps I could give him a leg-up, as it were.'

'Very charitable of you,' Harry replied, without so much as the hint of a smile. Then, glancing about the room, 'Nice little business you've got here. Fashionable location, fashionable clientele no doubt. Bit of a change from … what was it, medical electro-therapeutics was how Joey described it.'

'Well, as I said, I wasn't involved too much in that set-up,' Stansforth countered. 'This kind of show is more my cup of tea. Been here for a couple of years now, I suppose. The opportunity came up, previous owner got hit by the recession and I snapped it up for a song. As I said, this is my kind of business really. Dealing with people, that's what I'm good at. Gift of the gab, you might say.'

'Yes, I suppose you might,' Harry observed drily. 'Well, that's about all I need from you for the moment, sir. Oh, sorry, one last question. Couldn't help noticing a few droppings on your shelves. Looks like you might have mice. Or rats. I suppose you need to deal with them from time to time?'

Stansforth looked about the room, as if seeking evidence of the vermin himself. 'There might be a few around,' he responded. 'But they're not too bad.'

'I suppose you put out a bit of poison now and again?'

Stansforth nodded, eying Harry warily. 'Yes, now and again.'

'What do you use? Strychnine?'

'I don't really know. Just know I've got some stuff that's meant to do the trick. Mix it up with some mince and leave it on the shelves. Seems to do the job.'

'Yes,' Harry added.' My constable noticed a bottle of it on the shelf over there when he called the other day. He took the liberty of taking it away for analysis. Hope you don't mind.' Harry studied Stansforth's reaction closely as he spoke.

'Oh, really,' Stansforth replied, apparently unperturbed. 'I didn't notice it was gone. Your constable was wasting his time, but I don't mind if he wanted to take it away. Anything to cooperate,' he added as an afterthought.

Harry rose from his chair to indicate the meeting was over. The two men returned to the shop, where Willie was leaning against the counter, regaling Rachel on some particularly spectacular aspect of police work. He stood to attention as he spotted Harry.

'I trust Constable Milton hasn't been in your way, Miss Sharkey?' Harry inquired with mock severity.

'Oh no, not at all,' Rachel replied anxiously, then, noticing the smile appearing on Harry's features, she smiled too.

Outside, as Harry levered himself up into the trap, he said, 'Seemed pretty quiet out there. Apart from you gabbing on.'

'It was,' Willie replied. 'No-one, in fact. In twenty-five or so minutes. Maybe it's the time of day.'

'Or maybe Stansforth's crack at this business is going the same way as the last tenant's. Down the gurgler.'

'Maybe,' Willie concurred. 'But too hard to tell on the strength of one visit, I'd reckon.' Then, as he took the reins and sooled the pony into a trot, 'By the way, did you get a chance to talk to Effie about Rachel? You know, her interest in teaching?'

Harry smiled. 'I did indeed. And she's as keen as mustard to help. So we'll organise dinner at our place to talk about it.'

'Great!' Willie enthused. 'And I'll be there? Is that okay?'

'Crikey, mate! I couldn't invite you. That wouldn't be at all proper.'

'Oh, right. I suppose not,' Willie replied, downcast.

'But on the other hand,' Harry continued, 'if you were to turn up unexpectedly on police business, I suppose it would be very impolite for us not to invite you to join us. Wouldn't it?'

'I suppose it would,' Willie agreed, his enthusiasm instantly rekindled.

✕

Lydia took her friend's hand in hers and patted it gently.

'You poor thing, Eff,' she consoled. 'Such a terrible business. And so distressing for Michael and James too.'

'Yes, it was,' Effie replied. 'So awful. Poor Michael, he feels so guilty about the whole thing. Berating himself for not taking stronger action to protect Richard.'

'He shouldn't,' Lydia replied. 'There's nothing more he could have done.'

'To tell the truth, I rather feel the same way,' Effie confided in downcast tones.

'What do you mean, darling? How could you have done more?'

'Oh, I don't know,' Effie mused. 'Perhaps I should have been more insistent with Harry. You know, I had this feeling that something awful would happen. But I don't think he was prepared to take me seriously.'

'Really, I don't think that's quite fair. You can't blame Harry for what happened.' And Lydia eyed her friend a trifle more sternly. 'Your Harry is a very good policeman, you know.'

'I know, I know. But sometimes he doesn't trust my judgement on some of these things. It's just 'women's intuition' in his mind. Where's the evidence, he says. Well, sometimes you have to go on more than evidence, you have to go on your feelings. And sadly, when it comes to Richard Thames, my intuition was right, wasn't it?'

'Yes it was, dear,' Lydia reassured. 'Though I suppose it's too late to worry about things like that. It's up to Harry to catch Richard's killer now.'

'I know that,' Effie retorted, a slightly fretful note entering her voice. 'But he still won't take me seriously about that either.'

'Whatever do you mean?'

'It's obvious to me that Ramsgate fellow's involved. You know, the Collingwood doctor.'

'Really?'

'Yes, really. Robert Sharkey was injected with strychnine from Ramsgate's syringe. And according to Harry, he made no attempt to revive Sharkey when he was taken ill. Doesn't that point to him as the logical suspect? And then Richard is murdered in brutal circumstances, in what is clearly a crime of passion. Jealousy is the obvious motive. And Ramsgate fits the bill again. I mean, after all, he's single, not interested in women by all accounts, and according to Harry, has been acting strangely all along. You know, sometimes I think Harry tries too hard to look at all the possibilities when the answer is staring him in the face.'

'Now that you mention it,' Lydia replied, 'Ed was saying something similar about Henry Ramsgate. He thought his behaviour towards Sharkey was a bit strange too. And he described him as something of an odd fish. Apparently, he has a certain reputation among the medical fraternity.'

'There you go!' Effie declared triumphantly. 'I told you so. It's obvious!'

Lydia stirred her tea and mused for a few seconds. 'The question is,' she mused, 'what are we going to do about it? Perhaps you should talk to Harry again?'

'No point,' Effie replied gloomily. 'I know what he'll say. Where's the evidence?'

'Well, in that case there's nothing more to be done,' Lydia concluded. 'We'll have to let the case run its course. And trust in Harry to get it right.'

Effie glanced quickly around the Hopetoun Tea Rooms, then leant across the table. 'There is something we could do, you know,' she whispered conspiratorially.

Lydia stared at her friend, then found herself glancing about the room too. Though there was no need for secrecy, the tearooms were almost deserted on this Thursday afternoon.

'What did you have in mind?' she whispered back, eyebrows raised in expectation.

'We could get Harry's evidence for him,' Effie continued, still in a hushed whisper. 'Show him that Ramsgate is the one he should be pursuing.'

'And how do we do that? I don't quite understand.'

'I've been thinking about it,' Effie went on. 'If we can show Harry that Ramsgate is ... well, you know ... inclined towards men, surely that would put him at the head of Harry's suspects.'

'I see what you mean.' But Lydia sounded doubtful. And confused. 'But, Effie, perhaps the murderer isn't involved with Collingwood. And how do we know the murder was related to Sharkey's sexual inclinations, anyway?'

'Oh, that's all well-established,' Effie replied. 'Harry has already said he suspects it's an inside job. Because of the circumstances around Sharkey's murder, you see. And he also suspects Sharkey's and Richard's deaths are connected, for obvious reasons. You know, their romantic relationship. And if that's the case, the motive is surely jealousy, isn't it? We've already got him on board with all that. Now we just need to show him that Ramsgate is the jealous one, and the one he should be going after.'

'Goodness, you really have been thinking about it, haven't you, darling?' Lydia's voice was becoming animated. 'But what do you have in mind? How are you going to prove that Doctor Ramsgate is that way inclined? You know, romantically, I mean.'

'Well, I do admit that's the hard part,' Effie conceded. 'But I've been thinking about it quite a bit and I have a plan.'

'I rather thought you would have,' Lydia observed drily. 'Well, don't keep me in suspense, what is it?'

Effie needed no further invitation. 'Here's what we're going to do. Ramsgate doesn't know who you are, does he?'

Lydia looked surprised, then replied. 'I don't think so. I mean, I don't think I've ever met Doctor Ramsgate. And Ed doesn't know him very well. As I said, apparently he doesn't seek out the company of his fellow medical men.'

'Good. Well then, here's the plan. You're going to make an appointment to see Doctor Ramsgate. As a matter of urgency.'

'What?' Lydia sounded alarmed. 'Why would I do that? There's nothing wrong with me.'

'But there is, dear, there is. You're feeling very peaky. Have been for a little while. You thought it must have been something you ate, but it's been quite a few days now and you're feeling no better. A friend of yours had the same symptoms and told you that Doctor Ramsgate gave her a tonic that restored her to vitality in a trice. You seem to recall it was some sort of strychnine mixture. Or tablets, or something. Perhaps it might have even been an injection. Could the good doctor recommend something?'

'Heavens above,' Lydia declared, making no attempt to hide her alarm. 'I don't want to be injected with strychnine!'

'Don't worry,' Effie reassured. 'If it gets that far, you come up with some reason to avoid it. Perhaps you have a morbid fear of needles. You would much prefer a prescription for some chocolate-covered pills, you've heard they're very effective too. But don't you see, then we'll have our proof that Ramsgate does use strychnine on his patients. Despite what he told Harry, that he never carries the stuff with him.'

'Oh yes, I see,' Lydia said, then added, 'Really dear, that's rather clever. I think it might actually work. But what of the other? How are we going to uncover his romantic inclinations?'

'Ah yes,' Effie continued, 'that's the next part. At this point you tell him that actually, you had another reason for seeking him out. Turns out that a lady friend of yours, a very attractive, unattached lady friend, has formed an admiration for him from afar and is rather keen to make his acquaintance. But she's at a loss as to how to do so. So here you are, to do a favour for a dear friend by arranging an introduction.'

'Isn't that a rather unlikely scenario?' Lydia's enthusiasm was on the wane again. 'I mean, from what you and Ed say, this chap's hardly the kind of man to drive a woman to distraction from afar.'

'True, dear, very true,' Effie agreed. 'But let's hope Doctor Ramsgate doesn't recognise his own limitations. And I know how charming and persuasive you can be, so I'm counting on you to paint a picture of this mystery woman that no red-blooded bachelor could resist. So that if he does resist your invitation for a tête-a-tête with this lady, we'll know it's because he's got no interest in ladies at all, from that perspective anyway.'

Lydia considered the matter for a little while, then replied, still a touch doubtfully, 'Oh well, I suppose it can't do any harm, and it may achieve some good. But to be honest, Effie, you have thought about this such a good deal, I rather wonder whether it mightn't be better for you to play the part of the invalid. I'm concerned that I might slip up on some of the detail.'

'Nonsense, dear,' Effie declared. 'Ramsgate may well know who I am. And if he does know, or discovers later, that I'm Harry's wife, that would be a complete disaster, wouldn't it? Anyway, you're far more charming and convincing than I could ever be. No, it has to be you.'

'Very well, I'm up for it,' Lydia declared. 'When shall we spring the trap?'

'The sooner the better,' Effie replied. 'And while you're there, could you do one other thing for me? Doctor Ramsgate's office manager is a woman by the name of Margot Philips. I imagine she will be present somewhere in his office. If you get the chance, introduce yourself and have a chat.'

Lydia eyed her friend quizzically. 'Any particular reason for your interest in this woman?'

Effie smiled cryptically. 'No particular reason. It's just that Harry had cause to interview her a couple of times and he seems to have found her rather fascinating. I'm keen to understand the nature of that fascination.'

Lydia smiled archly. 'Perhaps jealousy is part of your motive, darling?'

Effie returned the smile. 'Possibly a tiny part of my motive, dear. But more than that, Harry thought she might have quite a bit in common with our interests. An independent woman, it seems. Perhaps a possible recruit to the cause?'

Lydia's smile broadened. 'Well, in that case, I'll certainly make it my business to introduce myself. That might be worth the visit on its own.'

14

THE FAINT REEK OF chemicals confronted Harry as he entered Fraser Sharkey's pharmacy on Johnston Street. The hustle and bustle of the street outside receded as the door swung shut. Not a customer in sight and only Fraser Sharkey behind the counter, pestle in hand, and desultorily grinding away at some concoction in a large stone mortar. He glanced up as Harry entered and his already grim expression darkened further.

'Oh, it's you again. What do you want? I told you everything I know last time. Don't tell me, you're here to tell me you've found out who killed my son. Somehow, I don't think so.' And he gave a thin, bitter laugh.

Harry ignored the jibe and replied pleasantly, 'No, Mr Sharkey. we haven't made an arrest as yet. But we're making progress and we might not be too far from a breakthrough. I've just got a couple of follow-up questions to ask. Any information you can provide might well help us to make that breakthrough.' And he raised his eyebrows in an encouraging way, inviting a positive response from Fraser Sharkey. But all he got was another caustic laugh.

'Well, in that case, you'll never find his murderer. If you need to rely on what I tell you. Because I can't tell you much at all. As I said before, Robert and I weren't on very cordial terms.'

Harry nodded sympathetically. 'Still, you never know, you may be able to recall something of importance. Sometimes what seems unimportant can be a vital clue. So I'm wondering, would you mind just shutting the shop for a short time while we have a chat? I promise not to take too long.'

To Harry's surprise, Fraser Sharkey responded to this request with equanimity. 'Very well, if you insist. Not that it matters much, we get precious few customers these days anyway. Not since things turned bad a few years back.'

He wandered across to secure the door and display the 'closed' sign. As he did so, Harry glanced around the pharmacy. The place had the stale smell of decline about it, the dusty shelves indicators of a business stagnating. Yet Harry also noted with some surprise that the shelves appeared to be still well stocked with medicines and the chemicals of the pharmacist's trade.

He turned his attention back to Fraser Sharkey, who had resumed his seat behind the counter. There was no invitation for Harry to be seated; indeed, there was no other seat in sight.

'And what about Mrs Sharkey?' Harry resumed. 'I mean, did Robbie talk with her much? Confide in her at all? You know, sometimes sons talk to their mothers when they can't talk to Dad.'

Fraser Sharkey glared at him and snorted. 'Fat chance! He hardly bothered to visit her either. Except when he wanted money. I forbade her to give him any, but she's a soft touch. I suspect she was giving in to him behind my back. Damn near broke her heart, it did, the way that boy treated her. Selfish young fool.' And he relapsed into gloomy silence, staring past Harry and apparently ruminating on his son's deficiencies.

'But I understand Robbie was more supportive of Rachel. From what she said, they had quite a strong relationship. He saw her more frequently?'

'Like she told you, only at the shop. And who knows, he might have been mainly going there to see the boss. That Stansforth fellow. I heard they were quite thick at one time.'

'Maybe,' Harry conceded. 'But Rachel seems to have been very fond of her brother.'

'I suppose so,' Fraser Sharkey admitted. 'But you'd expect that, wouldn't you? Her big brother, the Collingwood hero. What kid wouldn't be impressed by that? Pity she couldn't see the truth of what he was up to. The big hero, eh? What a laugh.' And he shook his head bitterly, absently picking up his pestle, as if to resume his grinding.

Harry contemplated the sad, embittered man in front of him. He's lost everything, he thought. First his son's respect, then his son's life. And by the look of it, his business seemed to be on its last legs too. Did Harry need to further tarnish his memories of Robbie Sharkey? Unfortunately, he did. He needed to know how much Fraser Sharkey knew of his son's secret life.

'Mr Sharkey,' he resumed solemnly. 'I need to ask you a question about your son's life that might be hurtful to you. Shocking even. But, for reasons that will become evident in due course, we need to understand whether you, or anyone in your family, was aware of … of a particular part of his life.'

Fraser Sharkey stiffened and stared suspiciously at Harry. 'What do you mean, 'a particular part of his life'? I've already told you, I knew about his gambling, and the trouble that got him into. Is there something else? Was he stealing? It wouldn't surprise me.'

'No, nothing like that,' Harry replied hastily. 'It's more his … his private life.' Harry paused again, as Fraser Sharkey continued to stare at him.

'Look, Mr Sharkey, there's no easy way to say this. Were you aware that Robbie was, well, attracted to men?'

Fraser Sharkey continued to stare, in utter incomprehension. 'What do you mean? What are you talking about? I don't understand.'

'I mean, sexually attracted to men. That he was, I think the term is 'homosexual'.'

Fraser Sharkey sat silent, the colour completely drained from his face, his mouth gaping open. He still seemed not to understand what Harry was saying. But eventually he managed to respond.

'Are you...are you trying to tell me that my son was...was a pervert? I don't believe you. You're lying!'

'I'm afraid not, Mr Sharkey, it's the truth. We have it from reliable sources. I take it, from your reaction, that you were unaware of that part of his life.'

Fraser Sharkey said nothing, staring past Harry, his eyes glazed. Eventually he started speaking, quietly, as if to himself.

'He must have been possessed. That must be the explanation. That's all it could be. The only possible explanation. He was taken over by the devil.' The bitterness had left his voice now, replaced by sad resignation. He hung his head and turned away from Harry, fumbling in his pocket and producing a handkerchief, which he raised to his eyes.

Harry resisted the urge to reach over and pat the poor fellow on the back. But when he spoke his tone conveyed his sympathy.

'There's no need for me to pursue that line of questioning further, Mr Sharkey. Again, I'm sorry to have had the need to raise it with you. But there is one other matter that I would like to check with you.'

Fraser Sharkey looked up from wiping his eyes. He looked a totally forlorn figure, but he struggled to regain his composure and when he spoke, it was still with a defiant edge.

'I will deal with it, Inspector, in my way. I will rely, as I always have, on the comfort of the Lord. Our family will pray for Robert's soul. It's clear to me now that he was driven by evil forces beyond his control. As to any other matter you wish to raise, I will help you if I can.'

Harry glanced around the pharmacy, at the dust-coated shelves laden with potions and pills. 'Looks like you're pretty well-stocked here, Mr Sharkey. You seem to keep up to date with all the latest medicines?'

Fraser Sharkey glanced around the room as well. 'I try to, Inspector, I try to. Though business has been so slow that, in some areas at least, I've had to reduce my stock. But I keep up as much as I can.'

'And you'd have a pretty good knowledge of what you have, and haven't got?'

'I should say so,' Fraser Sharkey replied, a hint of pride in his voice. 'I've got a detailed knowledge of everything here. You have to be on top of things in this business, I can tell you.'

'Well,' Harry proposed, 'I might test you out on that. I'm wondering if you can tell me about your supplies of strychnine?'

Fraser Sharkey's quick glance at Harry reverted to suspicious, but he answered readily enough. 'Well, Inspector, it depends on what form of strychnine you're talking about. For instance, up there, amongst the tonics, I have a variety of pills containing strychnine sulphate. Usually chocolate-coated to make them more palatable. And sometimes combined with arsenic and iron. They have been quite popular as a general pick-me-up.'

'Yes, I see you have quite a variety. Actually, I was thinking more of supplies of pure strychnine powder. That could be prepared for injection into the body.'

Again, Fraser Sharkey looked hard at Harry. 'Yes, I do,' he replied carefully. 'But there is far less call for that product. And I keep it behind glass up there for safety. It can be quite dangerous.' He pointed to a glass-fronted cabinet in the corner of the room.

'And you have supplies in stock?'

'Yes, I always keep just one bottle of the powder on hand. As I said, there isn't much call for it.'

'Would you mind checking?'

Fraser Sharkey rose and, pulling out the counter drawer, rummaged about and produced a key. He made his way to the glass cabinet, unlocked it and peered inside, running his eye along the lines of bottles and jars, stacked neatly in rows. After a few minutes of searching, he turned back to Harry.

'That's very odd,' he said. 'I can't find it.'

'Are you sure?' Harry queried. 'You haven't misplaced it?'

'Quite sure.' Fraser Sharkey asserted firmly. 'I know where everything is in here, and the strychnine is definitely missing. That's where it's meant to be.' And he pointed to a gap in the bottom row of bottles, the empty space indicating where a bottle had stood between the laudanum and the arsenic.

'A couple more questions, then,' Harry continued. 'Can you remember the brand of the maker? And can you recall the last time you saw it here?'

Fraser Sharkey looked nervously at Harry and shook his head. 'Not really. That is, I can't recall when I last saw it. I don't have much use for strychnine powder. Most of my strychnine tonics come already made up, as I said, chocolate-coated pills mainly. I'm sorry, Inspector.'

'I understand,' Harry replied. 'And the brand?'

'It would be Harper and Company. Imported from America. I get a good number of medicines from them.'

Harry produced his notebook from a pocket and scribbled the name down. 'I notice you keep this cabinet locked, Mr Sharkey.'

'Yes, I'm always careful about that.'

'And you always keep the key in that drawer?'

'Yes, always.'

'And who would know about that? Where you keep it?'

Fraser Sharkey stared blankly back at Harry. 'I don't know really. Nobody, I suppose. Unless they saw me take it from there.'

Harry wrote again in his notebook. 'Good. That'll do for now, I think.'

'I'm sorry, Inspector. I don't think I've been much help to you,' Sharkey said, looking rather downcast.

'Oh, I don't know about that,' Harry replied encouragingly. 'You might have been very helpful.' And he reached out to shake Fraser Sharkey by the hand. The man's grip, as he took Harry's hand, was surprisingly strong.

'Thank you, Inspector,' he said, looking directly into Harry's eyes. 'Our family will get through this. I will take comfort in my faith.'

'There's one other thing before I go, Mr Sharkey. Not related to the case, but I have a favour to ask of you.'

Fraser Sharkey looked surprised, and a little mystified. 'Certainly, Inspector. What is it you require from me?'

'Well,' Harry began, searching for the right words. 'It's about your daughter, Rachel.'

Fraser Sharkey's surprised expression grew more pronounced. 'Rachel? Really? What could you want from her?'

Harry paused again, wondering how to broach the subject. 'Well, Mr Sharkey, in the course of our investigations we've had reason to chat with Rachel. As part of our discussions with her employer, Mr Stansforth.'

Fraser Sharkey's expression changed from surprise to alarm. 'Rachel knows nothing about Robert's death. Nothing at all! You shouldn't be interviewing her, she's just a child.'

'I can assure you, Mr Sharkey, she hasn't been put under any pressure,' Harry replied. 'It's just that, in the course of chatting with her, she mentioned that she's very interested in the teaching profession. And my wife is a teacher, you see, and may be able to assist.'

Fraser Sharkey stared suspiciously at Harry. 'I don't quite understand. Rachel has perfectly satisfactory employment. She doesn't need her head filled with nonsense about other kinds of work. All probably pie in the sky too, no doubt.'

'Teaching is a very reputable profession,' Harry continued. 'And quite well paid too. I would think quite a bit better than her current employ. And this would be a real opportunity; my wife is well placed to organise a placement for Rachel.'

'What did you have in mind?' Fraser Sharkey asked curtly.

'Well, with your permission, sir, I'd like to invite Rachel to dine with us, so that my wife can discuss this opportunity with her. I was hoping Friday of next week would be convenient. In the evening.'

'Really, Inspector, that's too much,' Fraser Sharkey bristled. 'Exposing a young girl to the dangers of Melbourne at night. I couldn't allow it.'

'Don't worry,' Harry added hastily. 'I'll ensure she's under police escort, from your residence to ours. And back again. In fact, I will undertake to escort her myself. To ensure she's safe.'

Fraser Sharkey was silent for a few seconds. 'Are you a Christian family?' he said eventually. 'I don't want her exposed to any heathen influences.'

'Oh yes, most certainly,' Harry responded, trying to remember the last time he went to church.

Fraser Sharkey's stern expression softened slightly. 'Very well, Inspector. But she is to be home by nine o'clock. Not a second later. And you must promise that she'll be chaperoned at all times.'

'Righto,' Harry said, and again extended his hand. 'I'll pick her up at six. Thank you, sir.'

Bloody hell, Harry thought, as he swung the door shut behind him.

That's the hardest job I've had all week. The things I do to keep Effie happy. And Willie too, for that matter.

✕

'Well, Miss Smith, it seems to me that your vital signs are perfectly normal. Peaky, you said? Could you describe your actual symptoms again?'

Lydia endeavoured to put on a peaky expression, hoping that the excess face powder she had applied was giving her a convincingly sickly appearance.

'Oh, nothing that I could really put my finger on, Doctor Ramsgate. I'm just feeling tired, run down, a little woozy at times. Perhaps I've been working too hard, you know how it is.'

Ramsgate sat back in his chair and surveyed Lydia. She produced a handkerchief and coughed delicately into it, then glanced at him again. He didn't appear to be emanating waves of sympathy, but she pushed on.

'I think perhaps all I need is a tonic, a pick-me-up. The lady who suggested I come to you told me you prescribed her a wonderful cure. She was back to her best in no time at all.'

'Well, I suppose a tonic could do you no harm,' Ramsgate observed, ignoring her attempt at flattery. 'Though I'm far from sure it's necessary.'

'Oh, that would be splendid,' Lydia responded enthusiastically. Then, remembering her state of health, she added in a more tremulous voice, 'I think my friend mentioned something about strychnine in the tonic. I know that sounds dangerous, but she said it worked very well.'

Lydia's thought her words had some effect on Doctor Ramsgate. She fancied he paled somewhat, and his reply sounded strained.

'I don't think so, Miss Smith. Your friend must be mistaken. I'm not in the habit of prescribing strychnine for my patients.'

Lydia eyed him with what she intended to be a meaningful look. 'I'm sure that's what she said, Doctor Ramsgate. Are you saying that you never prescribe strychnine? I hear it's quite effective as a tonic.'

Ramsgate shook his head vehemently. 'No, never.' Then, after a short pause, 'Well, perhaps once or twice as chocolate-coated tablets, but only where patients have specifically requested them.'

'So you don't prescribe strychnine in liquid form?' Lydia persisted.

Now Ramsgate's demeanour changed from mildly nervous to outright suspicious. 'No, I don't,' he replied testily, eying her closely. 'And I'm surprised that you should be asking such questions, madam, given the recent horrific circumstances in our football community. To which I was directly exposed, I might add.'

Whoops, Lydia thought, suspecting she had gone too far. 'I'm terribly sorry, doctor, I wasn't aware of your involvement in that awful business. Please do forgive me if I've upset you.' And she reached across Ramsgate's desk and patted his hand sympathetically.

She felt the hand tremble slightly under her touch, before it was rapidly withdrawn from the desktop. 'I was not involved in that matter, except as an onlooker. I'd thank you to get your facts straight.'

'Of course,' Lydia replied quickly. 'I didn't mean to imply you were involved. But let's not discuss that horrible crime. There's something else I wanted to raise with you.'

'What do you mean, madam?'

'Well, Doctor, it's a rather delicate matter. I hesitate to mention it.'

Ramsgate looked at her nervously. 'Do you have another medical issue? Is it of a … shall we say, private female nature?'

Lydia smiled and waved her hand airily in Ramsgate's direction. 'Oh no, nothing like that. All's well in that department, I think. No, it's to do with you, doctor. A personal matter to do with you.'

Now Ramsgate looked mystified, as well as unsettled. 'Really, madam, I can't think what you mean. I'm not sure that …'

Lydia leaned in a little closer and adopted a confidential tone. 'Please don't think me impertinent, but I promised my friend I'd raise the matter with you.'

Ramsgate's pallid complexion seemed to blanch even more, and he recoiled back in his chair. The faintly sweet, but sharp, odour of carbolic, or something similar, wafted from his person.

'I can't think what you mean,' he said again. 'Are you … is she making some sort of accusation?'

Lydia smiled sweetly and reassuringly. 'Oh no, nothing like that. My friend is actually the same lady who recommended you to me.'

'Oh.' Some pink returned to Ramsgate's cheeks, but his tone remained suspicious. 'I am still at a loss to understand what all this is about. Please get to the point, I have patients to see.'

'In that case, I won't beat around the bush. My friend, who is a widowed lady of considerable social standing and, I might add, of charming appearance and character, is very keen to make your acquaintance.'

Ramsgate's air of mystification increased, and his colour again waned. 'I don't understand, Didn't you say she was a patient of mine? She must know me already, mustn't she?' Lydia noticed a tremor in Ramsgate's hand as he steadied it on the desk. Beads of sweat were forming on his brow.

'Surely, but not in the way she would like to be acquainted. To tell the truth, she is quite taken with you. No, perhaps besotted is a better description. But she is too well-bred to approach you directly. She has asked me to talk to you, to see if you would be interested in meeting with her. In a perfectly appropriate setting, of course.'

Ramsgate seemed confused. He spoke in an unsteady voice. 'Really, madam, this is … this is surely irregular?'

'Why do you say that?' Lydia replied. 'You're a well-known, confirmed bachelor. It's fair to say you're seen as one of the more eligible bachelors in our town. And as I said, my friend is a widowed lady of charming disposition and very independent means.'

Lydia examined Ramsgate's features as he sat there, seemingly struck dumb by the direction of the conversation. She wondered whether he was trying to reconcile the picture she had painted with the reality of his own life. Or the true nature of his own desires. Again, she was struck by how ill he looked, and how rattled by the whole tenor of the conversation.

He stood then, rather unsteadily, walked to the door and swung it open, his hand gripping the door knob so tightly that his knuckles turned white. 'Enough, madam,' he said, and his voice seemed unnaturally loud. 'This conversation is at an end. You're wasting my time, I have patients to see.'

Lydia's cool smile remained intact. She rose too. 'Of course, please excuse me for interrupting your busy schedule.' Then lowering her tone to a conspiratorial whisper, she said, 'But what shall I tell my friend?'

Ramsgate did not answer, instead rather roughly shepherding her out the door. 'Please see Miss Philips over there to make your payment,' he muttered gruffly as he pushed the door shut firmly behind her.

Seated behind a small desk in a corner of the room was an attractive, immaculately dressed young woman. She was set back into a small alcove, and Lydia hadn't noticed her when she'd entered the surgery and made herself known to the receptionist. Splendid, she thought, remembering the final part of Effie's instruction. Let's see if I can find out a little more about Miss Philips.

Was it her imagination, or was there some sympathy in Margot Philips half-smile and slightly raised eyebrows, as Lydia approached her desk?

'I seem to have got on the wrong side of the good doctor,' Lydia ventured brightly, as she took the silently proffered seat in front of the desk. 'Perhaps I'd better pay a little extra to get back in his good books.'

Margot's half-smile widened ever so slightly, as she replied, 'I shouldn't worry too much. Doctors aren't paid to be charming, are they?'

'I suppose not,' Lydia chuckled. 'Although I'm engaged to one who I'm gradually training in the arts of wit and charm. You may know him. Ed Brown?'

Margot's half-smile dissolved and she studied Lydia intently for a moment. 'I've not met Doctor Brown, but I've heard of him. He was there when Robbie Sharkey died, wasn't he? Robbie was a dear friend of mine.'

'Yes, that's right. You probably also know Harry Holloway. He's the inspector in charge of the investigation. He's married to a close friend of mine, Effie Holloway.'

Lydia fancied Margot's features softened as she replied, 'I've met Harry on a couple of occasions. A lovely man. Actually, he mentioned his wife to me in passing. He thought perhaps we should meet.'

'Effie tells me you made quite an impression on the good inspector. He couldn't stop talking about you. She said she almost felt jealous.'

Margot glanced up at Lydia and smiled. 'Oh, she shouldn't worry on that score. I can assure her I'm not interested in Harry in that way. He just seemed an interesting man.'

Lydia smiled back. 'I'm sure Effie was just joking. Anyway, I won't waste your time any further. How much is the consultation?'

While Margot was busying herself settling the account, Lydia sallied one further probe. 'It looks like you manage the surgery for Doctor Ramsgate. That must keep you busy.'

'It does,' Margot murmured, head remaining bent over the receipt she was writing.

'And does that include maintaining his inventory? You know, drugs and instruments and so on?'

'It does.'

'That's a big responsibility. Keeping up to date with the latest drugs, I mean.'

Margot sat up and handed Lydia her receipt. 'Well, of course I manage things in full consultation with Doctor Ramsgate,' she replied calmly. 'Any more questions, Miss Smith?' And a half-smile played around her lips again.

'No, no,' Lydia replied hastily. 'Sorry for being such a busybody.'

'Not at all. Thank you for your business and be sure to give my regards to Mrs Holloway. Tell her I would look forward to meeting her. If she so wishes.'

✕

15

SATURDAY 26 JUNE 1897

IN THE END, WILLIE Milton was unable to resist. A bitterly cold Saturday afternoon at Victoria Park and Willie was stationed on duty by the grandstand near the players' entrance. By one o'clock he was already bored stupid. Not to mention that all his extremities were rapidly approaching a state of frigid numbness.

Then, on the breeze came the smell of cooking saveloys from Tony's Sav Stand behind the grandstand, and Willie suddenly remembered that he hadn't had lunch. What's more, he was bloody starving. Today's game was against Saint Kilda, the bottom team, so there was a smaller crowd than usual for a Collingwood home game, and Willie was sure his colleagues could manage anything that cropped up in the next few minutes. Harry had told him to keep a sharp eye out for anything unusual from the Collingwood players, but there was no sign of any of them yet. A quick dash around the corner could do no harm.

There was already a fair queue lined up for Tony's famous offerings, but that was no impediment to a hungry policeman. Trying not to be too conspicuous, Willie approached the stand, keeping a discreet distance from the queue. Fortunately, Tony noticed him when he was a little way off, touched his cap in Willie's direction and grinned, all the while dolling out saveloy rolls to his eager customers. A quick word to Mrs Tony, stationed at the boiler, and two saveloy rolls were side-tracked, sauced and delivered into Willie's possession.

'Get that in ya, luv,' she invited. 'Cold as buggery, ain't it?'

'Thanks Ethel,' Willie replied, with true gratitude. 'Doesn't look like you're getting any trouble today?' This was Willie's quid pro quo: in return for a free sav or two, Willie, or one of his team, would occasionally check the ever-present queue at the stand to head off any trouble. Perhaps drunken patrons trying to queue-jump, or customers complaining about the quality of the fare, or even the occasional pickpocket working the line.

'No trouble, luv,' Ethel reassured him. 'Very quiet. Seems like no-one wants to barrack for the Saints these days. No-one likes a loser.'

'Suppose not.' Willie grinned and doffed his cap to her.

Resuming his position by the side of the grandstand, Willie pulled his cap further over his eyes, turned up his coat collar against the cold, and set about steadily demolishing his lunch. No sign yet of any Collingwood players, just a steady, thin stream of spectators wandering in from the turnstiles at the back of the stand.

Despite his efforts to keep a sharp eye out, Willie found his thoughts drifting away from the immediate task at hand to more pleasant prospects. Principally, to the prospect of becoming friendly, very friendly in fact, with a certain Miss Rachel Sharkey. Willie knew he was smitten and in the normal course of events he would be pursuing the courtship enthusiastically. But it was a delicate situation, given the poor girl's brother had just been murdered, and perhaps it would be bad form to be too forward in seeking out her company. But on the other hand, the investigation had given him a great opportunity to find reasons to call on her, and to make his interest apparent. And he fancied he had seen something in her eyes when she looked at him, and in her shy smile, that had quickened his pulse and raised his hopes. He felt his attentions were not unappreciated.

As he was ruminating on this romantic conundrum, Willie recognised one of the Collingwood players making his way through the crowd towards the players' gate. It was Danny Robinson, the curly-haired bloke who had been in the change room when Robbie Sharkey was brought in. Must be here early for a rub-down, Willie thought, remembering Robinson's injury complaint from that day. But to his surprise, Robinson walked straight past the gate, passing very close to Willie, and made his way towards the back of the stand.

Strike me, Willie thought, he's not after a sav this close to the start of the game, surely? Then he remembered Harry's instruction. This certainly came under the category of odd behaviour, so he followed Robinson around the corner, keeping at a discreet distance. Robinson walked straight past the sav stand and headed in the direction of an old groundsmen's shed that leant against the back of the grandstand. It was all very open and deserted, so Willie was forced to linger by the sav stand, which was now doing a reduced trade, with only a couple of customers in the queue.

'Back again, luv?' Ethel called out. 'You must be hungry. Want another one?'

Willie shook his head vigorously and put his finger to his lips, whereupon Ethel gave him a knowing wink and returned to her steaming pot of savs.

Robinson approached the shed, heading towards its far side. Willie stiffened as a figure appeared from behind the shed. Even at this distance, Willie had no trouble making out the dark features and hulking physique of Bill Hanrahan, the enforcer they had encountered at John Wren's tote. The two men came close together and engaged in animated conversation. Their body language told Willie that both men had a point to prove, with gesticulating, head-shaking and finger-pointing on both sides. This was not Wren's enforcer extracting a debt from one of their client's, Willie assessed. Instead, it seemed both men were negotiating some sort of deal.

After a few minutes, the deal seemed to have been successfully reached. The head-shaking turned to nodding, and then to a quick handshake, before Hanrahan produced a paper bag from within his coat and handed it to Robinson, who promptly turned on his heel and hurried back in Willie's direction.

Willie quickly parked himself at the end of Tony's queue and pulled his cap even further down, as he watched Robinson hurry past. No need to continue following him, Willie reasoned to himself. There was no point in picking him up now, despite the fact he was probably in possession of a fair wad of cash. He could have any number of reasonable excuses for that paper bag. No, best to let him get back to the rooms, then keep an eye out, the rest of the afternoon, to see what happened next.

'Blimey, Constable, you're on the tooth today! What'll it be, one or two more?'

Willie turned to see that the queue ahead of him had disappeared and Tony was waiting expectantly, bread roll in hand. No need to insult the man by refusing him, Willie thought.

'Thanks, mate, I reckon I could manage one more. Tell you what, they're bloody beautiful on a day like this.'

✕

'Well, she's certainly attractive. And a very confident young woman, she seemed to me.'

'That's how she struck Harry too, I think. Very cool and calm.' Effie sipped her tea, then relaxed back into Lydia's luxurious sofa. She loved

Saturdays, no school for two days, Alfie in the capable hands of Harry's mum, and the chance of a good old gossip at Lydia's place. Today she was very keen to hear the outcome of Lydia's surgery visit and what she was able to uncover about Henry Ramsgate. But Lydia had not yet finished on the subject of Margot Philips.

'I must say, she seemed very impressed with Harry. 'A lovely man' were her exact words.' And Lydia smiled knowingly.

Effie smiled back. 'She obviously has excellent judgement, don't you think?'

Lydia eyed her friend fondly. 'Not just a teeny bit jealous, darling?'

Effie was bursting to tell her friend the truth about Margot, but she remembered her promise to Harry. And besides, knowing Margot's secret allowed her to take the high ground, genuinely devoid of any trace of jealousy.

'Goodness, dear,' she replied, in mock admonishment. 'Surely you don't think I fall apart every time some woman smiles at Harry? I know he can't help being charming. But enough of Margot, tell me how you got on with Doctor Ramsgate. What did you find out?'

'Not a lot, I'm afraid. The good doctor wasn't very forthcoming.'

'Did you ask him about strychnine? And whether he had any in the surgery?'

Lydia frowned slightly. 'I did, but he denied it. And when you think about it, given what happened to Robbie Sharkey, I suppose he's hardly likely to own up to using the stuff. We were a bit silly to think that he would, I suppose.'

'I suppose we were,' Effie agreed, starting to feel rather foolish at their naivety. 'But what about the other?' she added, remembering the second part of their scheme. 'Did he like the idea of meeting your beautiful widow? Or did he seem revolted by the entire prospect?'

Lydia shrugged. 'Revolted, I'd say. Though I'm not sure that tells us anything. I had the feeling he'd become a bit suspicious of me by then. After I kept asking him about strychnine.'

'I suppose so,' Effie was forced to agree again. 'Well, that wasn't exactly a brilliant plan, was it? A waste of your time, really.'

Lydia topped up her cup from the elegant Dresden teapot, then replied. 'Not entirely, I think, dear.'

'What do you mean?'

'Well, I thought Ramsgate seemed really nervous about talking to me. Not just about the strychnine, but also when I was spinning that yarn about the wanton widow. He went really pale and started sweating. Either he thought I was onto him, or else he's a very, very nervous man.'

'Really?' Effie's enthusiasm was rekindled. 'That is odd. Perhaps there's something going on with Ramsgate after all.'

'He's definitely hiding something, I'm sure of it. But what that something is, I'm not sure. Still, I think you should mention it to Harry.'

Effie smiled. 'I will, but he won't be happy. He hates me getting involved in his work. 'Going off on a frolic', he calls it. Though more often than not, I'm on the right track.'

'He should be thanking you, shouldn't he, dear?' Lydia suggested. But the half-smile playing around her lips had Effie doubting her sincerity.

'That's right, I think he should,' Effie replied, a small, annoyed frown creasing her brow. 'He really should.'

✕

Harry watched as Willie made his way, beer in hand, through the smoke-filled Saturday evening cacophony of the Caledonian. Was it Harry's imagination, or did Willie seem to have more purpose in his step than usual?

'G'day mate,' Harry called, motioning Willie to the empty pew opposite. 'Must have been a boring afternoon watching the Pies towel up the Saints, I suppose?'

'Not really,' Willie rejoined, sliding into the vacant pew, and taking a swig of beer. 'In fact, it was a close go all day. And would you believe, the Saints got up!'

Harry whistled. 'Blimey, that's a turn-up. The Pies must have been off their game. Beaten by the bottom side.'

'Some of them certainly were. Off their game, I mean,' Willie replied. 'One in particular, actually. Danny Robinson put in a shocker. Gave away at least three goals through dead-set criminal mistakes in the backline. Could have done better myself.'

Harry whistled again. 'That's surprising. Danny's normally pretty reliable in defence.'

'Yeah, well not today. He got taken off halfway through the last quarter, but the damage was done by then. But you want to know why?'

'Why what?'

'Why Robinson put in such a shocker.'

'Tell me.' Harry leaned forward, his interest aroused.

'I reckon it was in his financial interest to play badly.' And Willie went on to describe the events he had witnessed earlier in the day.

Harry listened keenly. 'Well,' he said, when Willie had finished, 'kind of looks like he took a dive, doesn't it? Not that we can prove anything. Unless Danny boy's willing to confess, which is highly unlikely. He'd just say he was collecting some winnings, to explain the paper bag.'

'I suppose so,' Willie conceded, sounding a touch deflated.

'But I'll raise it with Ernie Copeland. He'll be very keen to hear what happened. After what happened with McInerney, the club's red-hot on stamping out that sort of thing.'

'Good idea.' But again, Willie sounded a little dispirited.

'Don't worry, mate, you did good work,' Harry said, reaching over and patting him on the shoulder. 'And in the broader scheme of things, it's a very interesting development. If Robinson's done a fix today, there's a good chance he's had another go in the past. Maybe he and Hanrahan tried to get a fellow gambler, Robbie Sharkey, in on a fix for the Carlton game.'

Willie whistled. 'I see where you're coming from, boss.'

'And maybe Robbie Sharkey refused to go along with it. So they made sure he took a dive anyway. Permanently.'

'Maybe they did!' Willie's enthusiasm had returned in force.

'Although that theory probably doesn't explain Richard Thames's murder,' Harry mused.

'It might,' Willie countered. 'Maybe Sharkey told Thames about the fix. It's possible, if they were as close as you reckon. Maybe Thames was suspicious when Sharkey got bumped off, and he had to be got rid of too.'

'Maybe.' Harry sounded unconvinced. 'But at least, we now know that Hanrahan was likely in on a match-fixing scheme. So that points to John Wren being involved too. So, well worth another visit to Johnston Street, I would reckon. Let's see what Mr Wren's got to say about Danny Robinson and what happened today.'

'Good idea!' Willie agreed. 'First thing Monday?'

'Steady on, mate,' Harry cautioned. 'Reckon we need to get back to Miller's missus first. That's our number one priority at this stage, tracking down Joey Miller. He's the one who holds the key to all this. Then perhaps we can pay another friendly visit to Mr Wren.'

✕

16

ERNIE COPELAND LOOKED AROUND the boardroom at the Grace Darling Hotel. The committee members looked back at him expectantly. A committee meeting on a Sunday was almost unheard of.

'Gentlemen, thank you for agreeing to meet at such short notice,' Copeland began. 'I know you'd all rather be spending today with your families, but the president and I have some important news for you.' He glanced toward the head of the table. 'Perhaps you'd like to address the members, Mr President?'

Beazley nodded briefly to Copeland. 'Thank you, Ernie. Gentlemen, there's been an important development in the Sharkey business. Specifically, in relation to Joey Miller.'

'What about him?' Jeremiah Wingard asked. 'Have the police found him?'

'No,' Beazley replied quickly. 'But we've had word from him.'

This news elicited a muted clamour around the table. Again, it was Wingard who spoke first. 'Really? You've seen him, Ernie? Where is he?'

'No, we haven't, Jeremiah. But he's sent a message via his wife. She turned up at Victoria Park yesterday, asking for Ernie.'

'Are you sure it was his wife?' Walter Stansforth asked. 'I don't reckon anyone's ever seen her. I certainly never did, in all the time we worked together?'

'I haven't met her before either,' Copeland observed. 'But she seemed to know a fair bit about Joey and what's going on.'

'What did she have to say?' Randolph Thames inquired. 'You said she had a message from Joey.'

'She did,' Beazley replied. 'It's a written note. And it indicates he wants to meet in confidence with Ernie and me. Just the two of us, he says. To explain himself.'

'Why just the two of you?' Stansforth asked. 'I don't know about the rest of you fellows, but as far as I'm concerned, if he wants to explain himself, he should explain himself to the whole committee.'

'Let's hear the note first,' Thames suggested. 'Before we make any judgements at all.'

'Agreed,' Beazley replied, and glanced at Copeland.

Copeland reached into his coat pocket and produced a dirty sheet of paper. Unfolding it, he began to read.

'Mr Beazley and Mr Copeland,
I reckon you all think I killed Robbie and I reckon the coppers do
too. But I never murdered him I swear it. I worked out I been stitched
up and I reckon I can show you how it was done. Am too scared to
go to the coppers. They won't believe me and I don't have enough
proof. But am willing to come in to talk to you two blokes and explain
what's happened. So you can help me explain it to the coppers. If you
say yes get a message back though Maud she knows where I am. And
please keep this note to yourselves just the two of you. Very important.
Joey Miller'

Copeland finished reading and looked around the room. To a man, the committee members stared back at him in silence.

William Beazley was the first to speak. 'As you can see, gentlemen, the note indicates that Miller wants to talk to Ernie and me only. But we don't think that's appropriate. We agree with Walter's view. As far as we're concerned, if he's got anything to say, he can say it to the whole committee. I hope you agree.'

There were murmurs of assent from around the table.

'Very wise, Mr President, if I may say so.' This time it was Walter Stansforth who spoke. 'This is indeed a matter for the whole committee. The question is, do we agree to his proposal? That we allow him to come in and explain himself. Before going to the police, that is.'

Beazley leaned back in his chair and folded his arms. 'That is indeed the question we have to resolve, Walter.'

'Well, I think we should,' Stansforth suggested. 'We should agree to that at least. I mean, if we think he's spinning us a yarn and he's guilty as hell, then we simply turn him in to the police.'

'We should not!' Wingard exclaimed emphatically. 'If you're proposing that we meet with him secretly without informing the police then I'm dead against it. It's not the right thing to do.'

'I don't know about that,' Stansforth suggested. 'After all, I'm not aware he's even necessarily under suspicion. That Holloway fellow just wants to talk to him, as I understand it.'

'Rubbish, man!' Wingard retorted angrily. 'It's obvious he's in it up to his neck. He knows he's in trouble and he just wants us to help him wheedle out of it. The proper thing to do is to turn him in to the police.'

Tom Sherrin, who had been sitting quietly, turned to Copeland. 'We should probably do the right thing and inform the police. But I'm a bit intrigued by that part where he said he's been stitched up. What does that mean? Did his wife give any explanation of that, Ernie?'

'Actually, I asked her about that,' Copeland replied. 'As well as quizzing her about anything else she knew. But she wasn't very forthcoming. I don't think Joey has told her much. Anyway, all she wanted to do was give me the note, then get away as quick as she could. Nothing to do with her, she said.'

'I know we could talk about this at length,' Beazley said, resuming control of the meeting. 'But I propose that I give you my opinion. And Ernie's for that matter, because we are as one on this. Then we'll have a show of hands around the room as to whether you agree with us.'

'Sounds a good idea,' Tom Sherrin commented. 'Otherwise we'll be here all day. I know what I think.'

'Very well,' Beazley continued. 'Here's my view. I have given an undertaking to Harry Holloway to keep him fully informed if we have any further information, and it is my strong believe that we should honour that commitment. I know some might argue we should have some loyalty to Joey Miller and give him the opportunity to have his say. After all, he is one of us. But I don't think that outweighs our duty to do the right thing by the police. It's my strong opinion that Harry is a reasonable man. If Joey has information about this matter that he thinks exonerates him, well, let him tell it to Harry. He'll get a fair hearing. That's my view, and it's Ernie's view as well.'

Copeland nodded in agreement, and there were a couple of other vigorous nods around the table. 'That's it in a nutshell, gentlemen. You can either agree or disagree with my view. Can I ask those who agree to raise their hand, please?'

A phalanx of arms rose into the air. Beazley clasped his hands together, in acknowledgement of this display of support. 'Thank you, gentlemen. I appreciate your very good sense. It's the correct way to respond.'

As arms were lowered, one remained aloft. 'Excuse me, William,' Thames said.

'Yes, Randolph, what is it?'

'I think there's another issue we must consider,' Thames suggested, looking less than comfortable. 'What are we going to tell Mrs Miller?'

Beazley looked at him with a puzzled expression. 'What do you mean? Isn't that obvious? We tell her that we don't agree to his proposal, and that he should turn himself in to the police.'

'But I'm not sure that's what Harry Holloway would want,' continued Sir Randolph. 'After all, won't that mean that Joey will just continue to go to ground? He's already told us he's afraid of the police, so it's unlikely he'll voluntarily turn himself in. More likely he'll just disappear.'

Beazley frowned and rubbed his head. 'I see what you mean. But what's the alternative? We've already agreed that we reject his request to talk to us.'

'There is another option,' Sir Randolph suggested. 'That is, we get the message back to his wife that we'll meet with him, and we alert Holloway to the meeting so he can be on hand when Miller shows up. That way he's guaranteed to apprehend him.'

'Capital idea!' Wingard exclaimed. 'Let him tell his lies to the police.'

William Beazley's frown deepened. 'I'm not sure I can agree to that,' he said slowly. 'It would be deceptive, and unfair to Joey. And after all, Walter has made the point, quite correctly, that we're not even sure he's a suspect. What do you think, Ernie? What should we do?'

Copeland did not respond immediately, but sat in silence for a good while, staring at the opposite wall in thought. Eventually, he turned back to face Beazley at the head of the table. 'I take your point, Bill, I really do. But I can see Jeremiah's point too. If Joey really is the murderer, or is involved in a murder plot, and if he flees when we reject his request, then we may be accused of warning him off. Of aiding and abetting a criminal. I think I have a solution to the dilemma that might be agreeable to you all.'

'Please, let's hear it,' Beazley said. 'I'm blessed if I've got an answer.'

'Well, I suggested to Maud Miller that I would visit her tomorrow at her residence with our answer. I understand she doesn't attend her stall at the market until the afternoon. But I propose that as soon as our meeting today ends, I call on Harry at Russell Street, or at home if necessary, and brief him on this new development. I'll suggest that he comes with me in the morning to speak to Maud Miller about her husband. He may seek her cooperation to lead him to Joey, or, if she's unwilling to cooperate, he may be required to employ sterner measures to force her assistance. Either way, we will have acted promptly and properly in accordance with the law and your pledge to Harry. And we will not have stooped to deception and trickery to lure Joey into the arms of the law.'

William Beazley sat back and lightly slapped the tabletop, relief flooding his features. 'A very wise suggestion. I don't know what we'd do without you.'

Copeland smiled gently at Beazley's words. 'Well, I hope it's the best way forward, Bill. It means we're really putting our trust in Harry Holloway to do the right thing by Joey. I'm confident he will.'

'So am I,' Beazley replied, now sounding far more enthused about the way forward. 'I take it the rest of you are supportive of Ernie's proposed approach? You'd better speak up if you're not.'

Murmurs of assent from around the table indicated consensus.

Beazley slapped his hands on the tabletop again, like an auctioneer bringing down the hammer. 'That's it then, we're agreed. We'll leave it to you, Ernie, to alert Harry Holloway forthwith. Let's settle this issue with Joey once and for all. Either he's been framed, as he claims, or he's involved in Robbie's murder and must face the consequences. Either way, we know that Holloway will get to the bottom of it. Now, gentlemen, I'll let you get home to your Sunday lunch.'

'You did the right thing coming to me, Ernie,' Harry said. 'I'm grateful to the committee for their trust in me.'

'I'm glad I caught you at the office. I thought you might have been having some well-earned time with your family on this day of rest.'

Harry Holloway leaned back in his chair and grinned. 'There's nothing else I'd rather be doing, mate. And nowhere else I'd rather be. But I'm under a lot of pressure to crack this case, I can tell you. It's all hands to the wheel at the moment.'

Copeland grinned too, but then his expression turned serious. 'Do you agree with what we're proposing, Harry? What if Maud Miller won't tell us where her husband is.'

'Oh, I think she can be persuaded,' Harry replied confidently. 'I haven't played all my cards with her yet. Not by a long shot. And it really isn't necessary to put your president in an embarrassing position by trying to trick Joey Miller into our clutches. No, I think what you propose is absolutely the best way forward.'

Copeland seemed relieved, relaxing back into his chair. He eyed Harry thoughtfully. 'I must say, I've got no idea what's going on with Joey, and all this stuff about him being framed. What's your view? Do you think he's guilty? Of killing Robbie Sharkey, I mean.'

'Actually, no,' Harry replied reflectively. 'I can't see how he had the opportunity and, more importantly, what's his motive? I can't find one. Not yet at least. No, I think there's a lot more to this business than just Joey Miller.'

'So, all his talk about knowing what really happened, do you think he does know who the killer is?'

'Not sure,' Harry replied thoughtfully. 'He may, or he may not. But I reckon he might have worked out what happened. That's why we're keen to find him and have a chat. I know he's scared of the police, there's probably a bit in his past that would justify him being nervous of us, and it could well be that he's not squeaky clean in this business as well. But murder? No, I don't think so.'

'Well, that's a relief,' Copeland sighed. 'He's a bit of a rough diamond, but I've got a bit of time for Joey. His heart's in the right place, I reckon. And it would be a big embarrassment for the club if it turns out one of our own killed Robbie Sharkey.'

Harry's expression became serious. 'I don't like to tell you this, Ernie, but the club should prepare itself for a fair bit of embarrassment in any event. And public scandal. Because everything I see indicates this is an inside job. As I told you last week, however Sharkey was injected, I can't see any way it could have been an outsider. It's highly likely that it was someone with a good knowledge of the club's procedures, and of Henry Ramsgate's medical set-up. My suggestion is the club should prepare itself for the worst.'

Copeland slumped back in his chair, crest-fallen. 'Yes, of course, I'd forgotten all that. Stupid of me. I suppose I was still hopeful you might be wrong.'

'It's always possible,' Harry replied. 'But don't count on it. Let's just push on, a step at a time.'

'A step at a time, it is, Harry. And first step, you and I visit Mrs Miller?'

'Yeh, first thing in the morning, I reckon. And hopefully she'll lead us on to Joey. So be in here by nine at the latest.'

17

MONDAY 28 JUNE 1897

ACCORDING TO ERNIE COPELAND, the Millers' residence was at 16 Coverlid Place, a mere five minutes around the corner from the Eastern Markets where Maud Miller plied her trade as Madame Zera.

Number sixteen turned out to be a run-down terrace cottage, one in a row of similarly decrepit dwellings, huddled incongruously between the back of a grand temperance hall on the Russell Street side, and the front of an equally pious gospel hall on the other side.

The residents of Coverlid Place did not seem to be thriving under the righteous inspiration of these establishments. Quite the contrary in fact, Harry thought, as he made his way down the narrow street towards number sixteen. The grimy bricks, peeling paint and crumbling facades all spoke of despair and despondency rather than spiritual upliftment. And the stench that assailed Harry's nostrils was the same that faced Melbourne's downtrodden poor everywhere: the grim odour of struggle and hopelessness.

'Not the most desirable spot to pitch your tent,' Harry observed to Copeland, as he swung open the rusty iron gate in front of number sixteen.

'Definitely seen better,' Copeland agreed, as they navigated the weed-strewn garden and tumbledown front porch.

There was no doorbell in sight, so Harry rapped firmly on the front door and waited. No response. He knocked again.

'Maybe she's out?' Copeland suggested.

Harry simply shrugged he wandered across to the sole window at the front of the cottage and peered in. Through the tatty gauze curtains, he could make out what appeared to be a bedroom, with the bed made up. Nothing out of the ordinary there. He went back to the front door and tried the handle. It was unlocked.

'Think I'll have a look,' he said quietly to Copeland. 'I reckon there's something wrong. You can stay out here if you like.'

'No fear,' Copeland replied immediately. 'I'm coming with you. If you don't mind.'

Harry nodded his agreement and slowly opened the door. Motioning to Copeland to stay back, he quietly edged his way through the tiny foyer towards the opposite door. It was slightly ajar and beyond it he could make out what seemed to be a small sitting room.

'This is the police!' he called. 'Anyone there?'

No response, the only sound Copeland's nervous breathing behind him.

Harry advanced, gently easing the door open. To reveal Maud Miller, spread-eagled on the floor of her dingy living room. Or more accurately, Madame Zera spread-eagled, her gaudy gypsy robes laid out around her like some bizarrely tasteless ornamental rug. Behind him, Harry heard Copeland's shocked gasp.

Harry leaned over and felt for a pulse at the woman's neck. Though it was scarcely necessary; the bloody mess that was the back of her skull was evidence enough of her state. Nothing, no pulse at all, and Harry's experienced eye told him she'd been dead for a little while. He stood erect and sighed.

'Is she ...? Has she been ... killed?' Copeland asked, almost in a whisper. Though there was no need for caution, her assailant obviously long since gone.

'Dead for some time,' Harry confirmed grimly, casting his eye around the room.

Everything appeared undisturbed, Maud Miller's few modest furnishings and ornaments untouched. Except for a brass oriental statue that lay on the floor by the dead woman, congealed blood spattered over its surface.

Harry took a couple of strides to the mantelpiece and examined its surface. A round clean mark amid the patina of dust indicated the statue's recent habitat, among a few other cheap knick-knacks.

'Taken from there, obviously,' Harry murmured, to himself really, as he endeavoured to imagine the violent sequence of events.

'Shall I put it back?' Copeland suggested, leaning down to retrieve the statue.

'No!' Harry exclaimed immediately, and Copeland recoiled in alarm.

'Sorry to scare you, Ernie,' Harry added hastily. 'But there may be fingerprints.'

'Fingerprints?' Copeland looked perplexed.

'Don't touch anything,' Harry explained. 'These days we can sometimes find a person's fingerprints on metal objects like that. And match them up against any suspects we might have.'

Copeland whistled quietly. 'Blow me, you fellows never cease to amaze me.'

'Yeh, it's a new technique we're starting to use more and more. Got a couple of boys back at headquarters who specialise in the business. So we'll leave that there for them to deal with. Never know your luck.'

'Of course, Harry, of course,' Copeland said hastily. Then, as some of the implications of the scene before them dawned on him: 'What do you make of it? A burglary gone wrong?' Copeland's tone indicated that his hypothesis was made more from hope than conviction.

Harry gave a slight laugh and replied grimly, 'No such luck, I'm afraid.' And with a sweep of his arm, 'Nothing worth nicking here, is there? No, it's pretty clear to me why she was done in. Someone, like us, was trying to find Joey Miller.'

'Oh, I see,' Copeland said hesitantly. 'But could it have been Joey himself? To prevent you finding him? What do you think?'

Harry said nothing, instead knelt by Maud Miller's corpse and lifted one of her arms. He pointed to her hand where two fingers were splayed backwards at impossible angles.

'I'll tell you what I think, Ernie. I think Joey had absolutely no reason to do this to her. No, whoever did this had one motive in mind. To find Joey Miller. And he had very persuasive ways of making her talk. I don't think she would have withstood having two fingers broken. And the promise of more.'

Copeland said nothing, just staring white-faced at the grue-some sight.

'She was killed to stop her identifying her attacker,' Harry explained. 'Once he had the information he needed, that was something he couldn't let happen. And I'd say he's past worrying about the prospect of murder. After all, he's killed before.'

'You mean Robbie Sharkey?'

'I do, Ernie.'

'Do you think he's murdered Joey too?'

Harry looked directly at Copeland and shrugged. 'I'm not going to speculate about that. All I know is that we have to get to Joey Miller, as soon as possible. There's no doubt he's in danger.'

'I wish I could help, Harry. But as I told you, I've no idea where he is either.'

'Think hard. Has he ever given you any clue as to where he might be? Or is there anyone in the club who might have had cause to visit him at home? Or who might have been given that information?'

Copeland rubbed his jaw slowly. 'Not really,' he responded doubtfully. 'I've asked everyone I can think of. No-one seems to know where he is. I suppose the most likely person might be Walter Stansforth. I mean, I think they were in business together before he came here. And I've noticed them together a bit at the club. You could try him. He's already said he doesn't know where Joey is, but he might remember something to help you find him.'

'Yes, he's told us that too, that he doesn't know Miller's whereabouts. But we might as well try him again, we might be able to jog his memory. It's a long shot, but worth a go,' Harry said. 'Though first we need to get this poor woman attended to.' He wandered over to the window and stared out at the tiny, overgrown back yard.

'Tell you what,' he said, turning back to Copeland. 'Here's what we'll do. We're only a few blocks away from Russell Street headquarters. Can I get you to dash up there and tell the constable on the desk I sent you, and to get someone down here quick as a flash? It'll only take you a few minutes. I'd go myself but I don't want to leave the body unattended, just in case her killer returns. Unlikely, I know, but better to be safe.'

'I'm your man,' Copeland declared stoutly. 'I'm carrying a few extra pounds these days, but I'll get along as quick as I can.'

'Good man. I appreciate your help. I reckon we're closing in on our murderer. He's clever, but he's also desperate. And desperate men make mistakes.'

✕

Rachel Sharkey smiled brightly at Harry and Willie Milton as they entered the premises of '*Walter Stansforth, Exotic Interior Design*'. Or more accurately, in Harry's estimation, she smiled brightly at Willie who returned her smile in equal measure.

'Excuse me, Miss Sharkey,' Harry said briskly, distracting her attention from his colleague. 'We're here to see Mr Stansforth. Rather urgently, as a matter of fact. Is he in?'

Rachel's smile evaporated. 'He is, sir,' she replied hurriedly, blushing as she spoke. 'He's in the back room. Would you like me to show you?'

'No need,' Harry replied briskly, striding towards the connecting door. 'We can make our own way.'

Walter Stansforth looked up from his desk as Harry flung open the door. He quickly began to rearrange the untidy mess of papers in front of him, but not before Harry spotted a small silver hip flask rapidly disappearing under the mound of paper.

'Good morning, gentlemen, you gave me quite a start. Excuse me, I'm trying to make sense of these damn accounts. A businessman's curse, I can tell you.'

'Sorry to burst in on you like this,' Harry began, 'but it's rather urgent that we catch up with Joey Miller and we thought there's a chance you might be able to help us.'

Stansforth sat back in his chair and swivelled it towards them. 'Goodness, Inspector, I thought we'd already been over this. If I knew where he was, I'd have let you know when you asked previously.'

'Yes, yes, I know that,' Harry continued hastily. 'But I thought you might be able to remember something from your time in business together. I understand he's been living apart from his wife for some time.'

Stansforth furrowed his brow in puzzlement. 'Not sure I can help, Inspector. I already told Ernie, I didn't even know he had a wife.'

Harry took a stab in the dark. 'What about your place of business?

Did that have any rooms attached to it? Did he sometimes camp there at all?'

Stansforth studied Harry coolly, now well and truly in control of the situation. 'Now that you mention it, there were rooms above the shop. And he did use them on occasion. But rarely, I believe.'

'Was the place rented after you left? Your business premises, I mean.'

'Not to my knowledge, Inspector. But you know, that was some time ago. Every chance they would have been leased out by now.'

'We'll check anyway,' Harry replied. 'Address, please.'

'61 Daly Street. Not far from here.'

'Thank you. Appreciate your cooperation.' And without further ado, Harry and Willie were gone, leaving Stansforth staring after then.

'Good luck!' he yelled belatedly, as he heard the front door slam behind them. He sat in contemplation for a good few minutes, before absently reaching for the small silver flask and raising it to his lips.

✕

The big recession had treated Daly Street badly and number sixty-one had not been spared the pain. At street level, the front windows were boarded up, the paintwork cracked and peeling and there were no signs of life. And glancing up to the first-floor facade, Harry could see that the living quarters upstairs were equally run-down. One of the two windows was smashed and, judging by the bird shit adorning the two sills, the only inhabitants were likely to be feathered.

'What a dive,' Willie exclaimed, as they stood in the street staring up. 'I'd say it's gone to rack and ruin after they closed down the business.'

'Probably not too flash when they were here, either,' Harry replied. 'Not the most salubrious neighbourhood.'

'Might as well have a look, boss?' Willie suggested.

Harry nodded his agreement and strode to the door. To his surprise, when he tried the handle it opened readily and the two men entered a filthy passageway, with an equally filthy room off to one side. Peering in, Harry could make out a couple of padded benches, thick with accumulated dust and bird droppings. Old, glass-fronted cabinets stood unsteadily against one wall. A range of bottles and medical-looking apparatus could be dimly seen through the grimy glass.

'My guess is that's the remains of Stansforth's business,' Harry observed. 'And I wouldn't want to speculate what he was up to.'

Willie nodded darkly. 'No-one's been in there for a while though. What about upstairs?' Indicating a flight of stairs directly ahead of them.

As they began to climb, Harry raised his finger to his lips, motioning to Willie to go softly and pointing to the steps in front of them. Here there were distinct bare patches in the middle of each dusty step, indicating the regular passage of feet. Willie felt his heart quicken as he followed close behind Harry, his body tensing as he peered up the flight of stairs. They reached the first landing and stood, listening. No sound, so they continued their cautious ascent, reaching the top landing where an open door lay before them.

Harry approached and leaned silently into the room, peering about. The room was dirty, but some attempt had been made to sweep away the years of accumulated dust. In one corner, an old mattress lay on the floor, with what looked like old sacking heaped over it. Nearby, an old packing case acted as a table, bearing a grubby collection of oddments: a spoon, a fork and a metal plate.

Harry entered quietly and stood stock-still inside, turning toward Willie and gesturing towards the far side of the room, where another half-open door could be seen. A sound drifted through the door, the unmistakeable shuffle of feet across the floor. A loose board creaked, then all was silent again.

Harry gestured towards the side of the doorway and Willie, instantly aware of Harry's intent, eased himself across the room and took up a position against the wall, adjacent to the door. Meanwhile Harry moved carefully across and stood directly in front of the doorway.

'Come on, Joey,' he said firmly. 'This is Harry Holloway. Time to give yourself up. Come on out and we'll have a chat. Nothing to be afraid of.'

There was no response from the next room, though Harry fancied he heard the sound of laboured breathing. He glanced across at Willie and nodded slightly.

'We're coming in, Joey,' he said, as calmly and casually as he could manage. 'Let's have no funny business.'

Harry had no time to move as a ragged figure burst through the doorway and cannoned into him, sending him sprawling. With remarkable dexterity, or perhaps driven by fear, the fellow was back on his feet and on his way down the stairs before Willie could bridge the gap and seize him. With a couple of bounds, Willie was on his tail and halfway down the first flight, before Harry hailed him. 'Come back, mate!'

Willie stopped, poised for pursuit, and turned back to his boss. 'You want to let him go?'

'Come back. It's not him. It's not Joey Miller.'

'Are you sure?' Willie peered back down the stairs, anxious to resume the chase.

'No, just some poor, half-crazy hobo. Reckon we put the wind up him good and proper.'

'Bugger!' Willie climbed back up the stairs, a good deal more slowly than he had descended. 'Thought we had him there. You don't reckon Miller's around here then?'

'No chance,' replied Harry, getting slowly to his feet and dusting himself down. His face hurt and he could feel a swelling to his cheek where the man's elbow had rammed into him. Nothing broken though, all in a day's work.

'Stansforth's sent us on a wild-goose chase,' he reflected ruefully. 'Though it was only ever an off-chance, I suppose.'

The two men stood together in the squalid room. 'Let's get out of here,' Harry said, his voice tinged with disappointment.

'Where to now, then?' Willie asked, equally dispirited.

'It's late. Let's call it a day.' Again, Harry spoke resignedly. 'Let's review where we're up to in the morning. It looks like we're not going to find Joey Miller anytime soon. So we might as well chase down a couple of other leads. Starting with John Wren and Bill Hanrahan. Let's find out what they know about Saint Kilda's surprise win the other day.'

18

'WE'LL TREAD CAREFULLY, MATE. Gently's the word,' Harry instructed as they headed down the side lane and prepared to negotiate the labyrinthine entrance to John Wren's tote.

Willie Milton tapped his nose with his forefinger. 'I understand. Big fish. Be a bit careful, eh?'

'No, no, mate,' Harry replied quickly, and with a hint of irritation. 'I don't mind taking on the big fish, if we have to. No, it's just that we don't have much to go on here. It's smelly as all get out, but where's the proof? Hanrahan might just have been making a winnings payment to Robinson, and even if he was trying to fix the game, how do we know Wren is involved? So leave it to me and we'll see how much Wren is prepared to give away.'

'Gotcha, boss,' Willie replied, suitably chastened.

This time it wasn't Hanrahan who responded to their knocking. Instead, a sharp-featured little fellow appeared, a fag drooping from the corner of his mouth and showing a significant reluctance to let them through the door into the courtyard.

'Bugger off, mate,' was his less than friendly greeting. 'How do I know you're not a cop?'

'I am a cop, actually,' Harry replied amiably, producing his badge from an inside pocket. 'But before you sound the alarm and send the punters scurrying for the boltholes, we're not interested in them. Or Mr Wren's business activities. We're here to speak to Mr Wren about another matter. If you need to check, go and tell him Harry Holloway wants to see him.'

At the mention of Harry's name, the little bloke relaxed considerably. 'You should've said who you were straight-up, mate. Mr Wren told us you're the only copper who's allowed in here without a warrant. Follow me.'

They followed the same circuitous trail to John Wren's office.

'Yes?' came the barked response to the tap on the door.

Their guide slipped into the office, shutting the door behind him. A muffled exchange followed before the door was opened again. 'He'll see you now.'

Again Harry was struck by how diminutive John Wren looked, seated behind his large desk. But the obvious authority of his demeanour, and the sharp glint in his eye, spoke of both business acumen and commercial success.

His greeting was abrupt. 'G'day Harry. Take a seat.'

'Sorry to interrupt you at work, John. But it's about the case we're working on. You know, Robbie Sharkey's murder. I thought you'd be keen to help clear things up for the club, as soon as possible.'

'Of course,' Wren replied. 'But I've told you all I know, Harry. Can't do more than that.'

'Well,' Harry continued, searching carefully for the right approach. 'It's just that there's been a development that may, or may not, be linked to the investigation. Involving one of your employees.'

'Who are you talking about?' Wren asked, fixing Harry with a steely look.

'Bill Hanrahan, actually,' Harry replied, studying Wren's expression closely.

Wren's impassive stare did not change. 'What's Bill done that's got you blokes interested?'

Harry considered the most circumspect approach. 'Well, it's just that we've been keeping a close eye on the club, and the players too. As part of the investigation, you see. And we noticed your bloke, Hanrahan, handing out a fair amount of cash at the footy to one of Collingwood's players, Danny Robinson. We wondered whether you could confirm it was a payout on a winning bet Danny might have had with you.'

Wren shook his head emphatically. 'No, it wouldn't be.'

'How can you say that?' Harry persisted. 'Without checking, I mean.'

'Because I'm not in the habit of sending my blokes out near and far to settle up. If customers win some money, they need to come to me.'

'So, no way Hanrahan would be settling a bet?'

'No way.'

'Well, what was Hanrahan doing, handing over that money?'

Wren eyed Harry disdainfully. 'I'd suggest you ask him.'

Harry bristled slightly at Wren's tone, but tried not to show it. 'He's your man, John. So, whatever he was doing, I assume it was on your orders.'

Wren's expression didn't waver. 'Well, Harry, your assumption would be wrong. Hanrahan works for me when I need him, but that's not all day, every day. He's got other irons in the fire.'

'You mean he works for others as well?'

'That's right.'

'Other bookies? Got a name for me?'

'George Winton, in the main. I'd reckon he puts in just as much time with Winton as he does with me.'

Harry looked at Wren doubtfully. 'You're not having me on, are you, John? Wouldn't you be worried about that arrangement? Like he might be giving away your trade secrets to the opposition?'

Wren smiled faintly and shook his head. 'Not really. I've got nothing to hide. Anyway, Bill's just a hired hand, he collects debts, does odd jobs, that's all. It's not as though he's privy to my whole operation.'

'I suppose not.' Harry suspected Wren was telling the truth. He remembered Hanrahan meeting with Robinson at the greyhounds. And Winton was there that day as well. It made sense.

'Anyway,' Wren added, with a touch of menace entering his voice, 'If I found out Bill was messing me about, he wouldn't last long with me. And he knows I always find out. Eventually.'

'I'm sure you do,' Harry replied drily, then added, 'Thanks, John, I'll get out of your way.'

'What's going on, Harry?' Wren asked, eying Harry keenly. 'George in a spot of bother?'

Harry smiled. 'Nice try, John, but you know I can't answer that. See you later. Hopefully we won't bother you again.' And he and Willie rose and left the room.

'What do you reckon, boss, is he having us on?' Willie asked, once they were out in the street.

'I don't think so,' Harry replied. 'No point in lying about something that can be checked so easily. No, I think Mr Winton might be the man we need to talk to about what you saw at the footy. In fact, I reckon I'll get him into the station, together with Hanrahan. And this time we'll be a bit more forceful in our approach. Shouldn't be too hard to drive a wedge between them and get to the truth.'

✕

'You really shouldn't have done that, dear. Or let Lydia do it, at least.'

Harry was trying to go softly with his wife, despite more than a twinge of annoyance at Effie and Lydia's recent antics.

'Well, we didn't think you were taking me seriously. About Doctor Ramsgate. We can't understand why you're not investigating him.'

Harry sighed and counted slowly to three under his breath, summoning all his patience.

'If it'll put your mind at rest, dear, I have been investigating him. Thoroughly.'

'And? What did you find?'

'Nothing. Well, at least nothing that would connect him with our investigation.'

'But don't you agree his behaviour was suspicious? With Lydia, I mean.'

'Not particularly.'

'How do you explain it then? He was all nerves with her. He was certainly hiding something.'

Harry settled himself back into the old armchair. Should he tell Effie? Why not, he knew she could be trusted to keep it to herself, and perhaps it would get her off Ramsgate's tail once and for all.

'You're right, dear, Doctor Ramsgate is hiding something. He's not a well man.'

Effie looked at him, clearly taken aback. 'Are you saying he's ill? And that's the cause of his strange behaviour?'

'He's a drug addict,' Harry declared flatly. 'Opium, actually. He's a frequent visitor to an establishment in Little Lonsdale Street.'

Effie stared at him incredulously. 'An opium addict? Surely not. The man's a well-known doctor.'

Harry smiled wryly. 'Well, you've had him tagged as a murderer, so addict doesn't seem so bad in comparison. But seriously, it's true. And believe me, if you went into one of those Chinese dens down there in Little Lonsdale, you'd be surprised at who you'd bump into. They're not just patronised by the down and out.'

'Oh dear.' Effie sounded mortified. 'How could Doctor Ramsgate be reduced so low? A respectable fellow like that.'

Harry shrugged. 'I don't know. A weakness in his temperament, perhaps. The pressure of work. Who can tell? The thing is, it's not uncommon for doctors to go down that rocky road. They've got ready access to all manner of drugs to ease the nerves. Morphine, sedatives of all kinds. And once you start down that path, there's no telling where you may end up.'

'I feel so awful about it,' Effie said quietly. 'Subjecting him to that grilling by Lydia. No wonder he was acting strangely, he must have wondered whether she was trying to find out his secret. For the newspapers or something.'

'I wouldn't worry too much about it,' Harry reassured her. 'He probably just thought she was a new patient being nosy. But his addiction raises a bit of a tricky issue for me.'

'What do you mean, darling?' Effie looked at Harry anxiously.

'Judging from his behaviour when Robbie Sharkey was crook, and also from what you say, there may be a real question about whether Ramsgate is still competent to practice medicine. And we know too that he gambles more than he can afford. So that could be another issue, for the financial stability of his practice. All of that is probably a matter for Collingwood to consider, I suppose. As far as his role there goes, I mean. But more importantly, I need to think about whether I report him to the Medical Board for investigation.'

'Really?' Effie's distress was evident. 'But don't you feel sorry for him, the poor man? As you say, it's an illness.'

'I do feel sorry for him,' Harry agreed. 'But I'd be even sorrier for a patient who suffered because Ramsgate made an error of judgement, due to his condition.'

'I've been such an idiot,' Effie murmured, almost to herself. 'Will you forgive me?' And she reached across and stroked Harry's arm.

'Always, darling,' Harry reassured her, easing her down onto his lap and hugging her tightly. 'But lesson learned, eh?'

'Two lessons, I think,' Effie whispered back. 'Number one, don't jump to conclusions. Number two, trust in Harry, he knows what he's doing. Always.' And she continued to hug him tightly, her arms wrapped around his neck.

19

WEDNESDAY 30 JUNE 1897

CRAWFORD MOLLISON'S OFFICE AT the Royal Melbourne Hospital was surprisingly ill-suited to a man of his brilliance. It was a pokey little dive, stuck at the back of the hospital on the first floor, lit only by a small window overlooking a grubby courtyard, from whence wafted the faint stench of hospital waste. A single electric globe hanging from the ceiling did little to alleviate the general gloom.

'Sorry about the surroundings, Harry,' Mollison said, waving his arm to indicate the room at large. 'Temporary only, I can assure you. I've told the hospital I'm relocating if they can't find me something better. They will.'

Harry shrugged. 'I've seen worse, Molly. Reminds me a bit of Russell Street actually. I could feel right at home here.' And he settled himself into a tatty leather armchair parked in front of the great man's desk.

'The boys at the office told me you've got something interesting for me,' Harry continued, dispensing with any further niceties. 'You'd better fill me in. I take it you've found something in Maud Miller's autopsy that might be helpful?'

'I did indeed,' Mollison replied.

'What was it? Something on the corpse, I assume. Relating to cause of death?'

Mollison shook his head. 'No, nothing like that. Cause of death was clearly as indicated. Head caved in after some pretty nasty preliminary work was done on the poor woman. And the brass lamp looks like the obvious weapon of choice. I've matched up the location of the blood spatter on it to the indentations in her skull. All quite straightforward.'

'Did you send the lamp on to our fingerprint boys?' Harry asked. 'Any results back? Do we have a print on it?'

'I've got their report back,' Mollison said quickly. 'And nothing to report, I'm afraid. Our man was no fool, they assume he was wearing gloves.'

'Well, what then?' Harry was beginning to feel that the hike over from Russell Street had been a waste of time.

Mollison grinned impishly; he was clearly enjoying building the dramatic suspense. 'I did find something on the body,' he replied. 'In the woman's clothing, to be more precise.' And he opened the top drawer of his desk and produced a small, tattered notebook. He tossed it onto the desk in front of Harry.

'I found this in a concealed pocket sown into her knickers,' he explained. 'I had a quick thumb through, it's got notes about various people. My guess is she used it as a cheat sheet on her customers. To help with her fortune telling.'

Harry picked up the notebook and opened to a random page. It was exactly as Molly had suggested, a name underlined at the top of the page and underneath various jottings that seemed to be memory joggers about the person's life and circumstances.

'I think you're right,' Harry agreed, looking up at the pathologist. 'But I can't see that it helps.'

'Go to the back page,' Mollison suggested calmly.

Harry did so and examined its contents. No name this time, just the initials 'JM' at the top, and underneath, the scrawl '17 Temple'. Harry whistled softly. 'Joey's address, I'd reckon. Or where he's holed up, at least.'

'What else could it be?' Mollison replied. 'Any idea where that street is?'

Harry nodded, head down as he thumbed through a few other pages. Nothing of note, just more on Madam Zera's clients.

'I know where it is all right,' he replied eventually. 'I'd say it's the Temple Street in West Brunswick. Just around the corner from Daly Street, where his shop was. That's no surprise. It's a pretty rough sort of neighbourhood, as I remember it.'

'I imagine you'd be in a hurry to get over there then,' Mollison suggested, rising from his desk in anticipation of Harry's imminent departure.

'You're right there,' Harry agreed, shaking Molly's outstretched hand. 'Thanks for this, my friend. It should be a great help.'

'Not at all,' Mollison replied, smiling contentedly. 'And sorry to keep you in suspense for a while there. It's a little game I just can't seem to resist.'

✕

Temple Street was just as Harry had remembered it. Rows of dishevelled terrace houses, many with windows boarded up or smashed in, others with rotting front porches, their rooves yawning crazily and seemingly on the verge of collapse. And everywhere the stench, of rubbish rotting in the street, of the overflow of grossly inadequate sewerage systems, of the despair of poverty.

Number seventeen was no different from its neighbours; the same down-at-heel terrace frontage, the same dismal ambience. Harry and

Willie approached the front door grimly. Harry was not expecting a good outcome. At best they would find the place deserted and Miller fled. At worst, another corpse to add to the growing list.

Harry gently tried the door. It creaked open inwardly against his hand. He looked down at the door latch. It was long since rusted away, the only security a rudimentary bolt on the inside of the door, but now slid back.

'Keep an eye out, mate,' Harry instructed quietly, as they crossed the threshold. 'No-one here, I reckon, but you never know.'

The interior of the dwelling was as run-down as its exterior. The narrow passageway exuded a mixed odour of damp and neglect. This was offensive enough, but there was another smell that also imposed itself on Harry's senses, a smell with which he was familiar and which always turned his stomach. And Harry knew they had found Joey Miller too late.

'Watch yourself,' he muttered to Willie as they approached the open doorway. 'This won't be pretty.'

Joey Miller was lying on his back in the middle of the room, staring unseeingly at the ceiling. A black pool of blood had congealed around his head in a grotesque halo. And the left side of his head was a pulpy mess. Joey Miller had entered oblivion in the same way as his wife, his brains bashed in.

Beside the body lay a short length of rusty steel pipe, one end covered in blood and gore. Obviously the murder weapon, and obviously brought onto the premises for that purpose. Not much point in looking for fingerprints there, Harry thought, our man's too clever for that. But we'll send it off anyway.

He sighed and looked about. The room was untidy and neglected, but it had not been trashed. Clearly Joey's killer had come with the sole purpose of obliterating him from the face of the earth. He was not searching for anything else. Good, Harry thought to himself, we might have got lucky. Small mercies, perhaps.

Harry turned to Willie. 'We'll leave him as he is. I'll get Molly down here as soon as possible. You stay here and secure the premises. And keep the rats away from him too, they've already made a start, I reckon.'

'Sure thing,' Willie replied steadily, though his now-pallid complexion betrayed his discomfort at the scene before him.

'But before I go, I think we'll have a quick look around,' Harry continued. 'It won't take long, there's not exactly a lot of stuff to go through.'

A quick glance in the tiny adjacent room that served as a bedroom promised little. A single bed occupied most of the room, and beside it a dilapidated bedside table. Harry produced a pair of cotton gloves from his pocket, donned them and inspected the content of the bedside table's single drawer. Nothing there of interest, just a tobacco tin, some cigarette papers, some dirty old betting tickets, a few other odds and sods, the accumulated detritus of Joey Miller's solitary life.

The living room was just as sparsely furnished, with a small table pushed against the wall, a cast-iron stove standing in front of a bricked-in fireplace, a stained porcelain sink sitting below a single water tap, a mantle above the fireplace, bare of any adornments, and a battered old cupboard or wardrobe against the far wall, one of its two hinged doors swung halfway open.

'Wonder if our man had a look in here,' Harry muttered, as much to himself as to Willie, as he approached the wardrobe.

Harry carefully swung both doors open, doing his best not to touch the metal handles. They creaked open on rusty hinges, revealing precious little within. The cupboard appeared to serve both as Joey Miller's wardrobe and kitchen dresser. On the top shelves, a couple of piles of clothing and on those below, a few plates, cups and cutlery, a saucepan or two and a dirty frying pan. On the floor of the cupboard lay a couple of pairs of shoes and an old umbrella.

Harry carefully felt through the clothing and ran his hand inside each of the shoes. Nothing. He knew what he was looking for and it wasn't here. He looked over at the table: it was bare. But then he noticed what was not visible from the doorway. The table had a drawer in one side, facing the far wall.

Here's hoping, Harry thought, as he gently pulled the drawer open.

'Blow me down,' he exclaimed under his breath, as he lifted two bottles from within.

One was unlabelled and half-filled with liquid. The second contained a white powder, and in contrast was clearly labelled, in faded red lettering: '*Strychnine, caution.*' And below it '*J.E.C.F. Harper and Co, Druggists, Madison, Indiana.*'

Harry turned to Willie, smiling grimly. 'Finally, mate, a break. Our man has got careless.'

'I'm not sure I follow,' Willie replied uncertainly. 'Are you saying this proves Miller was the murderer?'

'No, mate, just the opposite.' And Harry waved the bottle of liquid in front of his puzzled colleague. 'If this turns out to be what I think it is, it may well prove his innocence. Of murder, at least. Not that it really matters now, I suppose,' he added drily, with a glance down at the crumpled body on the floor.

✕

20

THURSDAY 1 JULY 1897

'MY GOODNESS, HARRY, YOU'RE good for business. I can hardly keep up with you.'

Crawford Mollison's attempt at gallows humour was lost on Harry this morning. He was tired and worn down, and the sight of Joey Miller, lifeless on the morgue bench, only added to his low spirits.

'Sorry, my friend, a poor attempt at humour,' Mollison added hastily, noting Harry's grim demeanour.

'That's all right,' Harry replied. 'Too many murders in too short a time, I'm afraid. A bit hard to see the humorous side.'

'Of course, Harry, of course.'

'But we're making progress,' Harry went on, endeavouring to put a bit more good cheer into the conversation. 'I'm hopeful this will be the last body you'll see. On this case at least. Now, what have you got for me?'

Mollison turned to the corpse. Miller was recognisable laying there, but only barely so. The left side of his head was largely caved in, the gory mess even more hideous than the sight Harry had witnessed yesterday. Mollison had been poking about in the wound, no doubt looking for evidence. Harry, for all his hardened exposure to this sort of thing, still felt a wave of nauseous revulsion.

Mollison pointed to the massive wound. 'Well, again you don't need to be a genius to work out the cause of death. Basically, a couple of decent whacks and he was done for.'

'And the murder weapon?'

Mollison indicated the steel pipe, lying on a bench nearby. 'You were right, Harry. That piece of pipe was undoubtedly the culprit. The indentations in the skull match its shape pretty well. I'm not sure that tells you anything you didn't already know.'

'True. But it's good to get it confirmed, at any rate.'

'Bit arrogant, our man, don't you think? Not even bothering to remove the murder weapon?'

'Yes, I suppose,' Harry agreed. 'Though when you think about, it was probably safer for him to leave it behind. He knew it wouldn't help us at all. I guarantee you found no fingerprints, right?'

'None whatsoever. Nothing to help identify the killer. Leaves us entirely in the dark, I suppose.'

'Not entirely,' Harry replied. 'Our man is smart, but he should have had a better look around Miller's joint. I'm hoping those two bottles I sent through to you will tell us a bit. Particularly the liquid. Have you had a chance to analyse it?'

'Of course, did it myself. No need to go elsewhere when I know more about pharmacology than anyone else around the place.'

Harry smiled slightly at Mollison's unabashed self-confidence. 'And you found?'

'Well, the powder was pure strychnine, as you would expect. But what I found in the bottle of liquid was rather interesting.'

'A strychnine solution?' Harry asked.

'Indeed it was. As per the note you sent through, I analysed a volume most likely to be used in an intramuscular injection and established the concentration of strychnine in that amount. I worked it out at two grains.'

For once, Harry felt himself in the dark. 'Doesn't sound much? Would that be enough to poison someone?'

'Damn near poison an elephant, I'd say. A twentieth of a grain is about as much as any doctor would apply for therapeutic purposes. So we're talking about forty times the safe level. Guaranteed to kill, that's for sure.'

Harry nodded slowly. 'Right, I see. That's helpful.'

Mollison assumed a puzzled air. 'Can't see how. Just seems to point to Miller as the likely killer. And he's now dead. So what's going on? An accomplice, you think?'

'Not necessarily,' Harry replied, then added, 'Your results eliminate a couple of other possibilities I've been working on. Thanks. As I said, very useful.'

Mollison smiled and patted Harry on the shoulder. 'That's all right, Harry, no need to tell me anymore. I can see you like to play your cards close to your chest. I can appreciate that, it's exactly the way I like to operate too.'

✕

Harry made his way around the Victoria Park terrace, his destination the small group of figures gathered together in front of the clubrooms, silhouetted against the glow of a single globe. In the gathering murk, he could just make out the burly figure of Bill Strickland out on the ground, leading the players in some sort of calisthenics.

As he approached the clubrooms, Harry recognised Ernie Copeland and Wal Lee, Copeland, as always, in his suit and rose-adorned lapel, and Wal Lee towering over him in his head trainer's large white coat. With them was Jimmy Johnston, his portly frame also squeezed into a white coat. All three men were watching the players out on the ground and it was not until he was close at hand that they noticed him approaching.

'Oh, it's you, Harry,' Copeland exclaimed and there was a discernible note of alarm in his voice.

Reasonable in the circumstances, Harry thought.

'What brings you out on a cold night like this?' Copeland continued. And then, more urgently. 'Do you have news about Joey?'

'I'm afraid I do, Ernie,' Harry replied, and got straight to the point. 'I'm sorry to say we found him yesterday at his premises. He'd been murdered.'

'Murdered? That's terrible.'

In the gloom, Harry couldn't clearly make out the expressions of the three men, but Copeland's tone betrayed his shock.

'So you were right,' Copeland continued sombrely. 'It seems Joey knew too much. Poor little bugger.'

'Certainly seems that way,' Harry replied. 'I'm sorry we couldn't get to him in time.'

'How was he killed?' Lee asked quietly. 'Was it … violent?'

'I won't go into detail,' Harry replied. 'Best you don't know, Wal.'

Copeland sighed. 'It just seems to go from bad to worse. It's just catastrophic for the club. Particularly since there's this dreadful suspicion that the culprit could be involved in the club in some way.'

'It's certainly alarming, to say the least,' Harry agreed. 'And that's why it's so important we track down the murderer urgently. So, I'd appreciate your thoughts about Joey Miller.' Harry glanced across at the two trainers. 'From all three of you actually, in respect of his work here at the club.'

Copeland looked at Wal Lee. 'You'd be best placed to inform the Inspector about that.'

The big man nodded and replied quietly. 'Certainly. What would you like to know?'

Harry looked out at the players on the ground, hardly discernible now in the chilly gloom. He wrapped his coat more tightly around himself, before going on. 'Well, it's come to our notice that Miller was previously involved in some sort of medical business. With Mr Stansforth, actually.'

'Really?' Lee replied impassively. 'I was unaware of that. What sort of medical business?'

'We're not entirely sure,' Harry replied. 'Treating people in some kind of way. The words 'medical electro-therapeutics' were used to describe his techniques.'

Lee shrugged. 'That's news to me. He never mentioned any of that, to me at least. What about you, Jimmy?'

Unexpectedly, Johnston responded vehemently, 'He was a crackpot, that's what he was! Always carrying on with all that rubbish. And trying to lord it over me, trying to make out he knew more than I would ever know. Good riddance, if you ask me.'

'Goodness me, Jimmy,' Copeland cut in quickly. 'If you had concerns, why didn't you tell me about them? Are you saying he was carrying out irregular practices here at the club?'

'I guarantee you he was not!' Lee interrupted curtly. 'You're not saying that, are you, Jimmy?'

'No, I'm not,' Johnston admitted sulkily. 'Not that I knew of, anyway. But he was always spouting on about his treatments and how they were the latest thing.'

'You really should have talked to me about this,' Copeland reiterated. 'I had no idea he had those kinds of ideas.'

'I couldn't really, Mr Copeland.'

'Whyever not?'

Johnston hung his head slightly before replying in an aggrieved tone, 'It's just that I knew Mr Stansforth brought him into the club, and

I thought I might get into trouble with him, and with you too, if I said anything.'

Copeland was about to remonstrate further, but Harry interrupted him. 'Never mind. No harm done. One other thing, Ernie. I couldn't help but notice that Miller's living conditions were rather, well … reduced. He appeared to be doing it very tough, in fact.'

Copeland shook his head. 'I'm sorry to hear that, I really am. But I knew nothing about his lifestyle, and it's really got nothing to do with us.'

Harry nodded. 'I assume he couldn't rely on his wage as a trainer here to survive.'

'Certainly not,' Copeland replied emphatically. 'We paid him a small allowance. To help cover his time here. But it wasn't much, about twenty quid over the season. We think that's very reasonable, but it's certainly not enough to live on. It's a labour of love here, after all.'

'Understood,' Harry replied. 'I'm not aware Miller had any other employment, and I was just wondering if he'd been seeking extra work around the club? He hadn't approached you, Wal?'

'He had not,' Lee replied firmly. 'And I wouldn't have offered him anything, even if I could. He did his job, but I didn't have a particularly high opinion of him.'

Copeland said nothing, just nodded slightly to confirm this assessment of Miller's character.

Harry saw that the footballers were making their way off the oval now, and one of them was loitering nearby. Danny Robinson made his way into the circle of light.

'Excuse me, Inspector.'

'Danny,' Harry replied encouragingly. 'Good to see you again. You want to talk to me? Privately?'

Robinson glanced around at the group of officials, shrugged and replied, 'No, it's all right, I've got nothing to hide. It's just that I might have some information for you.'

'Go on.'

'Remember, you mentioned to me out at the dogs about Robbie coming into some money?'

'I remember. You couldn't help me at the time. About any big wins he might have had.'

'That's right. But since then I've thought about what you said and I've remembered something Robbie said to me.'

'Go on, Danny. What did he say?' Robinson now had Harry's full attention.

'It's not about his punting. But we were talking in the pub once, and he winked at me and said, 'I've got a new sponsor. And he's going to be very generous."

'Really?' Harry looked at him keenly. 'That's all he said about it?'

'That was it. He wouldn't say any more.' Robinson looked slightly disappointed at the modest impact of his revelation. 'I know it doesn't sound much,' he added. 'But at the time I thought it sounded odd.'

'You're right, it was odd,' Harry reassured him. 'And it tells me a bit, I think. It's useful information, thanks for coming forward.'

'No trouble,' Robinson replied. 'Hope it helps to catch the bastard who did that to Robbie.' He turned and headed off towards the clubrooms to join his mates.

'Well, that's it, gentlemen,' Harry declared, turning back to the others. 'Thanks for your help, I'll let you get back to your work.'

'A word before you go, Harry,' Copeland said, motioning to the other two to head off and attend to their duties.

Once he and Harry were alone, Copeland spoke again. 'What do you make of what Danny was saying? Do you think Robbie was getting some sort of extra underhand payment from someone?'

'Don't know how you could interpret it any other way,' Harry replied sombrely.

'This could be very bad for the club,' Copeland continued anxiously. 'I hope it's not a sign of some degree of corruption. It's something Bill as president, all of us really, are most anxious to avoid. There's been too many scandals across the league in recent times.'

'To be honest, Ernie, it doesn't look good. But I don't think it's likely to be widespread corruption. More likely Sharkey indulging in a bit of friendly blackmail, I'd say.'

'Blackmail?' Copeland didn't sound relieved by this revelation.

'Yeah, I'd say so. Which, to my way of thinking, gives us a far better motive for murder, rather than an overly zealous lady barracker with a syringe instead of a hat pin, for example. Or even an SP bookie looking to recoup a bad debt.'

'I suppose it does. I must say, you seem to be making some progress on the case. Getting close to an arrest, do you think?'

Harry nodded. 'I think so. A couple more pieces of the jigsaw puzzle to fill in and we might be there.' Then he immediately wondered whether he had been too forthcoming. He trusted Ernie Copeland implicitly, but things were getting quite delicate. 'I can't say too much. In fact, I shouldn't really have told you that. Hold it in confidence for the moment, could you?'

Copeland rubbed his chin. 'I appreciate what you're saying, Harry, but I feel duty-bound to advise my president about the direction this thing is taking. It's likely to be of great significance for our club, and I feel as though we need to be prepared for whatever transpires. You know, once you're in a position to act and it all becomes public.'

'Fair enough,' Harry agreed reluctantly. 'Talk to Mr Beazley, by all means. But be as discreet as you can. And it's to go no further than you two.'

'Count on it, Harry.' Copeland sounded greatly relieved. 'Thank you, my friend and now I'll let you go. I know you've got a lot on your plate.'

✕

21

HARRY WALKED INTO THE interview room at Russell Street, sat down next to Willie Milton and surveyed the two men sitting opposite them. He fancied he had never seen two people less keen to be in each other's company. Bill Hanrahan and George Winton sat stiffly in their seats, both doing their very best to ignore the other's presence.

'Morning gentlemen,' Harry began convivially. 'Good of you both to make yourselves available.'

A surly greeting from Winton, an incoherent grunt from Hanrahan.

Harry grinned. 'No need to be down in the mouth, boys. After all, we're all friends here. I understand you two blokes know each other pretty well?'

'I don't think so,' Winton replied. 'I might have seen this chap around the track a bit, but that's about it.'

'Not what I've heard, George,' Harry replied, his smile still intact. 'In fact, I've been advised that Mr Hanrahan here is in your employ. On a part-time basis, but in your employ, nevertheless.'

Winton's florid hue deepened as he glanced quickly at Hanrahan. The latter said nothing and continued to stare ahead.

'Well, I suppose it's possible he might have done some work for me,'

Winton conceded. 'But only very occasionally, and it would have been a good while ago.'

Harry's smile disappeared and he leaned in towards Winton. 'We can easily disprove that. We have witnesses who will testify that you employ Hanrahan here on a regular basis. I would advise you to stop mucking about and tell the truth. Or things will go very badly for you.'

Winton stared at Harry, opening his mouth to speak, but no words came.

'Well then,' Harry continued, 'let me repeat the question. Is it accurate to say that Mr Hanrahan here is in your employ on a regular basis?'

Winton muttered an affirming grunt, again glancing nervously across at Hanrahan as he did so.

'Good,' Harry said, leaning back again in his chair. 'Make a note of that, Willie. Mr Winton was replying in the affirmative.'

Then turning to Hanrahan, Harry smiled again. 'Now, time to jog your memory too, Bill. I can see you're not a real talker, but let's see if you can at least help me with this.'

Hanrahan stopped examining his hands and fixed Harry with an angry stare.

'Tell me, are you acquainted with a fellow by the name of Danny Robinson?'

'Never heard of him,' Hanrahan spat out.

'Really?' Harry sounded surprised. 'Danny Robinson, the Collingwood footballer? You've never met him.'

'Never.'

'That's odd,' Harry went on, calmly. 'Because both I and Constable Milton here have witnessed you talking to Danny Robinson over the past two weeks. On two separate occasions. And not just a g'day either, a decent conversation in both cases. It seemed like you knew each other pretty well. Certainly, Danny Robinson told me he knows you.'

Hanrahan's stare turned from defiant to alarmed. 'You're lyin', copper,' he exclaimed. 'You never seen nothing. If you're so smart, tell me when I was meant to see this bloke.'

'Well, how does Sunday a week ago at the Plumpton, and last Saturday at Victoria Park sound to you? And if you want a bit more detail, how about last Saturday behind the groundsman's shed at Victoria Park? At approximately one o'clock.'

At this revelation, Hanrahan's attitude did an about-turn. 'So what?' he proclaimed vehemently. 'So what if I did meet with Danny? There's no law against that, is there? So bugger off, copper!'

Harry leaned forward slightly and when he spoke, his pleasant tone had evaporated. 'Actually, Mr Hanrahan, we're not so much interested in you meeting with Danny Robinson. What we're really wondering is why you handed him a very large amount of cash in a paper bag? Was that under instruction from Mr Winton here?'

'No, no,' George Winton exclaimed hurriedly. 'I had nothing to do with it. Nothing at all.'

For the first time Hanrahan turned to face Winton, and Harry noted the look of unrestrained fury on his face.

'You lyin' bastard!' he burst out angrily. 'You're not gonna dob me in for this, you fat turd!'

George Winton shrank back involuntarily, his normally florid features blanched with fear. 'Steady on, Bill,' he muttered, then turned back to Harry. 'I'm sorry, Inspector. I think I'm mistaken, actually. Bill was acting on my behalf. He was settling a bet for me.'

'Really?' Harry raised his eyebrows. 'Strange time and place to be settling a bet. I'm sorry, but I don't go along with that yarn. Want me to tell you what I think it was all about?'

Winton said nothing, just stared at Harry, open-mouthed. Hanrahan had adopted a sullen preoccupation with the far wall.

'See, George, this is what I think was going on. You and Bill here were conspiring with Danny Robinson to fix the game last Saturday. To get Saint Kilda up against the Pies. I have it on good authority that you were offering very attractive odds on a Collingwood win, far better than could be justified on form. And my people tell me that Robinson put in a real shocker on Saturday. So he was fulfilling his part of the bargain.'

Winton seemed to have recovered some equilibrium. 'Really, Inspector, that's just speculation. You can't prove any of it.' But he sounded far from confident.

Harry continued, 'And I reckon we'll have a real good chance of tracing some of the big bets held by John Wren on a Saint Kilda victory back to you, George. Through your mate here, or another one of your enforcers. You were going to clean up on both fronts.'

'You can't prove any of that! You're bluffing!' Winton protested vehemently, but his outrage sounded forced.

Harry just smiled benignly and went on, 'You haven't heard the most important part of my theory yet. You see, I reckon you blokes also tried to fix the result of the Collingwood–Carlton game two weeks before that. And you tried to rope in Robbie Sharkey to be part of your scheme. After all, you knew he was a mad punter, so it was well worth a go. And if he took a dive, there was a real good chance of Carlton getting up. But he pulled out at the last minute, so you went to more extreme measures. You bumped him off.'

Winton's restored bravado dissolved as quickly as it had appeared. 'No, no, I swear I had nothing to do with the Sharkey business. I mean, how could I have killed him? I wasn't even there!'

'I reckon you were in cahoots with Joey Miller, to slip Sharkey a dose of strychnine. And when Joey started to get a bit nervous about getting caught, you got your handyman here to bump him off too.'

'No way!' This time it was Hanrahan professing his innocence. 'No way! I might have been helping this clown to fix both those games, but no way I was involved in those two blokes getting done in.'

'Thanks, Bill,' Harry responded calmly. 'I'll take it that you'll be happy to swear to being part of the fixes?'

'Yeah,' muttered Hanrahan, less than enthusiastically as he realised the import of his words. 'But not the other business, you get me?'

'And what about you, George? Happy to confess to match-fixing?'

'I suppose so,' Winton replied, the front gone from him completely. 'But like Bill says, we had nothing to do with Robbie Sharkey. Or that Miller bloke. You have to believe us.'

Harry leaned back in his chair and folded his arms. 'I have to say, George, I'm amazed at your front. Pulling the same scan last Saturday as you tried to do the day Sharkey was killed. Even after you knew we were sniffing about.'

Winton scowled. 'It was Robinson's idea,' he muttered. 'I just went along with it. Thought you blokes'd be too busy on the Sharkey business to notice anything.'

'Nice to know we're underestimated,' Harry observed. 'Anyway, I'll get Constable Milton to get a statement from you both. We'll notify you in due course as to what charges may arise. As to the other, the Sharkey investigation, we're keeping an open mind about your involvement. You can be sure we'll be checking both your alibis. And we'll be calling you back in if we need to. So, I'll leave you with Constable Milton, and I'll bid you good morning.'

And Harry left the interview room, taking care that his satisfied smile did not appear until he had shut the door behind him.

The gold lettering on the polished oak door read, 'W D Beazley MLA.' Harry knocked firmly and waited. The door swung open to reveal the familiar round features of Ernie Copeland.

'Morning, Harry. Sorry to drag you away from the case, but Mr Beazley was most anxious to meet with you. He's rather worried about where all this will end up.'

'Understandable,' Harry murmured as he followed Copeland into William Beazley's parliamentary office.

That gentleman rose from his desk, shook Harry's hand cordially and invited him to be seated at a round table set off to one side. Harry settled into one of the comfortable leather chairs, smiled at the Collingwood president and waited. He had a good inkling of what was coming. The Collingwood leadership was obviously worried about the impact of the murders on the club's reputation. Harry suspected they would be a good deal more worried after he revealed what he had uncovered that morning.

'Thank you for seeing me at such short notice, Inspector,' Beazley began. 'I appreciate you're a busy man.'

'Always,' Harry replied. 'But more than happy to assist, if I can.'

'It's about this Sharkey business, of course,' Beazley continued.' I … we're very worried about its impact on the club.'

'Of course,' Harry agreed. 'Entirely understandable. But not much I can do about that, I'm afraid. Except sort the thing out as quick as we can and get it all behind us. The worst is always when it's still up in the air. That's when all the wild rumours start.'

'Yes, yes, exactly, I agree completely.' Beazley leaned forward intently. 'That's exactly what we can't afford: wild rumours. There's been enough scandal already in the football world – match-fixing, underhand payments, that sort of thing. We don't want any more. Not at Collingwood, at any rate. This club has been founded on the highest moral principles. I have great ambitions for us to be a model for the entire football league, indeed for the whole community.'

'Very commendable,' Harry murmured, hoping that his response sounded suitably complimentary. Though his experience of Collingwood supporters, and their various antics, rather flew in the face of the president's moral ambitions.

'And my committee is right behind me, of course,' Beazley continued. 'They too are very concerned about this terrible business.'

'Fair enough,' Harry agreed. 'But again, I can't see what that's got to do with me.'

'They, like me, want to get on top of the spurious rumours and innuendo that are flying about. To that end, they've asked me to report regularly on progress in the case, so that we can scotch some of the nonsense that's getting about.'

Harry wondered whether John Wren might have something to do with the president's concerns. Harry had heard a number of rumours that implicated Wren in Sharkey's death in various ways.

'Mr Beazley, I can understand why you and the committee would want to get on the front foot. For our part, the police would have no issue with the club publicly responding to unfounded rumours.'

Beazley leaned back and began drumming on the desktop with his fingers. 'That's just it. Inspector. We're not in a position to put paid to these rumours, unless we know they're untrue. And at the moment, we really know nothing about where the case is going. Except that Sharkey was murdered, and Joey Miller too, and there is some sort of intimation that the murderer may be someone with knowledge of the club.'

Harry realised where this meeting was going and to a great degree he empathised with William Beazley. The man was a straight shooter, a community-minded reformer, whose involvement with the Collingwood footy club was genuinely altruistic. But there was absolutely no way he could take Beazley, or the committee, into his full confidence about his growing understanding of the reasons behind Sharkey's death, and his rapidly narrowing list of suspects.

'I'm very sorry, but I'm just not in a position to give any further information to you at this time. We're at a sensitive stage of the investigation.' Harry hoped his words did not sound too much like he was fobbing off this very worthy man. Which he was, of course.

Beazley leaned back resignedly, then glanced across at Copeland, before resuming. 'I appreciate that, but are you able to tell us anything at all? For example, whether you expect to make an arrest in the near future? At the moment we're completely in the dark, and we have a committee meeting this afternoon at which my members expect to be briefed on where things are up to.'

Harry returned the president's gaze and considered what he should say. There were some things the committee definitely should not know about. But on the other hand, there might be other information that he could let slip that wouldn't impede the investigation, indeed might actually be useful.

'I completely understand your concerns, Mr Beazley,' he replied eventually. 'But you must appreciate that we're at a critical point in the investigation and I'm not at liberty to reveal the exact details you might be seeking. But I think I can reveal a couple of aspects of the investigation that may be of interest and may hopefully provide some comfort to your committee.

'Firstly, we are confident that all four murders that have occurred – Robert Sharkey, Richard Thames, Joey Miller and his wife – all these are linked, and are the work of one person. Secondly you can emphasise to your committee what I've already told Ernie, that we're very close to resolving the crimes and making an arrest. As I said to him, it's just a matter of fitting in the last couple of pieces of the jigsaw puzzle.'

Beazley seemed mildly pleased.

'That is comforting, Inspector,' he said. 'If anything positive can come of this horrible business, it's that we catch the villain responsible as quickly as possible, and get our lives, and the life of the club, back to normal. Though I doubt anything will be quite normal again after this.' Beazley rose from behind his desk and extended his hand.

But Harry didn't take it, instead motioning the president to resume his seat. 'Unfortunately, sir, there is another matter that I must advise you of. I'm afraid it will give rise to some … further difficulties for you.'

Both men looked at Harry, alarm writ large on their faces. 'What do you mean?' Copeland exclaimed. 'Has there been another murder?'

'No, no, Ernie, nothing like that. But it's something that will be viewed as a scandal within the football world, and it's something you blokes will need to act on quickly.' And Harry proceeded to inform them of the morning's revelations, and of Danny Robinson's involvement in the match-fixing scandal. As he spoke, both men listened grimly, their faces set.

'Thank you, Inspector,' the president said eventually. 'Rest assured we'll take immediate and strong action. Mr Robinson will no longer be part of our organisation.'

Copeland cut in, 'But are you sure the scheme was only limited to Robinson? In terms of the players, I mean.'

'I think so,' Harry reassured him. 'But, of course, we can't be sure at this stage. You'll need to make your own inquiries.'

Copeland continued. 'And from what you're saying, you think this match-fixing lurk of Robinson's had nothing to do with Sharkey's murder? Robbie wasn't part of their scheme?'

'I don't believe so,' Harry replied promptly. 'Although I'm sure they tried to rope him in. But I think Robbie refused. Not sure whether it was particularly out of loyalty, probably more that he was too proud of his own reputation to deliberately play poorly, in order to throw a game. Anyway, the fact that he laid a huge bet with George Winton on Collingwood to beat Carlton showed me he wasn't in on match-fixing, not for that game anyway.'

'But could he have been murdered for not taking part?' Copeland suggested. 'Getting rid of Sharkey would go a long way to pulling off their match-fix.'

'Undoubtedly,' Harry agreed. 'Believe me, I've thought long and hard about that possibility. But in the end, I don't think it's plausible. It's not Hanrahan's preferred style, for a start. He'd be more likely to give Sharkey a good old-fashioned bashing to put him out of action. And the other murders – Richard Thames, Miller and his missus – I'm sure they're linked to Sharkey's killing as well. And what would all their deaths have to do with the match-fixing scheme?'

Copeland nodded slowly. 'I see what you mean. That is hard to explain.'

'Tell me, Inspector,' Beazley interjected, 'what will the police do? About the match-fixing, I mean. Do you intend to take action against this bookmaker? And Robinson, for that matter?'

'We'll see what can be done,' Harry replied. 'In my opinion it should be a criminal offence, fraud actually, though it may be difficult to get a conviction. But we'll see. Now gentlemen, I'll leave you to it. We're all very busy at the moment.'

'That's for sure,' Copeland agreed, rising and shaking Harry's hand firmly. Beazley did the same, patting Harry on the shoulder to express his appreciation. Copeland accompanied Harry out into the corridor.

'Thanks Harry,' he said quietly. 'It's tough times, that's for sure. But we'll get through it. Let's keep working together.'

'Sure thing, mate,' Harry agreed. 'Hopefully we're getting close to seeing daylight at the end of the tunnel. I think I know what happened now. Well, pretty much anyway. I just need a bit more proof. It's like any investigation, there's a vast difference between knowing and proving it.'

'Of course,' Copeland replied. 'Can I tell the committee that? That you're in the know, but you need to prove it.'

Harry thought again, before replying. 'I can't see why not. Yes, there's no reason you can't say that. If you feel the need.'

✕

The hansom cab made its way down Pleasance Street towards number thirty-two. Inside sat Harry Holloway and Rachel Starkey, the latter looking demurely pretty in her best outfit. She had been surprisingly talkative during their journey, responding brightly to Harry's conversational overtures, all carefully aimed at future hopes and possibilities, and avoiding the recent tragic event.

'Here we are, Rachel,' Harry indicated, as they drew up at the Holloway residence. 'Come in and meet Effie.'

But Effie was not the first person they encountered as they entered the small lobby. Instead it was Harry's parents, Clem and Millie, on their way out.

'Oh, hello dear,' Millie greeted Harry. 'We've just dropped Alfie back. Effie said you had a visitor tonight.' And she smiled welcomingly at Rachel.

Harry performed the introductions, then began to shepherd Rachel into the house, as he bade his parents goodnight. But Clem was studying Rachel inquiringly.

'You look a bit familiar, love,' he observed. 'Have we met some-where before?'

'I don't think so,' Rachel replied, smiling politely.

Clem continued to gaze at Rachel in a puzzled kind of way, trying to place her.

'Where do you work?' he asked.

'At Mr Stansforth's shop in Johnston Street. Exotic Interior Design.'

'Blimey!' Clem exclaimed. 'We've never been in there, that's for sure. Oh well, perhaps we seen you in the street or something. We shop down Johnston Street as a rule.'

'I shop, you mean,' Millie chimed in. 'Precious little you do in that department, my man. Now come on, you old codger, you've probably got Miss Sharkey mixed up with someone else. Stop badgering the poor girl and let's get you home.'

And she proceeded to steer Clem out the door, but not before a parting word to Harry. 'Make sure you look after that wife of yours, Harry. She's had a long week, and she's very tired.'

'Come through and meet the boss,' Harry suggested to Rachel. 'She's giving the little fellow his dinner in the kitchen.'

They found Effie sitting at the table with Alfie, who was doing a sterling job of demolishing a plateful of stew. He offered a toothy grin to Rachel. Effie rose, intending to shake Rachel's hand.

'It's lovely to meet you,' she said. 'I'm so sorry for the loss of your brother. It must be terrible for you and your family.' And with that, she forsook the handshake and gave Rachel a warm hug instead.

'Right,' Harry said promptly, noticing the tears welling in Rachel's eyes. 'You two have a bit to discuss before dinner, so why don't I keep an eye on Alfie, and the roast in the oven, while you relax in the parlour? Effie will give you the good oil on what you need to do to become a teacher. I'll have this bloke tucked up in bed in fifteen minutes.'

Naturally fifteen minutes turned into thirty, but Harry didn't mind. He knew Effie had plans for Rachel that involved part-time work at Merton Hall while she worked her way through teachers' training college. And after that, a promise from the Misses Hensley for Rachel to join the staff, subject to satisfactory performance in her part-time role. From the kitchen, he could hear Effie prattling on excitedly, and the occasional quiet word or two from Rachel as she responded to some query or other.

Finally Alfie was fed, tucked up in bed, and read to. It must have been a big day at Nanna's because, barely two pages into his favourite picture book, he was sound asleep. Harry tiptoed from the room just as a loud rat-a-tat sounded on the front door.

Descending the flight of stairs in a few bounds, Harry was past the two women and into the lobby before Effie needed to rise.

'I wonder who that could be,' he said casually as he hurried past, managing to slip Effie a surreptitious wink at the same time. The door was opened to reveal Willie Milton standing there, scrubbed up and in his Sunday best, hair neatly plastered to his scalp.

'Am I late, boss?' he asked, a trifle breathlessly. 'I popped into the pub for a couple on the way, I'm in a little bit of a flap. Want to make a good impression.'

'Don't worry, mate, just sit there and look the part,' Harry suggested, grinning. 'Neither of us will be able to get a word in edgewise, anyway. Effie's off and running about the teaching game. She's got a captive audience.'

Harry showed the way into the parlour. 'Look who's turned up,' he pronounced to the room at large. 'Here on business, but he hasn't eaten, so I suggested he stay for dinner. You know what these bachelors are like. Don't know how to look after themselves, and there's plenty of tucker to go round.'

'Of course,' Effie exclaimed. 'That would be lovely. You're always welcome here, Willie, and I'm sure Rachel wouldn't mind if you joined us. Would you, Rachel?'

Rachel's pink glow and quiet smile seemed to answer the question, but she spoke up promptly. 'I don't mind at all. Constable Milton and

I have met a couple of times. At Mr Stansforth's, during his inquiries.'

'Delighted to see you again,' Willie said, putting on what he hoped was a charming smile. 'Though I think it'd be okay to go with Willie, rather than Constable, now we're away from work.'

'Good, that's settled then,' Effie proclaimed, getting to her feet and ushering her guests towards the dining room. 'Let's eat, shall we? Rachel has to be home by nine, so we'd best not waste time.'

With her husband and guests settled at table, Effie made her way to the kitchen, pausing to lean over Willie as she passed, and saying in a loud whisper, 'Goodness, that was a stroke of luck, you turning up like that, just as we were about to have dinner. You must have a sixth sense.'

And so the evening proceeded pleasantly, under the influence of roast lamb with all the trimmings, and for the men a couple of glasses of rum. Rachel was bright and animated, seeming to forget the sadness of recent weeks as she and Effie chatted about the possibilities that lay ahead. As predicted, Harry and Willie were called on to say very little. Not that Willie seemed to mind, he looked happy enough sitting there, gazing at Rachel. All too soon it was half past eight, the plum pudding had been consumed, and the allotted time had come.

'Well, Rachel,' Harry said, 'it's been very pleasant, but I promised your father I'd have you home by nine, so we'd better skedaddle. It's a good twenty minutes back to your place.'

'I'll tell you what,' Willie suggested hopefully. 'Why don't I take Rachel home in a cab? It'll save you the trouble of a trip there and back.'

'Nice try, mate,' Harry replied, 'but Rachel's dad wouldn't be too happy to see her turn up without her chaperone, and in the company of an unmarried man. Even if that unmarried man was a member of the force.'

'But you can join us for a lift home, if you like,' he added, noticing Willie's disappointed look. 'Can't see anything wrong with that. Besides, we need to have a little chat with Rachel about a couple of things on the way.'

Seeing Rachel's slightly panicked expression, Effie spoke up indignantly. 'You be careful, Harry Holloway. Don't put this poor girl under any more stress. She's had such a terrible time.'

'Don't worry,' Harry reassured. 'It's nothing too painful, I promise. Just a couple of details that she might be able to help with.'

'Well, make sure you go carefully,' Effie added sternly. 'Willie, I'm counting on you to keep him in check.'

'Absolutely,' Willie responded gallantly. 'I'll make sure of that.' And he smiled at Rachel before adding, 'Now, I'd better duck outside and find a cab or else we'll be late.'

'No need,' Harry replied. 'All taken care of. I told the cabbie to be here at half eight. He'll be waiting out there now.'

22

SATURDAY 3 JULY 1897

HARRY TUCKED INTO HIS fourth sausage with relish, fuelling himself for the long day ahead. Across the table, Alfie happily chewed on a piece of toast and jam, a fair portion of which was already spread over the table in front of him. Effie was keeping a watchful eye on him as she wandered around the kitchen, tea towel in hand, putting away the morning dishes. She was rumpled from bed and wrapped in her tatty old dressing gown, but Harry still found her confoundingly distracting. So tall and unselfconsciously elegant, her beautiful auburn hair partly free and framing her lively features, her longish nose and deep blue eyes. She caught his eyes following her around the room and broke into a smile. She liked it when she could sense his desire for her.

'She's a lovely girl,' Effie observed. 'And quite clever, I think. I'd say she's genuinely keen on taking up teaching too. It would be very good for her, I think. You know, a new start. Away from memories of the past.'

'Away from the family too,' Harry added. 'The old man's a bit strict, I'd reckon.'

'Do you think Willie's got good intentions? He's not just leading her on, is he? Not just flirting with her?'

Harry smiled, but then noticed Effie's concerned expression.

'Not if I'm any judge of character,' he replied, earnest now. 'From my experience, Willie's not a big ladies' man. I've seen him with the odd girl in tow, but nothing like this. I'd say he's smitten.'

'Good,' Effie declared, giving him a hug from behind. 'Now drink up your tea and get going. You said you had a big day.'

'Yeah, I'd better get a move on,' Harry agreed, glancing up at the kitchen clock, then rising to his feet.

'Did I hear you and Willie talking about going to the footy today? I thought you were too busy to take time off?'

'I am and we're not. Taking time off, that is. We're off to the G, Collingwood and Essendon. I reckon we're getting to the pointy end of this business and there's a couple of things I want to chase down. So, no Blues for me today.'

'Well, be careful,' Effie said softly, eying him with some concern. 'There's a very dangerous man out there somewhere.'

'There is indeed,' Harry agreed, leaning in to kiss her goodbye. 'And the sooner we get him behind bars, the better.'

><

Over lunch with her mother-in-law, Effie was just finishing her second cup of tea when they were interrupted by a knock on the door.

'Goodness me,' Millie exclaimed, starting slightly. 'Who could that be, dear? Is Harry home early?'

'I don't think so,' Effie replied. 'He said he'd be out all day. Anyway, if it was Harry, he'd let himself in.'

'Oh yes, of course. Shall I go to the door, dear?'

'No Millie, I'll get it.'

Swinging the door open revealed Rachel Starkey, standing there looking uncertain and nervous.

'Oh, hello, Mrs Holloway …'

'It's Effie, and hello to you too, Rachel. What brings you back so soon? Come in and have a cup of tea.'

Rachel shuffled nervously on the doorstep. 'Is Inspector Holloway in? I rather wanted to see him.'

'I'm sorry, he's off at the football. All day, I'm afraid. But come in anyway and have a cuppa. Perhaps I can help.'

Effie led the reluctant Rachel into the parlour, settled her down next to Millie, and went to refresh the pot.

'Now,' she enquired, as she set the cup down in front of Rachel. 'What did you need to see Harry about?'

'It's about this,' Rachel replied, producing a sheet of paper from her handbag. 'It's a letter from the football club. From Mr Beazley. Shall I read it out?'

'From Mr Beazley? That's odd. Yes, let's hear what he's got to say.'

'Here's the part that matters,' Rachel continued.

'The committee would like to make a presentation to you, in honour of your brother, immediately after today's game. If you could be at the gates of the MCG at five o'clock sharp, I will arrange for one of my staff to escort you to the Members' Lounge for a private ceremony.'

'Gosh,' Effie said, sipping contemplatively on her tea. 'That seems very strange, Mr Beazley inviting you to the club. Why not invite your father? I would have thought that more appropriate.'

'That's exactly what I thought too. But on the other hand, father has had something of a falling out with the club for some time now, so they might have been reluctant to ask him. I really think I should go. It would be very disrespectful not to. I was going to ask Inspector Holloway's opinion though.'

Effie rose and did a lap around the parlour, trying to think through this rather strange request. Rachel's eyes followed her around the room expectantly.

'Ah, I have it!' Effie said suddenly, coming to an abrupt halt.

She resumed her seat and took both Rachel's hands in hers. 'Here's what we'll do, if you're a bit worried about going alone. As I told you, Harry's at the MCG today on duty. You and I will go to the ground at the appointed time, perhaps a trifle earlier, and we'll get one of the officials to get Harry to come to the gate. I'll say we have an appointment with Inspector Holloway, that should do the trick. Then he can accompany us to the Members' Lounge to ensure that everything is above board. And he can take us home afterward.'

'Are you sure that will be all right?' Rachel was now looking decidedly worried. 'I'd hate to get in the inspector's way while he's working. Are you sure he wouldn't mind?'

'Quite sure,' Effie replied briskly. 'The game will be over by then, and he's bound to be free to meet us.'

Millie, whose concerned look was becoming more pronounced, now spoke up. 'Effie dear, that sounds rather exhausting. Are you sure you're up to it?'

Effie eyed her mother-in-law with a fond, but dismissive look. 'Really Millie, I'm not an invalid. It'll just be a pleasant Saturday afternoon excursion. And it will be lovely for Rachel to be presented with something to remember Robbie. It really is rather thoughtful of them.'

✕

Effie and Rachel laboured along Jolimont Road, from the tram stop towards the MCG gates. That is to say, Effie laboured while Rachel politely kept pace with her. Despite her confident assertions to her mother-in-law, Effie had found the journey rather tiring. As a result, they would not now arrive at the gates early as planned and would not have time to call for Harry before meeting with Mr Beazley's official. No matter, she was sure he wouldn't mind waiting while they summonsed Harry.

For some reason, a feeling of uneasiness had come over Effie as their journey progressed. Whether it was because she was feeling so tired, or perhaps because of the rather odd nature of their mission, but she couldn't help feeling strangely anxious. She said nothing to Rachel, of course, who was already anxious enough, but instead strove to calm herself, imagining the always safe presence of Harry, who would soon be at their side and as he always did, would make anxiety melt away with his relaxed self-confidence.

But then she happened to glance back down the other side of Jolimont Road and noticed a man strolling along, walking in the same direction as them, but fifty yards or so behind. He was wearing a large greatcoat and cloth cap pulled down over his eyes, and there was something vaguely familiar about his gait. None of that would have been of concern to Effie, except that she was certain she'd noticed the same figure loitering about while they were waiting for the tram at their Brunswick Street stop. But perhaps that was someone else. After all, she hadn't been paying close attention at Brunswick Street. She just had an odd impression that the man with a cap had been watching them.

Silently exhorting herself to buck up, Effie endeavoured to quicken her pace as they approached the park and the turn-off to the MCG. She glanced at the wristwatch Harry had given her for her birthday: five minutes past five, they were a touch late.

'We'd better get a move on,' she panted, quite out of breath, as they hurried through the park. They were heading towards the fenced laneway that funnelled to the MCG entrance area, and to the row of turnstiles flanked by large gates on either side. The game must have just recently ended because Effie could see that these gates had been opened to allow the patrons to exit. Already a largish number of bedecked supporters were streaming through and down the laneway towards them.

'This is a nuisance,' she exclaimed, as more and more spectators surged through the gates. 'Stay close to me,' she added. 'We'll just wait by the gate until they've gone through.'

But Effie had badly underestimated the size of the crowd pouring through the gates and pushing their way down the laneway. Quickly she realised that far from waiting it out at the gates, she and Rachel had no chance of even reaching them. And the raucous mob paid no heed to the welfare of the two ladies vainly striving to work their way into the ground. Pushing and shoving, shouting congratulations or commiserations to fellow supporters and abuse to the opposition, the human wave became a force too powerful to oppose. Effie felt herself pummelled and bumped, almost knocked down. Suddenly panic-stricken, she realised her only option was to turn back and join the crowd surging back out of the ground. She also realised she had let go of Rachel's hand. Through the melee she caught a glimpse of Rachel, some ten yards away from her and being rapidly swept further away by the force of the crush.

Effie called to her and tried to point back to the way they had come, but that was useless. She could scarcely hear herself above the din, and there was no chance she could make herself understood by Rachel. Suddenly Effie noticed something else. Amid the already boisterous crowd, a further hubbub seemed to be developing. In front of her she could see the crowd begin to move to either side, as if under the influence of some greater force. Then she saw what was happening. A very large man was forcing his way through the throng, shoving all and sundry to one side or the other as he went. And he appeared to be making a beeline for Rachel. As he burst past Effie, she could see the he had something half-hidden in his hand, perhaps a thin knife of some sort. She sensed his evil intent and tried to call a warning, but her voice could not be heard.

Just as the large man passed her, she became aware of an even larger fellow behind him, and in hot pursuit. She thought him at first some sort of accomplice, until he dived forward, crashing the first man to the ground in a perfectly executed tackle. In one swift movement he had seized the fellow's arm and twisted it behind his back, forcing the weapon from his hand. At the same time, a pair of handcuffs appeared, the other arm was twisted back to join its companion and the would-be assailant was rendered helpless.

Around them, the crowd was being quickly directed to one side or the other by a considerable number of uniformed constables, who had materialised, seemingly from nowhere. One such policeman now had Effie firmly in his grasp, his arms wrapped protectively around her. Instead of taking her to one side, he led her to the two men on the ground, one hand-cuffed and helpless, the other sitting astride him and firmly in control. And now turning anxiously towards her.

'You okay, Effie?' Harry asked, concern etched on his face. He held in his hand a hypodermic syringe, filled with a colourless liquid.

'I think so,' Effie managed to reply. 'But Rachel? Is she all right?' And she looked around for the girl she had taken into her care.

'All good there,' Harry replied, pointing towards the laneway wall where Rachel was being comforted in a more than professional way in the arms of Willie Milton, still in his greatcoat but now with his cap pushed back.

'What happened? Who is this?' Effie asked, still slightly dazed and thoroughly confused.

'This is our man,' Harry explained, pulling his captive to his feet and handing him into the care of two burly constables. 'His name is

Jeremiah Wingard and something tells me he's no longer welcome on the committee of the Collingwood Football Club.'

'And what's that?' Effie added pointing to the syringe.

'This? It's a hypodermic syringe, and I reckon that once we've analysed it, we'll find that it's filled with a lethal concentration of strychnine.'

23

SUNDAY 4 JULY 1897

EFFIE LEANED AGAINST HER husband and closed her eyes. Harry extended an arm around her shoulders and squeezed gently.

'Feeling better? Had enough adventure for the moment?'

Effie glanced up at him and smiled wearily. 'More than enough.'

In the armchair across from them, Clem Holloway shook his head. 'I still can't believe it,' he muttered. 'Jeremiah Wingard a murderer. And ... and one of them. I always took him for a real family man. After all that time, you'd reckon you'd know someone.' And he shook his head slowly, in complete bewilderment.

'Ah well, Dad,' Harry mused. 'Human nature, it's a mysterious thing. You never know what's going on with people underneath the surface.'

'It was very silly of you to go off and expose yourself to danger like that,' Millie admonished Effie. 'A woman in your condition.'

'Mum's absolutely right.' Harry added. 'You should have told me you were pregnant. If I'd known, I wouldn't have let you out of the house.'

'I'm sorry, darling. I was waiting until I was certain,' Effie replied contritely. Contrition was an emotion she rarely felt, and one which did not particularly agree with her.

'But I was trying to do the right thing,' she added. 'We thought the note was a bit odd when we read it. So I planned to call for you when we got to the ground. I just didn't reckon on that huge crowd coming out the gate.'

'Just as well you were onto him, son,' Clem observed. 'Might have been real nasty otherwise. He was obviously after that young lass with that needle.'

'You're right there, Dad, he was. And we were correct, turned out it was filled with strychnine. Highly concentrated. Seems like he got the idea from one of our first theories. That Rob Sharkey had been poisoned with a needle in the footy crowd at half-time.'

Something suddenly dawned on Effie. 'Hang on,' she bristled, 'Did you know that Mr Wingard was the killer? And did you know he would go after Rachel with that needle? I hope you weren't needlessly exposing her to danger.'

'Of course not,' Harry replied hastily. 'I mean, we didn't know what he was planning to do. But we did suspect him. And we were afraid that he'd come after Rachel. That's why I was keeping a close eye on him. And why Willie was doing the same to Rachel.'

Effie was not convinced. 'I just hope you didn't allow that to happen, just so you could catch him in the act,' she muttered.

'We didn't.' Harry was suddenly very serious. 'And trust me, you were never in danger. Willie had Constable Nelson with him, and as soon as you two left the house, Chas hot-footed it back here to warn me. So we made sure we had Wingard fully covered. And Chas had the job of making sure you came to no harm, if there was any confrontation.'

'You're forgiven then,' Effie smiled. 'But if you were so sure Wingard was the murderer, why didn't you just arrest him. Before he could threaten Rachel like that.'

'Good question, Eff. But the fact is, we didn't have enough evidence to arrest him, or prove our case. Though, as I said, we had a strong suspicion he meant harm to Rachel. So we just had to watch and wait. And hope he would do something rash. As it turned out, it was the best result, that we caught him in the act when we did.'

'You're right, dear,' Millie agreed. 'It was all for the best.'

Clem spoke again, a puzzled look on his face. 'What I don't understand, son, is why he was after the lass anyway. What had she done to him?'

'Nothing,' Harry replied. 'But she knew too much, although she didn't realise it. As I found out when Willie and I took her home on Friday night.'

'Go on,' Effie instructed, intrigued.

'She knew of her brother's relationship with Wingard. Well, not really, but Sharkey had sent her to the brickworks a couple of times to pick up a paper bag from Wingard for him. As you know, she worked close by. So Wingard got to wondering how much she knew. Was she just a courier, or did she know that the paper bags were full of cash, blackmail money? Even if she was just a courier, that's important evidence for us, if we found out. So he couldn't take the chance. And he'd already killed four times. What difference would an extra one make?'

'Right,' Effie mused. 'So he was the one who killed Rob Sharkey? And Mr and Mrs Miller? And who else? You're saying he killed Richard Thames as well?'

Harry nodded gravely. 'That's right, although I suppose technically it was Joey Miller who killed Sharkey. But in reality, it was Wingard who murdered him.'

'What?' Effie exclaimed. 'Now you're talking in riddles!'

'Well,' Harry explained, 'What I mean is, it was Miller who injected Sharkey with a lethal dose of strychnine.'

Effie was none the wiser. 'How could he have done that? Sharkey would surely have resisted.'

'Not at all. Sharkey was fully agreeable to being injected with strychnine. You see, he and Miller were in on this little scheme to boost his performance with a strychnine pick-me-up. Miller had come across this practice in his former dodgy medical dealings and sold the idea to Sharkey. Sharkey was desperate to boost his performance and he was nothing if not a risk-taker. In all aspects of his life, it seems.'

'So, Miller got hold of the strychnine, I suppose,' Effie suggested. 'From one of his former medical contacts?'

Harry shook his head. 'No, actually Sharkey stole the bottle of strychnine powder from his dad's pharmacy. He didn't visit often, but often enough to know where the key to the drugs cabinet was. And he knew that Fraser had little call for strychnine powder and was unlikely to miss it for a good while. When I saw that bottle missing from his cabinet, the penny really dropped.'

'Of course,' Effie murmured. 'But I still can't quite understand what Wingard had to do with any of that? You said it was he who really murdered Sharkey.'

'Wingard knew all about Sharkey and Miller's little scheme,' Harry replied. 'I suppose Robbie must have bragged about it to him at one time or other. He knew Wingard wouldn't rat on him, not with what Sharkey had over him.'

'What exactly did Sharkey have over him? What was their relationship?' Effie asked.

Harry glanced warily at his mother. 'I think their relationship was purely a business one,' he replied thoughtfully. 'I think Sharkey knew about … about the other side of Wingard's nature. And his inclinations. And he was making him pay to keep quiet about it.'

'But surely that's not enough for blackmail? And murder? After all, it would only be Sharkey's word against Wingard's. He could just say Sharkey was lying.'

'Obviously Sharkey had direct knowledge of Wingard's … appetites. I imagine they must have gone out on the town together, and one thing led to another and they ended up somewhere where various needs could be met.'

Harry paused and reached for his beer on the side table. A bit early in the day for Harry, but he considered it well-earned.

'And Sharkey must have had some convincing proof,' he continued. 'Witnesses perhaps, on some of their escapades together. And one witness in particular, at the end. Richard Thames. I'm certain Wingard became infatuated with him and was indiscreet in his approaches. And Sharkey would have been the first person Richard confided in.'

'The unwanted attention,' Effie said quietly. 'It was Wingard.'

Harry nodded. 'Exactly right.'

'But you still haven't told us how Wingard did it,' Clem interrupted.

'Easy,' Harry explained. 'He kept a close eye on Joey Miller and worked out where he was storing his bottle of strychnine solution in the rooms. Then he simply got an identical bottle, filled it with a highly concentrated strychnine solution, and swapped the bottles. Job done. And the beauty of it was that Joey thought he had accidentally poisoned Sharkey. And given what they were up to, he could scarcely reveal what had happened. And anyway, who would believe him? So he went into hiding.'

'Geez, Wingard was nothing if not cunning,' Clem exclaimed.

'That's for sure. Anyway, after a while Joey changed his mind,' Harry said. 'He thought about it, and thought about it, and he began to doubt that he had mistakenly killed Sharkey. Perhaps he realised he had used exactly the same solution he had used quite safely before.'

'Then he hit on the idea of having the solution tested by a pharmacist. We've checked around that part of Melbourne and found a pharmacist who can recall doing it. And of course, that test revealed a highly concentrated, fatal level of strychnine. Far higher than Joey had made up in the past. So he figured someone must have switched the bottles.'

'Did he work out it was Wingard who did the switch?' Effie asked.

'Not sure,' Harry replied thoughtfully. 'He might have. Perhaps he noticed Wingard hanging around the rooms before half-time and put two and two together. Joey told us he was sometimes required to pop down to the rooms to get something or other. Anyway, once he heard Joey wanted to talk to the committee, Wingard couldn't take the chance on how much he knew. For a start, he would know that Joey would spill the beans on how Sharkey was injected with strychnine. That would be bad enough, it would set us off on the right path to the truth. So he had to find him and get rid of him. And the only way to find him was via his wife, Maud, as we know.'

Effie looked at him quizzically. 'I can understand why Mrs Miller was killed. She would have identified him. But what about Richard Thames?'

'Similar reason. I assume Sharkey confided in him a fair bit, and Richard would have had his suspicions about what was going on. Anyway, Wingard couldn't take the chance. And I suspect that there was a fair dose of passion behind his actions as well. Anger at being spurned. And a fair degree of shame and self-loathing thrown in too, perhaps.'

Millie had been sitting silently through all these revelations, her features becoming paler and paler, and her expression more and more shocked. Harry noticed she now had tears in her eye.

'Don't worry, Mum,' he consoled her. 'It's all done with now. Let's not talk about it anymore.'

'Hang on,' Clem persisted. 'I don't want to harp on about it, but I'm blowed if I know how you settled on Mr Wingard as the murderer. And worked out how it was done.'

Harry glanced at his father, and then back at Millie. 'Well, just quickly then. First up, I had to work out how it was done. We had the 'needle in the crowd at half-time' theory as our first option. But the more I investigated that, the more fanciful it seemed. A poke in the bum with a hat needle is one thing, but injecting a big strong fellow like Sharkey would be much harder. Particularly given he came off after the rest of the team, when the supporter crush had dispersed.'

'Fair enough,' Clem interrupted. 'But why Mr Wingard?'

'Hang on, Dad, I'm coming to that. Anyway, then I got to thinking about those multiple bruises on Sharkey's bum that Molly pointed out after the post-mortem. And I got to thinking, what if they weren't hat pin marks, but instead multiple injection sites. And that would most likely mean that they had been administered with Sharkey's agreement.

'So I did a bit of research, spoke to a couple of experts in the field, and discovered that subcutaneous injection of strychnine is a known method for rapid stimulation of the muscles in the body. And has been used in a couple of notorious examples of athletes trying to get an unfair advantage. And I thought to myself, who would have both a knowledge of such a technique, and also the wherewithal to assist Sharkey in that way? And obviously, I quickly settled on Joey Miller. Who would be in any underhand scheme, if a bit of cash was forthcoming as a result.'

'Blimey, son. Well done!' Clem exclaimed. 'But how did you finger Mr Wingard? I can't see how he was connected to Miller and Sharkey.'

'No, it wasn't obvious,' Harry acknowledged. 'For a while there, I suspected Sharkey's murder was tied up with some sort of betting fix, but all our enquiries in that area came to nothing. And I just couldn't see why Sharkey would be murdered as part of a scam like that.

'Then I came around to the possibility that Sharkey had been injected voluntarily, on a number of occasions, and everything finally seemed to make sense. Actually, at first I thought perhaps his death was from an accidental poisoning by Joey, and that, somehow or other, he had got the concentration wrong. But then Richard Thames was murdered and given his connection with Sharkey, it just seemed like too much of a coincidence. And there was a piece of evidence from the post-mortem on Richard that eventually got me thinking very seriously about Jeremiah Wingard.'

'And what was that, smarty pants?' Effie interjected, looking up at her husband.

'Well, Molly pointed out a quantity of red dust on Richard's clothing. It seemed clear that he had been wrapped in something contaminated with this dust when he was transported to Albert Park. And I realised where I had seen dust very much like that. On many, many occasions.'

'Whereabouts was that?' Clem asked.

'On you, Dad. When you came home after a day at the brickworks. It was the bane of Mum's life when I was a kid. Remember, she always made you take off your clothes in the outhouse and wash up before you could have your tea.'

'Off course,' Clem clapped his hand on his knee. 'Of course, you're right.'

Harry continued. 'It wasn't hard to get Willie to pop out to the brickworks last week on the pretext of a routine interview with Wingard and gather a sample of brick dust on the way out. I had Molly compare it with what was on the clothing. A perfect match. So, I was certain we had our man.'

'I feel sorry for the Collingwood people,' Effie observed. 'Particularly Mr Beazley. I know he's a very fine person. He's done an enormous amount for his community and for ordinary working people. It must be so disappointing for him, this scandal in the club.'

'You're right, dear,' Harry replied. 'I know he'll be taking it hard. Ernie Copeland will be shattered too, no doubt. He's as straight as they come, and he's put his heart and soul into that club.'

'Is there anything you can do, darling? To help them, I mean.'

Harry nodded slowly. 'Hopefully, yes. I've managed to persuade the boss to issue a statement in *The Argus*, to the effect that we are confident this was an isolated incident and doesn't reflect any level of corruption in the club. You know, in relation to drug-taking, bribery and so on. That should help. And I'm catching up with Mr Beazley and Ernie tomorrow at the Grace Darling for a drink and a chat. I'll show them the statement and try to reassure them that it'll all blow over. Time heals everything, so they say.'

'Well done, darling,' Effie said, giving his hand a squeeze. 'I know they're the opposition, but they're part of the football family. We have to support them at times like this.'

✕

William Beazley finished reading the typed statement and handed it back to Harry. 'Thank you, Inspector, that will be most helpful. Hopefully it'll assist to put the scuttlebutt and lies to rest. It's not just among the football fraternity either, you'd be amazed where some of the comments are coming from. None of them supportive either, I can tell you.'

'I suppose not,' Harry offered. 'But it'll all blow over in time.' He hoped he sounded more positive than he actually felt.

'Not surprisingly, John Wren has been subject to a fair share of innuendo and rumour as well,' Ernie Copeland chimed in. 'They never miss a chance to have a go at him.'

'Yeah, I know,' Harry replied. He glanced again at the printed statement in his hand. 'You'll note we make it clear that illegal gambling was not the motive behind Sharkey's death. But, given Sharkey owed Wren so much money in the past, I suppose people will continue to speculate. As for the match-fixing issue, I'll leave that to you blokes to deal with. It's really more in your court than ours. But we don't mind if you mention George Winton by name. Otherwise all the rumours will turn to Wren again.'

'Good idea, Inspector,' Beazley agreed. 'We'll be certain to do that. Though I'm sure the mob will be after John anyway, no matter what we say.'

Harry shrugged. 'I suppose there's not much we can do if people with particular agendas continue to spread rumours.'

Beazley nodded his agreement and took a sip of his whisky. Again, he seemed to lapse into gloom. 'You know,' he observed reflectively, 'I'm not sure that Collingwood can recover from all this business. On top of all the other difficulties football's facing; you know, crowd violence, underhand payments and the like, it might just be too much for us.'

Harry eyed the two men, sitting despondently in their armchairs. All right, he thought to himself, remembering Effie's words. They might be Collingwood, but they're part of the footy family, and they're decent blokes. Time for a pep talk.

'You're taking this hard, gentlemen, and you've every right to. But I think you're being too pessimistic about its effect on the club. Think about what the club has achieved in the past few years with you fellows at the helm. You've gone from nothing to a premiership, you've got the most loyal supporters in the competition, and you're the best administered club in the League. It's going to take more than one bad apple in the barrel to ruin that record.'

Copeland looked up at Harry, a more positive look in his eye. 'I hope you're right, my friend.'

'I guarantee I'm right,' Harry continued. 'I'll tell you what. I'll bet you blokes that the Collingwood Football Club will still be around in a hundred years' time. And more than that, it will still have the most loyal membership and the most fearsome reputation of any club in this town.'

Copeland's face creased into a smile, as he raised his glass. 'Well said, Harry. Even better, coming from a Carlton man. Gentlemen, let's drink to that wager. None of us will be around to pay out, or collect for that matter, so what say we shout you a drink now? And we'll toast your forecast coming to pass. And while we're at it, let's also drink to the future success of Carlton. May your team survive and flourish into the future as well.'

And with smiles all round, and confidence restored, the three men clinked their glasses and sipped on the Darling's fine malt whisky.

AUTHOR'S NOTE

Death in Black and White is a work of fiction. All incidents and dialogue, and all characters, with the exception of some well-known historical figures, are products of the author's imagination, and are not to be construed as real.

Where real-life historical characters appear, including those associated with the Collingwood Football Club, the situations, incidents and dialogues concerning those persons are entirely fictional, and are not intended to depict actual events or to change the entirely fictional nature of the work. In all other respects, any resemblance to actual persons, living or dead, is entirely coincidental.

Death in Black and White is not a publication of, nor endorsed by, the Collingwood Football Club.

ACKNOWLEDGEMENTS

I would like extend my grateful thanks to my editor, Irma Gold, for her always constructive and incisive advice. And to Sandy Cull, for her brilliant cover and text designs.

Thank you to the team at Artslaw for their comprehensive and helpful advice on copyright and other legal issues.

Thanks also to Stephen Rielly from the Collingwood Football Club for his ready willingness to discuss and advise on the novel's content as it relates to the Club.

Finally, heartfelt thanks to Andrea for her ongoing support and always useful comments on the various drafts of this book.

www.ingramcontent.com/pod-product-compliance
Lightning Source LLC
Chambersburg PA
CBHW030527120726
47904CB00005B/1661